Written IN RED INK

A NOVEL

D0001820

Kieja Shapodee

ISBN: 0-9666189-0-4
LCCN: 98-93270

Cover by: Albert Chacon

Cover Photo Credits:
1-Courtesy of Albert Chacon
2-5-Courtesy of Brent Jones
6-Courtesy of Joyce Dix
7-Courtesy of Bernice Winslow

Award Publishing, Inc.
P. O. Box 3248
East Chicago, Indiana 46312
E-mail ivory@netnitco.net
www.spannet.org/awardpub

First Printing

Printed in the United States of America

10 9 8 7 6 5 4 3 2 1

Dedication

To my daughter, Karen Howard

Acknowledgements

My wonderful husband: Ivory Peterson.
Mother: Evelyn Ward
Sisters: Kathleen Peterson, Joyce Dix and Iris Dotson
Nieces: Andrea Washington and Kelly Ward
Nephew: Todd Peterson
Brother-in-law: Stanley Dotson
Aunts: Beatrice Johnson and Gladys Smith
Cousins: Fannie Mitchell, Jeannie Johnson, Pat Johnson,
Jeffery Johnson, Michael Johnson, Barbara Jean Mitchell,
Tia Evans
Friend and mentor: Evangeline Morse

A heartfelt thanks to all who provided information, proofread or
gave words of encouragement during the writing of this book.

Corine Morse Williams, Kim Okabe, Janet Hawkins Guydon,
Bobbie Christensen, Deborah Weaver, Tonia Morgan Oden,
Geraldine Wilson, Linda Smith, Grant Lewis, Jr., Phyllis Miller,
Sharon Jenkins, Dean McPherson, Michael Baisden, Major Seay,
Eileen Hartman, Jeannie Collier, Richard Asbury, Oletha Scales,
Audrey Jenkins, Clara Villarosa, Brent Jones, Bernice Winslow,
Beverly Washington, Adele Hodge, Tony Banks, Omar Tyree,
Dr. Francine Bellamy, Maria Mondragon, jessica Care moore,
Gregory Jones, Anthony Lindsay, Heather Lindsay, Marty Berg,
Jennifer Jones, Delores Luckett, Saundra Davis, Carol Reedus,
Jim Dunlap, Monique Berg and The SPAN organization

1

You'll be sorry!
the warning began the second Emily stepped from her car, but she
slung it away with a toss of her head and started for the hospital.
Halfway the parking lot, it was back.

"One hundred, ninety-nine, ninety-eight." She began counting to drown it out.
As she pushed through the revolving door, it howled in her head.

You'll be sorry! You'll be sorry! You'll be sorry!

Doubt descended over Emily and she stopped in her tracks.

How sorry will I be if I see my mother again?

"Can I help you, dear?" A lady with blue hair and apple red cheeks asked
from behind the reception desk.

"Leora DuPree," Emily said fast before she changed her mind.

"One moment." The lady flipped through a box and handed her a card.

"Thank you," Emily said and looked about. "Where're the elevators?"

"Past the pharmacy." The lady leaned forward, pointing. "And to your right."

"Thank you."

"You're welcome, dear," she said and returned to her steaming cup of tea.

Emily Douglas Bennett, tall, brown and beautiful turned heads as she strode with an air of confidence across the lobby. What they did not see was her trembling hand when she pushed the up button, nor did they hear the hostile words, nagging in her head like a childhood taunt.

You'll be sor-ry! You'll be sor-ry! You'll be sor-ry!

She began to count again.

"One thousand one, two thousand two, three thousand three."

On eight thousand eight, the elevator opened and Emily stepped in. Ten seconds later she stepped out into a pine scented corridor the color of a pale summer sky. Black arrows at corners pointed the way and she followed them past a few rooms already full of visitors until she reached Leora's closed door and started in.

You'll be sor-ry! You'll be sor-ry! You'll be sor-ry!

Emily needed reassurance she was doing the right thing and rummaged in her shoulder bag for the telegram from her elderly cousin, Maple Honey.

Why did Maple Honey send a telegram with news as important as this? Why didn't she call me?

Emily had called her several times and had gotten no answer.

Is this a trick?

The question flared then sputtered out like a damp match. Maple Honey loved her like a daughter and would never steer her wrong. Emily smoothed out the dog-earred page and read it once again.

LEORA LOW SICK. ASKING FOR YOU. COME AT ONCE.

She stuffed the message in her bag and pushed through the oak door into the heavy scent of roses and the deepest gloom. The only light came from strips over and under a short pair of drapes.

Leora loathed sunlight and had kept the house on Reese Street in the same state of perpetual dusk. Emily and Maple Honey's rooms were the only two where curtains billowed in the breeze.

Emily's eyes adjusted to the darkness and made out a figure propped on a mountain of pillows. She stood at the bed foot with her heart so full of joy, she thought it would burst. After twenty years, her mother had asked to see her.

Emily tiptoed to the window and pulled back a drape. Sunlight spilled in. Her eyes blinked shut. When she opened them, she gasped with surprise. Leora had hardly changed. She looked nothing like a sixty-year old woman with a thirty-eight-year old daughter.

To those who did not know her, Leora DuPree was a pretty White woman with shiny black hair past her shoulders, glowing peaches and cream skin accented by a beauty mark on her right cheek. Leora took pride in her appearance and certainly looked the picture of health. Only the phlegm rattling with each breath said otherwise.

Emily favored her mother, but with a wider nose and fuller and more sensual lips. Auburn hair accentuated her hazel eyes and vanilla wafer skin. She had no beauty mark, but a scar zigzagging like a lightening bolt down the right side of her forehead.

Emily dragged a high-backed chair to the bed and sat watching Leora sleep. *What if this is the only time we will have together?*

"Dear Lord." She prayed. "Please don't let her die."

Emily picked up Leora's hand, intertwining their fingers, comparing hand size, nail shape and her cookie-colored complexion to Leora's peaches and cream. Suddenly, a memory of her holding another peaches and cream hand streaked from a hidden place, bringing with it such horror, she dropped Leora's hand to the bed. Leora's eyelids fluttered twice and her eyes popped open.

"The light!" She screamed and clamped both hands over her face. "The light!" Emily leaped to jerk the drapes together and stopped the piercing shrieks.

"Sunlight hurts my eyes you know." Leora gazed at her visitor and smiled. Emily smiled back and sat down.

"Who're you?" Leora asked.

"Emily!" She whispered hoarsely. "Your daughter."

Leora's smile curved into a frown, turning her face into an ugly mask. Hate flowed from her green slitted eyes charging the space between them with a static electricity that seemed to crackle like fire.

"What did I do?" Emily cried. "Why do you hate me?"

Leora's wheezy breaths magnified in the silence.

"Whatever I did, forgive me...please forgive me!"

Leora raised up on one elbow. Her head bobbed weakly, but her eyes never wavered from Emily's as she coughed up yogurt thick phlegm, pursed her red painted lips and spat.

Emily thrust back to dodge the dull yellow gobs and trapped herself in the corner. She cowered out of reach until Leora went into a coughing fit and slumped back on the bed. Emily ran out sorrier than she ever thought she'd be. After a few minutes with Leora she was back to questioning her self-worth.

"I am a good and worthwhile person! Leora does not control me!" Emily pulled the old mantra from her mind's storage bin and chanted it under her breath, through the hall, down the elevator and across the lobby to the wall of telephones. She jerked up the receiver, dropped in a coin and punched Maple Honey's number. After no answer by the tenth ring, she headed for the parking lot and peeled away in her silver Mercedes, resuming the chant.

Westbound on I-20, Emily pulled into a filling station and called again.

"Hullo," Maple Honey answered with a country drawl.

Emily attacked. "Leora never asked to see me, did she?"

"Uh...uh no baby, she didn't."

"Why did you say she did?"

"I...I thought you needed to see her before—"

"Why did you send that telegram when you knew it was a lie?"

"You was gonna say no, if I called, so I sent it."

"I thought you loved me." Emily's voice quaked.

"I do, baby...I do."

"Then why did you lie?"

"I thought Leora might wanna beg your forgiveness."

"Ha! That's the last thing she wanted. She spat at me!"

"She what?"

"You heard right. She coughed up that filth and spat it at me!"

"Lordy Mercy! Lordy Mercy! Lordy Mercy!"

Tears filled Emily's eyes. She could not control the flood once it began and cried over the relationship with her mother for the first time in twenty years.

"I hate her! I hate her as much as she hates me!"

"Don't say that, forgive her. Her mind come and go."

"I don't care!" She beat her fist on the telephone. "I'll never forgive her!"

"Baby...baby." Maple Honey tried to console her.

"What did I do?" Emily sobbed. "What did I do?"

"I don't know," Maple Honey said.

"You know. I know you know!"

"No I don't. I ask but she refused to talk about it. Come to the house. We won't have to meet at the restaurant with Leora in the hospital."

"I'm way past Lacewell." She lied. "I'm almost home."

"Turn around, visit a while. I ain't seen you in so long."

"When I left Leora's house," Emily said flatly. "I swore I'd never set foot in it again...and I meant it." She found tissues and pressed them to her eyes.

"That was a long time ago. You don't have to come in, park in the driveway, I'll come out to you."

"No!" Emily snapped. "I told you no!"

"I see you still stubborn."

"I'm not stubborn. I just keep my word."

Silence filled the phone booth to overflowing.

"How them girls doin'? How Richard doin'?"

"He's fine." Emily's tone was friendlier. "They're all fine."

"That's good."

"Did you get the magazine article I sent?" Emily asked.

"I got it right here." Maple Honey read the caption, stumbling over some of the words. "Richard Edward Bennett named Doctor of the Year by the Board of Certified Ophthalmologists."

"I'm so proud of him," Emily said.

"My chest about to bust, too. I showed it to Nancy."

"How's Miss Nancy doing?"

"Fine. She say Richard is too handsome for words."

Emily laughed. Miss Nancy was seventy-nine years old.

"Richard a good husband ain't he?"

"Yes, he is," Emily said proudly. "The best."

"When you gonna tell him about your Momma?"

"Don't start that again."

"'S'pose he find out she alive and you lied to him?"

"How would he find out? I'm not telling, are you?"

"Baby, you know I won't...you missin' the point."

"What point? Before I got your telegram, Leora *was* dead to me; and as far as I'm concerned, she's back in that status."

"Don't say that about your Momma."

"I have no Momma. My Momma is dead."

"She just might be dead soon," Maple Honey said.

"Everybody has to die."

"Don't be so mean."

"How can you care about her?"

"'Cause she cared about me when I had nowhere to go."

"Ha! Leora never cared about anyone."

"That ain't true."

"You're her cook. Her maid." Emily taunted. "Her slave!"

"Lincoln freed the slaves." Maple Honey snapped back.

"He didn't free you."

"Now you listen here, girl. If I don't think I'm her slave, why should you?"

"I didn't mean—"

"You still havin' that bad dream?" Maple Honey asked.

"Not like I used to, only about once a week now." Emily wished it were only a bad dream and not the terrifying nightmare it really was.

"If you ask me." Maple Honey sucked her teeth. "That's once too many."

"I know."

"You need to see somebody and get some help."

"I know."

"Can't Richard recommend a good doctor?"

"He can but...."

"But what?"

"I don't know." She didn't want to admit she was afraid to see a doctor and maybe find out something bad about herself.

"I looked for Leora's journals again today."

"No luck, huh?" Emily said relieved to be away from talk of the nightmare. She shivered, thinking of the next one to come.

"Nope. Leora gotta have a secret room or something. I done turned this house upside down more than once, but I know they here somewhere."

"How many do you think there are?"

"Forty or fifty. Leora been writin' in them books since she was a girl."

"Do you think she wrote why she hates me?"

"Prob'ly. She say she wrote down everything ever happen to her."

"Maybe she destroyed them."

"Lord no. Leora saved just about everything she ever touched."

"Isn't that funny," Emily said. "Leora saved just about everything she ever touched and destroyed her only child. Don't you think that's funny?"

"I'm sorry baby. I shoulda left it alone and never sent that telegram."

"Before I got your message," She lashed out. "I was happy *and* pain free."

"Lordy Mercy! The pain done come back?"

"Yes."

"When?"

"The day I opened your telegram."

"Lordy Mercy! Lordy Mercy!"

Maple Honey moaned near tears and Emily regretted mentioning the pain.

"Don't blame yourself. I can handle it."

"I'm so sorry!"

"I'm the one sorry."

How could I say such mean things to the person who had protected me from Leora throughout my childhood?

"Forgive me!" Emily said.

"For what?"

"For talking so ugly to you."

"I should be askin' your forgiveness, for subjectin' you to Leora again."

"I don't want to talk about her anymore," Emily said. "When are you coming to visit me?"

"No time soon with Leora in the hospital."

"I thought we weren't talking about her. You need to worry about yourself."

"I forgot," Maple Honey said. "I take care of myself."

"You're taking your insulin like you should?"

"Uh huh."

"How's your blood pressure?"

"Good."

"That's good," Emily said.

"Sure wish you'd come spend some time with me."

"I have work to do at the store and I told Annette I'd be in."

"How that Annette doin'? She still crazy?"

"Crazy like a fox." Emily used Annette's favorite saying.

"Wel-l-l." Maple Honey sighed deeply. "I guess I'll let you go."

"Why don't—" Emily started to say meet her at Joyce's Cafe.

"What?"

"Never mind. I'll come back and visit you soon, okay?"

"Okay," Maple Honey said. "Bye, bye."

"Bye."

Emily pulled down the mirror to repair her water-damaged face and felt so foolish crying over Leora, she couldn't look herself in the eye. She jerked the car into drive and spun away, spewing gravel in her wake.

Cedartown-2, Iverson-40, Atlanta-60. Emily shot past the road sign.
Maple Honey sounded so hurt. Should I exit at Cedartown and go visit her?
Emily approached the exit and broke her speed to thirty. The ice pick stabs up and down her scar chose that second to begin. She took the pain as her answer and zoomed past the ramp for home.

2

By the time Emily exited on Wesley Chapel Road, the pain had gone. She parked in her space at, I Love To Read, the bookstore she co-owned with her oldest and dearest friend, Annette Marshall and headed inside. Wind chimes clanged overhead and immediately improved her mood.

"Good afternoon." She smiled at a lone man and nine women standing in two lines, flipping through their books.

"Afternoon." The man ogled Emily appreciatively.

Five women spoke. Two nodded. Two said nothing. The man continued to stare until she walked out of sight past floor-to-ceiling oak shelves filled with books in colorful jackets.

Emily looked about with a great sense of pride. Her business was responsible for six people making a good living wage. Kevin Adams and Hosea Hardy stocked shelves with the books received yesterday. Marsha Leigh assisted a customer. Robin Norton stamped sale prices on assorted books. Manager, Nora Price, and part-timer, Tasha Drew, rang up sales.

"Where's Annette?" Emily said. "I didn't see her car."

"She went to have her carphone installed," Nora said.

"Oh yeah."

"When are you getting yours?"

"Friday. However, I don't have to be reached at all times like Annette does."

"Annette sure doesn't want to miss a call, does she?" Nora laughed and pulled a dirty gray sack by a frayed string from behind the counter. "Here's the mail."

"Thanks." Emily headed for the office, towing it behind.

"I almost forgot," Nora said. "We're almost out of bags."

"Did you call, Mr. Webster?"

"Uh huh. He said we'd have them tomorrow."

"He told us tomorrow all last week." Emily returned to the counter. "How many do we have left, Tasha?"

Tasha counted silently.

"Ten large, seventeen medium and five small," she said. "Make that nine large." She filled a bag with four books. "People have really been coming in for the sale."

"Should I call him back?" Nora asked.

"No. Mr. Webster has been given too much slack as it is. I'll call."

When they'd bought the store, they had inherited Joe Webster with a four-year contract. His contract was now up. They would no longer have to endure his poor service, snide sexual innuendoes and whiskey breath. Emily slung the mail sack by her desk and dialed his number.

"Webster supplies." Joe Webster answered in his proper business voice. "Joe Webster speaking."

"Mr. Webster, Emily Bennett, how are you?"

"What do you want?" His tone was no longer business-like. "I told that other woman I'm looking for your bags to come in any day."

"Guess what, Mr. Webster?" She couldn't keep the pleasure out of her voice.

"What?" he asked warily.

"You're finished at I Love To Read!"

"You can't fire me." He snorted. "I have a contract."

"Not anymore," she said. "Your contract expired."

He snorted again. "My contract runs another year."

"I'm afraid not," Emily said. "It expired Friday."

There was a long pause before Joe Webster spoke.

"Maybe I can...uh...uh...find your order!"

"As of this minute, Mr. Webster, your services are no longer needed."

"What about all these here bags with your name on 'em?"

"You can keep all five thousand," she said and slammed down the phone. It rang immediately. She snatched it up ready for him.

"Now you listen here," she said venomously.

"Em," Annette said. "What's wrong with you?"

"I thought it was Joe Webster calling back."

"I'm calling from my car," Annette said.

"Nora told me you went to get it. How do you like it?"

"Sistergirl, driving and talking on the phone is so cool."

"Paying to have someone call me isn't so cool."

"You'll love it," Annette said. "Who are you giving your number to?"

"I don't know."

"Me either," Annette said. "I need to make up a list."

"If you're making a list of your men, that may take several weeks."

"I don't know *that* many men," Annette said.

"Sure." Emily laughed. "Sure."

"See you in a few," Annette said. "Bye."

"Bye."

Emily called another supplier and ordered yellow plastic bags with I Love To Read printed on a red heart.

Ten minutes later, Annette Marshall came in clutching a withered potted plant. Shorter than Emily's five-nine by three inches, she had the same hazel eyes and vanilla wafer skin and was always asked if they were sisters.

"I see you found an adoptee." Emily sorted the mail.

"I couldn't leave this baby at that store one more day." Annette pinched the dry soil then took it to the washroom for a drink of her special elixir, coffee grounds and egg shell water.

"Don't worry." She kissed the plant and made a space for it on the wrought iron baker's rack. "You're safe now."

"You and your children." Emily laughed. "I ordered new bags from Casey. He's bringing enough to last until we get them."

"Good." Annette kicked off her three-inch heels. One landed under her desk, one under the copier table. She dropped in her swivel chair, wiggling her toes.

"Guess what?" Emily zipped open an envelope.

"What?" Annette opened a compact and inspected her face.

"I gave Joe Webster the boot."

"It's time we were rid of that son of a bitch!" She powdered the freckles across her nose and pulled her dark brown hair into a ponytail.

"He didn't even know his contact had expired," Emily mocked him, laughing. "Maybe I can...uh...uh find your...order."

Annette propped her elbows on her desk and held her head with both hands.

"I guess he's satisfied now. I know I am." Emily flipped on the intercom to the stock room. "Hosea, our contract with Joe Webster is now null and void."

"We should celebrate," he said. "I'm going to Andrea's and I'll buy."

"I ate already. Let me ask Annette." She turned to her partner. "Hosea's going to Andrea's, do you want anything?"

"Umm umm, I'm saving myself for dinner. I have a hot date."

"No thanks, Hosea." She hung up and grinned at Annette. "So-o…who's the hot date with?"

"You don't know him...Bradley Malone."

"How long has this been going on?"

"A few days."

"Come on." Emily raised an eyebrow. "How many?"

"Six."

Emily laughed. "He must be buck naked ugly if you've known him six days and never mentioned his name."

"Well...he's not exactly a finey fine."

"If he's not fine, what does he have going for himself?"

"He's a plumber."

"A plumber?" Emily laughed. "And you have leaky pipes?"

"He lays pipe." Annette laughed heartily. "And I don't mean PVC."

"Oh-h." Emily shook her head sagely. "He's a *plumber* plumber."

"He's a five on the dick scale, but when he moves, he feels like a ten!" Annette closed her eyes. "Umph...umph…umph!"

"That good huh?" Emily said.

"Very good," Annette said. "Very good."

"Does he go on the husband prospect list?"

"Yes he does." Annette stood, twirling around. The long fuchsia and cream silk overblouse billowed from her sculpted body. "Is this okay to wear? He's picking me up here."

"Uh huh. Girl, you know you can wear a catsuit."

"Thanks." Annette knew she looked good. "I like that." She indicated Emily's black checked jacket.

"Thanks," Emily said. "Guess where I found it?"

"Hmm." Annette stoked her chin. "In Lisa's closet?"

"Bingo!" Emily snapped her fingers. "And it wasn't way in the back, mind you, but right in front. I found my denim dress in there, too."

"That shit happens when your daughter is built like a brick house and can wear your clothes."

"I may have to have Richard put a lock on my closet just to keep her out."

"Remember how you dressed in your Momma's stuff?"

"I never dressed in my mother's clothes." Emily tried not to sound as sad as she felt. "And I most certainly never acted like Lisa."

"Sure." Annette took the invoices from Emily and removed the checkbook from her desk drawer. "I bet Leora has a different story."

"Leora never cared about me."

"I forgot. I didn't mean to bring up unpleasant memories."

"It's a fact. Don't worry about it."

Emily wanted to mention her visit to Lacewell, but Annette would never understand how a mother could not love her child. Her mother, Queen Esther, worshipped the ground she walked on.

"This is for you." Emily handed Annette a blue envelope. Annette tore it open and read the bold scrawl.

"It's Lisa's thank you card."

"For what?"

"For the dress I gave her last month."

"Honestly. She said she'd sent a thank you card the same day."

"Ooops," Annette said. "She probably forgot."

"She didn't forget, she thinks she's slick that's what she thinks."

"They all think they're slick when they're fifteen."

"What's happening with young girls these days? When I was fifteen, I didn't know what slick was."

"You don't know what slick is now." Annette laughed.

"I do, too." Emily laughed with her.

"Lisa's just flexing her teenage muscles," Annette said. "You know adolescence is a crazy time."

"I know. I just hope we didn't make a mistake putting a private phone in her room. She'll probably be calling China."

"No, she won't," Annette said. "Lisa's the maturest fifteen-year-old, going on fifty child I know."

"That's easy for you to say. She's not your fifteen-year-old, going on fifty child."

"I wish I had a daughter just like her."

"You wouldn't if she was talking so mean and always rolling her eyes."

"Lisa's trying to see how far she can go," Annette said. "Pop that head like, Queen Esther, did me, that'll break that up."

Emily smiled at Annette's advice. She had never hit her girls and knew she wouldn't start now.

"I almost forgot. Tomorrow is awards day at school, I won't be in."

"I know," Annette said. "Lisa invited me last week."

Emily couldn't hide her hurt feelings. "She didn't even ask me."

"Kids are embarrassed having their parents at school."

"Michelle and Nicole aren't embarrassed."

"They aren't hanging with older kids like Lisa."

"Oh!" Emily said. "Is that why?"

"Uh huh."

"I thought at first it was a mistake to double promote her."

"See," Annette said. "I told you she'd do well."

"She's acing her classes, but her attitude stinks."

"Lisa's in a phase, testing her wings. She'll come around."

"I hope so," Emily said. "I hope she—"

The service bell buzzed with short impatient bursts.

"Is that a delivery?" Annette asked. "Is Hosea still at lunch?"

Emily went to the hall and looked toward the loading dock. Joe Webster stood eyeball to eyeball in the doorway with Kevin.

"What do we owe, Joe Webster?" Emily asked.

Annette flipped the account book open to Webster Supplies.

"Three hundred ninety-six dollars and thirty-four cents."

"Please write a check," Emily said and headed for the dock.

"With pleasure."

"I'm not going to say it again, boy. I want to see Miss Bennett."

"You don't work for us anymore," Kevin said with youthful exuberance and braced his arm on the door to stop it from shaking.

"I suggest you go get her!" Anger turned Joe Webster's ruddy complexion, redder. "Now!"

"I'll handle this, Kevin," Emily said.

He looked back relieved and let her move into his place.

"Uh...uh...Miss Bennett." Joe Webster's whiskey breath made her gag. "I found your order." He pointed to five boxes stacked neatly at the end of his navy cargo van.

"It's too late," she said coolly. "I'm not taking them."

"What you mean?" Joe Webster chomped on the cigar butt.

"What I mean," she said. "Is your contract has expired."

"Couldn't we...uh...couldn't we overlook that little matter?" His smile show-ed dingy yellow teeth. "I told you they got misplaced."

"You always have an excuse."

"I brought them didn't I?"

"But you brought them too late," she said. "We've already ordered from someone else."

"From the White man I bet."

"It could have been from you."

"Jacob coulda sold me this store." He took the cigar from his mouth and spat. Reminded of Leora, she stepped back.

"But he didn't Mr. Webster. He sold it to us."

Annette walked up and held out the check.

"This is what we owe you," she said.

He snatched it with such fury; a triangle of paper stuck between her fingers.

"What am I gonna do with all these goddamned sacks?"

"You can stick them up your—"

"Do whatever you please." Emily cut Annette off. "They're yours."

"You whores think you can just take over!" He hollered.

Emily slammed the door and fumbled with the lock. The second she turned the deadbolt, the door shook. Another blow rattled the hinges. It withstood the pounding, but could not shut out the verbal tirade.

"I ain't gone let you sluts keep me from makin' my livin'!"

"I'm calling the police, Mr. Webster!" Emily shouted.

"Call the goddamn police. I got somethin' for they asses, too!"

The battering stopped suddenly. Seconds later, they heard the van crank and drive away.

Emily took deep breaths to slow her galloping heart. "Go tell Nora what happened." She headed for the office. "I'm calling the police."

Five minutes later, two policemen took the report and told them the bad news. Before any charges could be brought against Joe Webster, he would have to do more than call them bitches and whores.

"I don't believe it." Emily fumed. "They can't do a thing until he hurts us."

"If he was going to do anything," Annette said. "He would have done it now."

"You think so?" Emily said.

"I know so," Annette said. "Joe Webster is a pussy with a capital P."

The wind chimes clanged. They glanced at each other and rushed to the front in time to see a woman enter with two small children. Relieved, they returned to the office but got little done. Each time the chimes sounded, they stopped work, listening for Joe Webster's angry voice.

At three o'clock, Emily headed home. She pulled onto Wesley Chapel. A navy van followed.

Is that Joe Webster?

Her heart beat like bongos.

Should I call the police? I wish I had my carphone.

She glanced in the rear view mirror,

Screeeeeeeeh!

She slammed the brake inches from the bumper ahead. She stopped at the light intending to turn onto Snapfinger. The van nosed into her lane. She panicked and U-turned in front of a speeding truck.

Beeeeeeeeeeeeeeeep!

She looked back and got the finger before she fled down the ramp.

Emily watched the rear traffic for the van. After five minutes passed and it didn't appear, she decreased her speed. With fear diminished and heartbeat normal, she felt secure enough to grocery shop and pulled into the Winn Dixie.

3

Emily drove home under a canopy of budding trees. Cones of sunlight slanted through the sparse foliage, dappling the car hood and the black asphalt with color like splashes of yellow paint.

Emily loved this area. A walk through the woods behind the house might reveal a deer nibbling tender shoots or rabbits scampering through the brush. She and Richard had looked for over a year before they had found their land. Another year passed before they had approved the blueprints for the two-story French Provincial house with a round stone turret on the west wall. Upon completion, Richard had smashed a bottle of champagne on the dark gray keystone and made a toast.

"I christen thee, Chateau Emily," he had said. "For my queen."

A genius at turning a piece of wood into something of heirloom quality, Richard got the workshop of his dreams and filled the house with his handiwork. Richard also liked to fish and received an extra bonus in the fact that their property bordered a swift-running stream alive with mullet and catfish. He and the two younger girls would often be found on the water's edge, waiting patiently for a bite.

Emily's dream kitchen contained a restaurant oven, a six-burner stove and a commercial refrigerator and freezer. Cobalt blue tile gleamed underfoot and on the spacious countertops. Copper pots dangled from iron racks suspended from ceiling beams. Richard made the cabinets lining the walls. He had also built shelves outside the pantry for her collection of cookbooks from around the world. A bath in each bedroom eased considerably the frantic knocks that used to prevail outside the two bathrooms at their old house in Atlanta.

Emily turned on her street. Sunday Lake Drive curved and dipped beneath the outstretched arms of ancient oaks that fell away at the rise and revealed Chateau Emily on the hill. The sight always sent a thrill up her back. She slowed and passed through the iron gates and rounded the semi-circular drive. She rummaged in her purse for the garage remote. The door rumbled up and she backed into her space. Up six steps she went with arms full of groceries and a dozen yellow roses. She unlocked the door. The first thing she saw were dishes in the sink topped with a pot glued white with grits.

"That girl!" Emily kicked the door shut and disarmed the security system. The cleaning lady wasn't coming today and she told Lisa to load the dishwasher.

"I'm not washing them. She can do them the minute she gets home," Emily said and snapped her keys on a tab on her shoulder bag. She hung it over the doorknob and put the groceries away.

In the pantry, she balanced on the stepstool and carefully removed one of her most cherished possessions from the top shelf. The crystal vase was an engagement present from her mother-in-law, Pauline Bennett had showered her with love from the first time they had met.

Why couldn't I have had a mother like Pauline?

Emily ran tepid water in the vase and added a pinch of sugar. Annette swore it kept the flowers fresh longer. She arranged the roses and held them to her nose. The aroma reminded her of Leora. She set them on the windowsill over the sink and let the sun cast rainbows over the ceiling.

The side door slammed. Nicole, thirteen, and ten year old Michelle bustled in dropping coats and books.

"Hi, Mommy." Nicole yelled. "I'm home."

"Hi, Mommy." Michelle mimicked. "I'm home."

"Pick up those books and hang up your coats."

"Ah-h, Mommy." They said but did as they were told.

"You passed by the hooks, why couldn't you do that in the first place?"

"We don't know." They sang, giggling.

Rail thin with brown eyes, pecan brown skin and two thick sandy-red braids down their chests, they looked like twins with Nicole the taller of the two.

"Mommy." Nicole tattled. "Lisa's with Kenya."

"She knows she's suppose to come straight home," Emily said with a frown.

"We told her you'd be mad," Nicole said. "Didn't we, Michelle?"

Michelle nodded and stuck her left thumb in her mouth.

"Lisa said they were going to the library, but I don't think so..." Nicole deliberately trailed off, leaving doubt.

"That girl!" Emily said. "That girl!"

"Is Lisa going to be in trouble?" Michelle asked.

"Big girls don't suck their thumbs." Emily evaded the question and gave each child a tight hug and a kiss. "Go change your clothes so you can eat."

They ran toward the swinging door.

"Walk, you two." Emily called. "And don't forget to wash your hands."

The girls slowed to a walk. The second they pushed through the door, they stampeded up the steps.

"Bet I can beat you changing." Nicole shucked her sweater.

"Bet you can't." Michelle took the challenge and tore at her clothes.

Nicole pulled on jeans and a sweatshirt. While Michelle looked under the bed for her other shoe, Nicole pulled a plaid cosmetic bag from under her blouses. Her eyes glazed over at the dazzling array of rings, bracelets, necklaces and earrings, all in precious fourteen-carat gold. She stuck a pair of tiny hoops through her ears and practiced her sexiest pose; lips half-parted with eyes half-closed.

"I win." Michelle stood by the door. "Come on, I'm hungry."

"Okay." Nicole turned from the mirror.

"When did you buy those earrings?" Michelle asked.

"Oh...the other day."

"You didn't go shopping the other day."

"I did, too." Nicole playfully hit Michelle's arm.

"O-o-w-w!" Michelle grimaced and shielded her left arm.

"What's wrong with you?"

"Nothing."

"Let me see." Nicole pushed Michelle's sleeve past a large, purple bruise. "How did you do that?"

Michelle dropped her head. Nicole made her look in her eyes.

"Lisa did it, didn't she?"

Michelle nodded. "She pinched me...hard."

"You should have pinched her back."

"Then she would have really beat me up."

"Yeah, I guess you're right," Nicole said thoughtfully. "You can't beat her by yourself, but we can beat her together."

"Wh-a-a-a-t?" Michelle's eyes grew big.

"The next time she does anything to either one of us, we'll beat her good!"

"Oka-a-a-y!" Michelle said enthusiastically.

"Are you afraid?"

"Uh huh, a little."

"Don't worry, together we can kick her ass."

"Ooo-we Nicole, you said a bad word."

"You're not going to tell Mommy are you?"

"No-o-o!" Michelle exclaimed. "No-o-o-o!"

"Come on, let's go eat."

"We're going to kick Lisa's ass." Michelle muttered under her breath all the way to the kitchen. "We're going to kick Lisa's ass!"

Seconds later, they sat eating ham sandwiches and sucking chocolate milk through elbow straws.

"Mommy," Nicole said. "When's the family meeting?"

"Tomorrow right after dinner."

"I'm voting for Ft. Lauderdale." Michelle voiced her choice for this year's vacation spot.

"I want to go some place new," Nicole said.

"You always want to go some place new."

"You always want to go to Ft. Lauderdale."

"I like visiting Aunt Valerie and Uncle Jerry."

"We should vacation in Rio," Nicole said.

"We could go to Denver and visit Aunt Cassie."

"We went there last year. We should go to Hawaii."

"You always want to have your own way." Michelle pouted.

"Whose way should I want to have, yours?"

"Girls! Girls!" Emily intervened. "Stop arguing,"

"I'm going to ride my bike." Nicole pushed her plate away.

"Me, too." Michelle slurped up the last of her milk.

"Have you two done your homework?" Emily said.

"I did mine at school," Michelle said,

"I did mine at school, too." Nicole said.

"No more homework at school. It's not homework if you do it at school."

"Okay, Mommy," Nicole said.

"Okay." Michelle answered, too.

"Let me see it before you two go anywhere."

Nicole wiped her hands on a napkin and showed Emily her homework.

"Good work." Emily kissed her forehead.

"Here's mine." Michelle held out her papers."

Emily scanned it and kissed her, too.

"Mommy," Michelle said. "Open the garage door."

"Open the garage door, what?" Emily said.

"Open the garage door, please."

"That's better." She felt in her bag for the remote. "You two stay in the yard."

"Mommy." Michelle whined. "We were going to Amy's."

"Not today. I said stay in the yard."

"We told Amy we'd come play with her." Nicole glowered.

"You heard what I said." She hugged them. They wiggled free, pouting.

I hate it when they're angry with me.

"Okay. You can visit Amy a little while."

Emily pressed the remote. The garage door rumbled up. Grinning, the girls grabbed their coats and ran down the steps. By the time she thought to tell them to be back in thirty minutes, they had pedaled out of sight.

Emily started dinner. She took a bowl from a high cabinet over the microwave. Taped to the side was a yellow note.

This entitles the bearer to mind blowing sex. Mr. Roscoe.

She stuck it in her pocket with a laugh and scribbled on a pink pad.

This entitles the bearer to freaky, freaky sex. Miss Nina.

She ran to Richard's workshop and stuck it under the jewelry chest he was making for Pauline's birthday.

Kenya Ross raced through the red light and turned right at the next corner. Lisa Bennett clutched the armrest and watched her wheel.

Will I ever be able to drive like this?

"I bet you been letting everybody in your pants." Kenya fished for information.

"Umm umm." Lisa pressed imaginary brakes.

"You can tell me." Kenya prodded. "Who you been fucking?"

"Nobody…yet."

"Serious?"

"Serious," Lisa said. "As a heart attack."

Kenya veered left with tires squealing. At the next street, she went right and skidded to a halt in front of a magnificent white brick house with black shutters and a bright red door.

"Who lives here?" Lisa asked impressed.

"Sebastian." Kenya drooled. "Sebastian Fabienne."

"Who is he?"

"Someone you've got to see. Fine as wine and I wish he was mine."

"I want to see this guy. You don't go nuts over guys. They go nuts over you."

"He doesn't know I like him." She slid from the car. "But he will today." Kenya led Lisa past the curbside mailbox up the cobblestone walk. "How old are you suppose to say you are?"

"Nobody's going to believe I'm eighteen," Lisa said.

"Just say it okay?"

Kenya rapped twice with the brass lion head knocker, counted to five then rapped five times more.

"Who knock?" A gruff, male voice asked.

"Kenya."

A man in a lime green plaid suit opened the door.

"State your business," he said.

"Sebastian invited me."

"Full name?"

"Kenya Ross."

He consulted his clipboard then ogled Lisa.

"Who's she?"

"My friend, Lisa."

"How old are you?" He scanned her again.

"Eighteen."

"Aw 'ight." He stepped back and let them in.

"Wow!" Lisa whispered. "He thinks I'm really eighteen."

"Apparently." Kenya led her on ankle deep carpeting to the kitchen.

Lisa hung back fascinated by the people around the table snorting cocaine.

I never thought I'd be in a real drug house. Stuff like this only happens in the movies. Twyla is going to flip.

A bald albino two inches shy of dwarfdom watched Lisa's every move from lashless pink eyes in an acne pocked face.

"Kenya." He hugged her with muscular arms and felt her hip. "What's up?"

"You." She squirmed free and couldn't help noticing the gun stuck in his belt. "Where's Sebastian?"

"Sleep." He nodded at the open door across the hall.

"Oh," she said. "Okay."

He took their coats and eyed Lisa's hourglass figure so brazenly, she wanted to ask for it back. Instead, she folded her arms across her breasts.

"You ladies help yourself." He pointed to the cocaine.

Kenya headed for the table almost before the words left his mouth.

"Who is that guy?" Lisa huddled behind her.

"Zebo."

"He's ugh—lee." She snickered. "He's—"

"Shhh!" Kenya looked back to see if he'd heard. He hadn't and her stomach settled back to normal. "Don't ever let him hear you call him ugly."

"Why? What will he do?"

"You remember Gwen Wilder?"

"Yeah. She was murdered."

"She called Zebo ugly."

"What!" Lisa's eyes got big. "He killed Gwen?"

"Shhh!" Kenya said. "You want him to hear you?"

"No-o-o!" She whispered with a new shot of adrenaline.

Not only am I in a drug house, I'm in a drug house with a gun-toting killer-midget. This is really going to wig Twyla out.

"Try some of this." Kenya cut a line of cocaine for Lisa.

"No, no thanks."

"Come on." Kenya sniffed it up. "You'll feel so-o-o good."

"No thanks. I'll just sit here until you finish." Lisa saw Zebo watching her and tugged unsuccessfully at the skirt halfway her creamy beige thighs. "Kenya." Lisa pulled on her arm. "I've got to get home."

"In a minute, in a minute."

"Kenya," Zebo said.

"What?" Kenya glanced back at him.

He jerked his head toward the door.

"In a minute." She leaned over for another hit.

"Now, goddammit!"

"Shit!" She muttered under her breath and joined him in the hall.

Neither one noticed Sebastian Fabienne awake on the bed within earshot of their conversation.

"What?" Kenya said with more attitude than she intended. She never wanted to be on Zebo's shit list.

"She's fine like you said." Zebo glanced back at Lisa. "But I thought I told you to start her on the shit."

"I'm trying. She won't do it."

"Make her." He frowned then smiled. "When they love it, they love me."

"I hope you don't want to fuck her now."

"Not today, but I want her soon."

"She's be at my party, Saturday. You can get her then."

"Good!" He pulled a vial from his shirt pocket. "Give her all of this, I want her groggy, but responsive."

"I understand." She stuck it in her pocket. "What about my payment?"

"You'll get it, after I get Lisa." He stared her down, daring her to complain.

"Is that all?" Kenya hid her anger well.

"That's all."

"What were you and Zebo saying about me?" Lisa asked.

"What makes you think we were saying anything about you?"

"I saw you looking at me."

"Zebo was saying how fine you are."

"Ugh! I don't even want him looking at me let alone calling me fine."

Kenya cut a line for Lisa. "Try some of this and feel like a million bucks."

"No-o!" Lisa looked at her watch. "I've got to get home."

"After you try this."

"If my father beats me home, I'll be on punishment and miss your party."

"Damn!" Kenya snorted the line and stood. "Come on."

Lisa snatched on her coat and hurried away from Zebo's prying eyes.

"You still coming to my party?" Kenya peeled from the curb, inquiring.

"Does rain fall to the ground?" Lisa laughed.

"You sure?"

"I'm positive!"

"Don't disappoint me now."

"How many times does my girl turn twenty-two?"

"Only once." Kenya bragged. "Only once."

Lisa walked in the kitchen and jolted Emily with her resemblance to Leora. She had the same lovely face, black hair, beauty mark and hateful green-eyed stare.

"Where have you been?" Emily asked.

"At the library," Lisa said sullenly.

"Why didn't you come home first?"

"If I had, somebody would have gotten the book I needed for my assignment."

"Okay," Emily said and gave Lisa a hug and kiss.

"Do you have to do that stuff?" Lisa twisted from her arms and swiped away the kiss.

"What stuff, sweetie?" Emily looked, baffled.

"Your slobbery kisses and bone-crushing hugs." Lisa tossed her luscious hair from her face. "That's what!"

"I slobber on you?" Emily's voice trembled. "I crush your bones?"

"You're always kissing and hugging."

"Only because I love you baby."

"Don't call me baby. I'm not a baby."

"Of course you're not a baby, you're my big girl."

"I'm not your big girl either! I'm almost a woman!"

"You're not quite a—"

"A woman? I'm closer to being a woman than a girl."

"Sweetie, stay a girl as long as you can."

"For what? I can never do anything or go anywhere."

"You'll have the rest of your life to do those things."

"I don't want to wait the rest of my life. I want to do them now!" Lisa shouted and ran out.

Emily looked at the sink and wished she had the nerve to call her back. Sighing deeply, she picked up the grit pot and began to scrape.

4

Emily heard the car pull in the garage and raised her eyes gratefully to heaven. Lisa was home. Dinner was ready. Richard wouldn't have to be a bear. She checked the rice and flipped on the intercom.

"Michelle, Nicole," she said. "Wash up for dinner and...and tell Lisa."

"Okay." Nicole's voice piped from the speaker.

Whenever Richard Bennett had a taste for banana pudding, he brought home bananas and milk. Today he carried a gallon of milk and a bag of bananas.

Walnut brown, six-two with wide shoulders and a waist kept trim with workouts at his club, he looked younger than forty-five.

"Hi, baby," he said in a warm baritone.

"Oh no." Emily turned her face up for his kiss. His thick, black, luxurious mustache tickled her upper lip.

"What?"

"I bought milk," she said.

He opened the refrigerator and added his gallon to the one on the door.

"And bananas." She added.

"Sorry." He laid his bunch in the fruit bowl full of bananas.

"Don't be sorry. This means we're on the same wavelength."

"A banana and milk wavelength?" Richard chuckled.

"A banana and milk wavelength is better than no wavelength at all."
He hung his trench coat in the mudroom and washed his hands.

"What's to eat?" He sat at the table. "I'm starving."

"Your favorite. Hawaiian pork chops, but if you can wait twenty minutes, I'll make you a banana pudding."

"I can wait," he said. "Did you get my suits from the cleaners?"

"I forgot. I'll get them tomorrow." She glanced over at him. His navy pin stripe suit looked as crisp and fresh as it had this morning. Some men had a flair for clothes and Richard Bennett was one of those men.

"I saw, Kenya, today," he said.

"Oh yeah?"

"She's so thin." He watched her measure sugar, flour and salt in a double boiler and add milk. "You *know* she's doing drugs?"

"Oh no!" Emily stopped stirring. Lisa idolized Kenya.
Were they doing drugs together today?

"Did you buy anything to drink besides milk?"

"Huh?" She only heard besides milk.

"Anything to drink besides milk?"

"Oh, uh huh, juice and soda."
He took out a grape soda, popped the top and guzzled it down.

"Where did you see, Kenya?" Emily got vanilla wafers from the pantry and bananas from the bowl.

"I stopped by Frank's office. She was there asking for money."

"What are Frank and Alice doing to help her?"

"Nothing. Ignoring her like always."

"Too bad. Did Lisa invite you to the award ceremony tomorrow?"

"Uh huh." He tossed the can in the trash.

"She didn't ask me." She lowered the flame, stirring constantly.

"Probably because she knew you were already going."

"What does Mr. Roscoe have for Miss Nina?" She held up the yellow note.

"It's about time. It's been up there a month."

"You've had thirty days to prepare," she said. "I'm expecting great things."

"Why wait? Give it to me right here against the frig."

"I bought eggs today. I can't have them explode from our body heat."

"I going to make you explode alright."

"Promises, promises," Emily said, laughing.

"I never make a promise," he said with a sexy growl. "I can't keep."

At seven-twenty, Nicole paced the foyer. A car pulled up ten minutes later and she jerked the door open before they had a chance to ring the bell. Lisa's study partners, Carlton Askew and Sean Favor, sauntered in. Both boys wore navy and gold Mitchell Prep jackets and that's where the similarities ended.

Carlton stood five foot eight. Pimples dotted his grocery bag brown face. A skin haircut made him look like a little boy. Round, horn-rimmed glasses forever slipping down his nose made him look like an owl. He dressed off the husky rack at Sears. Girls never gave him a second look.

Sean's baby smooth light brown skin stretched over an athletic six-foot frame. Curly black hair and curly long lashes surrounded dark, sexy eyes. His father's tailor made his clothes. Every girl in town wanted to give him some.

"Hi squirt." Carlton tweaked Nicole's cheek.

"I'm not a squirt." She slapped his hand. "H-i-i Sean."

"Hey, Kid." Sean pulled her braid.

"What's up?" Nicole giggled and scrunched her eyes.

"What's wrong with your eyes?" Sean asked.

"Nothing's wrong with my eyes."

"Then how come you keep doing that?"

"What?"

"Squinting like you're blind."

"I'm not squinting!" She snapped. "You're the one blind!"

"Chill, baby girl." Sean laughed. "Chill."

"Somebody has a crush on you, man," Carlton teased.

"This S. L. G. doesn't know what a crush is." He mock socked her jaw and tried to pull her braid again.

"I do too know!" Nicole knocked his hand away.

"Kid," Sean said. "Go tell Lisa we're here."

"Tell her your old stupid self." She stuck out her tongue and ran upstairs. Carlton and Sean looked at each other and laughed. Minutes later, Lisa skipped down the steps.

"Hello, guys."

"Hi, Lisa." Carlton said.

"Hey, S.L.G.," Sean said. "Where's Twyla?"

"Babysitting." She headed to the kitchen. "Come on in."

Sean washed his hands. Carlton sprawled at the table and reached for one of the submarine sandwiches Emily always fixed for Lisa's study session.

"What are you suppose to do before you eat?" Lisa asked.

"I forgot," Carlton said and joined Sean at the sink.

Lisa removed four orange sodas from the refrigerator and anxiously watched them devour the platter. She had studied hard and was eager to begin. Sean finished first and leaned back in the chair with a toothpick in his mouth.

"Let's see what you got, kid."

"I'm not a kid." Lisa hissed. "And stop calling me one."

Sean laughed.

"Do you have any questions for me?" Lisa turned to Carlton.

"Yeah. What year was the Emancipation Proclamation issued?"

Lisa didn't hesitate.

"January 1, 1863."

"What's the Pythagorean theorem?" Carlton asked.

"The square of the length of the hypotenuse of a right triangle equals the sum of the squares of the lengths of the other two sides," she said.

"Let's see what you got." Sean smiled smugly.

"Anything you can throw at me." Lisa countered.

"Spell exiguous," he said.

"Exiguous," she said. "E-x-i-g-u-o-u-s. It means meager or petty. She used it in a sentence. "Someone in this room is exiguous." She scowled at Sean.

"In what constellation is Betelgeuse?" Sean asked.

"Uh, uh," Lisa faltered.

"You don't know do you? I thought, Miss-Know-It-All, knew everything."

"The constellation Orion," she said tartly.

"What's the other name for Betelgeuse?" Sean got in her face. "Bet you can't answer that."

"That's the only name," she said confidently. "You're trying to trick me."

"Am I trying to trick her, man?" Sean asked Carlton.

"No."

"Give me a hint." Lisa's cheeks grew hotter.

"The initials are A. O.," Carlton said.

She didn't have a clue. She hated looking dumb, especially in front of Sean.

"I give up," she said. "I don't know."

"It's Alpha Orionis," Sean chided her. "Alpha Orionis."

Lisa wanted to defend herself, but Sean would harass her more so she swallowed her pride and kept quiet.

They quizzed each other for the next hour. Carlton missed the formula for acetone. Sean didn't miss any of his questions.

Carlton patted Lisa's back. "Good session."

"Thanks," she said. "You did good, too."

"Not bad S.L.G." Sean gave praise in one breath and took it back in another. "Not bad for a little kid."

Lisa exploded. "Watch this little kid beat your SAT scores."

"In your dreams." Sean sneered. "In…your…dreams."

"I *know* what I can do!" She laughed in his face. "Just you wait."

Nicole came in and stood by Sean's chair.

"What do you want, Nicole?" Lisa said.

"None of your business!"

"You'd better get out before I hit you in that pig nose."

"You do." Nicole returned. "And tonight you die."

Lisa jumped up, heading for Nicole. Sean leaned back, ready for the show.

"Girls." Carlton jumped between the sisters. "Chill."

"You just wait!" Lisa pushed through the door. "Daddeeeeee!"

"What?" Richard called from the family room.

"Come to the kitchen, please." She glared at Nicole. "Just you wait."

"Humph!" Nicole rolled her eyes.

Richard entered with a book under his arm. Sean and Carlton came to attention.

"Hello, Dr. Bennett," they said together.

"Hello, boys," he said. "Kiddy Widdy—"

"Daddeeeeee!" Lisa shrieked. "Don't call me that."

"Why are you screaming like you're crazy?" Richard asked.

"Nicole is interrupting my studying."

"Kitten, come out so Lisa can finish."

"I wasn't interrupting anything, Daddy. I came to get something to drink."

"Stay out of the kitchen when Lisa's studying."

"How come she has to study in here?" Nicole asked. "Why can't she study somewhere else?"

"Daddy," Lisa said. "Tell her to stay out of my room, too."

"I haven't even been in your old stupid room."

"You're always snooping in my room and if anybody's stupid, it's you."

"Nip it," Richard said. "Nicole, get your drink and finish your homework."

"I'm finished." She bragged. "And I don't need a tutor."

"I'm not being tutored!" Lisa yelled. "I'm studying!"

"Sure." Nicole smirked. "Sure."

"Daddeeeeee!" Lisa protested. "Make her stop!"

Richard looked at his watch. "Isn't it past your bed time?"

"Daddeeee!" Nicole was horrified to have Sean know she went to bed so early. "Why do you always embarrass me!"

"Move it, Nicole," Richard said.

"You take up for her every time."

"That's enough." He turned to go. "Just do as I say."

The minute the door swung shut, Nicole stuck out her tongue. Lisa hit at her. Nicole dodged and headed for the door.

"I'm sure glad." She jeered. "I'm not dumb like you!"

At ten thirty, Emily walked bare foot across the varnished floor into Lisa's room. She lay in a ball in the middle of the twin bed, her pink blanket a heap on the floor. Emily spread the cover over her and touched her head. Lisa mumbled something unintelligible and turned away. Emily took it as another rejection and retreated.

Next door, Nicole and Michelle lay in a full sized bed with legs criss-crossed in silent battle. Emily untangled the yellow blanket, furled it into the air, and watched it settle over her children. She listened to their soft breathing a while then went to her room.

Richard lay in bed reading. A smile crossed his face when Emily locked the door. She continued on into the bathroom and turned on the shower. She stepped under the spray and scrubbed with a loofah mitt until her skin tingled. She rinsed off the thick lather and patted herself dry. Emily surveyed her body in the mirror. Nipples big as blackberries jutted from firm upturned breasts. She gave them a loving squeeze and frowned at her stretch marked stomach far, far from pancake flat.

Emily sat naked at her vanity. Richard stopped reading and turned off his lamp. He lay with fingers interlaced behind his head, watching her beauty ritual with half-closed eyes. Each night was the same play, yet somehow different. He never tired of watching her perform.

She pressed a dispenser. Pink lotion squiggled in her hand. Languidly, she rubbed them together and massaged her upper body, being careful not to get any on her nipples. Richard said it tasted like bad medicine. She pointed her toe skyward and slid the moisturizer along one shapely leg, then the other. A dab of *Joyous* perfume on each pulse point completed the ritual.

"Did you enjoy the show?" She turned to Richard.

"I always enjoy the show." He held out his arms. "Come here and let me show you how much."

Emily crossed the room.

"On or off?" She hesitated with her hand on the lamp chain.

"On. I want to see your eyes when I make you come."

She laughed. "I want to see your face contort like a rubber mask when I make you come."

"Come on then baby, make me contort."

She pointed at a high pulsing area of the cover.

"What's that?"

"Mr. Roscoe."

"Why is he jumping like that?"

"He's excited about something."

"What?"

"Miss Nina.

"This Miss Nina?" She touched her pussy.

"Yes baby, that Miss Nina. Bring her on over here."

"Are you prepared to blow my mind?"

"I'm not only ready, I'm willing and I *am* able."

"I shall see." Emily crawled in bed and molded herself to his body. "Make me scream your name!" Her hot tongue flicked in and out of his ear.

"I'll do my best." He flung the cover back and caressed her damp tangle of russet pubic hair.

She wormed her hand through the slit in his shorts and freed Mr. Roscoe. Their kiss transferred a bitter trace of earwax as their tongues played hide and seek. Her nipple grew marble hard under his finger and even harder when his mouth covered it with scorched breath. Emily squirmed and opened her legs. His fingers strummed her pussy lips then slipped inside.

"Mmm...ssss." She moaned and pushed against his hand. Richard slid the shorts down his hips and kicked them into the rumpled bed-clothes, awaiting her cue.

"Ssss, ooooh! Now! Mr. Roscoe, now!"

He maneuvered over her, aiming Mr. Roscoe at her pussy door. One thrust, had him in. "Ssssss." Another thrust put him in to his balls.

"O-o-o-oh, Richy." Emily moaned. "O-oh yes-s, yes-s-s."

They moved in perfect unison, gaining speed.

She grabbed his hips and held him tight against the feverish grind of her pelvis.

"We can make our boy tonight." She whispered. "I feel it! I feel it!" Richard's erection fell flat. He tried to rise.

"Don't stop!" She wrapped her legs around his body. "Don't stop!" He snatched away and rolled off the bed. In five strides, he was in the bathroom, slamming the door. Emily squeezed her thighs tight, trying to hold the good feeling before it escaped completely.

Richard came out and searched the bed covers for his shorts. He sat on the chaise lounge across the French windows, put both feet through the openings and stood, snapping them around his waist.

"Richy...honey...what's wrong?"

"Don't start." He dropped to the seat. "Don't even start."

"All I said was we could make our baby boy."

"I've had this baby boy obsession of yours." He measured past his head. "Up to here."

"Honey!" Her voice quivered. "Don't you want a son?"

"I don't need a son to feel like a man. You're the one making me feel like a sperm donor. Is that all you need me for?"

"You know better than that. I love you." Emily slipped from bed and knelt in front of him. "Come on, Honey." She tried to free Mr. Roscoe.

"Stop that!" He shoved her hands away.

Her sobs began softly then intensified as if for a dead loved one. Ashamed of himself for being so harsh, Richard pulled her close and asked the question he already knew the answer to.

"Why is having a boy so important to you?"

"I...don't...know!" She wailed. "I...don't...know!"

"Don't cry." He led her to the bed. They began to make love again. This time, Emily did not mention the baby boy.

Hours later, a vicious blow to his lower back jolted Richard awake. He leaped up and pulled on the lamp. Emily thrashed about in deep sleep with her mouth opened in a silent scream. Fingers curved like talons, clawed at an invisible enemy. He grabbed her and kept her from falling off the bed.

"Wake up!" He shook her until her eyes opened.

"Help me, Richy! Help me!" She tried to fight off the nightmare's effects.

"You're awake...stop struggling...hold still...hold still."

"My eyes! My eyes!"

He rushed to the bathroom and returned with eye drops and a warm towel.

"Hold still." He unscrewed the peaked cap. "I'm putting in the drops." He squeezed three drops into each eye then covered them with the towel.

"Emily. You need to do something about these nightmares."

"I know."

"You always say I know, but never do anything."

"I'm afraid."

"Afraid? Of what?"

"I might find out something bad about myself."

"Baby." He pulled her into the warmth of his arms. "What bad thing could you have done? You're too kind to do anything bad."

"Richy."

"Huh?"

"You take such good care of me." She turned lazily on her side and sank into a deep sleep.

5

Richard came in the kitchen humming a merry tune.

"You're mighty chipper this morning." Emily set a plate of bacon and eggs before him and pushed down two slices of bread in the toaster.

"Great sex makes me chipper." He sat and opened the paper.

"Hush. You're always chipper."

"That's because you always give me great sex." He growled. "But..."

"But what?" She juggled the toast onto a saucer and set it by his plate.

"I think you know."

She poured coffee. He said grace and sipped at the scalding, black brew. Emily poured coffee for herself and sat, stirring in sugar and cream.

"Richy, honey," she said in her sweetest voice. "I…"

"Don't try to sweet talk me. You either see somebody about your nightmares, or I'm getting twin beds."

"Okay." She sipped her coffee. "I will."

"I mean it! I can't take those kicks anymore." He massaged his back.

He sounds like he really means it this time. I didn't want twin beds. I love to roll across the king-sized mattress and snuggle next to his gorgeous body.

"Okay," she said. "I'll see someone about this nightmare."
He stopped eating and looked at her.

"Everytime I threaten to get twin beds, you say the same thing."

Lately she had been seriously thinking about seeing someone about the nightmares. Every day she wondered. Is tonight the night it comes? She was sick of the stress, the anxiety of awaiting each one. Over the years, she had tried to figure out what triggered it. She had recorded her activities. Foods eaten, the times eaten. She had even kept a record of the times she went to bed and how long she slept. She had even tried comparing the nightmares with the phases of the moon but was never able to pinpoint anything specific and had finally given up.

"I mean it this time. I'm making an appointment."

"Uh huh." He never stopped eating nor looked her way.

"I mean it. I'm sick of waking up frightened out of my mind with my eyes on fire and not knowing why."

"You've been saying that for how long now? Sixteen, seventeen years?"

"I mean it this time."

"If you do mean it." He took her hand. "You should see Rachel."

"Rachel Chambers?" She jerked free and rolled her eyes.

"If Rachel can't help you," he said. "No one can."

"Humph," she said and snatched the paper up to her face.

"How many times do I have to say it? There has never been anything between Rachel and me. There's no reason for you to be jealous."

"So what if your sister is married to her brother?" She lowered the paper. "You're a man, she's a woman!"

Richard debated with himself before he spoke.

"Rachel's a woman, but she's also a lesbian."
Emily looked at him with pure astonishment.

"She's a what?"

"You heard me," he said and sipped his coffee.

"You've known this about her and never told me?"

"I made her a promise—"

"You made her a promise. What about your promise to never lie to me?"

"I didn't lie, I just never told you. Plus, I made my promise to Rachel long before I made one to you."

"So her promise had precedence over mine?"

"No baby, it's just that Rachel had more at stake."

"Like what?"

"Her career for one."

"So?"

"All you were was a little jealous."

"Jealous?" She screeched. "I was never jealous."

"You were insane with jealousy and you know it."

"I was not."

"You were too."

"So why are you breaking your promise now?"

"It wasn't fair to have you thinking there was even the remotest possibility Rachel and I might be involved."

"I never thought you were involved with her"

"Sure." He laughed. "Sure."

"I didn't," she said. "I trust you implicitly."

"Right."

"Rachel Chambers is too beautiful to be a lesbian."

"They don't all wear overalls and butch haircuts."

"How long have you known about her?"

"A long time."

"How long?"

"Emi-lee-e." He dragged out her name, annoyed.

"You shouldn't have mentioned it if you weren't prepared to discuss it." She flared. "Now, how long have you known?"

Richard sighed and blew out his cheeks.

"Since we were kids."

"Kids?" she asked. "How old?"

"Around eighteen."

"How did you find out about her?"

"She told me."

"Why?"

"She wanted me to tell Junior why she broke their engagement."

Emily's mouth gaped open.

"Ralph was engaged to marry Rachel Chambers?"

"Yes."

"What happened when you told him?"

"He was heartbroken."

"Poor baby! How did *you* feel when she told you?"

"I considered her a freak who'd hurt my big brother."

"But you're still friends. Why?"

"She made me understand she hadn't chosen the lesbian lifestyle, the lesbian lifestyle had chosen her."

"The Bible says homosexuality's an abomination."

"I think they're born like they're born, like everyone else."

"It's hard to believe anybody would be gay if they had a choice. You know how some people treat them."

"Yeah, I know," he said.

"Did Ralph ever get over Rachel?"

"I guess. I only talked about her with him once."

"When was that?"

"One Thanksgiving when we were all home."

"What did he say?"

"I don't remember. That was when you were driving me nuts."

"I never drove you nuts."

"Yes, you did. I came to Atlanta looking for you like crazy."

"Did you find me?" She teased.

"Yes." He grinned. "Remember the first time we made love? I couldn't believe what was happening to me."

"Stop it!" Emily covered her ears with her hands. "Do I have to hear this for the rest of my life?"

"You were fantastic." He caressed her arm. "You hadn't had sex in a long time, had you?"

"No," she said with a laugh.

"You were in dire need of some good sex weren't you?"

"Why do you talk about things that happened so long ago?"

"Because my little apple pie, our first time was incredible."

"Stop it." She changed the subject. "You should introduce Ralph to some of your female colleagues."

"Junior's a big boy." Richard drank the last swallow of coffee and wiped his mouth and hands on a napkin. "He can find his own women."

"Well, I'm going to introduce him to Annette."

"Wild Annette and cool Junior?" He laughed. "Get real."

"Annette would make Ralph a fine wife."

"She's not his type."

"Opposites attract. Annette's fire, Ralph's water."

"Yeah, they'd make steam and blow each other away."

"They would not."

"Stay out of Junior's love life," he said. "Are you going to see Rachel now that you know she doesn't want my body?"

"No," she said glumly. "She'll probably want mine."

"No, she won't."

"How do you know?" Emily helped him into his jacket and fluffed the hand-kerchief in his breast pocket.

"Rachel's world renown and very much in love with someone."

"Who? Who?"

"Nobody you know."

"I might know. Who?"

"I'm not telling you," he said. "So stop asking."

"You might as well tell. I'm going to pester you until you do."

"You can see Alfred Keenan."

"Is he good?"

"Yes, but he can't touch Rachel's expertise."

"He can't?"

"Nope." He kissed her and headed for the door.

"Maybe I should wait a while."

"I can have those beds in our room before noon."

"You wouldn't?"

"I will, now who will it be, Rachel or Alfred?" He waited for her answer.

Can Rachel Chambers help me? She is world-renown. Maybe she can.

"I don't know," she said.

Richard returned and pulled her to him. "Do you think I'd send you to some-body I thought might try to get my good pussy?" He felt it through her robe. Emily said nothing.

"Well, do you?"

"No."

"Who will it be then? Rachel or Alfred?"

"Rachel, I guess."

"You're sure now?"

"If she looks at me funny once, I'm out of there!"

"Fair enough." He went down the steps, laughing.

Although leery about seeing Rachel Chambers, Emily was also intrigued. *Who is the person she's in love with? Do they have great sex? Is she the man or the woman? Does her mother and brother know about her? Are they ashamed? Did she and Ralph ever do it? Did she like it or was it awful? Can Dr. Rachel Chambers separate business from pleasure?*

6

Wednesday, February 11, 1981

Lisa fell across the bed with her virginity heavy on her mind. Since she'd turned fifteen, doing it was all she thought about. She and her best friend, seventeen-year-old Twyla Burns, were the last virgins in their class if the talk in the girl's locker room could be believed. Everybody said they had done it at least once. They would be in a huddle talking about the good feeling they got when a boy touched their stuff. Lisa knew some were lying. Dina Hudson wasn't. She was four months pregnant. Lisa didn't want a baby. She just wanted to see if it was as good as everyone said. When school started Monday, she intended to be an ex-virgin.

Lisa rolled off the bed and sat at her desk. Lover prospects called for something special. She pulled out the light blue stationery with her initials in gold across the top and in thirty-seven seconds had six candidates from her class.

1. Danny Bell
2. Yusef Ruff
3. Romaine Williams.
4. Joey Marvane
5. Aaron Dillworth
6. Kent Davis

She closed her eyes, picturing each one and lined Romaine off first. He referred to girls as cunts. Danny went next for dirty fingernails. Yusef followed. His hair stayed full of lint balls. Joey's head came to her shoulder. Aaron wore thick glasses and Kent had acne.

Shit! Who is left? Teddy Hicks?

She didn't even write his name. He told everything he knew.

She tossed the paper in the wastebasket and took out a new sheet. This time she drew a line down the middle and one across the top. On the right, she wrote pros. On the left, cons. Her pen poised over the paper, awaiting a name. Carlton came to mind. She wrote his name at the top. Under pros, she put grade in school: senior, time known: all my life, I.Q., very smart. On a scale of one to ten for sex appeal she had to put a zero. Carlton was more like a brother. She tossed that paper and chewed the pen.

Who else? Who else? Sean? Naw. He makes me sick. Thinks he's so smart.

Lisa sometime talked to Sean on the phone, but she always called him. He never called her. She knew it amazed him she was so smart. She also knew he considered her a kid. She heard Sean had lots of sexual adventures but didn't give play by play descriptions the next day in the boy's locker room.

Let's just see how things look.

She wrote Sean Favor at the top of the sheet. Under pros, she put discreet.

Sean played basketball, football and ran track. She sometimes attended those events but never missed his diving competitions. She loved to watch him stride confidently to the end of the board and stand there like a lean, clean, diving machine, waiting for silence. Suddenly he would leap into the air, execute the dive and enter the water so smoothly there was hardly a splash.

She remembered how the water glistened on his taut frame and trickled to the bulge between his legs. She shivered, wondering what that bulge would feel like in her. Under pros, she wrote great body and packing large. His taunts at her study session came to mind and under cons, she put egotistical and brash. However, she was willing to overlook these faults because then and there she decided Sean Favor was the one she wanted to burst her cherry.

"Well." She dialed his number. "Here goes."

"Hello," Sean said.

"Hi. This is Lisa."

"I know it's you, S. L. G."

"I don't want to be called sweet little girl anymore."

"What should I call you? Kiddy Widdy?"

"Don't you dare call me that!"

"Chill out, chill out!"

"You don't tell me to chill out! I'm always chilled."

"What do you want?" He said annoyed.

She lost her nerve.

"Dina Hudson is having a baby."

"Where have you been? Everybody knows that."

"I bet you didn't know Benny says it's not his."

"That's news. Dina never looked at anybody but Benny."

"I know," she said. "But he still says it's not his."

"Maybe he knows something we don't." He chuckled. "But if my girlfriend was having my baby, I'd be the happiest man in the world."

"You would?"

"Yeah...then I'd have my extension."

"What's that?"

"A child from me is my extension...I'd be immortal."

"Immortal? Come on, Sean."

"Yeah. Daddy says he's an extension of his father, I'm an extension of him, my baby would be an extension of me, his baby an extension of him and so on. Favor blood until the end of time equals immortality...get it?"

"Yeah," she said. "Heavy stuff."

"Yeah!"

"I don't know what I'd do if I got pregnant."

"One thing for sure."

"What?" She expected him to say something smart.

"You'd have a beautiful baby."

"You think so?"

"A baby girl that looks like you. Wow!"

"A baby boy that looks like you." She returned the flattery. "Too fine."

"Yeah, he would be, wouldn't he?"

"Just think if we had a baby together." Lisa got carried away.

"Us?"

"Just kidding. I don't ever want a baby."

"Our baby would be a god, Lisa," he said. "With you as his mother and me as his father, our baby would be the most beautiful baby in the world."

"Yeah, it would."

"Isn't there something we have to do before we had a baby?" He teased.

"That's what I want to talk to you about."

"What?"

"I...I..." She stammered nervous. "Uh...uh...I...want."

"Spit out what's on your little mind."

"Little mind?" She hissed. "I knew not to ask you."

"Ask me what?" he said quickly.

"Nothing."

"Come on, what?"

"Forget it."

"What is it?"

"I said forget it."

"I'm sorry about what I said, tell me."

"No!"

"Forget it then. I've got to go."

"Fine." Lisa slammed the phone down.

It rang immediately.

"Hello." She answered.

"What do you want to ask me?" Sean said.

"I thought you weren't interested."

"I am. What is it?"

"I want you to make love to me."

"Wha-a-at?" He had expected something silly.

"I want you to make love to me."

"I can't do it to you."

"Why not?" She never considered he would refuse.

"Because." He hedged.

"Because what?"

"Li-sa."

"That's okay, I'll ask somebody else."

"Who?"

"What's it to you? You're not interested."

"You're just a kid."

"A kid!" She shrieked and slammed the phone down again.

Sean hung up bewildered. Juveniles were always flirting with him, blatantly offering to fuck him anytime, anyplace, anywhere.

I haven't popped any of them though. After all, I'm a senior. I have a reputation to uphold. If any of my homies found out I was doing a juvey, I'd never hear the end of it.

Lisa flashed through his mind. His dick began to swell. It had never done that before when he thought of her. He always considered her a little girl and now she wanted him to fuck her. Sure she was a senior and acted older, but she was still a juvey, a fifteen-year-old kid. The more Sean thought about Lisa, the harder his dick got.

Maybe I could tap it once. This is crazy. Suppose I get caught with her?

His dick throbbed in measured beats.

It's better for me to pop her than some stranger.

His dick pressed like a steel pipe against his jeans. He picked up the phone.

I didn't ask her. She asked me.

"Hello," Lisa said.

"Hey."

"What do *you* want?"

"I changed my mind."

"Don't do me any favors, Favor!"

"It's not a favor. I want to."

"Oh. What made you change your mind?"

"I don't want you exposing yourself to the shit in the street," he said. "You need someone to watch your back."

Smooth Sean, very smooth.

"Okay," she said. "When?"

"What about tonight?"

"You know I can't get out on a school night."

"Well when then?" He was anxious to proceed.

"I'll be at Twyla's this Friday."

"That's two days away. Can't you say you're going to the mall, tomorrow?"

"Maybe," she said.

"How much money do you have?"

"None, why?"

"I'll need twenty-five for my man at the motel."

"Twenty-five dollars? Where am I going to get twenty-five dollars?"

"This was your idea. That's your problem."

"Okay, okay I'll get it."

"I'll pick you up after last period."

"I have to come home first."

"Damn!" Sean said. "Why?"

"Because my father said so."

"I'll pick you up as soon as the bus drops you off."

"Okay."

"I've got to go. I'll talk to you later."

"Don't go."

"I've got something I need to do."

I don't know if I can wait until tomorrow, her voice has me on fire.
Lisa's hands shook so. She could hardly dial the phone.

"Hello." Twyla Burns answered on the first ring.

"Guess what?"

"What?"

"Sean's going to make love to me."

"Sean who?"

"Sean Favor."

"You mean football star, class president, fine, fine Sean Favor?"

"Yes, I do."

"How did you manage that?"

"I asked him and he said yes." She didn't go into his initial refusal.

"Sean is going to do it to you?"

"Don't sound so sad."

"I'm not sad." Twyla pretended to cry. "I'm jealous."

"You'll do it soon."

"But it won't be with Sean."

"It'll be with somebody you like."

"Nobody likes me."

"Carlton likes you. You could do it with him."

"If Carlton's so great, why don't you do it with him?"

"Wel-l-l-l," she said. "I asked Sean first."

"Carlton's a fumbler."

"How do you know that?"

"Who do the girls hang all over, Carlton or Sean?"

"Sean but—"

"I rest my case."

"There're more guys to choose from than Carlton."

"Name one."

"I can name six."

"Who?"

"Romaine, Yusef, Danny, Joey, Aaron and Kent."

"I might halfway consider Aaron but the rest are losers."

"Dang, Twyla. You're too hard to please."

7

"**M**ommy." Nicole told as soon as she got in the house. "Lisa's in the front talking to Sean."

"She knows I don't like her hanging on the front with boys." Emily marched to the foyer and jerked open the door. Lisa leaned in Sean's car window. Their heads touched conspiratorially.

What are they up to? They're planning something.

Emily disliked Sean and thought he was so full of himself, he might explode at any moment. She heard he was spoiled rotten and believed it just by looking at his red Porsche parked inches from her prize roses. No teen-aged boy needed a car that cost more than some people earned.

"Mother?" Lisa asked. "What do you want?"

"Invite your friend in for some refreshments," Emily said.

"Mrs. B," Sean said. "Any other time I'd be delighted to eat some of your delicious cooking, but I can't today."

Emily lingered at the door

"Mother!" Lisa snapped. "He doesn't want anything!"

Emily went inside without another word.

"Why do you let her talk to you like that?" Nicole asked. "She just blew you off in front of Sean."

"Nicole, please," Emily said and went upstairs.

Lisa went in the kitchen wearing painted on jeans, a poured in sweater and more make-up than a clown. She took Emily's wallet from her shoulder bag and removed three tens.

"What are you doing?" Emily asked.

Lisa spun around, clutching the bills.

"Uh, uh," she stammered then said boldly. "Sean's taking me to the mall. I needed some money."

"Put that money back. You're not going anywhere."

"I'm going." Lisa smirked. "I'm going."

Emily wanted to slap the smirk and the make-up from her face. Her eyes filled with tears, she knew her voice would quake and turned away.

Reveling in her new power, Lisa strutted for the door.

"Where do you think you're going?" Richard's stern voice jerked their heads to the garage door.

"Daddy," Lisa said. "You're home early."

"I stood here just to see how far you'd go." He glared at Lisa then looked at Emily. "Are you all right?"

Emily nodded and wiped her eyes.

"Hand it over," he said and leveled his palm under Lisa's nose.

"What?" Lisa said.

"The money you stole from your mother."

"Money?" She lied with a straight face. "I...I didn't steal—"

"Don't even try it! Hand it over!"

Lisa dug out a ten and laid it in his hand.

"Don't you play with me, girl!"

"Daddy, I...I...I..." Lisa gave him the remainder of the money.

He gave it to Emily. She stuffed it in her bag.

"You're grounded for thirty days."

"Thirty days?" Lisa wailed. "That's not fair!"

"You're lucky it's not forever."

"I'm suppose to go to Kenya's party Saturday."

"You're not going to Kenya's party and you're not going to see her again."

"Why, Daddy, why?"

"Because I said so that's why."

"Damn!" Lisa muttered under her breath.

"What did you say?" Richard asked.

"Nothing," she said, rolling her eyes.

Richard grabbed her collar with such force, he lifted her off the floor.

"Daddy! Please!" Lisa cried. "Chok...ing...me...ow...ow!"

He dragged her toward the laundry room.

"Let her go!" Emily screamed. "You'll break her neck!" She pried at his grip and was dragged along, too.

Richard grabbed a face cloth from the table and turned on the hot water.

"Daddeeeee!..Daddeeeeee! Plee...eeze! Plee...eeeze!"

"Let her go!" Emily shouted. "Let her go!"

He shook her off and jerked Lisa to the water. Steam billowed in her face. She struggled to escape. He squirted in a golden line of liquid soap and turned on the cold water. Bubbles threatened to overflow the sink. He turned off the water and pushed Lisa's screaming face through the suds.

"You'll drown her!" Emily hammered at his back. "Let her go!"

Hunching his shoulders, he forced the cloth in Lisa's mouth, scouring inside like he was washing a dirty cup.

"Next time, you'll think twice before you curse me." He pulled her from the water. She sucked in sweet air seconds before he redunked her head and scrubbed her face clean. Satisfied, he let go. Lisa slumped to the floor, sobbing.

"Mommy! Mommy...Mommy!"

Emily pulled her into her arms. "Shhhh shhhhh."

Richard looked at his child with no compassion and turned to leave. Nicole and Michelle flanked the door, bug-eyed.

"If either of you says a curse word or wears make up after I've told you not to." Richard's voice bounced off the walls. "The same thing will happen to you, understand?"

"Yes, Daddy." They moved back to let him pass.

"Let's get you out of these wet things." Emily peeled off Lisa's sweater and unsnapped her bra.

"What are you looking at?" Lisa held a towel over her breasts.

"That's what we're trying to figure out." The sisters sang together.

"Mommy!" Lisa whined. "Make them stop looking at me!"

"Who wants to look at your old naked self?" Michelle laughed.

"Come on, Michelle," Nicole said. "Let's go tell Sean, Lisa can't go with him because she's all wet."

"Mommeeee!" Lisa shrieked. "Make them leave me alone."

"Go along now." Emily shooed them away and helped Lisa into dry clothes.

"My eyes burn," Lisa said, pitifully.

"I have some drops in my medicine cabinet. Come on."

Mother and daughter walked up the stairs arm in arm.

"Mommy, I can't believe he dunked my face in the water!"

"It was a horrible thing for him to do."

"I didn't have that much make-up on, I didn't deserve that."

Emily knew it wasn't only the make-up, it was the money she'd stolen, plus he said she'd cursed him, but still, dunking her face. She dropped the medicine in Lisa's eyes as her anger at Richard escalated to fury.

"Oww, owww!" Lisa jerked away. "That burns."

"I know, but it'll feel better in a minute." Emily placed a damp cloth over Lisa's eyes. "Lie here and rest. I'll come back later to check on you."

Emily went to confront her husband and knew exactly where he would be. She went to the garage and opened the door behind her car. Richard bent over the worktable, sanding the back of the jewelry chest. She walked closer and saw her love note a crumpled pink ball in the wastebasket. She folded her arms across her breasts and glared until he looked up.

"What?" he said and blew away a fine layer of sawdust.

"You know what!"

"Don't start with me! Don't even start!"

"That was totally unnecessary."

"I don't understand you." He spread his hands. "You're angry because I chastised Lisa, yet you let her get away with murder."

"I do not."

"I know you heard her curse me."

"No, I didn't!"

"You had to hear her. You were standing right there!"

"Well, I didn't!"

"Well I did!" he said harshly. "But it should have been you dragging her to wash that gunk off her face, not me."

"Lisa's only fifteen—"

"That's right, she's only fifteen." Richard threw a cloth over the jewelry chest. "So why weren't you all over her?"

"I...I." Emily stammered ashamed of her weakness.

"You never told her to stop seeing Kenya. She planned to go to her party."

"Uh...I was going to. It's hard telling Lisa to give up a friend she's known all her life; she can't see the unsavory things in Kenya we do."

"Lisa is to stay away from Kenya. I've seen some of her friends and frankly they scare the hell out of me."

"If you tell her to stay away, she'll want to see her that much more." Emily used Annette's analogy. "Lisa's in a phase, testing her wings." She doodled in the sawdust.

"I'll say. She stole your money and you didn't even whimper."

"I was going to say something."

"Before or after she starts robbing banks?"

"That's not funny."

"I know its not. You need to put your foot down."

"If I tell Lisa no, she gets angry with me. They all do."

"Let them get angry. A mother's job is to tell her kids no when they need to hear it. That's how Momma did us, and when we overstepped her bounds, she beat our butts."

"I could never spank them."

"Who said spank? Beat 'em 'til they bleed."

"That's not funny, either."

"I'm sorry."

"I don't want them to...hate me."

"Kids don't hate their folks when they're disciplined, they hate them when they're not."

Leora never disciplined me. Maple Honey did. I hate Leora. I love Maple Honey. Maybe there's something to what he says.

"You think so?" She stopped doodling and looked at him.

"I know so," he said with conviction and a kinder tone.

She perked up at the change in his voice.

"We have great kids, don't we?" She reached across the table and touched his hand. "Did you see the "A" Lisa got on her assignment?"

"What assignment?" he asked.

"The assignment she researched at the library, Monday."

"I've been meaning to talk to you about that."

"What?"

"Lisa didn't go to the library, Monday."

"What do you mean?" she asked.

"I mean she wasn't at the library, Monday."

"Yes, she was." She insisted.

"No, she wasn't."

"But she said—"

"I found out today she was in Atlanta with Kenya."

"But Lisa said—"

"I know what Lisa said. She swore she was at the library."

"How do you know she wasn't?"

"Junior dropped by the office today and happened to mention seeing Lisa and Kenya in Atlanta Monday at the time she swore she was at the library."

"Couldn't he have been mistaken?"

"Emi-lee-e...please." The look on her face made him sorry he'd been so blunt but she needed to understand how their girls always managed to deceive her.

"She told me she was at the library. Are you sure?"

Richard's voice rose like a thundercloud. "You're asking me...if...I'm...sure?"

"Yes, I am," she said. "Are you?"

Richard marched from the workshop, she followed.

"Well, are you sure?" Emily asked again in the kitchen.

"Goddammit!" He whirled around. "You let our girls do what ever the hell they please and you ask me if...I'm...sure?"

"I'm sorry." She tried to make up. "I was trying to—"

"You as much as called me a liar!"

"I didn't mean to." She turned from his fury and looked at the roses on the windowsill. "I know you'd never lie."

"You didn't seem to think so when I told you about Lisa."

"Honey, I was sorry as soon as I said it."

Emily spun around, but he already stormed through the swinging door, cutting off her apology. Sighing, she slumped against the sink.

Why can't I discipline my children or see through their deceit?

8

Richard arrived home early for the monthly trip to Athens to visit his parents. Usually, Emily enjoyed seeing her in-laws, but today she dreaded going. Everything was not fine between her and Richard and she didn't want to pretend it was. They still weren't speaking. They'd never gone this long without making up, but she didn't care. The way he'd screamed goddammit at her, she should never speak to him again in life.

Dinner was a glum affair. Michelle and Nicole picked at their food. Lisa said she wasn't hungry but Richard made her sit at the table anyway.

"May I be excused?" Lisa asked when the meal was over.

"Yes," her father said.

Lisa ran to her room. Richard threw down the napkin and followed.

"Come in," Lisa answered the knock to her door.

"I want to talk to you," Richard said.

Lisa jumped from the bed, pleading the second he came through the door.

"Can I start my punishment next week?"

"Wrong doers don't choose their punishment time."

"I'm suppose to go over Twyla's house tonight."

"You're grounded. You won't be spending tonight with anybody but us."

"Please, Daddy." She hugged him.

"I said no."

"I never get to do anything!" She fell on the bed, crying.

"That's right and as long as you're irresponsible, you won't. "

"Daddy, let me go for a few hours. I won't even ask for all night."

"No. So you might as well call Twyla and tell her you won't be coming."

"My punishment is too harsh," she said crossly. "Thirty days is too long."

"You'd better watch your tone. I'm not your mother. I'll use my belt on you."

"I'm sorry."

"Stealing from your mother's purse." He shook his head. "I'm so ashamed of you, I don't know what to do."

She scrambled off the bed and hugged him again.

"I'm sorry, Daddy...I love you."

"Don't try to butter me up." He took her arms from around his waist.

"I'm not trying to butter you up. I do love you."

"I love you, Lisa Marie." He lifted her wet face up to his stern one. "But remember this, if you remember nothing else."

Uh oh! When he uses my first and middle name, he is truly pissed.

"What?" she asked.

"If you ever take another dime from your mother like you did yesterday, there will be no place for you to hide from me, do you understand?"

"Yessir, I'm sorry."

"You should be."

"I'm really sorry."

"Don't tell me you're sorry," he said. "Tell your mother. Now get ready so we can go." He closed the door on the way out.

"Damn!" Lisa said way under her breath.

I thought surely I could have talked Daddy into letting me spend tonight with Twyla. How am I going to explain to Sean why we can't meet? I can already hear him calling me a 'widdle baby'.

She called Sean and got a busy signal. Two minutes later, it was still busy.

"Damn!" She called Twyla.

"Hello."

"I can't meet Sean tonight."

"How come?"

"I'm on punishment."

"For what?"

"For wearing a little make-up and some more stuff."

"It's for the best. Aren't you afraid to have Sean stick his pee-pee in you?"

"Twyla," Lisa scolded. "Don't say pee-pee, say dick."

"I could never say," she spelled. "D-i-c-k!"

"Dick rhymes with sick and pick. Don't you say those words?"

"Yes, but—"

"Twyla, it's only a word, Je-sus Chr-ist!"

"Don't use the Lord's name in vain."

"Twyla," Lisa said. "Sorry!"

"You're forgiven...You're so brave, I'd be scared to death."

"Women have been doing it since the beginning of time."

"I know but what if it hurts so bad you pass out?"

"It's not going to hurt *that* bad," Lisa said with more assurance than she felt. "Talk to you later. I have to reschedule with Sean."

"Okay, bye."

Sean's number was still busy. Lisa called Kenya.

"Hello," Kenya answered.

"I can't come to your party."

"Why?"

"Daddy said I couldn't."

"I thought you were looking forward to your first grown-up party."

"I was."

"I guess you'll miss all the fun."

"Yeah. I guess."

"Too bad," Kenya said. "Baby parties are your speed anyway."

"They are not!" Lisa said. "I'm coming to your party."

"Oh yeah. How're you going to do that?"

"I'll slip out after everyone's asleep.

"Don't get caught now."

"Hey...this is Lisa Marie...the Kid."

"Lisa!" Richard bellowed through the intercom. "Let's go."

"I've got to go. See you Saturday."

Lisa tried Sean again and hurriedly dialed Twyla's number.

"I couldn't get Sean," she said. "Do me a favor."

"What?"

"Call Sean. Tell him I had to go to Athens and I'll call when I get there."

"Let me get a pencil." Twyla rummaged in her desk. "I can't find a pencil."

"Lisa, let's go!" Richard shouted.

She jumped up and pressed the intercom. "Coming, Daddy. Twyla how can you not have a pencil? Use a lipstick, a crayon, something!"

"What's the number? I can remember it."

"555-6378."

"555-6378," Twyla said. "Got it."

"You're sure?"

"Of course, 555-6378."

"Lisa." Richard warned. "If I have to come up these stairs."

"I've got to go," Lisa said. "Tomorrow I'll still be a virgin."

"Don't be so sad. I'll still be one, too."

Loud footsteps sounded on the steps.

"I'm coming, Daddy!" Lisa jumped off the bed and slammed the phone down so fast, she never heard Twyla ask.

"Is Sean's number 6578 or 6978?"

Michelle sat between her silent parents chattering about her upcoming ballet recital. Nicole hugged the right rear door. Lisa steamed on the left.

What could Sean and I be doing right now? Hugging and kissing at first and then...and then.

Lisa angrily folded her arms over her breasts and sucked her teeth.

"Suck your teeth again and it's going to be me...and....you. Understand?"

"Yes Daddy."

I'm still doing it. I'll have Sean meet me at Kenya's party.

Lisa wanted a party when she had turned fifteen. All she'd gotten were some presents and taken to dinner.

'Your sixteenth birthday is the important one,' her mother had said. Her sixteenth birthday was over six months away. Kenya's party was Saturday and was going to be the party she didn't have last year.

I think I'll even try some cocaine.

The sun had set when Richard steered his black Mercedes into the back yard at his parents' home and parked.

Pauline Bennett stepped on the porch, wiping her hands on her apron.

"I knew ya'll were coming today."

Michelle and Nicole scrambled from the car up the steps into her open arms.

"Where's Grandpa?" Nicole asked about her favorite person in the world.

"In the living room, honey," Pauline said.

Nicole yanked open the screendoor and hurried inside.

"Gram." Michelle tugged at her arm. "Guess what?"

"Hmm?" Pauline gazed into her bright eyes.

"Lisa's on punishment. She didn't come home and wore a lot of make-up."

Pauline peered in the car and got a hateful look from Lisa.

"Gram." Michelle ran down the steps to a wooden swing suspended from a stout oak branch. "Come push me."

"It's chilly out here and getting dark."

"Just a few, plee…eeze."

"Hello, Momma." Richard came up the steps next. "How's my favorite girl?" He lifted her hefty five-foot, cocoa-brown bulk off the floor.

"Put me down, boy." Pauline laughed. "You got to be strong as a bull to lift all this weight."

"Momma." He kissed her cheek. "You're perfect to me, just perfect."

"Sonny, you always know exactly what to say."

"How's Daddy doing?"

"Fine as long as he takes his medicine like he should."

"Let me go holler at him," he said and went inside.

"Hi." Emily walked into Pauline's arms. "How're you doing?"

"Just fine, just fine."

Emily's hug went on and on.

"What's wrong, baby?" Pauline patted her back.

"Richard is so angry with me. He says I doubted his word."

"Don't tell me about my son and his word."

"If you can't trust a man's word," they said Richard's adage, laughing. "Then what can you trust?"

"I'm having problems with, my girls, too." Emily said.

"What kind of problems?"

Emily told how Michelle and Nicole pouted when she told them no, how Lisa had been acting, but left out her brazenly taking money from her wallet. *I hope Richard won't mention it either. I feel like such a wimp.*

"How long has this been going on?"

"For awhile."

"I love these chil'ren, but they need their buds nipped, that's what they need."

"I don't want them to hate me."

"Hate you, why would they hate you?"

"I don't know."

I never want my children to feel about me the way I feel about Leora.

"Smack their faces and let them know you're the boss."

"I have never hit my children." She shook her head. "And I never will."

"Never say never, my girl." Pauline warned. "Never say never."

"Mommy, push me, please." Michelle sat on the swing, sucking her thumb.

"We'll talk later." Emily went to the swing and sent Michelle soaring.

Pauline hobbled down the steps and opened the car door.

"You think you're the only one ever been punished for doing something stupid?" she said to Lisa.

Can't you see I want to be left alone?

"You hear me talking to you, girl?"

"Yes, ma'am."

"Move over." Pauline climbed in beside her.

Oh no! Not another lecture.

"I remember the time I sneaked off to a dance."

"You sneaked off to a dance?" Lisa said. "Wow!"

"Yep. I stole Papa's car."

"You stole a car?" Lisa couldn't believe her Gram, a stickler for honesty, was a car thief.

"Sure did. Dumb! Dumb! Dumb!"

"Wow!" Lisa said. "Was the party worth it?"

"That was the grandest party." A happy glow lit up her face. "I met your Grandpa at that party."

"You did?" Lisa said. "Tell me, tell me!"

"It's getting chilly. Come on inside, I'll tell you later."

"Tell me a little bit, plee...eeze?"

"Well-ll. I got to the party, Herb Strong, the boy I liked tried to get me out to his car. When I wouldn't go, he took off with Gloria McGrew."

"Oh, Gram, how awful."

"I was a virgin." She snickered at the memory. "I couldn't compete with those fast girls that...that—"

"Gave it up, Gram?" Lisa offered.

"Yes." Pauline looked at Lisa. "Have you given it up?"

"No, ma'am," Lisa said. "Not yet."

"Remember, your body is a precious gift."

"It is?"

"You don't give presents to just anybody, do you?"

"No ma'am."

"The same applies to your body. These are dangerous times. There's diseases, and this new thing called AIDS."

"Did you bake a pineapple-coconut cake?"

"Have you heard a word I've said?" She took Lisa's hand.

"I heard."

Pauline looked at the darkening sky with a silent prayer.

Watch over this child, Father. Please watch over this headstrong child.

"Will you promise to save yourself for someone you love who loves you?"

"I promise to save myself for someone I love who loves me." Lisa kissed Pauline's hand. She always treated her like the woman she almost was. She was glad she'd come. She thought of Sean…well almost glad.

"Tell me about how you met Grandpa."

"He asked me for a dance." She swayed to the music in her head. "It was like we'd practiced together all our lives. We were so smooth. The floor cleared and it was just us dipping and twirling."

"Too bad you can't dance with Grandpa anymore."

"Oh, I dance with your Grandpa all the time."

I don't believe that. How can a paralyzed man dance?

"Come on," Pauline said. "I did make a pineapple-coconut cake."

"Mmm," Lisa said. "Yummy."

"Listen to your parents, girl. They only want the best for you."

"I know, Gram, I will." Lisa took Pauline's hand. She wouldn't have to steal her Daddy's car tomorrow night. Kenya only lived three blocks away.

"Don't stay out too long." Pauline called to Emily and Michelle.

"We're coming." Emily grabbed the ropes, bracing herself against the to and fro momentum of the swing until Michelle jumped out and ran ahead. Emily strolled toward the two-story brick house, admiring its solid beauty. She loved Pauline's home: The spacious rooms. The crannies. The nooks. It suddenly occurred to her: Pauline's house was identical to Leora's. She laughed out loud at the irony. How could two houses so alike be so different? Pauline's house was filled with love. Leora's house was filled with hate. Emily removed her coat before she went through the back door. Ezell stayed cold and Pauline kept the thermostat at eighty degrees year round. She hung her coat in the closet off the kitchen and went to see her father-in-law.

Never without a deck of cards, Ezell Bennett placed a red queen on a black king on the tray clipped to his chair.

"How're you doing?" Emily gave him a hug.

"Not bad for an old man." He stopped playing to return her kiss.

"You're not old."

Ezell laughed a big man's laugh, deep and resonant. His jovial nature and good looks eclipsed the wheelchair he'd been confined to for over thirty years. He kept his mind sharp playing cards, his body lean with daily workouts and his fingers limber playing piano.

"Mommy." Michelle called from the kitchen. "Come here."

"Tell this old body that." He laughed.

"Mommeee," Michelle said. "Come here, please."

"Let me see what this girl wants. I'll be right back."

Pauline put an LP on the stereo. Nat "King" Cole's velvety voice filled the room singing *Unforgettable.*

"Lisa." Pauline called out.

"Yes ma'am?"

"Come here, please."

Lisa stood in the doorway.

"Watch this baby." Pauline tapped Ezell's shoulder.

He looked up from his game.

"Excuse me. May I have this dance?"

"Yes, beautiful lady."

Pauline settled on his lap and put her arms around his neck. His honey brown arms bulged as the wheelchair moved in time to the music. Lisa watched a few seconds and ran to the kitchen.

"Mommy." She pulled Emily by the arm. "Come see Gram and Grandpa dance...come see them dance!"

Michelle and Nicole followed. The four of them sat on the sofa beside Richard, watching Pauline and Ezell glide over the polished oak floor.

"How romantic," Lisa said. Her grandparents were really something.

"Mommy," Michelle said. "You and Daddy should dance?"

"Yeah Mommy," Nicole said. "You guys dance."

Emily looked at Richard. He continued to stare straight ahead.

"Not now," she said. "We'll just watch them."

The music stopped and everyone applauded.

Pauline kissed Ezell and got up. "That was fun."

"Put on Count Basie, baby and let's jitterbug."

Ezell spun his chair around. Pauline did some fast dance steps.

Everyone laughed.

"You guys are something else," Lisa said. "Something else."

"Does that mean we cool?" Pauline returned the LP to its cover.

"You're cool." Lisa laughed. "Real cool."

"Grandpa," Nicole said. "Dance some more."

"Yeah Grandpa." Michelle added. "Dance some more."

"No more dancing...for me." He pretended to gasp.

"Ah Grandpa," Lisa said. "Show us a jitterbug."

"Yeah Grandpa," Nicole said. "Show us."

"Yeah Grandpa," Michelle said around her thumb. "Show us."

"The next time you come, I'll do the Charleston."

Richard, Emily and Pauline laughed. The girls looked perplexed.

"I've got a lure that make fish jump in the net," Ezell said.

"This I've got to see." Richard followed his father to the hall closet for the tackle box.

Emily went to Pauline's room to see the clothes she bought for her trip to see her daughter in Denver. Nicole went to the den to watch television. Lisa went to the kitchen for another piece of cake. Michelle went to the dining room to look at photo albums.

"Get out of my chair." Lisa commanded.

"You don't own this chair." Michelle countered and continued to leisurely leaf through the album.

"I was here first." Lisa set her cake on the table and folded her arms.

"So?"

Nicole heard the squabble and came from the den.

"You don't have to get up, Michelle!" she said.

"You shut up, Nicole!" Lisa glared at her then turned back to Michelle. "Get up. I'm not telling you again."

"Why can't you sit in the other chair?" Nicole asked.

"Because I was sitting in this chair."

"Too bad," Michelle said. "I'm still not getting up!"

"I'm counting to three," Lisa said.

"Count to a thousand and three. I'm still not getting up."

"I mean it, Michelle," Lisa said. "I'm not playing."

"Don't blame me because you're on punishment."

"Onetwothree!" Lisa said and delivered a stunning back blow.

"Oww!" Michelle cried and looked at Nicole.

Has the chance to kick Lisa's ass come so soon?

Nicole nodded. They jumped Lisa and wrestled her to the floor.

"Stop it! Ooww! Ooww! Oowwwwww!" Lisa screamed beneath the flying fists. "Daddeeeeee! Daddeeeeee!"

"What the hell?" Richard pulled the girls off Lisa and shook them like rag dolls. "Have you lost your minds?"

"They jumped on me, Daddy." Lisa cried on the floor. "They jumped on me."

"She hit me in my—" Michelle started to explain.

"I can't believe it, fighting like animals." He shook them again.

"She's always mean to us," Nicole added. "She's—"

"I'm so ashamed I don't know what to do! Get ready so we can go!"

Nicole and Michelle rushed from his sight.

"You okay, Kiddy Widdy?" He helped Lisa stand.

"Daddeee." She sniffed. "Don't call me Kiddy Widdy."

"Sorry."

"They jumped on me for no reason."

"Can you walk?"

"I think so." She took a few baby steps and limped to the kitchen.
Richard watched her go and shook his head.

"See what you started." Nicole accused.

"What I started?" Lisa screeched.

"Yeah," Nicole said. "You pinched Michelle's arm."

"She messed up my Michael Jackson tape."
Nicole scowled at Michelle. "You didn't say you deserved the pinch."

"I was going to," Michelle said. "But you didn't let me."

"I'm not sleeping with you anymore," Nicole said. "I want my own room."

"Please," Michelle begged. "You know I'm afraid to sleep by myself."

"Lisa Marie, Nicole Yvette, Michelle Renee!" Richard roared. The room got
pin drop quiet. "Shut up and get ready!"
He went down the hall and tapped at his mother's door.

"Momma. We have to go. These girls have lost their minds."
Emily, Pauline and Ezell followed Richard to the kitchen. Lisa, Nicole and
Michelle sat in their coats, mopping their sweaty brows with paper towels.

"These three were fighting," Richard said.

"I wasn't fighting." Lisa cleared herself. "They were."

"Fighting?" Pauline shook her head.

"You were fighting?" Emily gaped at her girls.

"Can you believe it, Momma?" Richard said. "Fighting like wild animals.'

"She started it." Michelle pointed at Lisa.

"I did not," Lisa said. "They started it."

"No matter who started it!" Richard barked. "You know what's coming."
Nicole and Michelle groaned. The "no activity" punishment was the same as
a death sentence.

"You're both grounded for two weeks," he said. "School and church only."
Lisa laughed.

I won't be doing time by myself.

"Don't laugh," Richard said. "You have two more weeks added on."

"Why?" Lisa's smug look vanished. "I didn't do anything."

"You weren't at the library, Monday."

"Yes, I was." She lied smoothly. "Yes, I was."

"I happen to know you were in Atlanta."

Lisa blinked, dumbfounded. "Please, Daddy no!"

"My class has a trip to Birmingham." Nicole whined.

"My class, too!" Michelle began to cry.

"Too bad!" Richard said.

"Daddy, Michelle and I saved all year for this trip."

Emily thought the punishment too harsh, but held her peace.

"Too bad, so sad. Goodnight, Momma, goodnight, Daddy."

"Goodnight," Ezell said.

"'Night, son." Pauline returned his hug and kiss.

"Say goodnight, girls!" Richard said and went out the door.

"Goodnight," they sang and ran out behind him.

Emily hugged her in-laws and followed her family.

What kind of children am I raising? Fighting of all things. I can't beat them like Pauline suggests, but I have to do something. What can it be?

With everyone angry at Richard, the temperature in the car hovered near freezing. The girls dozed off immediately, leaving their parents to stare silently at the dark road. The only friendly voice came from the radio until Richard pushed in a cassette and practiced his Spanish. To while away her time, Emily counted semi-trucks. She was up to three hundred and fifty-one by the time they exited at Panola Road and fifteen minutes later pulled into the garage.

"Wake up, sleepy head." Richard shook Michelle. She mumbled something and snuggled deeper into the seat. "Come on, Pumpkin." He carried her inside and left Emily to get the other two in as best she could.

Richard lay on his side, trying to ignore the clinks and squirts associated with Emily's toilette. He longed to turn and watch, but would not give her that satisfaction, not tonight.

Emily's gown swished over the carpeting. She knelt to pray. She climbed in bed, the mattress dipped under her weight. A click set her alarm clock. Another click plunged the room into darkness. *Joyous* perfume wafted over Richard. He almost took her in his arms.

Was I sure?

"You have an appointment with Rachel, Monday," he said dryly. "Her offices are on the twenty-fifth floor of the Lawson Building."

He's talking to me. Maybe we can make up. I need some bad.

"Oh?" she said. "What time?"

"One o'clock." He jerked the covers to his chin and made such a to-do of turning on his stomach, she forgot about them making up or making love.

"Thank you." She stared in the corner the moonlight could not reach, waiting for sleep to come.

Turned low, Lisa's phone rang many times before she awoke.

"Hello." She whispered.

"What the fuck happened to you?"

"Sean, I'm sorry. I tried calling you, but your line stayed busy."

"You left me hanging. I waited for you for hours."

"Didn't Twyla tell you?"

"Tell me what?"

"I had to go to Athens."

"Twyla didn't tell me shit!"

"What! I told her to tell you what happened."

"Well, she didn't."

"I called as soon as I got to my Gram's house."

"I wasn't home! I was waiting for you!"

"Don't be mad. I'm sorry."

"Sorry don't cut it, Lisa."

"What else can I say?"

"You can say when we can set up something else."

"I don't know." She reached over and pulled her blanket off the floor.

"You don't know? How come you don't know?"

"I'm on punishment."

"Punishment?" His laughter split her ears. "Shit!"

"Haven't you ever been on punishment?" She cracked back.

"Yeah." He boasted. "When I was a kid."

She started to say meet her at Kenya's party, but he laughed again.

"What...is...so...damn funny?"

"You are." He teased. "You're a widdle baby."

"I'm not a baby and you'd better stop calling me one!"

"Or what?" He scoffed. "What will you do?"

"Call me a baby again and see!"

"Is the widdle baby mad at Poppa?"

Lisa slammed the receiver down and called Twyla. The phone rang twelve times before she hung up.

"I am pissed with you, Miss Burns, I am truly pissed with you!"

9

A t ten past midnight, Lisa peeked out her bedroom door. All was quiet. She hurried downstairs in bunny slippers and a pink terry robe hiding a red velvet dress that stuck to her body like static cling. She kicked the slippers in the closet and stepped in black heels. She applied the forbidden make-up by the dim foyer light, shook her hair into a wild do and donned her beloved Mitchell Prep jacket. With one last admiring glance, she cut the security system and left.

Very little light shone on Sunday Lake Drive at night. Shadows loomed on both sides of the street like inky monsters, but Lisa was not afraid. She was too excited to be afraid.

A short cut past the Todd residence put her on Kenya's street. The Ross' eight columned colonial house usually resembled a matron in satin and lace. Tonight with rap music peppering the chilly air like machine gun fire and lights ablaze at every window, it seemed a whore in leather and fishnet hose.

Lisa crossed the threshold onto a trembling floor and marijuana smoke so thick she immediately began to cough. She followed the quaking boards to the living room.

Oh boy!

Mrs. Ross' Louis the Sixteenth furniture stood haphazardly by the wall blanketed with her Persian rugs. Eight lines of dancers moved in sync to music blasting from colossal speakers on each side of the fireplace. Lisa searched the room for Kenya. The first person she saw she knew was Zebo. He spotted her and pushed through the crowd. He lost her in a grove of damp bodies, jumped on a yellow damask chair for a better view and saw her leave the room.

During a lull in the music, Kenya's distinctive cackle drifted down the hall. Lisa waded through hips gyrating to a samba beat and found her bent over the baby grand, snorting.

Man, does she look bad.

Kenya's parchment colored skin seemed glued to a skeletal frame. Her hair, tipped with cocaine, hung in strings over eyes sunk deep in her head.

"Hey," Lisa said.

"Hey girl. I didn't think you were coming."

"And miss the party of the year? No, no, no, no, no."

Hot and sweaty, Lisa tied the jacket around her waist and surveyed the room. Zebo stood in the doorway.

Is he following me?

"Let me get you something to drink," Kenya said.

"I'll have some of this." Lisa held up a bottle of sangria. She liked the delicious sweet wine Kenya had introduced her to.

"I have something special for you," Kenya said.

"What?"

"Something you'll love," Kenya said.

She by-passed paper cups and assorted liquor bottles and crossed the room to a tall armoire and returned with a goblet filled to the brim with a creamy brown liquid. Lisa took a sip.

"Mmm," she said. "This tastes like chocolate milk."

"It's creme de cocoa. Drink it. I have a surprise for you upstairs."

"What?" Kenya was always giving her nice gifts.

"You'll see." She pointed to the cocaine. "After you try some of this."

Lisa suddenly felt dizzy.

I'm already getting high from the marijuana. I'm not trying cocaine. I'm here to party, not become a drug addict.

"No thanks."

"Come on, girl, try it."

"No thanks," Lisa said. "What's my surprise?"

"You'll get it, after you try this." She grabbed Lisa's arm to pull her to the piano and knocked the glass from her hand. It bounced unbroken off the thick carpet, splashing the contents at their feet.

"Shit!" Kenya screamed. "Look what you made me do!"

"I'm sorry." Lisa picked up the glass. "I'll get some paper towels."

"Forget that." Kenya yanked her to the piano. "Try this."

"I said no!" Lisa jerked free. "What…is…wrong…with…you?"

"I'm cool." Kenya held up her hands. "I'm cool!"

"What did you have to show me upstairs?" Lisa asked.

"Nothing." Kenya cut a line. "Nothing now."

"Okay," Lisa said dismally. "Where's your friend, Sebastian?"

"How the hell should I know?"

"You don't have to bite my head off." Lisa plucked the damp dress from her body and went in search of something cold to drink.

"Lisa." Earl Young pulled her on the dance floor. "What you doin' here?"

"The same as you, having a good time."

His underarm funk made breathing hard. She turned her head and removed his hands from her hips.

"You feel that?" He rolled against her.

"How could I miss it?"

"Let me give you this log." He whispered. "I been saving it just for you."

"I don't think so, Earl."

He leaned back and looked at her with wild, dark eyes.

"You think you too good to give it to me?"

"It's not that," she said the four magic words she had heard from the girls at school. "My period is on." It seemed nobody liked bloody stuff.

"Too bad." He walked off and left her standing on the dance floor.

"Asshole!" She yelled at his back and continued to the kitchen.

Lisa lingered at a counter full of liquor bottles, hoping to find more creme de cocoa. She opened the refrigerator to disappointment. There was no cold water anywhere. The Ross' always had a jug or two on the door shelf. Lisa gulped a glass of tap water wondering where Kenya's parents were this time. *Europe, Asia, South America?*

Kenya gave a party each time they traveled, handing out their food and liquor probably as punishment for always being left behind.

Lisa saw Zebo headed her way. She turned to go and bumped into a tall, well-built man dressed in black from his cowboy hat to shiny snakeskin boots. *Who is this honey? He is too fine.*

"Ex…cuse me." She gazed into his handsome face.

"Pardon me, Mademoiselle," he said with a lovely accent.

Lisa glanced back. Zebo was nowhere in sight. She turned around for a closer study.

The bulge in his tight pants got her attention first. A cross flashed in thick chest hairs under a suede shirt unbuttoned to the waist. A neatly trimmed mustache and goatee surrounded full, luscious lips. Perfect white teeth gleamed against skin, the color of fine sand. Ebony dreadlocks snaked down his shoulders. Dark eyes bored into hers so intently, she got weak in the knees.

"Are you okay?" He popped his fingers to the fast music.

"Yes."

"Let me introduce myself, I'm Sebastian—"

"Sebastian!" She squealed. "You're *the* Sebastian?"

He is fine as wine. Why isn't Kenya clinging to his arm?

"Yes, I am." He laughed. "And you are?"

"I'm Kenya's friend. We were at your house the other day."

"Hello, Kenya's friend."

She laughed. "I mean I'm Lisa...Lisa Bennett."

"Enchanted." He took her hand. "I'm Sebastian Fabienne."

"Sebastian Fabienne." She savored the name in her mouth. "Where're you from?" She noticed for the first time, a tiny diamond in his right ear.

Cool.

"Jamaica."

"Jamaica?" she said. "I've been to Jamaica on vacation."

"Is that right? Where did you go?"

"All over. Kingston, Ocho Rios, Montego Bay."

"My country is beautiful, is it not?"

"It's very beautiful," she said.

"You're very beautiful."

A blush covered her cheeks. Guys called her fine, but never beautiful.

"Thanks you," she said. "I love your accent."

"And I," he said with a chuckle. "Love yours."

Lisa laughed. It never occurred to her, she had an accent.

"Have you been in America long?" she asked.

"A few years, but not much longer. My business is almost complete."

"Oh." She sipped the water to hide her disappointment.

The fast music stopped. A slow song began.

"Would you like to dance?"

"Yes," she said. "I would."

Sebastian led her through the crowd, not to the stifling living room, but out the sliding glass door to the deserted deck.

A single light illuminated the bushes swaying in the wind. Lisa forgot about her jacket until he helped her in it, took her in his arms and sang the sensual lyrics to the song in her ear. A delightful new warmth enveloped her body and she never wanted the music to stop. A fast song came on. Sebastian led her down the steps to a bench.

"Why are you out so late, little one?"

"Don't call me that." She bristled. "I'm not a child."

"My apologies, Mademoiselle Leesah."

"Apology accepted."

"Your head would be on your pillow if you were home, would it not?"

"I'm not home. I'm exactly where I want to be."

"Home is the safest place from those who aren't what they seem."

"What's that suppose to mean?"

How will it feel to kiss him?

"It means people are not always what they seem." He leaned back. Light filtered through the budding shrubs on her face.

"I know that. What people are you talking about?"

"Are you a virgin?"

"That's none of your business!" She jumped up.

"I did not mean to pry." He stood, too.

A slow song came on. He danced her deep into the garden until the rough bricks on the back wall pulled at her wool jacket, stopping them. He leaned against her. His dick pressed into her stomach.

What does a dick feel like? What will he do if I touch his?

Afraid to risk his anger, she put her arms around his back and languidly rubbed his shirt. He tilted her chin and kissed her lips.

I shouldn't be kissing Kenya's man.

She jerked away.

"I...I can't...I—"

His mouth stopped her protests. His tongue flicked at her lips until they parted and she tasted peppermint saliva.

"Trust me." He whispered. "Trust me."

Lisa's head spun. How could she trust a total stranger she'd just met at one of Kenya's parties? She was probably the only one in the entire house who hadn't done jail time.

Sebastian's hand crawled under her dress and crept inside her pantyhose. A fire ignited in her stuff she had never felt before.

"Sssssso-o-oh." She moaned. "O-o-o-o-o-o-oh!"

I promise to save myself for someone I love who loves me.

The pledge to her Gram popped in her mind.

How could I know it would feel this good?

"Please!" She pulled halfheartedly at the hand in her panties.

"Leesah, Leesah." He tried to kiss her again. She let him.

Remember. Pauline's words hit like stones. Lisa tried to turn away. His body held her captive.

"You want me." His words burned her ear. "Admit it."

"Yes!" she said almost against her will. "Yes."

"Then give yourself to me completely."

"I can't." She went limp. "I can't"

Sebastian leaned off balance to look at her. She shoved with all her strength and knocked him in the bushes.

"Stop!" Sebastian called. "Leesah, wait!" By the time he climbed from the shrubbery, she had disappeared in the house. He went through the rooms looking for her.

"Have you seen, Leesah?" he asked Kenya.

"Why do you want her?" Anger darkened her eyes. "When you can have me?"

"I should tell Lisa about your deal with Zebo."

"What are you talking about? What deal?"

"I heard you outside my door bargaining for Lisa. How could you sell out your friend?"

"I couldn't find anyone else." Her voice was hard. "And business is business."

"I should tell her what you've done."

"Tell her." She laughed. "She won't believe you."

"I'll make her believe me."

"Call her then." She spouted Lisa's phone number.

"Maybe I will."

"When did you become such a crusader? You never cared about the others."

"I should have," he said sadly. "I should have."

"You better stay out of it. Zebo wants Lisa bad, now."

"He won't rape this one."

"He will and he'll kill you if you interfere."

"Not bloody likely," he said. "Not bloody likely."

"Sebastian." Kenya's voice turned to silk. "When are you going to give me some of this?" She touched his crotch.

He knocked her hand away.

"I wouldn't fuck you with somebody else's dick!"

"Fuck you!" She trailed him through the crowd, cursing every step until he jumped in his car and sped away.

"Goddammit! How the hell did I get involved in Zebo's affairs?"
He hadn't meant to listen when he'd lain across the bed and heard Kenya and Zebo bargaining for Leesah. It made him sick to his stomach how they could so casually decide her cost while she stood no more than twenty feet away totally unaware of her peril.
Why does Leesah intrigue me so? Is it her looks? Her sophisticated naiveté?
He was not sure what he would do until the drugged glass fell from her hand. He took that as a sign from the Blessed Mother to save her from Zebo and appointed himself the one to sever her hymen.

With a racing heart, Lisa slipped in the front door and hung up her jacket. She put on the robe, kicked the shoes in the closet and stepped in her slippers.
So far. So good.
After the make-up came off, she tousled her hair and started up the steps.
If anyone sees me, I'm coming from the kitchen for a snack.
  "I'm not doing that shit, again." Lisa glanced in the mirror and could not get over how normal she looked. Where was the guilty face she should see for letting Sebastian kiss her and touch her stuff? She crawled in bed with a heavy heart, reliving the memory of his lips and hands.
Is this what Gram was talking about? Is this how it feels to love someone? Does Sebastian feel the same way?
She drifted off to sleep. The low ring of the phone pulled her awake.
  "Hello," she said hoarsely.
  "Leesah?"
  "Sebastian?" She sat up ashamed she'd run away.
  "Chéri, I want to see you again."
Kenya will kill me. Tell him no! Tell him no!
  "I...I...want to see you, too." She heard herself say.
  "When can we meet?"
Her family would be gone the whole day, first to church then to Athens for her Gram's birthday party. If she could stay home, it could be done.
  "Today!" she said without hesitation. "This morning."
  "Catch a cab to my house," he said. "I'll leave enough money in the mailbox for your fare and a tip."
  "Okay," she said. "What's your address?"
  "789 Iris Lane."
  "I'll be there at ten thirty."
  "Sweet dreams."

"Sweet dreams to you, too." Lisa flopped on her pillow, quivering.
In a few hours, I'll be in Sebastian's arms. I have no doubt I'm giving myself to someone I love who loves me.

10

"You didn't arm the security system last night." Emily slammed a plate stacked four high with pancakes in front of Richard.
I'll make you talk to me whether you want to or not.
"Yes, I did," he said.
Lisa laid her head on her folded arms.
How could I forget to reset the security system?
"It was off when I came down," Emily said.
"I know I turned it on." Richard stopped pouring syrup, trying to remember.
"You just thought you turned it on."
"I'm sure I did," he said. "But I guess I didn't."
Hurry up and notice me, Mommy, before I get too cool.
"I hope we don't wake up with every thug in the county in the house." Emily set pancakes in front of Lisa. "What's wrong with you?"
"I...I...don't feel so good." She closed her eyes to half-mast.
Emily felt her forehead.
"You're burning up."
"My head and eyes ache, too."

"Sounds like the flu." She patted her arm. "Go back to bed, I'll bring your breakfast up."

"Just juice and toast." Lisa shuffled toward the door. "I may be able to keep that down."

Lisa retrieved the hot water bottle wrapped in a towel from the hall closet and hurried to her room. She held it to her face until she heard her mother coming and tossed it under the bed.

Emily set a tray on the desk and felt Lisa's forehead again.

"You feel like you're getting hotter!"

"I feel dizzy, too," she said to add the right touch.

"That's it," Emily said. "I'm staying home."

"No-o!" Lisa moaned. "You've been looking forward to Gram's party."

"Don't be silly, I can't leave you here sick." Emily gave her two cold tablets and a glass of orange juice.

"I'll stay in bed." Lisa gulped them down and slumped back on her pillow. "Don't let me spoil your day."

"I don't know." Emily debated between staying and going.

"Please go." Lisa assured her. "I'll be fine."

"You're sure you'll be okay?"

"I'm sure." She smiled weakly.

Emily's chest swelled with pride.

This is my old Lisa, thoughtful and considerate.

"Okay, now eat your toast." Emily admonished with a shake of her finger. "And stay in bed."

"I will, Mommy, I certainly will."

Lisa watched her father's car go through the gates and drive out of sight. The first thing she did was drop a disposable douche packet in her purse. It was one she'd taken from her mother when she thought she and Sean would do it. Today she would finally get to use it. She called a cab before she showered. By ten o'clock, she had dressed. At ten twenty, she was headed to Atlanta. At eleven, she knocked on Sebastian's door.

He greeted her in a long, burgundy dressing gown with matching scuffs.

I bet he's naked under there.

"Permit me." He pulled Lisa into his arms for a kiss. "I dreamed of doing that all night."

"Me, too," Lisa said breathlessly. "Me, too."

"Are you hungry?"

"I'm starving." The toast and juice had done nothing for her, but her mother knew she could never eat when she was sick.

He hung up her coat and ushered her to the kitchen. Today it smelled of golden delicious apples.

"Where is everybody?" Lisa asked.

"Sunday is my day." He pulled out a chair. "Relax until I fix your food."

"I'm not hungry for food." Lisa looked where the dressing gown fell open at his thigh.

"What are you hungry for?"

"You," she said. "I'm hungry for you to make love to me."

"Are you now?" Sebastian chuckled at her boldness. He swept her in his arms and carried her across the hall into a room full of indigo shadows.

"What's that for?" She pointed to a white towel midway the bed.

"A gift I will treasure." He set her on the spread and kissed her parted lips.

"Will it hurt a lot?"

"At first. Then it will get better."

She looked apprehensive.

"When Fabienne tells you something, what are you suppose to do?"

She looked blank.

"Believe it, Chéri, believe it."

"Okay."

"The pain will come once. The pleasure will last a lifetime."

I love the way he makes plain words sound extraordinary.

"Okay."

"Are you afraid?"

"No," she lied.

"With me there is nothing to fear."

"Okay."

"Je vous vois, Vous me voyez, je t'invite pour un jour d'amour."

"What did you say?"

"You see me, I see you, I invite you for a day of love."

Sebastian shook off the robe, revealing chiseled pecs, abdominals and obliques. His arms and legs resembled coiled steel. Lisa noticed none of this. Her eyes stayed glued to the throbbing, veined dick, standing in a clump of thick black hair.

"Ooooh we!"

"Do you want to touch it?"

She nodded and got to her knees.

"It's...it's so big!" Fear radiated from her eyes.

"Don't be afraid, trust me." He tried to reassure her.

She reached to touch it, then hesitated.

"Go ahead." He commanded. "Touch it."

Lisa touched it. It moved under her hand. She jumped with a shriek.

"It won't bite." He laughed. "Touch it."

Lisa mashed the tip.

"Owww." He pulled away. "That's too hard."

"Sorry," she said and used feather strokes. "Like that?"

"Yes." He closed his eyes. "Just like that."

Lisa marveled at how his dick could be so hard and his nuts so chamois soft. She made a game of trying to catch the little things inside, but they always slipped away.

Sebastian removed her dress. With one deft snap, her bra fell away. Her huge nipples reminded him of succulent red berries on mounds of cream. His tongue circled the tips and drove her mad.

"O-o-o-oh!" Lisa moaned. "O-o-o-o-o-h!"

Sebastian slid off her pantyhose and panties and slipped his fingers in her stuff. Delightful spasms took her breath and left her panting.

Sebastian removed petroleum jelly from the nightstand. Lisa watched fascinated as he rolled on a condom and smeared it with the lubricant. More went on his fingers to cover her stuff. She opened her legs as wide as they would go.

Disguising his eagerness, Sebastian climbed on top of Lisa. He wanted her first time to be perfect. He pushed at her vagina. It resisted. He pushed again, applying pressure. Slowly she began to open.

"Owww!" She screamed. "It hurts! It hurts!"

Sebastian sat back and massaged her clitoris.

"Relax." He whispered. "Relax, relax."

"O-o-o-o-o-o-oh. Sssssssssso-o-o-oh!"

He mounted her again and sank into her sweet tightness.

"Owwww, it hurts!" She started to protest.

Sebastian caressed her stuff again and pushed.

"It hurts, it hurts, o-o-o-o-o-o-o-o-oh, sssss." She groaned until pleasure mingled with pain and she couldn't tell which was which. She squirmed beneath him, moaning his name.

His breaths increased with each thrust. Sweat poured from his face in hers. The cross pendulumed over her mouth.

"I love you!...I love you!...I love you!"

He knew she wanted him to say he loved her too, but he couldn't go that far.

"Thank you."

"Ssss...o-o-o-oh...sss...o-o-o-oh, I think...I'm...coming."

"Come on...come on." He urged. "Let it...go."

The orgasm pulled her to the mountain peak and hurled her over.

"O-o-o-o-o-o-o-o-o-o-o-oh." She spiraled in a free fall of glorious new sensations and flopped back, spent.

Sebastian raised her legs, working for his climax. His sweat burned her eyes. The cross hit in her mouth, leaving the metallic taste of gold.

When is he going to finish? Why is he so heavy?

Lisa shifted. Another orgasm bloomed and began to grow.

"Sssss." she hissed.

Goddamn! I'm working on one nut. She's headed for two.

Lisa's journey to the mountaintop was swift. She leaped into the chasm with outstretched arms and floated from one current of ecstasy to the next until she settled in the valley, totally consumed.

"Sssssss aaaaah," Sebastian yelled. "Sssssssssh hmmmmmmmm!" He shot his load and collapsed on her out of breathe.

"That was the most beautiful experience I've ever had." Lisa gushed.

"That's the first of many beautiful experiences you will have in your life."

"I'm so glad I met you." She wrapped her arms around him.

"You have given me a priceless gift." He showed her the blood stained towel.

"I have?"

"Your virginity is a gift I will treasure."

"You will?"

"When I am a very old man reflecting over my life, I will remember the gift a young woman named Leesah gave me and I will smile with great joy."

"You will?"

He kissed her tenderly. "Yes, I will."

"I'll never forget you Sebastian."

"Nor I you. Who are you going to tell about your experience today?"

What a strange question.

Lisa looked at him puzzled. "My friend, Twyla, why?"

"No one else?" he said casually. "Not Kenya?"

"Why do you ask that?"

"No particular reason. Are you hungry now?"

"Yes," she said. "Starving."

"Come, let us wash and I will prepare you the most scrumptious meal."

Sebastian made pancakes and sausage. Lisa took two bites and pulled him back to bed. She had two more orgasms before he sent her home.

Lisa scrubbed away the makeup and surveyed her face in the mirror.

Now I'm officially a woman.
Each time her stuff jumped, it reminded her of exactly what it felt like to be filled to capacity with a dick. Now she understood the talk at school. The only difference, they had done it with boys. She had done it with a man.
If I don't tell someone what happened to me, I'll explode.
Lisa called Twyla and got no answer.

"Damn!" She slammed the phone down. "Where is she?"
Normally Kenya would have been her second call, but she didn't dare tell her she'd done it with the man she loved. With no one else to share her secret, Lisa got in bed with a book and read until the words merged and she fell asleep.
The giant telephone on Mt. Everest rang shrilly. Lisa grabbed the miles long cord and began to climb. Halfway up, she awoke to the ring of her phone.
Sebastian?

"Hello." She answered breathlessly.

"I'm tired of waiting on you," Sean said. "When are we going to do it?"

"I changed my mind."

"What?" He yelled.

"I changed my mind."

"You can't change your mind."

"Pardon me? This is my mind. I can change it if and when I choose. That's my prerogative."

"To hell with your prerogative! You asked me to fuck you. Now you want to back out, oh no you don't, baby, oh...no...you...don't!"

"Why are you so upset? You didn't want to do it to me in the first place."

"I didn't ask you goddammit, you fucking asked me!"

"And now I've changed my mind."

"You got somebody else to fuck you, didn't you?"

"No." She hoped she sounded sincere. "I decided to wait like you said."

"You're lying, Lisa! You're fucking somebody! I know it!"

"I am not. I decided to wait. Please believe me."

"I don't believe a goddamn thing you say."

"I'm sorry you feel that way." She hung up and left the phone off the hook. When the staccato noise got on her nerves, she unplugged the line and went back to sleep.

11

D r. Rachel Chambers leaned back in the blue suede chair and scanned the information on her newest patient.

Full name: Emily Mona Bennett.

Recommended by: Richard Bennett.

Have you seen a psychologist before? No.

Do you consider hypnosis a valid therapy? No.

What is your favorite color? Blue.

Ahead of her time in her use of unconventional equipment and techniques, color therapy was Dr. Chamber's latest experiment. She felt color affected everyone and had eight suites in different hues. She took her theory so far as to have eyeglass frames and lab coats to match.

What kind of patient would Emily Bennett be? Difficult? Easy?

I hope I can help her.

She pressed the intercom.

"Yes, Doctor?" Millie said.

"Send Mrs. Bennett in please."

Emily came hesitantly in the room.

When is Dr. Chambers going to make a move on me? How does she keep her skin so clear?
Her caramel face was flawless.
Who does her hair?
Her dark brown hair was cut in a short sleek style.
Where did she buy that bad necklace?
The gold tube studded with diamonds had to cost a fortune.
Who is her lover?
Emily imagined Dr. Chambers in bed with a woman. An embarrassing blush spread across her cheeks.
"Hello," Dr. Chambers said.
"Hello." Emily sat in front of the desk, shredding a tissue.
"I see you have trouble sleeping. Can you tell me about it?"
"It's not really trouble sleeping...I...sleep...I just have this...this nightmare." Emily rolled the tissue into balls.
Is she looking at me funny? Is she sizing me up for the kill?
"How long have you had this particular nightmare?"
"Since April 17, 1951."
Dr. Chambers glanced at Emily's date of birth and subtracted.
"You've had this nightmare since you were eight years old?"
"Yes," she said. "It started on my birthday."
"I see," Dr. Chambers said. "Do you have the dream—"
"It's not a dream!" Emily said harshly. "It's a nightmare!"
"Excuse me. Do you have the nightmare every night?"
"I used to have it every night, now at least once a week."
"Does it repeat in a sleep session?"
"Pardon me?"
"Do you have more than one nightmare a night?"
"No, once I have it, I don't have it again that night."
"Tell me about the nightmare." Dr. Chambers leaned back. She had become intrigued years ago when Sonny first mentioned his wife's sleeping problems.
"I can't," Emily said meekly.
"Why?"
"I can't remember it when I wake up."
"None of it?"
"None of it," she said. "All I can remember is the fear."
"Then tell me about the fear."
"It's like a huge monster on my chest, crushing me, overpowering me. I can't explain it."

"Is it always the same fear?"

"Yes."

"Hmm," Dr. Chambers said. "Have you ever been hypnotized?"

No way I'm letting you hypnotize me! No way!

"Hypnotized?" Emily laughed nervously. "No never."

"In a hypnotic state, you may be able to remember."

"What will you do? Swing a pendulum and tell me I'm getting sleepy?"

The doctor's laugh sounded sweet and light like any other woman's.

"It's not done that way anymore. It's done electronically."

"Electronically?" Emily said. "How about that."

"A brain wave synchronizer puts you in an altered state." She pointed to a stainless steel machine next to a navy blue recliner.

"Is that right?" Emily said. "What will they think of next?"

"It's quite reliable."

"I'm sure it is." She fidgeted with her purse and talked about her children, the bookstore and said not another word about her nightmare.

Dr. Chambers stopped taking notes and stood.

Is she going to make her move now?

Emily scooted to the edge of the chair set to run.

"I see our time is up," Dr. Chambers said.

Emily glanced at her watch.

Where did the time go?

"See my secretary about an appointment next Monday." Dr. Chambers came around the desk with her hand out.

Here it comes!

Emily jumped up.

"Follow these instructions." She handed Emily a blue card.

Emily shoved it in her handbag and shook the offered hand. Dr. Chambers gave her hand a soft pat. Emily jerked free and hurried away.

Emily called Richard from the car. He was still in surgery. She hung up disappointed she couldn't share with him the details of her first session.

What was I thinking when I questioned his word about Lisa?

Miss Nina throbbed, reminding her she hadn't had sex in almost a week.

She stopped by Karen's Soul Food Deli and picked up everything Richard liked. Roast chicken, dressing, macaroni and cheese, collard greens, cornbread muffins, potato rolls and chocolate chiffon pie. She unloaded the bags just as Nicole and Michelle came in the door.

"I smell chicken." Nicole smacked her lips. "I'm starved.

"Me too," Michelle said. "Yummy, yummy give me a spoon."

"Change so you can eat. Daddy and I are eating alone tonight."

"In the dining room?" Michelle asked.

"Uh huh."

"How romantic," Nicole said.

"Where's Lisa?" Emily looked at her watch.

"I don't know," Michelle said.

"Me neither." Nicole shrugged.

"Wasn't she on the bus?" Emily asked.

"No." Nicole answered. "Maybe she's with Kenya again."

Emily groaned and hoped not.

"Well." She sighed. "Change your clothes so you can eat."

"Okay," they said and ran up the stairs.

Michelle lathered her hands and rubbed bubbles on her face.

"Can you keep your eyes open in soap suds?"

"Don't ask me." Nicole laughed. "Ask Lisa."

"Girls, hurry up." Emily spoke over the intercom. "Michelle stop playing in that water."

"How did she know I was playing in the water?" Michelle asked awed.

"I don't know. But she always does."

Nicole and Michelle ate hungrily. Emily watched the clock.

Lisa wouldn't be foolish enough to disobey her father's curfew would she?

At five o'clock, Lisa strolled in without a word. She got a soda from the refrigerator and leaned against the sink sipping it, waiting for a comment from her mother. Emily pretended not to notice and she left.

"What's wrong with her?" Nicole asked.

"She needs a spanking, Mommy." Michelle swept the floor.

I wish it were that simple then I'd some how find the courage to spank her.

"Lisa, are you going to eat?" Emily asked twice over the intercom and got no reply. "Michelle, go see if Lisa's going to eat."

She ran upstairs, yelling Lisa at the top of her voice. Minutes later, she was back, crying.

"What's wrong?" Emily drew Michelle on her lap and wiped her tears.

"Lisa, called me a bad name."

"What'd she call you?" Nicole asked.

"She called me a little b—"

Emily covered Michelle's mouth.

"Never mind. Words can't hurt you, forget what she said."

"You said we shouldn't say bad words." Nicole couldn't believe her mother would so casually dismiss something as serious as bad words.

Michelle slid off Emily's lap. "I'm telling, Daddy."

"Don't tell Daddy. I'll talk to Lisa." Her eyes pleaded with them. "Okay?"

"Okay." They agreed, nodding their heads.

"Look at the time." Emily grabbed each girl by the hand. "I need to get dressed before Daddy gets home. Michelle, you can find me something to wear. Nicole, you can style my hair." She led them to her room, hoping the flurry of activity would keep their minds off the fact she was letting Lisa get away with a lot more than she should. "Help make me pretty for Daddy."

"But you're already pretty," Michelle said.

"Thank you, sweetie. Choose a dress, while I shower, okay?"

"Okay." Michelle ran to the closet. Green was her favorite color. A jade gown sparkled inside a clear bag. She tried to open it, but couldn't reach the zipper.

"Did you find me something to wear, sweetie?" Emily came from the bathroom in a terry robe with her head wrapped in a towel.

"Uh huh." Michelle answered. "A pretty one."

Emily sat on the vanity bench next to Nicole.

"My nose is gigantic isn't it?" Nicole pinched it to a point.

"Your nose is perfect," Emily said. "Can you do anything with this hair?"

"Leave it to me." Nicole combed Emily's hair back and twisted it into a chignon at the base of her neck then pulled two tendrils loose by her ears.

"You look pretty like Auntie Annette."

"Thank you, sweetie. You did a good job."

"You're welcome," Nicole said. "Daddy'll be home soon. I'll set the table."

"Thank you." Emily went to the closet. "Which one did you choose?"

"This one, Mommy," Michelle said. "This one."

Emily groaned. Loaded with sequins, the strapless gown weighed a ton. She had only bought it because she liked the color. She stepped in it and the matching shoes and returned to the vanity to apply her make-up. Michelle slid on the bench beside her.

"Mommy?"

"Huh?"

"How did you get that scar on your head?"

"Car acci..." She started to give the answer she always gave, but this time she told the truth. "I don't know."

Michelle looked puzzled.

"You don't know how you got your booboo?"

"I can't remember how I got this booboo."

"It must have hurt a lot. Do you think you cried?"

"I probably cried a lot." She traced the broken lines and tried to force the memory of how she got the hideous scar to the surface of her mind.

"Daddy's home!" Nicole called through the intercom. "Hurry! Hurry!"

Emily ran down the steps and stood at the door when he came from the garage.

"Hello." Emily watched his eyes widen with surprise.

"Hello yourself," he said.

"Are you ready to eat? I have all your favorite foods."

He nodded and she helped him remove his coat. After he washed his hands, she led him to the dining room. Blue candles flickered next to her best place settings on mirrored placemats.

"The table is beautiful, Nicole."

"Thank you," she said and fussed with a napkin until it set properly.

"How was your day?" Emily tried to draw Richard out.

"Fine," he said and silently ate his food.

"Who's ready for dessert?" Nicole asked.

"I am," Richard answered.

"Almost," Emily said.

"Let me take it, Nicole," Michelle begged. "Let me."

"Okay but be careful, these are Mommy's expensive dishes."

"I'll be careful."

Nicole held the door. Michelle walked slowly to the table and served her father. He took a forkful and moaned with pleasure.

"Are you ready for your dessert, Mommy?"

"Yes, I'm ready."

Michelle walked in solemnly with the pie. She approached the table and tripped over nothing at all. The dish flew from her hands and stuck to Emily's bare shoulder like a medal.

"Aaaah!" Emily screamed at the chilly contact.

The plate fell to the table, wobbling toward the edge. She tried to catch it without messing her gown, but it slipped over and shattered on the parquet floor.

"Mommmeee." Michelle ran out with eyes wide with dread.

Nicole hurried in with damp paper towels and picked up the mess.

"Don't cut yourself." Emily warned and wiped the pie from her body. She helped Nicole rinse the pieces, hoping it would glue together. From there, she looked for Michelle and found her hiding in the hall closet.

"Honey, please come out."

"I'm sorry I broke your plate. I didn't mean to."

"I know you didn't." Emily crooned. "I love you more than some old plate."

"You do?"

"Of course I do, come on out now and help Mommy put her dress away." She coaxed Michelle out and they returned the dress to the safety of the garment bag. By the time Emily changed to a sweatsuit and returned to the dining room, Richard had left.

"Let me help." Emily wanted her dishes safely back in the breakfront.

"Don't worry." Nicole shooed her away. "They're in good hands."

Emily wandered into the family room. Richard sat on the sofa, reading the paper. She dropped on the opposite end and thumbed through a magazine.

"Did you enjoy your dinner?" she asked.

"Yes," he said dryly. "Thank you."

"I'm sorry." She scooted over and pulled his stiff body to hers.

"Oh!" He continued to read until she turned his head and kissed his unyielding lips.

"I'm really sorry!"

"How sorry?" he said.

"This much." She extended her arms out as far as they would go.

"Not sorry enough."

"I'm sorrier than this plus the couch combined."

"Not sorry enough."

"I'm sorrier than my arm's length, the couch and this whole room."

He appraised her outstretched arms, the couch and the room. "And?"

"Uh...uh...all that plus the length of the hallway."

Richard decided to forgive her. He was tired of being angry.

"Your sorrow is big enough," he said.

"I'm forgiven?"

"Forgiven." He nibbled her ear.

She kissed him passionately, thinking of the sexual fireworks to come.

"Where's our problem child?"

"In her room."

"Was she home on time?"

"Yes," she said. "Yes, she was."

I seem to be lying more and more.

"How was the appointment with Rachel? I thought about you all day."

"It was okay," she said. "I wasn't impressed."

"Give it a chance. I still think Rachel can help you."

"I'll give her five sessions."

"What can you expect to accomplish in five sessions?"

"That's all I'm giving." She held up her hand "Five!"

"Okay, okay, five is better than nothing. At least you're there."

"That's right."

"By the way, did Rachel hit on you?"

"Maybe, I'm not sure."

"Maybe." He laughed. "She either hit on you or she didn't."

"She patted my hand like this." She demonstrated the handshake.

He laughed again. "Rachel always shakes hands like that."

"Honestly?" she said.

"For as long as I've known her."

"Maybe it wasn't a bad touch."

"Bad touch." He shook his head. "Je-sus Chri-ist!"

"I'm sorry I was so jealous of, Dr. Chambers."

"How could you think I'd go with Rachel? She's practically family."

"I'm sorry."

"You should be."

"Richy," she said his name with such guile, he sat up and looked at her.

"What are you up to?" he said with a grin.

"Who is Dr. Chamber's lover?"

"I'm not telling you, so quit asking."

"Why not?"

"Rachel doesn't need her sexual preference spread over town."

"I won't tell."

"You'd be obliged to tell Annette, and Rachel might as well go on TV."

"I won't tell Annette a thing."

"Sure."

"Cross my heart and hope to die." Emily wet her index finger in her mouth and crossed her heart. "If I should ever tell Annette or anybody."

"No."

"Why are you being so difficult?"

"There's more at stake than your curiosity. I don't want to see Rachel hurt, plus—"

"Plus what?"

"Knowing her identity could undermine your efforts to stop the nightmares."

"Why do you say that?"

"You'd be so busy wondering what Rachel does when she's with her lover, you couldn't concentrate on the reason you were there."

"I could too."

"I'm not telling you," he said defiantly. "So don't ask me anymore."

"Okay." Emily copped an attitude. "I won't.

Nicole and Michelle came in to watch TV. Michelle zonked out first and Richard carried her to bed. Eight-thirty grew near. Nicole began her protest.

"Daddy, can I stay up until nine?"

"No," he said. "We go through this with you every night."

"I'm not a baby. I can stay up later than eight thirty."

"Sure, Nicole."

"I can," she said, emphatically. "Let me plee...eeze?"

"Nope."

Nicole stomped upstairs. Emily looked in on her five minutes later. She was sound asleep.

Richard stopped by Lisa's room. She'd fallen asleep studying. He walked her to the bed and laid the covers over her shoulders.

"Goodnight, baby." He kissed her cheek. "Sweet dreams."

"'Night, Daddy." She mumbled and went back to sleep.

The low insistent ring of the telephone pulled Lisa awake.

Sebastian? It's about time you called me.

She grabbed the receiver.

"Hello." She squinted at the clock.

"Hey," Sean said.

"Why are you calling me at three o'clock in the morning? In fact, why are you calling me at all?"

"When are we going to fuck?"

"Must you be so vulgar?" she asked with a yawn.

"To hell with vulgar. When are we going to fuck?"

"How many times do I have to tell you, I changed my mind?"

"You're a goddamned tease, Lisa, that's what you are!"

"I'm a tease because I changed my mind?"

"Yes, goddammit!"

"I'm not a tease," she said. "Besides, plenty of girls want you."

"I don't want plenty of girls, I want you."

"You can't have me, so stop calling me, you hear?" She hung up and snuggled under the blanket. "Damn, why is Sean tripping?"

12

E arl told Lisa about Kenya's beating at school.

"What happened?" she asked him.

"All I know…" He paused for drama. "…Is a midget kicked her ass like a football."

"Nobody did anything? Nobody helped her?"

"Shit, the man was insane." Earl couldn't keep his eyes off Lisa's nipples poking against her blouse.

"As good as Kenya is to you." She folded her arms over her breasts. "You let Zebo beat her up?"

"Don't start that hero bull shit with me. The dude was packing."

"You could have done something."

"Why didn't you do something your damn self?"

"I'd left already, but if I'd been there, I would have!"

"Sure, Lisa, sure."

"I would have," she said fervently. "How's Kenya doing?"

"Okay I guess, Kenya's tough."

"I called," Lisa said. "Her mother said she moved out."

"Moved my ass, she got thrown out."

"What? Why?"

"Serious damage was done at that party. Cigarette burns on the furniture, holes knocked in the walls."

"Oh yeah?" Lisa cringed, remembering the drink she had spilled.

"A lot of stuff came up missing."

"Like what?"

"Two TV sets, a VCR, plenty liquor."

"Man!" Lisa said. "Do they know who took it?"

"Naw, but it was probably that roguish ass Harvey Parks."

"Is Kenya really okay?"

"She must be, I heard she'd be at the party, Saturday."

"Party." Lisa perked up. "What party?"

"Tricia's party," he said. "You going?"

"Tricia lives across town. I can't get way over there."

"You can go with me." He licked his lips. "Then we can fuck."

"Sorry," Lisa said. "I can't make it."

"See ya," he said and walked away.

Anxious all day about Kenya, Lisa called her the minute she got home.

"Kenya doesn't live here anymore," Dr. Ross said.

"Where does she live?"

"I have no idea."

"If she calls home, will you tell her to call me?"

"Lisa?" he said.

"Yessir?"

"Maybe you should find a friend closer to your own age."

"Why? I've known Kenya all my life."

"I know you have, but sometimes..." He searched for the right words. "Sometimes people will do things to break your heart."

"Kenya would never do anything to hurt me."

"I hope you're right," he said sadly. "I hope you're right."

Lisa hung up worried about Kenya, hoping Sebastian would be at the party. This time when he saw her, she wanted to look better than delicious, she wanted to look scrumptious. She headed for her mother's closet and tried on the royal blue dress. The crepe de chine hugged her hips like a second skin. She buttoned the silver and black beaded cuff around her neck and looked in the mirror. The dress screamed "Sexy! Sexy! Sexy!" so loud it hurt her ears.

Her wardrobe chosen, Lisa went to her room and plopped at her desk, doodling and daydreaming about Sebastian.

"Hello." She stopped to answer the phone.

"What are you doing?" Twyla asked.

"Nothing. What's up with you?"

"Nothing. Are you sure you're not still mad?"

"About what?"

"Because I didn't tell Sean you couldn't meet him?"

"Don't worry about it," Lisa said cheerfully. "Everything was for the best. If I had done it with Sean, I would have never done it with Sebastian." She drew a six-inch heart on her notebook and printed L. B. vs. S. F. inside.

"Was it really as good as you said?" Twyla asked.

"Words can't even describe it."

"They can't?"

"No, they can't."

"Lisa?" Twyla said.

"Huh?"

"Aren't we best friends?"

"Yeah."

"Shouldn't best friends share?"

"You want Sebastian to do it to you, don't you?" She opened the notebook and covered a sheet with Mrs. S. F.

"You said he's a virgin's dream come true."

"He is, but I love him. I'd be crazy with jealousy."

"You know I'm afraid and need help."

"Twyla, some things you just don't ask to share."

"Lisa, please."

"You wouldn't use some one else's toothbrush would you?"

"I'd let you use my toothbrush if you needed it."

"Get real."

"Suppose I let you have my new lace dress."

"A lace dress for Sebastian, are you cra...zy?"

"What about my new watch?"

"I love Sebastian. He is not for sale at any price."

"What about," Twyla said softly. "My diamond studs?"

"What?"

"My diamond studs," she said louder and held her breath.

"You'd give up your diamond studs?"

"Uh huh," Twyla said.

"I'm not promising a thing. He might not want to do it to you."

"Couldn't you call him and ask?"

"I can never get in touch with him," Lisa said, sadly. "I went to his house and nobody answered."

"You think he left town?"

"He would have told me," she said indignantly.

"Don't go off on me."

"Sorry. He'll probably be at Tricia's party. You want to go with me?"

"You're on punishment."

"So?"

"You are too cool," Twyla said. "Too cool."

"What can I say?" Lisa bragged. "What…can…I…say?"

"How are we going to get there?" Twyla asked.

"We could go with, Earl," Lisa said sweetly.

Twyla shrieked. "I wouldn't be caught dead with Earl Young."

"If you weren't so picky, Earl would be perfect to do it with." She laughed. "He's always trying to give somebody his log."

"I'll die a virgin first."

"Maybe you could give it to Sean."

"I sure would." Twyla sighed. "In a hot minute I would."

"I wish somebody would, so he'd leave me the fuck alone."

"Your mouth is so filthy."

"Fuck! Fuck! Fuck!" Lisa hissed. "Isn't that's what you want Sebastian to do to you?"

"Yes…but."

"No buts, you either want to be fucked or you don't. Now which is it?"

"I…I want to…to…be…fucked."

"Now that that's settled, I'll call Shelly for a ride."

"Not Shelly." Twyla complained.

"Why not?"

"She has a lot of car accidents."

"Do you want to go to this party or not?"

"Yes."

"Then chill." Ten minutes later, Lisa called back. "We can ride with Shelly."

"Great," Twyla said without much enthusiasm. "What time?"

"Twelve sharp."

"Twelve?" Twyla said. "My Dad is still up at twelve."

"What time does he go to bed?"

"I don't know around one, I think."

"Are your parents light or heavy sleepers?"

"Light, I think."

"That's not good. My folks sleep like the dead."

"Maybe I shouldn't go."

Lisa thought of the diamond studs.

"Of course you should go," she said. "You just have to be careful when you leave. I'll call Shelly for a later pickup."

Lisa called back with a new pick-up time.

"I'll ring you twice at one thirty, you come out and we'll pick you up at the corner down from your house at one forty."

"I don't know," Twyla said. "Suppose my Dad isn't asleep?"

"Then you have to ask yourself a very serious question."

"What's that?"

"How badly do I want to be fucked?"

"You're vulgar and cruel, Lisa, vulgar and cruel."

"No, I'm not. You need to be there to plead your own case."

"Okay. Three rings at one twenty. I go to the corner of the house."

"Twyla," Lisa said. "Maybe you need to write this down."

"That's not right?"

"No it's not. I'll ring your phone twice at one thirty, you'll meet us on the corner down from your house at one forty."

"I've got that."

"Are you sure?"

"You'll ring twice at one thirty, I'll meet you on the corner from my house at one forty."

"That's right."

"What are you going to wear?" Twyla asked.

"Something totally kicking."

"Is it new?"

"Yeah," Lisa said. "It's my mother's."

"I wish my mother had pretty clothes like yours. All she buys is sweats."

"What about your pink lace dress?"

"Oh. I forgot about that."

"Now," Lisa asked. "What time is pickup?"

"One forty," Twyla said, but not like she meant it.

"And Twyla," Lisa said before she hung up. "I want those earrings in my hand before we leave."

Maybe I'm not in love. I just bargained Sebastian away for a pair of diamond studs.

Saturday, February 21, 1981

Lisa stood at the head of the steps, waiting to hear the television go off. Someone was coming. She scampered to her room and jumped in bed. Excitement coursed through her body at the thought of seeing Sebastian again. Her stuff fluttered so she thought she might have to disappoint Twyla and do it with him herself, diamond studs or no diamond studs. The clock said ten-twenty.
Damn! I'm ready to go. Now!

Her door opened. Emily came in with a basket of clean clothes. Lisa lay as still as her super charged body would allow, listening to her mother put clothes in the dresser drawers.

Tonight of all nights. You should be asleep. Why are you taking so long? What are you looking for in the closet? God! I hope not your new dress.

Lisa burrowed in the pillow to wait her out. Emily left a few minutes later. Lisa did not hear her go. She was fast asleep.

Lisa jerked awake and watched the numbers on her clock change from two nineteen to two twenty. She yanked up the phone and called Twyla.

"Hello." Twyla sounded sleepy.

"Did you get Shelly's call?"

"Are you at the party?"

"No! I'm not," Lisa said pissed she'd fallen asleep like a little baby.

"No," Twyla said. "I fell asleep."

"Me too." Lisa admitted with an embarrassed laugh.

A car horn blew once outside the house. Lisa carried the phone to the window and looked out.

"Shelly's here now. Are you going?"

"I...I'm afraid," Twyla said.

"Suit yourself. I have to go."

Lisa grabbed her party clothes and hurried downstairs. Before she could get her jacket and disarm the security system, the car drove out of sight.

"Shit!" Lisa went to the kitchen for a glass of orange juice and dropped dejected in a chair.

Will I ever see Sebastian again?

She drained the glass and cut off the lights. Halfway up the stairs, she remembered the dress and shoes and returned in the dark for them. An eerie blue light floated across the room. She flipped the switch. It was the ornament on her mother's keys. Her car keys! In that instant, Lisa decided to take the car. She dressed hastily and turned off the security system. She unsnapped the keys from the bag and hurried to the garage.

"Damn!" She ran back for the remote in her mother's bag and turned out the kitchen lights. She pressed the remote and slid under the steering wheel. The garage door groaned up. She groaned, too. It was pitch dark outside.

I've never driven at night.

"I can do this," she said for courage and turned the key. "Where are the lights?" Lisa pulled a knob on the dashboard. Water squirted over the windshield. She pulled another. The lights blazed on. While she was at it, she turned to her favorite radio station.

She yanked the Mercedes into drive and pressed the gas. The car shot forward. She slammed the brakes and hurtled into the wheel. Pain shot across her breasts. She pressed the gas again. The car lurched forward. She hit the brakes and slammed into the wheel again, worsening the pain.

Maybe I should forget about this.

The memory of Sebastian's churning body above hers spurred her on. She gently mashed the gas and crawled away.

Lisa waited for the green light at Wesley Chapel Road and Snapfinger and remembered she forgot to close the garage door.

Oh Lord! Suppose Daddy comes down and finds it open? Suppose the thugs Mommy talks about happen by?

Before she could worry about her father or thugs, a police car skidded to a halt in the next lane.

"Oh God...Oh God!" Lisa stared ahead and squeezed the steering wheel.

Suddenly, the cruiser shot through the red light onto Rainbow Drive and disappeared into the night. Lisa trembled so hard she couldn't move even as car horns honked angrily behind her then pulled around and sped away.

"Relax...relax...relax." Lisa flexed her hands until the feeling returned and went left. She turned onto Tricia's street. Cars jammed both sides of the road. She parked two streets over and walked back to the party house.

The odor of bodies jammed like sardines in a tin formed a wall of funk to the ceiling. A haze of marijuana smoke set Lisa coughing as she pushed through the crowd looking for Kenya or Sebastian, but mainly for Sebastian. Someone took her hand. She spun around expecting to look up into Sebastian's handsome face but looked instead down into Zebo's hideous one.

"Hey, pretty thang." He shouted.

"Hey."

Zebo threw his arms around her waist and pinched her hip.

"Stop that." She backed up.

He did it again and grabbed her hand.

"Let me go!" She tried to wrench free. His grip tightened.

"I let you go once already!"

"You let me go!" Lisa pried at his fingers. "Let me go!"

He plowed past dank bodies, towing her behind.

"Help me!" Lisa screamed. "Help me somebody!"

She grabbed a sleeve here, an arm there, anything to stop herself from being taken by this man. Some looked in her direction but no one did anything. Lisa dragged her feet. He jerked her along with an incredible strength and kicked open a door. Lisa caught sight of a rumpled bed and renewed her efforts at escape. Zebo shoved her in the room. Sebastian pulled her out.

"Sebastian!" She cried with relief. "Make him leave me alone!"

"She's mine, mother fucker!" Zebo pulled the gun from his waist.

Sebastian grabbed Zebo's wrist and held the weapon skyward.

They stumbled around the room, bumping into dancers unaware anything was amiss until Zebo pulled the trigger. The bullet ripped across the nose of one young woman and lodged in the arm of another. Their soprano screams pierced the loud music and pandemonium broke out. People ran in all directions. Sebastian wrestled the gun away. It dropped to the floor. Zebo bent to retrieve it. Sebastian grabbed Lisa's hand and pulled her toward the kitchen. He glanced back and saw Zebo knocked beneath the stampede. His screams were ignored the same as Lisa's.

Sirens wailed in the distance. Sebastian led Lisa along the edge of the woods. Dogs strained at leashes, barking. Motion lights flicked on, casting their shadows over the ground. They stopped by some bushes, gasping for breath.

"I have...to get...my mother's...car."

"You drove...here?"

"Uh huh," she said with a bit of pride.

"Where...is it?"

"A few streets over."

"Which way?"

"I don't know." She pointed the way they came. "That way...I think."

"Come on!"

Lights flashed on three squad cars and two ambulances in front of Tricia's house. Lisa and Sebastian stood in the shadows, watching paramedics load a sheet covered figure in an ambulance and drive off with sirens silent.

"Was that Zebo?" Lisa shivered, wishing she were home in bed.

Sebastian *knew* it was Zebo.

"I don't know," he said. "Let's go."

They found the car. Lisa thrust the keys in Sebastian's hand.

"I hope to hell it's not reported stolen. If we get stopped, I could do serious jail time."

"Don't worry, Mommy's, asleep."

"Right!" He yelled. "Why the hell were you at that party?"

"I came to see you," she said mystified by his displeasure. "Why are you mad at me? Why was Zebo acting like that? Why did he pull a gun on you?"

"Did you tell Kenya you were no longer a virgin?"

Baffled, she shook her head "No." she said. "I—"

"Why not?" he said roughly.

"I never got a chance to talk to Kenya," she said on the verge of tears. "She moved and I didn't know how to reach her. I wanted to see you."

"Kenya is not a friend to you. Do not trust her ever again."

"What are you talking about? She's my big sister."

"She set you up."

"Set me up? For what?"

"Kenya was suppose to hook you on cocaine."

"Kenya would never do such an awful thing."

"Kenya supplies young virgins for Zebo. He pays her with cocaine."

"I don't believe you!"

"Kenya brought you to my house for Zebo's approval."

"That's not true."

"I heard them making plans outside my bedroom door."

Lisa remembered them whispering and looking at her.

"Didn't you think it was strange for her to go across the room for a special drink for you?"

"I thought about that...but."

"The drink Kenya gave you was drugged."

Marijuana didn't make me dizzy. My drink was drugged!

"Zebo beat her because she knocked it from your hand and didn't get you started on cocaine."

Lisa began to cry.

"Shh, little one, shhh." He reached out and pulled her close.

"How could she do that? We've been friends since I was a little girl."

"Sometimes those we admire disappoint us." He hugged her tight but could not stop her tremors.

"I...I...trusted her!"

"I know you did," he said. "I know you did."

"I'll never trust anybody else again!" She wailed. "Never!"

"Yes you will." He took a flask from his jacket. "Sip some of this."

"What is it?" she asked warily.

"Something to relax you."

"What is it?"

"Rum, Jamaican rum."

She hesitated, afraid.

"Please," he said. "Let me be the first person you trust."

"I...I—"

"Please?"

Lisa took the flask and looked at Sebastian.

"Can I really trust you?"

"I would never do anything to harm you."

She wanted to trust him. His voice pleaded for her trust. Lisa raised the flask to her lips and swallowed. The liquid burned like hot sauce down her throat.

"Aaah." She handed it back. "Yuck."

"Take another small sip." He urged.

"Umm umm." She coughed. "It's nasty!"

Sebastian took a swig and returned the pint to his pocket.

A delicious warmth spread with the speed of a brush fire from her stomach and headed in all directions. It consumed her stuff and rushed down her legs, up to her breasts, out to her fingertips. When it reached her head, she seemed to move in slow motion.

"Maybe I'll have another little sip." She got the flask and took a long pull.

"That's enough for you." He took the flask and drank the rest.

"Are we going to your house?" she said.

"I'm taking you home."

"No-o-o-o-o!" She cried. "I want you to make love to me."

"It's late," Sebastian said. "And you're drunk."

"I...am," she said with slurred speech. "Not...drunk!"

Sebastian laughed but stopped when she unzipped his trousers with a steady enough hand and worked his growing dick free. She squeezed the tip like he'd taught her so expertly, he could hardly concentrate on driving.

She's sober enough.

He turned on a dead end street, darker than a cave and parked. He rolled on a condom and moved to the passenger side. He pulled Lisa on his lap and kissed her deep. His fingers started a hole in her pantyhose and worked it large enough to play in her vagina.

"Sssssssssh!" Lisa hissed. "O-o-o-o-o-o-o-o-oh!"

"Sit on it." He helped Lisa hike her dress and straddle his thighs. He pulled the elastic of her panties aside and pushed. She was too tight. He played with her until she became slippery wet. He tried to enter again. Slowly she opened and took him in bit by bit.

"Sssssss!" Lisa hissed. "Sssssssss." She unbuttoned the cuff and pulled down her bodice. Her breasts bobbed in his face. He took a nipple in his mouth.

"Ssssssssssssssssh!"

"Move like this." He commanded.

Lisa followed his instruction and lifted herself up and down, increasing the wonderful sensation in her stuff. Seconds later, she jerked against him, exploding.

"Sssssssooh! Sssooooooooooooooh!"

"Hmmmmmmmm!" Sebastian clamped her hips down and exploded, too.

They collapsed in each other's arms, panting. Sebastian took out a handkerchief and cleaned up. Lisa used tissues from the box on the seat.

"I have something to tell you," he said.

"What?"

"I'm leaving tomorrow."

"Leaving?" She stared at him in the dark. "Why? Why?"

"My business here is finished. It's time to go home."

"Don't leave me...don't leave me...I love you...I love you!"

"You don't love me."

"Yes I do! I do!"

"There's someone special out there waiting for you."

"No! No!" She threw herself on him. "I love you!"

"Please Leesah, it's time to go."

She tightened her arms around his neck. "If you leave, Zebo will get me!

"No, he won't."

"How do you know?"

"I know."

"I'm afraid."

"Do you trust me?"

"Yes," she said with a small voice.

"If I say Zebo won't bother you, what are you suppose to do?"

"Believe it," she said then gasped. "That was Zebo in the ambulance, wasn't it? He's dead, isn't he?"

"Yes."

"Oh God!" Her arms dropped from his neck. "Oh God!"

She stared out the window in a daze.

"Lisa, get dressed." He slid under the wheel. "Do you hear me? Get dressed."

She slowly pulled the top over her breasts and buttoned the cuff.

"What's your address?" He wiped the foggy windshield and started the car.

"48950 Sunday Lake Drive." She mumbled.

He picked up the phone and dialed.

"Hello." A sleepy male voice answered.

"Fabienne here, I need your help."

"Name it."

"Pick me up at 48950 Sunday Lake Drive in thirty minutes."

"It's done."

"Thanks, man." Sebastian hung up and pulled off.

They rode in silence with Lisa's head on his shoulder.

"Sebastian," she said quietly.

"Yes, my pet."

"I promise I'll never make love again unless it's with you."

"Leesah...Leesah...don't make that promise."

"I swear it," she said. "I'd swear it on a Bible, if I had one."

He almost laughed and remembered she was fifteen and her heart was broken.

"Chéri," he said gently. "If it is our fate, we will meet again."

13

Emily fell asleep with something she was suppose to do nibbling at her mind. The nightmare woke her at three. She tossed fitfully and jolted awake at five, remembering the blue card Dr. Chambers had given her Monday. She had forgotten it completely.

She hurried to the dark kitchen and fumbled in her bag. The garage door rumbled down.

Did I press the remote?

She felt for it. It wasn't there. She scanned the room. The red light on the security system was off. For a reason she could not explain, she didn't think of thugs, she thought of Lisa and quietly turned the doorknob to the garage.

Bathed in moonlight, Lisa stood next to her car in her new dress.

Emily flipped the light switch.

Lisa froze.

Daddy?

Emily stepped on the landing and Lisa relaxed.

It's only Mommy. I know how to handle her. I'm as much woman as she is now. What pet name will I call my stuff? Miss Stacy? Miss Mimi?

She laughed and started up the steps. Emily started down until they stood a step apart. It was like looking into Leora's slitted green eyes, but Emily held her ground.

"Get out of my way!" Lisa spat.

Rum fumes drifted up Emily's nose.

She's drinking, too?

Emily added this offense to Lisa's hateful attitude and her disobedience and her meanness and her selfishness and her cruelty and her thievery.

Lisa moved sideways. The distinctive odor of sex flared Emily's nostrils. Fury hotter than a steel mill furnace surged to her hand and slapped Lisa's face.

"Mommy?" Lisa looked astonished. "What's wrong with you?"

The next blow buckled her knees. Lisa grabbed for the banister. The car keys and garage door opener flew from her hand. She tumbled down the steps and landed in a heap on the cold, gray concrete. Pain coursed down each leg and shot up her spine.

"You hurt me, Mommy." Lisa struggled to her feet. "Look, I'm bleeding."

Quarter sized circles of blood dropped from her hand and dotted the floor.

Emily marched down the steps. Instead of consoling Lisa, she punched her with both fists.

"Mommeeee...sto-o-p!" Lisa raised her arms to protect her head. "Sto-o-o-op! Sto-o-o-o-op!"

"I'll kill you...I'll kill you...I'll kill you!"

"Stop, Emily, stop!" Richard shouted from the landing.

Emily never looked up. Her hands slipped around Lisa's neck and squeezed. Richard ran down the steps and tried to pull her off and ended up prying her hands away finger by finger.

Lisa clutched her throat and dropped to the floor, gulping in air.

"I'll kill her...I'll kill her!"

Richard had never seen Emily this angry and had to man handle her to keep her from attacking Lisa again.

"Emily...stop it! Stop it!"

"I'm finished...I'm finished with her!" She threw up her hands and slumped to the steps. "I'm finished with her!"

"Are you okay?" He knelt by a sobbing Lisa.

She nodded.

He got tissues from the car and applied pressure to stop the bleeding.

"Daddy...Daddy!" Lisa croaked.

"You've been drinking!" He shook her savagely. "You've been drinking!"

"I'm...sorry...Daddy...I'm...sorry!"

"I suppose you're doing drugs, too?" He shook her again.

"I don't do drugs!" she said with hurt feelings. "How could you think that?"

"Why shouldn't I? You're doing every goddamn thing else."

"I'm sorry, Daddy. I'm sorry."

"Lisa Marie Bennett." Richard shook his head. "I don't want to talk to you right now. If I do, I'll hurt you, so just get out of my sight!" He moved away, wiping the blood off the floor.

"Mommmmeeeeee." Lisa extended her arms to Emily. Emily made no attempt to comfort her. Lisa didn't know what to do. Neither parent seemed to want to have anything to do with her. She crawled across the floor and tried to lay her head on her mother's heaving breast. Emily pushed her away.

"Mommy. I'm sorry."

"Let's clean up this mess and get to bed." Emily stood.

"I'm almost finished," Richard said. "You two go ahead."

By the time they reached Lisa's room, black and blue bruises had formed around her neck and across her face.

"You're paying for this!" Emily threw her bloody dress in the wastebasket.

"I will, Mommy, I will."

"Where will you get three hundred dollars? Out of my wallet?" Ashamed, Lisa dropped her head.

"I'll never do that again, I'll...I'll cash in some of my bonds."

"Humph!"

"I will, I will. I promise!"

"Where were you tonight?"

"I...I—"

"A lie better not come out of your mouth!" Emily shook a finger in her face. Lisa didn't know what to do. Her mother had never been this mean to her. She didn't know how to handle this new person.

"At...at a party." The words raced across her lips in a rapid confession. "But I won't ever do this again, I know now it was wrong. Please forgive me."

"Who were you with?"

"Nobody, Mommy, nobody!"

"Don't lie to me!" Emily's nose wrinkled with disgust. "You've had sex with somebody. I smell it all over you."

Oh God. Busted by my mother. Sebastian could go to jail if she finds out we made love, but if she beats me again, I'm not sure I can keep his name a secret.

"I'm sorry."

"Who was it?"

"I...I..."

"I know it was that smart mouth, Sean Favor!"

"Sean," Lisa said. "What...what makes you say Sean?"

"You think I don't see S. F. loves L.B. all over your books."

"Uh...uh." Lisa stammered. "Yes, it was Sean."

"We'll see about this." Emily mumbled to herself.

"What are you going to do?" Lisa tugged at her arm. "Please don't say anything to Sean, Mommy, please don't say anything to Sean!"

"How many times have you been with him?" Emily jerked Lisa's face around. "Hold still!" She cleaned the dried blood crusting below her nose and applied cocoa butter to her neck. "Well, how many times?"

"How many times, what?" Lisa asked stupidly.

Emily smacked her head, hard.

"Ow!" She cried, rubbing the spot. "Tonight was the first time."

"Tomorrow," Emily said. "You go on birth control pills!"

"I'm not doing it anymore. I don't need birth control."

"Oh yes you do and I'm personally putting them in your mouth!"

"Okay," Lisa said with her mind already made up to spit them out.

With Sebastian gone, what's the use?

"I'm finished with you."

Lisa looked in the mirror at her swollen jaw. Her brain whirled, composing excuses to explain the incredible damage to her neck and face.

I'll say a maniac attacked me. A maniac did attack me. I never knew Mommy possessed such rage. Can this be the same gentle woman tucking me in bed?

"I love you, Mommy."

"I love you, too, but right now I don't like you very much."

"Mommy." Lisa grabbed her in a bear hug. "How long will it take for you to like me again?"

"I don't know," Emily said. "You'll just have to wait and see."

Emily soaked her gown in cold water and showered off Lisa's blood. She returned to the kitchen just as Richard came in from the garage.

"Did you see a blue—"

"This?" He pulled the card, keys and remote from his robe pocket.

She dropped the remote in her bag and snapped on the keys.

"This is why I came down in the first place." She fingered the card. "Why were you here?"

"I couldn't remember if I'd turned on the security system."

"It was off when I came in," she said. "Now we know why it was off when I accused you of forgetting the last time."

"It's a good thing I came down. You would have killed her if I hadn't."

"I should have. I wonder how many times she's stolen my car?"

"I don't know, I checked it out. It's not damaged."

"I want to know how she backed in the garage?"

"Did you see her backing in?"

"No, I only heard the door going down."

"Did she say where she'd been?" he asked.

"A party somewhere across town."

"She drove across town?" he said incredulously.

"That's what she said."

"And you believe her?"

"Yeah, I believe her," she said. "She thinks she's slick!"

"One thing Miss Slick won't be doing," Richard said.

"What's that?"

"She won't steal *your* car again. Mine maybe, but definitely not yours."

"Humph!"

"I didn't really mean it when I said beat 'em 'til they bleed." He chuckled. "Chokes and punches were not quite what I had in mind either."

"I know, I lost my head."

"You sure did! I've never seen you so angry. You scared me!"

"I scared myself. All I wanted to do was inflict as much pain as I could!"

"Considering you never hit her before, I think you succeeded."

"Humph!"

"You're not afraid she'll hate you?"

"I don't care if she hates me or not."

"I think we might begin to see our old Lisa again."

"Humph!"

"Drinking, sneaking out, stealing your car. Is she doing drugs, too?"

"I hope not." She looked at Richard. "But add had sex to that list."

"Had sex?" He looked at Emily, stunned.

"Didn't you smell it all over her?"

"No-o."

"She's doing it with Sean."

"I'll break that punk's neck."

"Somehow I don't think he's totally to blame, Lisa probably asked him."

"I can't believe it," Richard said. "My Lisa is having sex."

"She tried to tell me she wasn't going to do it anymore, like I'd believe she'd stop once she'd started. I want her on birth control before the sun goes down."

"My baby girl having sex," he said somberly. "Are you sure?"

Emily remembered Lisa's look, challenging her woman to woman. "Believe me, I'm sure."

The grandfather clock chimed six-thirty.

"I might as—" The ice pick stabs began so suddenly, Emily lost her train of thought.

"What's wrong?" Richard asked.

"Nothing." She lied. "What do you want for breakfast?"

"Whatever you cook."

"I haven't cooked your favorite in a long time."

"What's that?"

"Fried hot dogs, grits and cheese eggs."

"Yummy."

"I love an easy to please man." She gripped the table, enduring the pain.

"I love a woman who pleases her man." He kissed her and went upstairs.

Emily laid her head on her folded arms. To distract herself from the pain, she counted each tick of the clock. By the time she'd reached one thousand forty-three, it had eased enough for her to read the instructions on the blue card.

1. Avoid caffeine drinks after 4 p.m. (Coffee, colas etc.)

2. Refrain from drinking alcohol after 6 p.m.

3. Retire at the same time nightly.

4. Record any feelings, impressions upon awakening.

Starting today she would follow these directions to the letter. Right now Lisa was all she could think about. Having sex, drinking, stealing her car, driving without a license and quite possibly doing drugs. God help us.

14

I Love To Read expansion had been postponed long enough. Plans to use the vacant room for seminars, book clubs discussions and book signings were finalized. Today was furniture shopping day.

Emily pulled in front of Annette's house and blew the horn. Annette came out dressed to impress in a pink coat over a navy pinstriped pantsuit. She looked like a beautiful gangster with the gray fedora cocked to the side of her head.

"Sistergirl." Annette got in the car. "I am ready to shop 'til I drop."

"You are too tough!" Emily fingered the fine linen cloth.

"I do look delicious," she said with a laugh. "Don't I?"

"Yes, you do."

"Let's ride."

First, they stopped at Office World.

"Maple Honey had this same chair in her room." Emily rubbed the oak rocker.

"How's Miss Maple Honey doing?" Annette asked.

"She's fine. I keep meaning to visit her, but something always comes up."

"When you do go, I'll ride with you."

"Okay," Emily said.

"How's Miss Hotsy Totsy doing?" Annette said.

"I have my foot on Lisa's neck so tight, she can feel my toes every time she moves."

"Got-damn!" Annette laughed.

"To school and back," Emily said. "That's *all* she can do."

"Is she on birth control?" Annette asked.

"Every morning I personally put a pill in her mouth."

"Does that boy...what's his name?"

"Sean?"

"Yeah," Annette said. "Does he still come around?"

"So Richard can break his neck? The asshole should be glad he's not in jail!"

"I know I didn't hear the A word come out of your mouth?"

"Hush." Emily laughed. "I can say asshole."

"I know, sugar." Annette patted Emily's arm sympathetically. "It just sounds so funny when you do."

"Let's buy these rockers," Emily said. "They'd be great in the reading room."

"Why not."

They purchased the chairs and set out again.

"What's for lunch?" Emily asked. "Chinese or Mexican?"

"Chinese."

Emily headed for the Golden Dragon. A blue van flashed by just as she pulled in the parking lot.

"That looked like Joe Webster."

"Where?" Annette jerked around.

"I thought I saw his van." She drove to the street. A blue van was nowhere in sight and she promptly threw Joe Webster from her mind.

A tiny waitress in red and black satin pajamas escorted them to a table overlooking the rock garden.

"Beef and broccoli." Emily gave her order.

"I'm hungry." Annette ordered a combination plate of cashew chicken, shrimp fried rice, lobster egg foo young and sweet and sour pork.

"I envy you," Emily said. "I wish I could eat all that and still keep my figure."

"You envy me?" Annette said. "I envy you."

"Why in the world would you envy me?" Emily asked. "You're beautiful. You date great guys. You're smart, successful."

The waitress returned with two dainty blue willow cups and a matching teapot. Annette poured for both of them and stirred in sugar.

"Don't forget single." She sampled the tea. "Mmmm. This is delicious."

"You're single by choice." Emily sipped her tea. "This *is* good," she said. "You could have married many times. What's going on with Bradley Malone?"

"Don't mention that dogsnake."

"The plumber is fired?" Emily asked.

"Yes, he is."

"What happened?"

"He's married."

"When did you find this out?"

"Last night," she said sadly, then laughed uproariously. "I saw him and his family at the grocery store. He saw me coming down the cereal aisle and lost three complexions." She laughed again. "You should have seen his face. He was this color." She held up the white cloth napkin. "I thought he was going to pass out."

"Did his wife notice?"

"Hell no! She was too busy comparing corn flakes with oat bran."

"How does she look?"

"A cute, short, brown thing. He spit his two boys out."

"You weren't serious about marrying him, were you?"

"Hell, no!" she said. "But do you know that son of a bitch called after I got home to say that was his sister and her kids?"

"No, he didn't."

"Yes, he did."

The waitress set the hot plates on the table and they stopped talking.

"Em, look at me," Annette said when she walked away. "Is there a flashing neon sign on my forehead saying fuck Annette?"

"You're crazy." Emily laughed so hard, tears rolled down her face.

"I don't feel like a fox. I'm lonely. I want what you have."

"What?"

"A husband, a home, children."

"You can have that."

"I don't want to marry somebody just to say I'm married. I want a man who makes me cream thinking about him."

"Girl." Emily laughed. "You don't want wet panties all day."

"I'm serious, I want romance and somebody who loves my dirty draws like Richard loves yours."

"You wouldn't think he loved me at all a few weeks ago."

"You made up, didn't you?"

"Passionately." Emily smiled big. "Passionately."

"I want that, too. Passion and great big sex, if you know what I mean."

"I know what you mean. You need to meet Richard's brother."

"Richard's brother has great big sex?" Annette stopped eating and stared at Emily. "How do you know?"

"I don't know exactly. But if great big sex genes run in the Bennett family then we can expect blood brothers to be equally hung, can we not?"

"I guess. Why haven't you mentioned this big dicked man before?"

"I know I've told you about him, but he just moved back to Atlanta."

"Umm umm."

Should I tell her about Ralph and Rachel? Richard didn't swear me to secrecy.

"You don't have any idea who her lover is?" Annette asked.

"No, and Richard won't tell."

"Forget Dr. Chambers and her lover," Annette said. "How does Richard's brother look?"

"Just like Richard," Emily said.

"He's fine then."

"Ralph is fine alright."

"Ugh." Annette made a face. "Did you say Ralph?"

"Yep, but if you don't like Ralph, you can call him by his first name."

"Which is?"

"Ezell."

"Ugh. That's worse than Ralph."

"Everybody in his family calls him Junior."

"How can a grown man let himself be called Junior?"

"What's wrong with Junior?"

"It's something you call a little boy."

"Believe me." Emily laughed. "Ralph is no little boy."

"What else does he have going for him? What does he do?"

"He's a lawyer with Love and Crews."

"Hmmmm."

"You've seen Ralph."

"Where? When?"

"About eighteen years ago when we were in Athens."

"Eighteen years ago." Annette laughed. "Hell, I don't remember what my face looked like yesterday let alone somebody else's eighteen years ago."

"He was at the Blue Lights the Friday after Thanksgiving."

"I don't remember."

"Do you remember the dance contest?"

"No, I don't remember the dance contest." Annette laughed.

"Ralph won it."

"So he can dance and he's hung. What else can he do?"

"Annette!" Emily said exasperated.

"Main question. Is he seeing anyone?"

"I don't know."

"Has he ever been married?"

"Not that I know of."

"How come you can't answer the important questions?"

"If I ask Richard anything, he clams up, saying I'm trying to matchmake."

"Well, aren't you?"

"Wel-l-l...yes." She laughed. "Yes I am."

Their light giggles made patrons at surrounding tables look in their direction and smile.

"How old is Ralph?"

"Forty-seven."

"Forty-seven is a good age."

"Where did he move from?"

"Chicago."

"What side?"

"Side?"

"Northside? Southside? Westside?"

"I don't know."

"Damn, Em, how am I going to marry this man if you can't give me any information?"

"Sorry." She laughed.

"Richard did say Ralph dated a lot of women but never found anyone to compare with Rachel Chambers."

"When a woman breaks a man's heart, the woman he ends up with gets fucked every time."

"That's something you just made up. Isn't it?"

"No, baby doll." Annette tapped her heart. "That's experience."

"Well so much for romance." Emily looked at her watch. "We have time for one more place. Where else can we go?"

"There's a furniture outlet on Covington."

"Okay, let's ride."

Traffic moved at a fast clip down Covington Highway. Emily pulled out to pass and noticed the blue van.

"Is that Joe Webster?"

Annette started to turn around.

"Don't turn around." Emily warned. "Okay, go ahead, see if it's really him." Annette peered through the rear window and easily read Webster Supplies across the hood.

"It's him, it's him!" She screamed. "It's him!"

The van closed in inches from her bumper. Emily pulled out and jumped behind a lumber truck. She attempted to pass. Oncoming traffic kept her pinned behind the keen ended logs slanted dangerously in her direction. Ahead the road became four laned. The van pulled alongside them, swerving to close. Emily dodged left.

"Call the police!" She screamed "Call the police!"

Annette grabbed the phone. The van swerved toward them again. Emily ducked. The phone flew from Annette's hand and dropped under Emily's feet. She accelerated and pulled away. The road suddenly became two laned again. She stomped her brakes to avoid the ditch and laid on her horn. She shot past two cars and narrowly missed the semi fender, returning to her lane.

"Where is he?" She screamed at Annette. "Where is he?"

She tried to think of a plan, but panic had taken charge. All she knew to do was to go as fast as she could from the danger.

"He's coming!" Annette sank to the floor. "He's coming!"

Emily mashed the gas pedal. She did not see the patrol car until it spun out behind her with sirens wailing and lights flashing. Relief flooded her and she jammed the brakes. The Mercedes fishtailed, grabbing for traction. Emily steered to the shoulder of the road. As soon as the car stopped rolling, she was out, running toward the cruiser. The officer hopped out, unsnapping his holster.

"That man is chasing us...he's chasing us!"

"Who?" He looked where she pointed. "Who's chasing you?"

"Him!" She yelled. "Go after him! Go after him!"

In the distance, the blue van U-turned and drove out of sight.

"Calm down, ma'am," he said. "Calm down."

"He tried to run us off the road!" She slumped against his fender. "You let him get away!"

"I'd like to see your driver's license." His eyes roamed her body behind dark green sunglasses.

Who does she remind me of?

"You should be chasing him, not harassing me!"

"Just get your license!" He snapped.

"It's in the car." She looked where Joe Webster turned and rolled her eyes.

"I don't like your attitude." He folded his arms across his chest. "Now get your license."

Emily pushed away from the cruiser and marched to her car. He followed five paces back, watching her hips sway.

"Is he gone?" Annette asked.

The officer bent down and saw her huddled on the floor.

Let the church say a man. Got-damn, he's fine!

"Yes!" Emily jerked open her door and fumbled in her bag. "He's gone."

Annette checked her makeup and climbed from the car.

"Am I glad to see you." She dusted off her suit. "You saved my...our lives."

Emily handed the officer her license. He opened his ticket pad.

"Don't give her a ticket," Annette said. "We were running for our lives."

"Why was that man chasing you, ma'am?"

"I just love the way you say ma'am," Annette said and explained about Joe Webster. She could not help checking the officer out and followed her Daddy's advice. She looked first at his shoes, black leather polished to a high sheen. A good sign. Bluish-gray trousers held a knife crease. A light blue shirt, starched to perfection was another good sign. Cropped black hair could just be seen under a wide campaign hat, but best of all, a handsome mahogany face, clean-shaven and blemish-free behind the sunglasses made him look as sexy as hell.

Got-damn! Got-damn!

"Are you?" Annette asked and smiled her best smile.

"Am I what?" he asked.

"Giving her a ticket, silly."

"Not this time." He looked at Emily and closed his book. "But if I catch her going eighty-five on my road again, she'll be going to jail."

"Thank you," Emily said dryly and reached for her license.

"Is it my imagination." He held onto the license. "Or did I give you a break?"

"Thank you," Emily said sweetly and he let the license go.

"I've seen you before." Annette flirted openly. "What's your name?"

"Officer Trotter," he said.

"I see that." She boldly flipped his nametag. "Your first name, silly."

"Don't touch," he said with a frown. "My name's not silly, it's Milo."

"The Ivory Oaks Country Club." Annette snapped her fingers. "That's where I've seen you."

Milo's demeanor changed to friendly. His smile showed movie star white teeth.

"Yeah. I joined about eight weeks ago."

"How do you like it so far?" Annette said.

"It's great, but I can never get a court."

"Basketball, handball or tennis?" Annette asked.

"Tennis." He put his sunglasses in his shirt pocket and looked at her with intense black eyes. "You're a pretty good player."

"I'm okay," Annette said. "But she's the club pro." She grabbed Emily's hand and held it over their heads.

"Annette," Emily said. "You're embarrassing me."

"Maybe you can help me with my game." He looked at Emily.

"Maybe I can squeeze you in."

"Are you sisters?" Milo looked from Emily to Annette.

"Yes." Emily answered. "Yes, we are."

"I thought so."

Annette scribbled her home number on a business card. Before she finished with Milo Trotter, she knew his middle name-Elgin, religion-Baptist, age-29, marital status-single, and ambition in life-chef.

"You can cook?" Annette asked.

"I'll whip up something." He looked Emily up and down. "And you ladies can sample my wares."

Emily glanced at her watch. "We have to go, Annette."

"We're going to take you up on that." Annette shook his hand.

"I want you to." He looked at scowling Emily and remembered who she looked like.

The White woman Daddy picked up before he dropped me at my piano lessons.

"Thank you, officer." Emily reluctantly shook his offered hand.

"Don't mention it." He opened her door. "Drive carefully now, you hear?"

He sounded fatherly, however, his eyes traveling her body said something else entirely. Emily hung up the phone and started the car.

"Annette." Emily glanced at her watch again. "We have to go."

"Okay," Annette said, and continued to talk to Milo.

"Annette!" Emily said with an annoyed tone. "Let's go."

"Okay, okay." Annette ran around the car and hopped in. "Bye Milo."

"Bye," he said and waved.

Emily pulled off. Annette waved back and got on her knees, peering out the back window. "Got-damn, he's fine!"

"Sit down, Annette," Emily said. "Your tongue is hanging out."

"He's still looking. I think he likes me."

"Quit it," Emily said. "You're old enough to be his—"

"I know you're not going to say mother?"

"Big sister." Emily laughed. "I was going to say big sister."

"Nobody says one word when a man dates a younger woman."

"Suppose Joe Webster comes after us and there's no one to stop him?"

"Do you think he was going to hurt us?" Annette said.

"What do you think?"

"I think Joe Webster is all bark and no bite."

"He's never chased us down the highway before," Emily said.

"There's nothing the police can do until he kills us."

"Great," Emily said. "Let's just wait for him to do that."

"Are you going to tell Richard?"

"No way! If I told Richard this, Joe Webster, would be dead by nightfall."

"Then you definitely should tell him." Annette laughed.

"I can just see the headlines, now." Emily laughed. "Doctor Kills Man Who Chased Wife Down The Highway. You know what Richard did to, Wally Key, and he only felt my arm."

"I like a man who'll defend his woman."

"If Wally sees me coming." Emily laughed. "He crosses the street."

"That'll teach him to keep his hands off you," Annette said. "Tell Richard, Joe Webster touched your titties."

"I don't think so." Emily shook her head, laughing.

"Joe Webster is a pussy," Annette said. "A real man would have killed us that day at the office."

15

"I think about Milo all the time." Annette wrote a check and put the checkbook away.

"I thought we agreed," Emily said. "At thirty-eight, you're too old for him and at twenty-nine, he's too young for you."

"I know," Annette said. "But I can't get him out of my mind."

"You can't?" Emily said. "Poor baby."

"Do you think he'll call me?" Annette propped her elbows on the desk and held her head with her hands.

"I hope not, for your sake and his."

"I at least used to see him at the club Saturday afternoons."

"Maybe you should come Saturday mornings," Emily said.

Annette perked up. "He's there Saturday mornings?"

"I see him hanging around the tennis courts."

"You do? Why didn't you tell me?"

"You know why. I shouldn't have told you that little bit."

"Do you think he can cook?" Annette asked.

"I guess so, if he wants to be a chef."

"You two would have a lot in common, in the kitchen."

"You would too, if you tried."

"I am not, I repeat, not Annette the homemaker, you are."

Emily laughed and looked at her watch.

"It's time for me to leave. See you later."

Annette did not answer. She stared into space, daydreaming of Milo Trotter.

Emily arrived at Dr. Chambers' office for her fifth and final session. She felt she had given herself adequate time to discover something significant about her nightmares and hadn't. When she kicked Richard during the next one, he would have no reason to threaten her with twin beds.

"Hello, Doctor." Emily walked in and sat in her favorite chair.

"Hello Mrs. Bennett," Dr. Chambers said. "How are you today?"

"Fine, thank you."

Dr. Chambers got down to business.

"Quickly," she said. "Say the first word that comes to mind."

"Reese Street." Emily laughed. "You said say one word."

"Two words are fine. Anything about Reese Street you want to talk about?"

Emily paused as the sad memories grew in her mind.

"I spent my childhood on Reese Street."

"Anything specific about your childhood?"

"How about when I realized my mother hated me?"

"Do you want to talk about it?"

Recollections of that time leapt into Emily's head as vividly as the events of last night, but she could not go quickly to the exact second she knew Leora hated her. She could never rush the memory. She had to let it play slowly, savoring her sweet childhood innocence before the dreadful knowledge rose naked from the graveyard in her mind.

"I was coloring on the front porch." Emily saw herself as an eight-year-old child that beautiful spring day in Lacewell. She lay on her stomach across the planks of the porch and outlined the shape of a ball with a stub of blue crayon. It was her birthday. She expected to get new crayons and a pair of black patent leather shoes. She looked at her scuffed white sandals. Maybe she would get new sandals, too. Sweat balls rolled down her face, united under her chin and formed grotesque shapes with each drop to the page.

Bored with coloring, she scooted to the end of the porch, being careful of splinters and noticed the cardboard box under the steps. She jumped down and pulled it out. It made a perfect convertible. She stepped over the door onto a black leather seat and drove around town. Suddenly, the box turned into a boat tossed in a violent storm. She gripped both sides for dear life. Waves slammed the port side and washed her overboard. She clung belly down to the flattened vessel until it floated ashore. Before Emily could catch her breath, the boat became a rusty metal and wood railroad flatbed car. She dug her toes in the grass and pushed herself over the yard.

"Woo woooooooo." She pulled the whistle chain. The mournful sound floated over her head. She stopped by the magnolia bush and took on peaches. At the rotted stump speckled with toadstools, she picked up timber. A final push past the oak tree brought her to the edge of the yard.

She peered over Stone Mountain at the cheering thousands, awaiting her dare devil feat. She would the first to ride a flatbed car down the granite dome.

"Laaadies…and…Gentllemen." She yelled. "The…Ama…zing…Emi…ly will slide to the bottom of this mountain." She cast off down the kudzu covered hill.

Two vehicles turned onto Reese Street at the same time. The driver of the black Buick felt the power of the car and accelerated. The farmer in the rusty green, pick-up truck loaded with fruit and vegetables slowed down to keep his produce from bouncing out. The Buick jumped the hill. The driver's mud red eyes popped from his licorice face. A child hurtled down the slope directly in his path. Ash dropped from the cigarette before it fell from his mouth to the floor. The brakes whined like a high soprano scream.

Emily flung both arms out beyond the flattened box, grasping for anything to stop her descent. Her hands clutched and tore the kudzu vines from the ground. A final grab stopped her so suddenly the momentum flipped her over and she watched the car pass a heartbeat from her body.

The Buick jumped the curb and gouged a deep gash in the bank in front of Miss Payley's house. The driver broke from the car. The farmer jumped from his truck. They ran toward Emily and reached her at the same time.

"You all right, young un?" the farmer asked.

"Yessir," Emily said low.

"You all right young un?" he asked her again.

"Yessir," she answered louder.

"Thank you, Jesus!" The man from the Buick babbled. His mud red eyes no longer bulged with fright. Sweat still poured from his face and he pulled a blue bandanna from his back pocket and mopped it away. Emily tried to sit up, but she couldn't open her fists. The farmer pried her right hand loose. The Buick driver freed her left. She wiped them on her sun suit and stood on shaky legs.

Leora marched toward them. From afar, she looked very angry. The Buick's driver began to plead his case.

"Missus...Missus...I didn't hit her...I didn't see her...until it was too late, but I...I...didn't hit her...she just scared...ain't you baby? Tell Momma you...just scared!"

Leora came closer and all could see anger was not the emotion stamped on her face. Hatred was. Pure and raw it glowed from her eyes like deadly radiation into Emily's brain. The men shifted nervously and looked at their shoes.

"Mister, mister your car on fire!" The farmer yelled.

Black smoke and orange flames billowed from the window. The Buick driver ran with relief from Leora. The farmer followed close behind.

"Get that cardboard and get to the house." Leora's pointed red nails stabbed Emily's back. Each time she turned around to see the fire, she got another jab. Leora let her stop long enough to toss the flattened box under the steps before she jerked her to the porch and shoved her in a wicker rocker.

"Sit there and don't move until I say so."

Leora went in the house. Emily turned the chair so she could see the burning car. Orange flames reached like long fingers from the interior, competing with rolls of dark smoke. Miss Payley ran back and forth across her yard with hands clamped tightly to her ears, anticipating an explosion. Even the farmer moved his ancient truck past the house, out of harm's way.

The man dragged a black hose full of kinks down Miss Payley's steps. Water trickled out. He turned it like a jump rope, yanking out the crimps. Water gushed in a powerful stream. He placed his finger over the end. An arc fell on the hot roof, dancing and hissing until it turned to steam.

The man smothered the last flame and stood by the charred skeleton slowly shaking his head. He and the farmer walked past Emily. The red-eyed man turned his malevolent stare on her. It vaulted across the street loosing in her mind a frightening memory of another red-eyed man. Disregarding Leora's orders, Emily ran to her room and burrowed beneath the protective folds of the heavy chenille spread.

Who is the other red eyed man? Did Leora always hate me or is today the first time I noticed?

She drifted to sleep with these thoughts and had the nightmare that would terrorize her for the next thirty years.

"Mrs. Bennett," Dr. Chambers said softly. "Mrs. Bennett."

"Yes." Emily answered in a daze.

"Time's up."

"I hadn't thought of that day in so long. It hurts to remember."

"In order to find out why you have this nightmare, you may have to dredge up more painful memories."

"I'm prepared to do whatever it takes. I'll see you next Monday."

"I'm glad to hear that," Dr. Chambers said. "Good bye, Mrs. Bennett

"Good-bye." She shook her offered hand. "Please call me, Emily."

16

The telephone woke Richard.

"Emily." He jostled her. "Get the phone."

"Huh?" She mumbled lost in sleep.

"Emily, get the phone." He shook her harder. "Get the phone."

"Okay, okay." She groped for the receiver. "Hello."

"Brace yourself for bad news!" The woman sounded ancient and tired.

"What?" Emily raised up on one elbow. "Who is this?"

"Nancy Bowles, Maple's friend."

Emily's heartbeat increased. She tossed the covers back, swung her legs over the side of the bed and turned on the light.

"What's wrong Miss Nancy?"

"Maple passed ten minutes ago."

"No! No! No!" Emily's screams jolted Richard fully awake. "No-o-o-o-o!"

"What's wrong?" He sat up. "What's wrong?"

"Maple Honey!" She wailed. "She's dead! She's dead!"

"Oh no!" He scooted over and pulled her in his arms. "What happened?"

"Miss Nancy." She sobbed. "What happened?"

"She had a stroke."

"A stroke?" she said blankly. "But she's in good health."

"No baby, she wasn't. She didn't want to worry you."

"She didn't want to worry me? Oh God! She called last week and said she was doing fine."

"She was sick when you visited your mother."

Did Richard hear Miss Nancy mention my mother?

She moved the phone to her other ear.

"She was talking about coming to visit me."

"She couldn't walk. She could hardly do anything for herself."

"Oh no, no-o-o!"

"She's with Jesus now. She's with Jesus."

"Who'll love me?" She wept against Richard's chest. "Who'll love me now?"

"I'll love you, baby." He hugged her tighter. "I'll love you."

"When are you coming down?" Miss Nancy asked.

"As soon as I can get packed."

"Come to my house. You remember how to get to Lacy Acres don't you?"

"Yes, ma'am, I think so."

"Put your grief in the Lord's hands and He'll soften it."

"Yes, ma'am, I will," Emily said. "Miss Nancy?"

"Yes, baby."

"Was she in a lot of pain? Did she suffer?"

"No, she wasn't. She was talking about you." Miss Nancy's voice broke and she wept softly.

"It's okay, Miss Nancy." Emily consoled her now. "It's okay."

"And she was gone, just like that."

Emily heard a loud fingersnap.

"It's okay, Miss Nancy. You hang in there, you hear me?"

"I will, bye bye."

"Bye." Emily clung to Richard sobbing. "She's gone, Richy, she's gone!"

"I know, I know, I'm sorry. I'm so sorry!"

"My champion is gone!"

"Get some rest."

"I can't rest now. I might as well get up," she said but made no attempt to do so. "Who can we get to stay with the girls?"

"I'll call, Momma."

"Ezell needs Pauline more than we do."

"Daddy can take care of himself," Richard said. "I'd go with you, but I've got surgery scheduled today and all next week."

"Maybe I could ask, Annette."

"Momma'll come." Richard looked at the clock. "She should be up now." He picked up the phone. "You know she'll do anything for you."

"I know." She crawled from bed and went to take a shower.

Richard watched her drag out ten minutes later and slump at the vanity.

"Maybe I should go with you," he said.

"No!" she said much too sharply. "I'll be all right."

Having Richard in Leora country is marital suicide.

"I could come down later," he said. "Saturday, maybe."

"No, no, I'll be fine. The girls need you here."

She finished her grooming and dotted on *Joyous*, a present from Maple Honey. She pulled open a drawer. The sweater on top was one Maple Honey had knitted. The navy silk robe she wore was a "just because" gift. Just because Maple Honey knew she would like it. Everywhere Emily looked she saw reminders of Maple Honey and began to cry.

Emily left at seven o'clock. She lost time to road construction ten miles before Greensboro and ran up on an accident involving an overturned semi near Union Point. She reached the Lacy Acres section of Lacewell at eleven forty and pulled on Packard Street trying to remember the blue and white house Maple Honey had taken her to when she was little. She entered the six hundred block and saw Miss Nancy sitting on her front porch like a cotton headed sentry. Emily parked beneath the crab apple tree and ran up the steps into her arms.

"How're you doing?" Emily hugged her tight.

"Fine. I've put myself in the Lord's hands."

"Miss Nancy, I can't believe she's gone!" Emily's eyes watered.

"I can't believe it either." Miss Nancy rose with the aid of a walker and hobbled through the door. "Come on in."

"Let me get my clothes." Emily got a bag from the trunk and went inside.

"Put your things in the front bedroom and come eat a little lunch."

"I ate already." Emily threw the suitcase on the bed and began to unpack

"I have to eat now because of my diabetes."

"You go ahead."

"When you finish," Miss Nancy said. "Look through Maple's papers."

"What papers?"

"Some papers she wanted you to see."

"Okay."

"Maple must have known she was leaving this miserable, old world."

"What do you mean?" Emily set her bag in the closet and went to the kitchen.
"Because she brought her papers with arrangements for her funeral."
"What?" Emily said amazed.
"She wrote down everything she wanted done."
"Everything?"
"Everything." Miss Nancy pointed to the Queen Anne buffet. "Open the top middle drawer and take out everything you see."
Emily pulled out a yellow spiral notebook, a gray photo album and an imitation brown leather portfolio. All were held together with a beige rubber band.
"Look in the notebook first," Miss Nancy said.
Emily sat at the dining table and slid the rubber band off the notebook. Funeral Arrangements for Maple Alice Reed headed the top of the first page. Emily leafed through the sheets full of pink, yellow and white receipts all stamped paid in full. The following page had the instructions.

1. Wilburn Funeral Home-Lacewell, Georgia
2. Coffin-dark oak, brass handles, lined in pink satin
3. Funeral dress-White chiffon gown/ Order of Sheba sash.
4. Hair and Makeup-Ruthena Ellis
5. Organ music-Harvey Greene (no piano)
6. Songs-*I Want Jesus To Walk With Me, Peace Be Still, I Will Trust In The Lord Until I Die*
7. Singer-Carrie Buck
8. Headstone-Georgia Granite
9. Sermon-Rev. Glen F. Carson-Worship Baptist Church
10. Interment-Harmony Cemetery Plot number 2349
11. Reading glasses on chain around my neck
12. Holy Bible in my hand
13. Obituary-Lacewell Lecturer-Use photo from album.
14. Pillow under my head
15. Pall bearers-Ned Buck, Albert Massey, Leon Duff, Marcus Sims, Bobo McCready, Al Tom
16. Flowers-Yellow rose casket spray

Miss Nancy came in and sat next to Emily.
"Maple was the most organized person I ever knew."
"Yes, she is," Emily said sadly. "Yes, she was."
"Get the phone baby, we need to start calling these folks."
She got the phone from the hall and set it on the table. Emily had never made funeral arrangements before. "Where do we start?" She asked.
"First we call the funeral home and set a day, then go from there."

The earliest the funeral could be held was Tuesday. They spent the rest of the day calling those on Maple Honey's list to see if they could participate. Leon Duff was in Detroit for his daughter's wedding. Miss Nancy called Bob Fisher. After Bob said he'd be proud to carry Miss Maple to her final resting place, everything was set.

People started dropping in around six thirty. By ten o'clock, the kitchen was filled with every food from coconut cake to collard greens and okra. It was past midnight before the house was quiet again and Emily opened the photo album. Thick black sheets held pictures pasted at each corner with black triangles. She turned a page. Maple Honey and Leora in long white dresses with arms hooked at the elbows smiled at her.

"Who is this?" Emily pointed at a White looking woman.

"Your grandma, Mona."

"Is she dead?"

"No, she's up in Chicago."

"She must be pretty old, huh?"

"Uh huh."

"Who is this?" A handsome man with a handle bar mustache and a plain woman with expressive eyes looked back at her.

"Your granddaddy Jimmy and his wife, Della Mae."

"Are they still living?"

"Jimmy's been dead. She's over in Alabama with her sister."

"They never had any children?"

"No, they didn't."

"Who is this?"

"Your Uncle Campbell." She pointed to the lovely woman beside him. "And this is your Aunt Emily."

"Am I named for her?"

"I don't know, maybe."

"Who is this?" A dark-skinned, good-looking man smiled at her.

"Oh that's, Walter Lee, Maple's husband."

"Maple Honey had a husband?" Emily said shocked.

"Uh huh."

"Why wasn't she with him? Were they divorced?"

"Maple left Walter Lee a long time ago, but they never divorced."

"How come she left him?"

"For the oldest reason in the world, a low down woman."

"What happened?" Emily asked.

"It's a long story, but I don't mind talking about it." Miss Nancy sipped her coffee. "Maple was six months pregnant and doing poorly. Walter Lee sent for Dovie Thompson to help with the cooking and cleaning and such. Walter Lee said she was his cousin." Miss Nancy nodded with a knowing smile. "Maple believed that mess, but I knew they weren't bit more cousins than the man in the moon. I knew Dovie was a low life slut, pardon my French, the minute I laid eyes on her, wearing her dresses so tight you could see the outline of her draws." She laughed. "That is…when she wore draws."

Miss Nancy leaned forward. Her voice grew softer.

"Now, I never saw her do this myself, but I heard plenty folks say whenever a man was around, Dovie would pretend she was picking something off the floor just so he could look up her dress. After they got an eyeful of her hairy hole, she would stand up laughing."

Miss Nancy gave a deep sigh.

"Anyway, that heifer hadn't been in Maple's home two weeks before she had it tore up worse than the cyclone I saw destroy Jethro William's house."

"What did she do?" Emily asked.

"A convict escaped from the chain gang over near Malltown. Maple's sister, Daisy, lived in Malltown. Toby, Daisy's husband, was in Athens on business. Maple was worried sick about her sister over there all alone and drove over to stay with her. When she got there, Toby was back so Maple went home and guess what she found? Walter Lee and Dovie laid up in her bed."

"Oh no!" Emily clamped her hand over her mouth.

"Maple stabbed Dovie several times and sliced Walter Lee across the chest. She cornered Dovie on the back porch and was about to stab her again, when Walter Lee knocked her down the steps."

"Wha-a-at?"

"He knocked her down the steps. Maple always said it was an accident but…"

"You think it wasn't?"

"I don't know. I'm just talking," Miss Nancy said. "Anyway…Maple broke both hips and lost the baby."

"That's why she walked with a cane. Poor Maple Honey."

"Maple got out of the hospital and Daisy took her home. She and Toby nursed her back to health. I got to hand it to Toby, he and Maple never could stand each other, but he did his best by her."

"I was at Daisy's house the day that fool, Walter Lee, came by. Can you imagine after all he had done? We told him to get on way from there."

'Maple is my wife,' he said. 'I'm here to take her home where she belongs.'

"He started cursing and bamming on the door. Maple took Toby's rifle off the wall. You didn't know she was a crack shot, did you?"

Emily shook her head, no.

"Maple snatched open that front door and shot twice through the screen. Walter Lee's feet didn't touch either step when he flew off that porch." Miss Nancy roared with laughter. "Maple took careful aim and creased the side of his head. Walter Lee ran past his car like a scalded dog. He never asked Maple to come back after that and hair never did grow in that crease. He got teased so much he always wore a hat, even in his own house."

"What happened to, Walter Lee?" Emily asked.

"He had a heart attack. Talk was, he died humping Dovie. I don't know if its true or not, but Dovie began acting strange afterwards. She started picking up paper in the street, saving it in her purse and talking to herself. When she took off all her clothes that Sunday at church and ran naked into the pulpit, her folks took her straight up 441 to Milledgeville. That's where she died."

"Poor Maple Honey." Emily wiped her eyes. "Will any relatives come in?"

"All her people are dead except you and Leora."

"Is Leora going to be at the funeral?" The question had nagged her all day.

"I doubt if the nursing home will bring her way back up here."

"When did she go to a nursing home?" She asked out of curiosity not caring.

"Shortly after you went to see her."

"Where is she?"

"Down in Allison."

"Where's that?"

"I don't know exactly, somewhere down Macon way."

"Why so far?"

"Leora had to leave the hospital," Miss Nancy said. "Maple had to put her somewhere. It was the only place that had a bed."

"I see," Emily said.

"Maple wanted to look it over but she was too sick." Miss Nancy handed Emily a colorful brochure. "This is where Leora's staying."

A handsome building of red brick surrounded by blooming flowers and lush shubbery dominated the front cover. A two legged sign with Blue Pine Nursing Home in black print stood on the manicured lawn. Beneath, in red cursive were the words The Elderly–Our Most Valuable Resource. Robust patients played shuffleboard and table tennis. Emily tossed the pamphlet on the table glad to never have to see Leora again.

Miss Nancy handed Emily an envelope labeled last will and testament.

"It's time I showed you this," she said.

Emily opened it and scanned the top page. "Bless her heart," she said amused. "Maple Honey made me the beneficiary of her estate."

Miss Nancy pulled the rubber band off the portfolio. It expanded like an accordion to show compartments labeled Insurance, Bonds, Bank Accounts, Real Estate and Guardianship.

"What's all this?"

"Maple's estate," Miss Nancy said. "Finish reading the will."

Emily's mirth quickly turned to awe. Miss Nancy would receive two thousand dollars monthly for the rest of her life. Fifty thousand dollars went to Worship Baptist Church building fund. Another fifty thousand went to the Pearls of the World Scholarship fund, but the bulk of the estate, over six hundred thousand dollars went to Emily Douglas Bennett.

"What?" Emily stared at the will. "I can't believe this!"

"Believe it, it's all yours."

"All this is making me dizzy." Emily looked through the portfolio. "Rental houses in Atlanta. A two hundred-acre farm. An insurance policy valued at fifty thousand dollars. A savings passbook with eighty-two thousand four hundred forty-one dollars and six cents. Maple Honey owned all this!" she asked. "Where did all this come from?"

"From Walter Lee."

"Where did he get this kind of money?" Emily asked.

"Loan sharking, making moonshine and running it north," Miss Nancy said. "Walter Lee was a scoundrel, but he sure knew how to make money."

"I'll say." Emily picked up the phone. "Richard's not going to believe this." Miss Nancy took the receiver from her and hung it up.

"Why did you do that?"

"Maple dictated this letter to me." Miss Nancy held out a yellow envelope.

"I knew it!" Emily squealed and practically snatched it from her hand. "I knew she'd written me a letter!"

January 13, 1981

Dear Emily,

If you are reading this letter, I have gone to meet my Lord. I know I should have discussed the matter of your Momma with you, but I could never bring myself to make you sad. One-minute Leora's mind is sharp, as can be, the next, she can't remember her name. She needs someone to look after her and you are the best choice. By now you have read my will. I leave my possessions to you with one provision: You will become Leora's legal guardian and take her to live in your home—

"What?" Emily looked at Miss Nancy. "She wants me to do what?"

—where you will give her good care. I know this is an underhanded way of going about things, but I could think of no other. Don't let a lie stand between

*you and your husband. Confess to Richard about Leora. I know he will
understand. See Lawyer Samuel Swan to become her legal guardian. I know
you will do the right thing. Always remember, I love you.*

Maple Honey

Emily slammed the letter on the table so hard, crystal glasses in the china
cabinet, clinked together, chiming.

"Leora in my house!" She screamed. "No way! No way!"

"Emily! Emily!"

"I'm suppose to tell *my* husband my mother is alive after I've lied to him all
these years? No way, Miss Nancy, no way!"

"Emily—" Miss Nancy tried to calm her.

"If Maple Honey were here, I'd sure tell her a thing or two! I can't believe
she'd try to bribe me to be Leora's guardian."

"Maple thought it was the only way to get your consent," Miss Nancy said.
"I know it's a difficult decision—"

"It's not difficult at all." Emily fumed. "Maple Honey can keep her land, her
money, insurance, her everything because if helping Leora is the only way I'll
inherit, then I'll never inherit!"

"You're not giving all this up. I know you'll do the right thing."

"Ha!" Emily screeched. "I'm not going to be suckered with that do the right
thing line again. When I was down here last month, I thought I was doing the
right thing. I went to the hospital to see Leora and what did I get for doing the
right thing, huh? Spat at, Miss Nancy, that's what I got, spat at like a dog...and
now you...and Maple Honey want me to do the right thing again? No, N-O!"

"I'm sorry for what Leora did to you but—"

"No buts, Miss Nancy, I don't care what's involved, I'm not helping her."

"You don't mean that."

"If Leora was bleeding to death in the street." Emily's voice trembled. "And
all it took to save her was lifting one finger." She held up her pinkie. "Then
she'd die where she lay!"

"So much hate is not good."

"Don't tell me about hate; I lived with the queen."

"So you won't become Leora's guardian?"

"And have her at my house?" She snapped. "No, I won't!"

"That's your last word?"

"That's my absolute last word."

"Then I'll say no more about it." Miss Nancy got up and hobbled to her room.
"Goodnight, Emily," she said before she closed the door.

"Goodnight."

How could Maple Honey ask this of me? She of all people knew the abuse I suffered at Leora's hand. How could she ask me to jeopardize my marriage and confess to a man who made his motto, Truth Is My Only Shield into a wooden plaque and hung it in our foyer for the world to see?

Emily looked at her watch. It was twenty after two, but she dialed Annette's number anyway.

"Hello." Annette answered with a sleepy voice.

"Hello," Emily said glumly.

"What's wrong with you? You sound pissed."

"I am!"

"Why?"

"Maple Honey made me the major beneficiary in her will."

"That's great."

"It's not great, she left me money, income property, bonds."

"What?" Annette squealed. "So what's the problem?"

"I can't take it."

"Why not?"

"In order to inherit, I have to become Leora's guardian."

"What's so hard? Become her guardian, and put her ass in a nursing home."

"I'll have to bring her to live in my home."

"Your own home?"

"Yes, my own home."

"Let me understand," Annette said. "Miss Maple Honey left you property, money and stuff but in order to get it, you have to take Leora into your home?"

"You got it."

"Looks like you'll be telling Richard your mother's alive," Annette said.

"If I told Richard this, I'd be divorced before the week was up. Even if he did know about Leora, I still wouldn't bring her to my house."

"Why?"

"Because I hate her too much. Maple Honey thought I'd be dazzled by everything she had to offer and run to sign guardianship papers, but I'm not."

"You're going to give up your inheritance?"

"Yes, I am."

"The state of Georgia is going to love you," Annette said. "If it was me, I'd take her in."

"It's not you!" Emily snapped. "It's me!"

"Excuse the hell out of Annette. If you didn't want my advice, why did you wake me up in the middle of the damn night?"

"Sorry," Emily said. "It's been a long day. I'm tired. I'm mad."

"Before you go," Annette said. "Let the church say, a man."

"A man," Emily said. "Who?"

"Who have I been praying for?"

"I hope you haven't heard from that child."

"Milo is not a child. So what if he's a few years younger?"

"If you want to date a man the same age as your baby brother, go ahead."

"If Milo was sixty-five, you wouldn't be saying anything."

"Yes, I would, then he'd be too old for you."

"Em," Annette said sadly. "Be happy for me."

"Oh sweetie, I'm sorry. If you're happy, I'm happy."

"Guess where he took me for dinner?" Annette said eager to talk about her new man.

"Mmmm," Emily said. "Roberta's?"

"Cold."

"The Circle Room?"

"Freezing," Annette said with a laugh.

"I give up, where?"

"The Ca–ba–ret."

"Wow!"

"Milo and I looked so delicious, everyone stopped eating to check us out."

"I know they did."

"He asked me to go with him to Miami."

"Get out!" Emily squealed like a teenager. "What's in Miami?"

"State Patrolman's convention."

"Are you going?"

"Does a bear shit in the woods?"

"I guess that means you're going?"

"It sure as hell does."

"When are you leaving?"

"Our flight leaves at nine this morning."

"How romantic," Emily said. "Is he paying your way?"

"Of course he's paying my way." Annette got huffy.

"You're sure?"

"Sure, I'm sure." She changed the subject. "Where do you think Milo is on the dick scale?"

"Hmmm, he's tall and built, I'd say polish sausage."

"Wrong." Annette giggled.

"Bigger?"

"Much."

"Hmmm, paper towel tube?"

"No-o-o!"

"I give up," Emily said. "How big?"

"B-O-L-O-G-N-A!"

"And how do you know all this?"

"I saw it, felt it, took it." Annette bragged.

"Say what? When?"

"I gave him some tonight."

"On your first date?"

"I couldn't help myself."

"Sure!"

"I couldn't."

"Was he worth it?" Emily asked. "Was he any good?"

"Was he any good?" Annette laughed. "If I start forgetting things and acting strange, it's because the brother fucked my brains out."

"Girl you better cool your sex jets."

"What?" Annette asked in mock shock.

"You know about this AIDS disease everyone's talking about."

"Only gay people get that," Annette said.

"You still need to be careful."

"Would anyone fine as Milo have a disease?"

"Men finer than him have diseases."

"Nobody's finer than Milo and he's mine!"

"You're crazy."

"I'm crazy like a fox about Milo."

"Please," Emily said. "You can't be crazy about him already."

"Girl, I'm in love."

"You can't be in love. You've only known him twenty minutes."

"Love has no time frame. Twenty years, twenty months, twenty minutes."

"Get real, Annette."

"Love can happen in a millisecond."

"You just made that up, didn't you?"

"Richard told me he fell in love the first time he saw you."

"He told me that, too, but no one falls in love at first sight."

"Well, let me tell you, you can," Annette said. "I did."

"You're always falling in love."

"What's wrong with falling in love?"

"Nothing except every man you fall in love with is an uh uh..."

"Is "asshole" the word you're searching for?"

"That's the word exactly." Emily laughed.

"I'm finished with assholes. I have Milo."

"I hope so," Emily said. "I certainly hope so."

"I know so! Soon you'll be my matron of honor."

"That's what you said about Ron Adams."

"Ronny was a son-of-a-bitch!" She snorted. "Milo isn't."

"I hope you're right."

"Em," Annette said softly.

"Huh?"

"Joe Webster's been following me."

"What?" A shiver of dread ran down Emily's back.

"Today when I went to the store, I noticed him behind me."

"Has he said anything to you? Has he threatened you?"

"No, he just follows."

"Did you call the police?"

"Yes."

"What did they say?"

"The same thing they said last time. He's committed no crime."

"What does he have to do? Kill us first?"

"You already know what I think he is."

"Annette, please be careful."

"I will," she said. "I'm going to tell Milo."

"He can be your personal bodyguard."

"And what a fine body it is."

They laughed.

"I'm beat," Emily said. "I've got to go."

"Get some rest, sistergirl."

"I will. Annette, please be careful."

"I will, bye-bye."

"Bye."

Emily climbed in bed distraught about Joe Webster stalking Annette, but the second her head hit the pillow, she was sound asleep.

Next door, Miss Nancy stared at the ceiling worried sick.

Lord, what will Emily do if she finds out she's on file at the nursing home as Leora's daughter and the one to contact in an emergency?

17

"I can take a cab home." Lisa argued with her father in the parking lot of South DeKalb Mall. "I'm not a baby."

"I brought you here," Richard said sternly. "I'm picking you up and taking you home."

"Daddeee." She whined. "Come on."

"I'm giving you a break as it is. Your mother said not to let you out of my sight. Keep it up and I'll take you straight back to the house."

"Ok-a-a-y." She grabbed her purse and jumped from the car.

"You'd better call me." He hollered before he pulled off.

"I will." She waved and walked free for the first time in over forty days.

Lisa's first purchase was the denim dress she had seen in the paper. She needed bras and panties and bought a blue and yellow set. A pink cashmere sweater that accentuated the green of her eyes sang a siren's song and she plunked down her father's credit card for it, too. By the time she got over to Rich's, her arms ached from carrying so many bags.

"Lisa!" Sean Favor shouted over the buzz of noise. "Hey...Lisa!"

She walked toward him with her brain whirling.

Did Mommy speak to his mother about us doing it? He doesn't look mad. He's smiling. He doesn't know a thing.

"Hi Sean."

"You bought the whole mall didn't you?" He laughed at her many bags.

"Almost." Lisa dropped her things by the spurting fountain and plopped on a concrete stool.

Sean sat one stool over and pitched pennies into the water.

"Man, it's hot." She removed her jacket and tossed it on the bags.

"Yeah."

"You're making an awful lot of wishes." Lisa fished a coin from her purse, flipped it in the water and made a wish.

"There're a lot of things I want."

"Oh yeah?"

"Yeah," he said. "I think one of them is about to come true."

"Good for you." She began to gather her bags.

"Where're you going?"

"To call my Daddy to come get me."

"I can take you home." He jumped up to help her with the bags.

"Thanks, but I have to call him."

"I can save him a trip."

"That's okay. Will you watch my stuff?"

"Sure." Sean's dick got stiffer, watching her switch away.

How will Lisa look naked?

His dick threatened to burst his pants. He jerked a bag on his lap and peeked inside. The cashmere sweater felt so soft he couldn't stop stroking it.

"You want to wear that?" Lisa walked up and caught his hand in the bag.

"Hell no." He snatched his hand out. "Is your Dad coming?"

"He wasn't home."

"I'll drop you off." He gathered all of her bags and walked away.

"I can't." Lisa watched him leaving with her new clothes. "Daddy said call him." He had also forbidden her to ride with Sean.

"You're not afraid of me are you?"

"What?" She cupped her ear.

Sean walked back, grinning.

"I said you're not afraid of me are you?"

"I'm afraid of no man! So why would I be afraid of you?"

"If you're not." He walked away, laughing. "Come on then."

Lisa hesitated a second then ran ahead to hold open the door.

"Isn't it a pretty day?" She held her face to the sun.

"Yeah." Sean eyed her body in the filmy dress. "Pretty."

"Where's your car?"

"Over there." He nodded toward Candler Road. "Get my keys out of my jacket, will you?"

"Sure." She got them and hurried to unlock the car.

Sean tossed her bags behind the black leather seats and slid under the wheel. Lisa unlocked her door and got in and jumped out fast.

"What's wrong?" he said.

"Oww! I burned my thighs on this seat."

"Use this." Sean pulled a red and green, plaid blanket from under her bags and spread it over the seat. "I wouldn't want those fine, creamy thighs burned." He patted the seat. "Get in."

Lisa got in. Sean jetted across the parking lot.

"You could at least let me close the door." She crossed her legs, shortening her dress. "What's your hurry?"

"No hurry." He careened onto Rainbow Drive. "I'm just taking you home." They streaked across Wesley Chapel onto Snapfinger and narrowly missed a car pulling from the church lot.

"Slow down!" She buckled her seat belt. "You're going too fast."

"This ain't fast." Sean accelerated. "This is fast."

The Porsche embraced the curves and roared past Panola Road going eighty.

"Hey" Lisa yelled. "You passed my turn off!"

"Did I?"

"You could have dropped me at the corner."

"Chill, Kiddy Widdy." He glanced too long at her thighs and veered over the solid line.

"You don't call me Kiddy Wid—watch out!" She braced for the collision.

Sean stayed on the wrong side longer than necessary then pulled back. The approaching car shot past. Its horn sounded one long blare.

"Are you cra-zy?" Lisa yelled. "You almost hit that car!" She now knew why her father had forbidden her to ride with him.

"Did I hit it?"

"You came close."

"Close only counts in horseshoes." He barreled past the Henry County line.

"Where're you going?"

"Did you know your mother told my mother to make me stay away from you." A menacing tone had replaced his carefree manner.

"She did?" Lisa gulped. "I wonder why?"

"I think you know why."

"No, I don't. What are you talking about?"

He reached over and fondled her breast.

"Stop that!"

"Stop what?" He did it again.

"I'm not playing, Sean." She moved against the door. "Stop it!"

"I wonder where your mother got the idea we were fucking?"

"Uh…uh…listen, Sean." Her voice quivered. "I can explain."

"Explain?" He chuckled. "What's to explain, if you say I fucked you, then I need to fuck you, don't I?"

"Stop this car!" Lisa shrieked. "Let me out of here!"

"Hold on. I'll let you out real soon." He slowed down and turned on a road full of ruts and overgrown bushes. Lisa unbuckled her seat belt, lifted the lock and jumped from the car before it stopped rolling. She turned and headed for the highway. Sean kicked his door open paces behind. He grabbed at her. She sidestepped and crashed through the underbrush.

Brambles pulled at her dress. Supple green switches whipped her bare legs. A root snarl slowed her down. He seized her arm and spun her around. They eyed each out of breath. Lisa recovered first and jerked free. He grabbed her again. She socked him in the mouth.

"Oww!" He pinned her arms and hauled her kicking and screaming to the car.

"Let me go you son of a bitch!"

"Such words from such a refined young woman."

"Fuck you, fuck you!" Lisa screamed.

He opened the car door and reached for the blanket. She broke free and headed for the woods.

"Shit!" He caught her before she got ten feet and dragged her back. "Take off your clothes!"

"I'm not taking off my clothes!" She gasped out of breath.

Sean seized her jacket sleeve. Lisa pulled out of it. He threw it down and grabbed her dress, ripping it to the hem. He wrenched the delicate material, trying to take it off. She fought to keep it on.

Sean gave a strong tug. The dress tore from her body. Goose bumps grew over her skin and she shivered in panties and bra.

"Everything off!" Sean commanded.

"No!"

He grabbed her bra. With a mighty jerk, the three hooks pulled open. He snatched it off, baring her breasts. She crossed them with her arms.

"Fuck you!" She hissed. "Fuck you!"

"You got that wrong S.L.G, I'm…the one going to fuck you."

He grabbed her. She yanked away. He pulled her back, molding himself in the curves of her body. His dick pressed against her hip. His hot breath puffed in her ear and she stopped struggling.

"Let's not do it like this," Lisa said.

"How do you want to do it?"

She leaned back seductively.

"Let's make this special, something we'll always remember."

"Let's do that." Sean relaxed the hold on her waist and twisted her nipples into hard balls. "Your nipples...are...so big."

"You like touching them?"

"Uh huh."

"Touch me there," she said.

His hands slid down her stomach, exploring under the elastic.

"Oh-h, Sean." She moaned. "That's so go-o-ood."

"You like that?"

"Oh-h yes." She faced him and rested her hands flat on his chest. "Kiss me." She whispered and lifted her face.

He leaned with closed eyes to comply. She kneed at his groin and missed.

"You bitch!" He shoved her back.

She fell and hit her head a glancing blow on a rock hidden in the spiky grass.

"Stop Sean. Don't do this." She groaned in a daze. "Let me go."

"Not a chance." He dropped his clothes piece by piece until he towered over her in just socks and shoes. "Is this what you told Mommy I fucked you with?" He ran a hand along his thick dick.

"No, Sean, please no."

"Yes, Lisa, yes." He tore off her panties and dropped to his knees.

"Stop...it!" Lisa screamed. "Please stop!"

He leaned down for a kiss. The blow to his lip surprised him. He pinned her hands and sucked a nipple.

"Mmm." His breaths came faster. "Does...that...feel good?"

"No! Sean, please don't do this to me."

"I've waited a long time for you S.L.G." He played in her forest of pubic hairs. "Now I've got you where I want you."

"Stop! Please stop!"

She turned from his searching fingers. He flipped her back. She held her legs together. He wedged them open with his knee. He rammed his tongue in her mouth. She bit down hard enough to draw blood.

"Bitch!" The slap left his hand imprinted on her cheek.

Lisa's screams soared higher than the trees.

"Shut…the…fuck…up!" Sean clamped a hand over her mouth and grabbed the rock by her head. "If you fucking scream again I'll…I'll…"
Lisa's terrified eyes slid past the butterfly shaped birthmark above his wrist to the weapon hovering above her head. The scream died in her throat.

"That's more like it." He stuck his tongue in her mouth unbitten. He sucked her breasts unencumbered. He kneed her legs wider and lunged savagely into her tight pussy. Lisa shuddered with pain, but made no cry.

"Ssssssss!" Wild animal grunts began deep in his throat. Seconds later, he exploded with a satisfied groan and rolled off her out of breath. He grabbed her torn dress and used it to wipe away the come.

"Now you can say, Sean Favor, fucked you."
Sobbing, Lisa lay on the ground with the dim faces of murdered girls from TV floating before her eyes.

Will I be on the evening news? Is Sean going to kill me?

Lisa heard peeing behind a bush and got up. Gingerly, she took a step and nearly tripped over their clothes scattered over the grass. Groaning, she bent down and gathered everything in a bundle and went on wobbly legs to the car, feeling for the keys. They weren't there, but dangled in the ignition like an open invitation. She got under the wheel, locked the doors and wiped the sticky come as best she could. Lisa put on the new dress. When Sean started toward the car, she turned the key. The Porsche rumbled to life and she pulled away.

"Hey!" Sean grabbed the door handle. "Lisa, you better stop!"
He kept up until she pulled on the highway. After she accelerated to forty, he had to let go and doubled over, gasping for air. Fifteen feet ahead, Lisa skidded to a stop and dangled his clothes from the window.

"You bitch!" Sean charged. "You ugly bitch!"
Lisa let him almost touch the door again before she pulled away.

18

ean used my trust and raped me. How I hate him! How I hate him! My promise to Sebastian is shattered in a million pieces. Should I tell Daddy? No. He'll kill Sean and go to jail. I don't want my Daddy in jail. I don't want anybody to know what Sean did to me. I won't be ridiculed like Corvetta Stewart, after she said Jimmy Dill raped her. I'll never be that foolish.

Lisa returned to the mall. She stuffed Sean's clothes, his car keys and her mangled things into a bag and dropped it in the first trash can she saw.

She called her father and while she waited, she put on panties and combed the grass from her hair.

Please God. Let Gram still be visiting her friend. She'll know something's wrong the minute she sees me.

Lisa spotted her father's car coming down the incline and gathered her bags

"So how was your shopping spree?" Richard said.

"Okay."

"That's all you have to say?"

"Uh huh." She didn't want to draw attention to herself and have him notice she wore a different dress.

They rode home in silence. Richard pulled in the garage and helped her carry in her things.

"Dinner's almost ready." He looked in the oven at the baking chicken.

"I'm not hungry." Lisa pushed through the door and started to run up the stairs. Pain in her stuff slowed her to a walk. In her room, she undressed and jammed everything, even her Mitchell Prep jacket, into a bag for disposal. She wanted no reminders of what happened today.

Lisa stood under a shower of near scalding water. She scrubbed inside her mouth to wash away the taste of Sean's kisses. She rubbed frantically between her legs to clean away his come.

I hope I won't be sorry I spit out the birth control pills. Don't let me get pregnant. Please don't let me get pregnant.

Tears filled her eyes followed by hacking sobs. She put her head under the spray and wanted her mother's arms wrapped tightly around her more than anything in the world.

"Where's Gram?" Lisa peeked in the kitchen door.

"At Miss Evelyn's," Nicole said.

"Too bad." She came in the kitchen. "I wanted her to see my clothes."

"I want to see." Michelle opened a bag. "What's this?"

"I'll show you." Lisa removed the cashmere sweater.

"Pretty." Michelle rubbed it against her face.

"What's in here?" Nicole snatched a shoebox.

"Can you wait?" Lisa grabbed it back.

"What did you do to your hair?" Richard asked. "Didn't you just get it done last Saturday?"

"Yes." Lisa avoided her father's eyes. "I didn't like it."

"You think I'm made of money?"

"No, Daddy."

"I'm not spending another dime on your hair."

"That's okay. I'll do it myself."

"If it gets done, you'll do it."

Lisa held an orange mini dress up to her body, modeling.

"Do you like this?" she asked Michelle.

"I love it."

"Me too," Nicole added.

"What about you, Daddy?" Lisa asked.

"It's very pretty," Richard said. "Why are your eyes so red?"

"Are they red?" She looked at him. "I guess I got shampoo in them."

"They're really red," he said. "Like you've been crying."

"Crying?" She laughed. "Why would I be crying?

"I don't know. They just look so red."

"Daddy," Lisa said. "When is Mommy coming home?"

"Wednesday."

"I miss her."

"I miss her, too," he said.

"I miss Mommy the most," Michelle said.

"No you don't." Nicole challenged. "I miss her the most."

"I miss her bigger than this house." Michelle said.

"I miss her way bigger than this whole street." Nicole added.

"Girls," Richard said. "Nip it."

It became very quiet.

"Let's go to our room." Michelle suggested.

"Good idea." Richard said.

"Don't you want to finish looking at my clothes?" Lisa asked.

"Later." Nicole and Michelle went upstairs to continue the argument as to who missed their mother the most.

Lisa showed the rest of her clothes to her father glad to have something to do to take her mind off Sean. The image of him running down the road in just socks and shoes intruded anyway and she laughed out loud.

"What's so funny?" Richard asked ready to laugh with her.

"Nothing," Lisa said. "Can I call Mommy?"

"Uh huh. The numbers on the refrigerator."

Lisa dialed, praying she'd be there.

"Hello," Miss Nancy answered.

"May I speak to Emily Bennett, please?"

"Just a minute, Emily, telephone."

"Hello," Emily said.

"When are you coming home?" Lisa gripped the phone.

"I'll be home Wednesday."

"I miss you."

"I miss you, too, sweetie."

"I love you, Mommy!"

"I love you, too," Emily said slowly. "What's wrong?"

"Nothing's wrong," Lisa said. "What makes you think anything's wrong?"

"You sound funny."

"Funny, how?

"You sound different."

"Different?"

"You sound sad."

"I'm not sad." Lisa laughed again. "I just miss you that's all."

"You're sure that's all?"

"Uh huh."

"I'll be home Wednesday when you get out of school, okay?"

"Okay?" Lisa said. "I love you."

"I love you, too. Let me speak to Daddy."

"Mommy wants to talk to you." She got her clothes and went to her room.

"Hello, baby," Richard said.

"Is Lisa okay?"

"As far as I know, why?"

"She sounded funny. I hope she's not trying to see that Sean."

"You told his mother to keep him away from her, didn't you?"

"Yes, and she assured me she would."

"Well then."

"Would you stay away from me if your mother told you to?"

"Oh Lord."

"Keep an eye on her."

"I will. You doing okay?"

"I'm okay, it's almost over." Her voice got shaky.

"Don't cry, baby, don't cry."

"I won't," she said. "Where are Nicole and Michelle?"

"Upstairs arguing about who misses you the most."

They both laughed.

"Want me to call them?" he asked.

"No, just give them a hug and kiss."

"I will."

"Maple Honey left me—" She almost mentioned the inheritance. *I'll never be able to tell Richard this.*

"Maple Honey left you what?"

"She...she left me with a lot of good memories."

"That's good, that's good."

"How's Pauline?"

"Fine, she's over Mrs. Ward's. The girls were driving her nuts."

"After she gets them to school Wednesday, she can go home."

"She'll be glad to hear that."

"You're sure Lisa doesn't sound funny?"

"No," he said. "She did look like she'd been crying though."

"Crying, when?"

"When she got back from the mall."

"When was she at the mall?"

"This morning."

"Who with?"

"By herself."

"She went by herself?" She screamed. "I told you to watch her."

"Let me finish," he said. "I took her and picked her up."

"How long was she gone?"

"About four hours."

"She could fly to Chicago and back in four hours!"

"Sorry," he said. "I thought she needed a break."

"Watch her from now on."

"I will," he said. "What's all that noise?"

"People partying." She held the phone to the open door. "Can you hear?"

"Sounds like a convention."

"It looks like one. Maple Honey knew everybody," she said. "Did you ask Dr. Chambers about my make-up session?"

"She said come in Wednesday at the same time."

"Good, I really need to talk to her."

"I really need you to sex me up." He whispered. "I might have to come to Lacewell tonight!"

"I dare you to come." She challenged, knowing he wouldn't.

"I will," he said huskily. "I need your body."

"I need yours, too but I've got to get back with these folks."

"Okay," he said. "I love you, bye-bye."

"Love you, too. Bye."

Emily hung up worried. Lisa was probably slipping, trying to see Sean. Richard didn't know the games young girls played like she did.

"Kiddy Widdy." Richard knocked on Lisa's door.

"Daddeeee. Why do you insist on calling me Kiddy Widdy?"

"Kiddy Widdy is my special name for my special girl," he said.

"Don't call me that silly, baby name anymore."

"I won't," he said. "Your favorite movie is coming on."

"A Warm December?"

"Uh huh. Come on down and we'll watch it together."

"Maybe."

Lisa had stayed in her room mostly to avoid her Gram. By six o'clock, she felt confident enough to face her and went to watch the movie. Afterwards, she returned to her room and fell on her bed, trying to plot the perfect revenge for Sean, but could think of nothing vile enough.

At nine o'clock, the ringing phone made her jump. Suppose its Sean. She started not to answer.

"Hello," she said.

"Sean's missing?" Carlton said.

"Missing? What happened?"

"I don't know, his mother called around four, looking for him. She just called back. I haven't seen him all day, have you?"

"Me? No I haven't seen Sean in a long time."

"I hope he's okay," Carlton said.

"He's probably laying up with some hot momma."

"If that's the case, he'd at least call his mother. He knows how she worries about him."

"He will as soon as he can get a way." Lisa regretted the slip as soon as it left her mouth.

"What do you mean a way?" Carlton asked.

"I said...away." She stammered. "Not a way, he's probably with a female far away from a phone."

"I hope you're right."

"I've got to go." She rushed to hang up before she said something really dumb. "I just washed my hair. It's dripping all over. Talk to you later."

"Sure."

"Keep me informed."

"Okay, bye now."

"Bye, bye."

Lisa hung up, happy she'd caused Sean some grief. It wasn't as much grief as he'd caused her, but it was a start. She was going to get even with Sean Favor and she didn't intend to wait on the what goes around comes around payback method her Gram talked about either. She didn't care if it was a thousand times worse than anything she could dream of, she was personally going to make Sean Favor sorry he ever knew her name.

"Lisa! Lisa!" Michelle's frantic screams came from the intercom. "Come down here quick!"

Lisa went as quickly as she could to press the button.

"What's wrong?"

"Sean's on TV! Sean's on TV!"

"What?"

"Sean's on TV. Hurry down here before he goes off!"

Oh God! My fingerprints are all over Sean's car.

She inhaled slowly to calm herself.

Chill, Lisa chill. Sean comes to my house. I sit in his car. Of course my prints would be there.

Lisa went in the family room. Everyone looked sad for Sean. Nobody felt sorry for her.

I never wanted to have sex with Sean. He raped me!

"What happened?" Lisa asked.

"Shhh," Richard said. "Let me hear."

Lisa eased on the sofa next to her grandmother.

Sean's grim face filled the screen. The camera pulled back. He wore a tattered yellow shirt torn at the sleeve. Sizes too large, it flowed off his shoulders. He gripped the pants at the waist to keep them on. They stopped inches below his knees. Lisa stifled the laughter threatening to bubble out.

A reporter from channel five faced the camera.

"Today around two o'clock, young Sean Favor was kidnapped from South DeKalb Mall." She stuck the microphone in Sean's face. "What happened?"

"A White man stuck a gun in my side," he said with a straight face. "And made me drive to the country."

"Can you identify him if you saw him again?"

"Yes. He's about six feet tall with black curly hair and a beard."

"Why did the man take your clothes?" The reporter asked.

"He said if he took my clothes, he could get further away."

"Were you sexually assaulted?"

"Hell no!" Sean barked then added greater emphasis. "Hell no!"

"Did he harm you in any way?"

"No. He just took my car."

Lisa almost lost it then and started out.

"Where're you going?" Michelle asked.

"He looks so pitiful," Lisa said. "I can't watch." She rushed to her room and fell on the bed with both pillows over her face to muffle her hyena laughter.

Lisa dreaded going to school. All weekend, she tried to think of an excuse to stay home and ended up using what always worked with her mother. She held the towel wrapped hot water bottle to her head before she went in the kitchen.

"Gram," she said. "I don't feel so good."

"What's wrong, hon?" Pauline asked.

"I'm hot and feverish. I think I have the flu."

"Stick out your tongue."

Lisa stuck out her tongue. Pauline felt her face and neck.

"Hmmm," Pauline said. "That's strange."

"What?"

"Your face is hot but your neck is cool."

"What do you think it is?"

"I think it's an excuse to stay here with your old Gram."

"No it's not." Lisa whined. "I'm really sick."

Pauline laughed and set Lisa's book satchel by the door.

Every red car sent Lisa's heart racing. At school, she surrounded herself with friends, hoping someone would stop Sean before he killed her.

After gym class, Lisa walked up on Sean with a group of his friends. A dangerous look swept across his face. She scurried past with the vivid memory of the rock raised above her head.

What will Sean do to me now? I know he wants to hurt me bad.

She looked fearfully over her shoulder. He wasn't following her this time, but she knew he eventually would. She needed to do something to stop him from doing her more harm.

I know. I'll write an insurance letter and tell everything Sean did to me.

Tuesday, March 31, 1981

There's the bitch responsible for everything bad that's happened to me.

Sean saw Lisa pass by his classroom a few minutes into third period. She was the cause of him being on television in clothes stolen from a scarecrow. She was the cause his car was broken into and the radio and cassette player and ten of his best tapes stolen. She was the cause he had to have his ignition rekeyed. She was the cause he spent time at the police station looking at line-ups of tall, bearded White men with black curly hair and angry blue eyes. She was the cause his folks worried everytime he left the house. Most of all, she was the cause for the total ridicule he suffered from his homies who refused to believe the man he said took his car didn't fuck him up the ass.

You're going to pay bitch and you're going to pay big time.

"Yes, Mr. Favor?" Mrs. Vince acknowledged his raised hand.

"May I be excused?"

"Yes."

Sean sprang from his seat and followed Lisa like a stalking tiger. She looked back and ran terrified into the front office.

"Yes," the secretary said.

"Miss Hill sent this." She gave her a folder and glanced out the door. Sean was gone.

"Thanks. I was just on my way to get this." She examined the papers and looked up. "Is there anything else?"

"No ma'am."

Lisa walked out with her hands balled into fists on the alert for Sean.

"I'm going to get you." He stepped from the restroom and grabbed her arm.

"If anything happens to me, I have a letter saying you're a rapist."

Sean let go and stepped back like she had the plague. Lisa continued on her way. He trailed incensed. Before she went in Miss Hill's classroom, she turned on him with her most ferocious look.

"Now *you* can say, Lisa Bennett, fucked you!"

19

Emily went to I Love To Read, hoping work would take her mind off of Maple Honey.

"How're you feeling?" Annette hugged her. "You look so sad you make me want to cry."

"I'm okay," Emily said. "I'm fine."

"I'd tell you about my trip but you look so unhappy."

"I'm okay tell me." She knew Annette was anxious to talk about her new man.

"Sistergirl!" Annette plopped in her chair, grinning.

"What?"

"Sistergirl! Sistergirl!" Annette swooned, hugging herself.

"What? What?"

"Sistergirl! Sistergirl! Sistergirl!"

"If I have to come around this desk," Emily stood with her hand raised. "I'm slapping you silly."

"If there was an award for eating pussy." Annette strutted about the room. "Milo would win three!"

"Shut up!"

Annette held up her hand for attention.

"You know the thrill that hits you all at once and your pussy jumps remembering...you know?"

"Yeah, I know."

"Lizzie's been jumping all morning." She dropped in her chair and fanned under her dress. "Chile! Chile! Chile!"

"You are so crazy." Emily laughed.

"Like a fox." Annette tapped her head. "Milo asked about you."

"Oh?"

"He wants to know if you'll help him with his tennis game."

Emily groaned. Milo was the last person she wanted to instruct.

I hate the way he looks at me.

"You promised, remember?"

"I know."

The phone rang.

"I Love To Read, Annette speaking."

"Hi baby," Milo said. "How's the most beautiful woman in the world?"

"Flattery will get you everything." Annette's voice got sexier. She winked at Emily and swiveled in her chair. "How are you?"

"Better since I'm talking to you."

"I enjoyed our trip very much," she said.

"My fellow officers still talk about the fox on my arm."

"Oh really now?"

"Uh huh, when can I have you on my arm again?"

"You can take me to lunch."

"You're on," he said. "What time?"

"Twelvish?"

"Twelvish it is. How's your friend?"

"Who, Em?"

"Yes, Emily."

"She's fine. We were just talking about you."

"Something good I hope."

"Uh huh." She laughed. "Something very good."

"When can she give me some help with my game?"

"Hold on." She pressed hold. "When can you help Milo with his game?"

"I'm booked this Saturday. What about next Saturday at ten?"

Annette clicked Milo back on.

"The earliest she can take you is next Saturday at ten."

"Great!" He hung up without saying good-bye.

"Did I tell you Milo is teaching me to drive a stick shift?"

"Oh yeah, what does he drive?"

"A Bentley."

"A Bentley?" Emily asked. "How can he afford such a car?"

"I don't know. It's sharp. It's burgundy—"

"Bob Quill is the only one I know who drives a burgundy Bentley."

"Now you know two," Annette said with an annoyed tone.

"Don't go getting an attitude."

"Attitude? Me? I'm in too good a mood for attitude." She made the gear shift motions. "Shifting gears is so cool!"

"I bet you jerked every bit of the way."

"I did not."

"Right."

"I didn't."

"Tell me about Miami," Emily said.

"The part inside or outside the hotel room?"

"The part outside."

"There was no part outside the hotel room, so ha!"

"Umph! Umph! Umph!" Emily said. "You are so bad."

"Milo thinks I'm so good." Annette laughed.

"Has Joe Webster been following you?"

"No."

"Milo let me shoot his pistol." Annette bragged.

Emily hated guns and made Richard keep his in their bedroom safe.

"Was it loud?"

"Loud and heavy."

"Did you close your eyes when you fired?"

"No, but I should have."

"Why?"

"Then I wouldn't have seen the sparks."

"Sparks?"

"Yeah, I held it like this." She pointed up. "And pulled the trigger, sparks fell on my hand. I put that bad boy down fast."

"Has Joe Webster been following you?" Emily asked.

"You already asked me that," Annette said. "And if he did, I'd take Milo's gun and shoot him in the balls. Joe Webster is a—"

"I know...I know," Emily said with a laugh.

"Have you ever been to the Castle?"

"Once for our tenth anniversary. Why?"

"Milo is taking me there this weekend."

"He must be loaded if he can take you there," Emily said. "Richard says he has to save ten more years before we go again."

"What am I going to wear?" Annette looked at her watch and stood. "Milo dresses finer than I do. I need to go shopping just to keep up with him."

"Save your money. You don't need to shop, you need to co-ordinate," Emily said. "You can dress from the clothes in your closets for the next five years and not wear the same thing twice."

"I wish," Annette said. "You want to see something?"

"What?"

"I don't know where Milo gets his money, but he sure likes to spend it on Annette. Look what he gave me." She removed a huge emerald ring from her purse and slid it on her finger.

"If this is an engagement ring," Emily said, "I'm impressed."

"It's just a present. But it's so...so—"

"Is "big" the word you're looking for?"

"Yeah! Do you think it's real?"

"It looks real, but what difference does it make if it's real or not? It's the thought that counts."

"You're right," Annette said.

"Where does Milo live?"

"In RobHen North," Annette said. "That big modern place you can see from the road?"

"That's Dr. Quill's house. I don't think he sold it."

"You're probably thinking of another house."

"No, I'm not."

"Em," Annette said with a nasty tone.

"Okay...okay."

"Inside he has all types of furniture. French Provincial, oriental, modern. eclectic I think they call it and girl you should see his kitchen. It's gorgeous!"

"Has he cooked anything for you?"

"Uh huh!"

"Can he really cook?"

"Better than Momma and you know Queen Esther can burn."

"He *should* open a restaurant if he cooks that good."

"He plays piano beautifully and serenaded me on a—"

"A white Steinway?"

"Yes, a white Steinway," she said peeved. "In a foyer with—"

"Black and white tile?" Emily answered for her.

"Em!" Annette huffed. "Do you want to hear this or not?"

"Okay, I'll be quiet. Go ahead."

"Anyway...Milo serenaded me. His singing isn't so great, but it was so romantic. He led me up this long sweeping staircase into this black marble bathroom and slo-oo-ow-ly undressed me and sponged my body with coconut soap. Then he lifted me soaking wet and carried me to a king sized bed."

"And then what?" Emily asked.

"And then...and then." Annette shut her eyes tight.

"What? What?"

"And then he fucked my brains out again!" Annette said fast. "Ssssssh! Shit!"

"My." Emily laughed. "You were a busy little bee."

"He thought I was going to him head, but I wasn't about to put that hugey in my mouth."

"You're crazy." Emily laughed.

"Uh huh, like a fox." She tapped her head. "I'm only going to give my husband head. Do you give Richard head?"

"No comment." Emily laughed.

"Don't pull that 'no comment' bull shit with me. Does Richard eat you?"

"No comment."

"Don't you love it?"

"No comment." Emily laughed.

"I love it and you love it, too." Annette got her purse and keys and headed for the door.

"Where're you going?" Emily asked.

"Home to change. I want to look delicious when Milo shows up."

"You look delicious now."

"No sistergirl, right now, I only look good."

"You're crazy."

"Yeah, like a fox." Annette tapped her head and laughed. "Ta ta."

"Ta ta."

"Come in." Emily looked up in answer to the rap on the door pane. Milo stood there looking finer than fine in a fuchsia sportcoat over a white shirt, black slacks topped off with a black and melon tie.

"You just missed, Annette." Emily stood and offered her hand. "She'll be right back."

"Hello." He removed his shades and held her gaze and her hand longer than necessary. "How can you be more ravishing than the last time I saw you?"

Emily laughed and pulled her hand away.

"Thank you," she said. "Please have a seat."

"So this is Annette's little business?" He walked around with his hands clasped behind his back.

"No, this is Annette's and Emily's big business."

"I stand corrected." He turned to look her up and down.

She felt nude under his gaze and sat behind her desk.

"What is that bewitching perfume you're wearing?" he said.

"Joyous."

"Doesn't Annette wears that, too?"

"Yes, she does."

"Long ago someone else I knew wore that same scent."

"Oh?"

"She looked exactly like—"

"Da da-a-a-a!" Annette sang her entrance. She looked way past delicious in a navy double-breasted suit with a pleated skirt above her knees.

"Baby! Baby! Baby!" Milo crooned. "How can be more ravishing than the last time I saw you?"

"Oh-h-h, Mi-i-lo." Annette giggled and took his offered arm.

Emily rolled her eyes at his lack of a better line and watched the beautiful couple leave. Before Milo closed the door, he looked back with a sly grin and winked. confirming her gut feeling. He was not the man for Annette.

I'll be glad when this affair runs its course and is over.

Emily left the store in good spirits. By the time she walked in Dr. Chamber's office, she was crying so hard she could hardly see.

"What's wrong?" The doctor escorted Emily to her usual chair.

"I should have gone to see her...I should have gone to see her!"

"Whom should you have gone to see?" Dr. Chambers offered a box of tissues.

"Maple Honey!" Emily jerked out three. "My, Maple Honey!"

"Do you want to talk about your Maple...Honey." She seemed to question the name.

"That's not her real name," Emily said. "I started calling her Maple Honey when I was eight years old." She wiped her eyes, laughing at the memory.

"Why did you call her that?"

"It's a long story," Emily said.

"Do you want to talk about it?"

"Well," Emily said. "She arrived that morning in a black and white cab. The driver jumped out and pulled two brown suitcases and a cardboard box from the trunk. He set them at the curb then scurried around the car and opened the back door. A large, dark skinned woman struggled to get out of the seat but every time he tried to help, she slapped his hands.

'I can do it myself.' She told him.

'I ain't got all day!' He pushed his cap back on his head.

When she finally stood, she leaned on a silver handled cane.

'Where's my money?' He held out his hand.

'You ain' through with me. How am I gonna get these cases up that hill?' He glared at her but fitted the box under his arm and picked up both suitcases. He marched up the slanty brick steps cut in the clay bank, then up the green painted steps and set them on the porch. It took her a long time, but she struggled behind him until she made it.

'It's about time,' he said. 'Where's my money?'

She opened a big black purse and slapped fifty cents in his hand.

'Where's my tip?' he asked.

She printed something on an index card and handed it to him.

'What's this?' he read aloud. 'Do unto others before you have to be told.'

'That's your tip, buddy,' she said. 'That's your tip.'

'Listen here you old bat.'

'Who you callin' a old bat?' She threw the cane in the air, caught it half way and turned it into a weapon.

"That driver ran down those steps so fast, his cap fell off and he never stopped to pick it up." Emily doubled over with laughter.

'Hi." She turned to me and said. 'I'm Maple, Honey.'

"I thought Honey was her last name and said. "How do you do, Miss Honey? She laughed so hard her stomach shook like jelly."

'Baby, I just know we gonna be good friends.'

"I fell in love with her that second and the hole in my self-esteem began to close."

"She sounded like a delightful person," Dr. Chambers said.

"She was," Emily said. "She was the only one who loved me like a mother should."

"How should a mother love?"

"She...she...should love you no matter what."

"Maple Honey loved you no matter what?"

"Maple Honey loved me unconditionally...Leora not at all."

"Who is Leora?" Dr. Chambers asked and leaned back in her chair.

"Leora?" Emily looked surprised. "Did...did I say Leora?"

"You said Maple Honey loved you unconditionally...Leora not at all."

"I...I...didn't mean to say Leora."

"Whom did you mean to say?"

"I don't know why I said Leora."

"Who is Leora?"

"Leora." Emily picked at a crease in her skirt. "Is my mother."

"Do you want to talk about your mother?"

"No. She's dead."

"How long has she been dead?"

"Since...since 1966."

"What month did she die?"

"Month? Uh...uh July."

"What date?"

"July uh...uh fourth! The fourth of July!"

"How do you feel since your mother died on such a festive day?"

"I...I..." Emily touched her burning cheeks. No one had ever cross-examined her about her mother before. Everyone else accepted her word, which it seemed Dr. Chambers was not going to do.

Emily wanted to tell the truth. It was so embarrassing being caught in a lie. "My mother's in a nursing home. Richard doesn't know. He'd never forgive me if he found out."

"Why was it necessary to say your mother was dead?"

"She hates me, so I just say she's dead."

"Why do you think your mother hates you?"

"I don't know." She told her about the incident at the hospital.

"I see."

"I told you about the time I almost got hit by the car."

Dr. Chambers nodded.

"Did your mother ever tell you she hated you?"

"She didn't have to. She showed it with each curse until Maple Honey came."

"The abuse stopped when Maple Honey came?"

"Yes."

"Why do you think it stopped then?"

"Because Maple Honey wouldn't permit it."

"How do you feel since Maple Honey died?"

"Sad," Emily said. "Abandoned."

"That's only natural."

"And angry. I'm so angry with her, I could scream."

"Scream if you wish."

"I won't really scream, but Maple Honey has done something so mean."

"What has she done?"

"In order to inherit her estate, I have to bring Leora to live at my house."

"And you can't do that?"

"No." Emily's voice became icy. "No, I can't."

"Why not?"

"I hate Leora so—" Emily rubbed her forehead.

"Are you experiencing the pain, now?"

"Yes."

"Do you need to lie down?"

"It's not as intense as it usually is. I can continue."

"Do you still think the pain is connected to your hatred for your mother?"
Emily answered without hesitation. "Yes, I do."

"Do you want to keep the pain?"

"Keep it?" Emily flared. "Of course, I don't want to keep it!"

"If you think your pain is caused by your intense feelings for your mother, then the longer you hold onto these feelings, the longer you will have the pain."

"I don't know if I can stop. I've hated her so long."

"You can do anything you put your mind to." She stood. "Time's up."
Emily looked at her watch and stood, too. "Times just flies when I talk to you."

"That's a good sign." Dr. Chambers laughed. "Now, I want you to think about what I said about exorcising the pain."

"I'll think about it."

"Good." Dr. Chambers walked her to the door. "See you next Monday."

"Okay. Bye-bye."

"Bye."
Emily thought about how much she hated Leora and resigned herself to always have the pain.

20

Richard chipped mud off his golf shoes and tossed them in the trunk. The aroma of roses in bloom floated in the garage. He inhaled deeply. It was a glorious day to be alive. He glanced at his watch.

I should have been gone, if Junior and I want to tee-off at eight.

Just as he slid under the wheel, the phone rang. He started to ignore it, but didn't want it to wake Emily and got out to answer.

"Hello."

"Emily Bennett, please."

"She's unavailable, would you like to leave a message?"

"Have her call, Mrs. Shelton, at the Blue Pine Nursing Home."

"What is this about?"

"I need to speak to her about her mother."

"That's impossible. My wife's mother died years ago."

"I'm sure this is the right number, 404–555–1258?"

"That's our number but—"

"Is your address 48950 Sunday Lake Drive?"

"Yes it is, but—"

"That's the phone number and address for, Leora DuPree's, daughter."

"That's her name but—"

"Can you have, Mrs. Bennett, call me? Perhaps we can straighten this out."

"I'm telling you," he said. "You have the wrong, Emily Bennett."

"Do you have a pencil?"

"Yes." He took out his pen and patted his pockets for something to write on. He pulled a receipt for a drill he needed to return from the board. "Go ahead."

"Have her call, Mrs. Shelton, at 912–555–3188. Anytime after one"

He scribbled the message and repeated it.

"I'll tell her."

"Thank you, good-bye."

"You're welcome, good-bye."

He wrote, Leora DuPree, three times and circled it. Emily always regretted not having her mother, now somebody was trying to give her one. He jumped in the car already seeing her laughing her head off.

Emily fired a tennis ball to her opponent. Justine French leaped high and missed, ending the game.

"You did it again." She ran to the net to shake Emily's hand. "But watch out next time."

"Promises, promises." Emily laughed. "All I hear are promises."

They walked off the court and met Milo Trotter by the tall chair. Emily glanced at her watch.

At least he's punctual.

"Ladies." He posed with hands on hips and a smile more dazzling than his whites.

"Hello," Emily and Justine said together.

"Justine French, Milo Trotter, Milo, Justine." Emily introduced them.

"How do you do?" Justine smiled and shook his hand.

"How do you do?" Milo looked her up and down and held her hand until she pulled it away.

"I've got to run," Justine said. "It's nice meeting you."

"Nice meeting you, too," Milo said.

"Okay," Emily said. "Work on your backhand."

"I will." She waved with her racket and headed for the locker rooms.

"Another one bites the dust." Milo watched until she turned the corner.

"You just missed, Annette," Emily said.

"I'll see her later." He sauntered onto the court. "I'm ready for you now."

Emily sent a ball to his service box. Milo returned it with an overhead smash. Back and forth it went until her hand stung and she realized he wasn't there to learn from her. He was there to beat her butt.

Emily knew she couldn't beat Milo with physical strength; his returns were savage, but she could slow him down. She gripped her racket with both hands to give her shots power. When he approached the net, she sent lobs back court. When he ran back court, she dropped shots inches from the net. To confuse him further, she varied her spins from top to under to flat. Milo was in excellent shape but the exercise she meted out kept him chasing the ball and she easily won the set.

"Good...game." Milo ran to the net, huffing like an exhausted dog. "Damn good...game"

"Thank you." Emily offered her hand, smiling. She would not give him the satisfaction of knowing it throbbed with pain even when he crushed it in an unsportsmanlike grip.

"Most men... can't return... my volleys."

"I'm not most men." She shot back and strutted off the court.

"You definitely are not." He followed, admiring her legs. "I love a challenge, especially a challenging woman."

Emily stopped at a bench under a vine covered arch and pulled on her sweater.

"I've been watching you kick ass on the court."

"Is that right?"

"Yeah, that's right."

Emily moved back from his body, smelling of cologne and sweat. His hand went up against the wall. She turned the other way. His other hand went up, trapping her inside his bulging muscles.

"You're good on your feet. I want to see if you're as good on the sheet."

He ground into her. Emily shoved him back, stunned.

"Tongue tied?" He laughed.

"No, asshole, disappointed!" She put her entire body into the slap to his face and stalked off to the sound of his laughter, echoing over the court.

She'd given up all hope of him being Mr. Right for Annette the day he winked at her, but she hadn't thought he'd be a dog and a snake and try to bed her, too. *This is going to break Annette's heart.*

Emily showered, changed then went to find her husband. She stood at the French doors until she spotted Richard and Ralph having drinks at an umbrella table on the balcony. Richard waved. She waved back and weaved through the maze of black clothed tables, stopping occasionally to speak to friends. She reached the table. Richard and Ralph stood.

"Hi, baby." Richard kissed her lips and pulled out a chair.

"Hi, guys." She sat and crossed her legs.

"Hello, lovely Emily," Ralph said.

"How was your game?" Richard asked.

"Great. I beat the stuffing out of a state trooper named Milo Trotter."

"Those macho guys never learn do they?"

"Nope," she said with a laugh. "They never do."

"Where're my girls?" Richard asked.

"Shopping with, Annette." She looked at Ralph. "I want you to meet her."

"I'm always eager to meet a beautiful woman."

"How do you know she's beautiful?" she asked.

"Sonny, told me," Ralph said.

She looked at Richard. "Now who's matchmaking?"

"All I said was she's beautiful." Richard sipped his drink.

"I'll bet." She looked at Ralph. "Annette's from Chicago, the Southside."

"Is that right?"

"Watch it, Junior." Richard laughed. "You're being set up to be married."

"Richy, stop that." She playfully slapped his hand.

"I'm telling you man, you'll be married so fast your head will roll off."

"You're scaring him to death." She slapped his hand again. "Don't listen to him, Ralph."

"He's already scared to death," Richard said with a chuckle.

"Who's scared? Not me." When Ralph laughed, his eyes crinkled shut just like Richard's.

"You'd better be, Junior." Richard warned him with a laugh.

"I'd love to be married," Ralph said. "To the right woman."

"See!" Emily stuck out her tongue at Richard.

"The girls didn't want to be around us old folks, huh?" Ralph changed the subject.

"If they had known their favorite uncle was here, wild horses couldn't have kept them away."

He laughed. "Did they like the outfits?"

"You know they loved them, they wore them today."

"I'm glad," Ralph said pleased. "I was hoping they would."

"You Bennett boys have excellent taste." Emily looked from one to the other. "We love everything you buy us."

"Thanks." Richard and Ralph said together.

Richard patted Ralph's back affectionately and signaled for a waiter.

"When are you going to settle down and have your own kids?" Emily ignored

Richard's frown and maneuvered the conversation back to marriage.

"Oh, I don't know...when I can find a woman like you."

"Sorry, Junior, you'll never find another like Emily. She's one of a kind and she's mine." He patted her hand.

"Thank you, darling." Emily patted his hand back.

Their waiter waltzed up with goblets of ice water and red tasseled menus.

"Would Señora like a drink?" He turned his handsome face to Emily and bowed slightly. His accent was beautiful. His aim was to please.

"No thank you Julio, I'm starving. I'm ready to order."

"Si, Señora." Julio held his pen ready to write her desire.

"I'll have baked chicken, broccoli casserole, a salad with French dressing."

"Something to drink?"

"Coffee," she said.

"Are the gentlemen ready to order?" He looked first at Richard then Ralph.

"I'll have the porterhouse steak, medium rare," Ralph said. "Baked potato with sour cream."

"Would you like a salad?

"Yes, with Thousand Island dressing."

"Anything else?"

"No," Ralph said. "Just remember steak medium rare."

"Si, Señor." Julio turned to Richard for his order.

"I'll have the same thing he's having except I want my steak well done, no pink at all, got it?"

Past experience told him his tip would be generous if the steak orders for Dr. Bennett and his guests were perfect.

"Si, Señor." Julio finished writing the order. "Something to drink, perhaps a nice burgundy?" He paused, looking from one man to the other.

"Either of you want wine?" Ralph studied the wine list.

"Just coffee for me," Richard said.

"I'll have a glass of burgundy," Ralph said.

"Si, Señor." Julio collected the menus and left.

Richard looked at his watch and called him back. Julio stopped short and returned to the table.

"Si, Señor?"

"Will you bring a telephone, please?"

"It would be my pleasure."

Julio returned minutes later and plugged in the phone.

"Something funny happened this morning." Richard chuckled and opened his wallet. "She said call after one."

"Who?" Emily took the calling card and unfolded the paper. Leora DuPree sprang at her like a cobra. The blood drained from her face. She reached for a goblet. It tipped, spilling water over the tablecloth.

"Careful." Richard dabbed water off the receipt. "I can't get this wet."

Emily knew if she spoke, her voice would betray her. She took a large swallow of water from Richard's glass along with several pieces of ice.

"What's this about?" She mumbled.

"A Mrs. Shelton called from the Blue Pine Nursing Home." Richard laughed. "She wanted to speak to you about this woman. How could they make such a mistake?"

Emily drank more water.

"Mistake like what?"

"She says Leora DuPree is your mother."

"That's impossible. It's probably a wrong number."

"That's what I said. Then she read our phone number and address to me."

"They'll realize they made a mistake," she said.

"That could take forever. You need to call and straighten this out."

"Right now?" She forced herself to look in his eyes.

"I'm curious to know what this is all about, aren't you?"

"Can't it wait?" she said. "Our food will be coming soon and I'm starved." She looked as casually as she could from Richard to Ralph.

"I'd think you'd rush to know what's going on," Richard said.

"It's just a silly mistake." She stroked his hand. "I'm famished."

"Okay," Richard said. "After we eat."

Is it my imagination, or is Ralph looking at me funny? Can he see I'm panicking? Maple Honey!! How could you give them my phone number and address?

Julio served the meal and returned later to inquire about the food.

"Is everything satisfactory?" he asked.

"Yes, thank you." Richard made an okay sign. "Perfect."

Julio looked at Ralph.

"Mine is excellent," Ralph said.

Julio eyed Emily's uneaten meal and could see the huge tip he always got from the doctor flying away.

"And Señora is not pleased?"

"I have the worst headache," she said. "I can't eat a thing when they start."

"I'm sorry," Julio said relieved to know she wasn't displeased with the food or his service. "Some aspirin, perhaps?"

"Yes, thank you." She hoped taking them on an empty stomach wouldn't really make her sick.

"Right away." He was back in seconds with aspirin and refilled her glass.

"Thank you." Emily swallowed the pills. "You're very kind."

"It is my pleasure."

"Since you're not eating," Richard said. "You can call Mrs. Shelton."

"My husband is learning Spanish." Emily tried a stalling maneuver. "Maybe he can practice on you, Julio."

"It would be my pleasure," Julio smiled.

"No…no," Richard said. "I just started, later maybe."

"Si, Señor." He picked up Emily's food and left.

Please! Please! Please! Emily prayed to the god that fixed dumb situations people sometimes found themselves in. She dialed the first nine numbers and misdialed the last two.

"No answer." She hung up after the fifth ring. "I'll try later."

"No answer?" Richard said. "What kind of nursing home doesn't even answer the phone?"

"I sure wouldn't want my folks in a place I couldn't even reach by phone." Ralph looked at Emily.

"Me neither." She dropped the crumpled receipt in her bag.

"I need that." Richard held out his hand. "Write the number on something else, okay?"

Reluctantly she added the name and number to her address book and watched Richard return the receipt to his wallet.

A flash of bright color pulled Emily's attention to her right. Milo Trotter stood inside the French doors, surveying the room behind dark glasses. He had changed into a double breasted azure blue jacket over a cream shirt and slacks with a yellow and blue tie. He strolled to the bar and ordered a cognac then leaned on the counter, touching Emily all over with his eyes.

Emily tried to avoid looking his way, but every few seconds, an invisible magnet seemed to pull her head in his direction. Each time it did, he smiled. Her imaginary headache now throbbed for real.

"How is your headache, Señora?" Julio set a doggy bag next to Emily.

"Getting worse each minute," she said glad for the interruption. "Thank you for asking." She got her purse, the doggy bag and stood. "I'm going home."

Ralph and Richard stood, too.

"Take a nap." Richard gave her a kiss. "You'll feel better."

"Okay." She turned to Ralph. "Are you coming home with Richy?"

"It depends." He laughed.

"On what?"

"On what's for dinner?"

"It'll be a surprise." Emily laughed and started toward the door. Out of the corner of her eye, she saw Milo headed her way and outfoxed him with a U-turn down the balcony steps.

When I tell Annette what you said, buddy. I've seen the last of you.

21

A tantalizing aroma greeted Annette and the Bennett girls at the door.

"Mmmm." Nicole drooled. "Spaghetti."

"Mommy, we're home." Michelle yelled and lugged a shopping bag full of new clothes to the family room.

"Mommy." Nicole peeked around the kitchen door. "Come see what, Auntie Annette, bought us."

Emily came out in a flowing saffron caftan.

"O-o-oh, Em." Annette touched the silky fabric. "I like this."

"Thanks. Richard brought it back from New York." Emily twirled about like a high fashion model.

"Great taste." Annette whispered. "And great sex, how can you stand it?"

"It's hard," Emily said with a haughty toss of her head. "But what can I do?" They laughed.

"Look what, Auntie, got me." Michelle pulled two sacks from the overturned bag. "Look, Mommy, look." She turned Emily's face in her direction.

"Michelle!" Emily scolded. "Can't you see I'm talking?"

Michelle's eyes teared up and her mouth curved down.

"Come here." Emily hugged here. "What you did was rude."

"Sorry," Michelle said glumly and became excited again. "Look, Mommy." She held up an apple green jumper with her name embroidered in gold.

"It's beautiful." She held the fabric to Michelle's face. "You look gorgeous in this color."

Michelle beamed.

"Where's Lisa?" Emily asked.

"In my car," Annette said. "That girl knows she loves a car."

"I know." Emily laughed. "Believe me I know."

"Look, Mommy." Nicole modeled a denim skirt and matching cowboy shirt.

"That's lovely. I hope you thanked, Auntie."

"I did," Nicole said.

"I did too." Michelle chimed in.

"You spoil these girls rotten. You're worse than Ralph."

"What are Aunties for?" Annette laughed. "If not to spoil pretty little girls?"

"I have something to tell you," Emily said.

Annette's laughter faded at Emily's serious expression.

"What?" she said. "What is it?"

"Let's talk in the turret room."

They walked down the hall in silence and went into a circular room filled from floor to ceiling with books. Annette sat on the leather sofa. Emily sat across in a wing chair.

"Milo hit on me today after our tennis lesson," Emily said.

"Oh that?" Annette laughed. "Milo told me he was playing around with you."

"He told you he was playing around?"

"Yeah, he said you might misunderstand."

"Misunderstand? I know when I'm being hit on."

"Well I know what Milo said he said!" Annette got agitated.

"Would I lie about something as serious as this?"

"I don't know!"

Emily stood. "You've known me twenty years and him a hot minute and you don't know?"

"I think you're making something out of nothing," Annette said casually.

"You think I'm lying? Is that what it is? You think I'm lying?"

"I don't think you're lying, I just think you misunderstood what Milo said."

"You're good on your feet. I want to see if you're as good on the sheet." Emily said. "Now tell me what part I misunderstood?"

"I know Milo didn't say that."

"You think I made it up?"

"I don't know."

"I see." Emily marched to the door and snatched it. "Get out!"

"What?" Annette jumped up. "You're throwing me out?"

"I don't want anybody in my house who calls me a liar."

Annette flounced from the room. Emily hurried to open the front door. Lisa and Carlton stood on the steps talking.

"What did I say about hanging outside with boys?" Emily flew into Lisa. "Carlton, you know better!"

"Sorry, Mrs. Bennett."

"We were only talking, Mommy," Lisa said.

"You can talk inside and I'm not going to tell you again."

"Sorry." Lisa walked in. "Come on in, Carlton."

"Naw, I've got to go anyway. Bye." He went down the steps.

"Bye." All three said at once.

"What's wrong with her talking out here?" Annette asked.

Emily tore into her. "How can you be an authority on teenage girls and a fool where grown men are concerned? I know what's best for my child so keep your pitiful advice to yourself!" She stalked to the kitchen and left Annette and Lisa standing there with their mouths ajar.

"Well, excuse me!" Annette said.

"What's wrong with, Mommy?" Lisa asked.

"She's upset about something." Annette snatched her purse off the hall table and started out the door.

"Auntie," Lisa said. "You don't have on any shoes."

Annette looked at her feet and laughed.

"I left a bag in your trunk," Lisa said. "Can I get it?"

"I don't know," Annette said. "You might steal *my* car, too."

"I won't." Lisa held out her hand. "I promise."

Annette looked in her purse and gave her the keys. "And don't lock them in the trunk, either."

"I won't." Lisa laughed and ran out.

Annette found her shoes and opened the front door. Her heart sputtered to a halt. The triple fine man, towering over her with muscles like a lumberjack had to be Ralph Bennett. He smiled down on her. She got lost in his deep, dark brown eyes, crinkling in a taffy brown face. His hair was the same shiny black as the mustache growing luxuriously over lips made for kissing.

"Annette." Richard steered her back inside. "I'm glad you're here. I want you to meet my brother."

"Annette Marshall, this is Junior...uh Ralph."

"Pleased to meet you," she said.

"I'm pleased to meet you, too."

"What should I call you Ralph or Junior?"

"Call me either one." His laughter boomed over the foyer. "As long as you call me.

"Didn't I tell you she was beautiful?" Richard said.

"Very beautiful!" Ralph said.

"Shucks," Annette said. "You're making me blush."

"You and Emily look like sisters."

"Uncle Junior!" Michelle screamed and slammed into his body.

"Uncle Junior!" Nicole ran into his arms and laid her head against his chest. "When did you get back?"

"Yesterday."

"Girls stop that." Richard swatted their bottoms. "Where're your manners?"

"Sorry." Ralph held the girls close, apologizing. "My nieces adore me."

"I don't blame them," Annette said. "I'd adore your fine self, too."

"Direct and to the point." Ralph laughed, again. "I like that."

"Come see what I got." Michelle pulled Ralph's arm.

"Me, too." Nicole tugged the other one.

"It was very nice meeting you." Ralph smiled bashfully at Annette and let his nieces tow him away.

"The pleasure was all mine," she said. "All mine."

I love a man who loves kids. Does Milo love kids? I'll ask him when he picks me up tonight.

"Where's Emily?" Richard flipped through the mail on the hall table. "She wasn't feeling good when she left the club."

"She's in the kitchen," Annette said with an aching heart.

How could Em misunderstand something Milo said in jest? I should go in that kitchen and slap some sense in her head.

"Come on in and help her cook."

"I can't today. I have to leave."

"You're not staying for dinner? I was hoping you and Junior might hit it off."

"I'd love to stay," she said. "But I have a date, please tell Em I'm gone."

"I'll walk you out." Richard took her arm and escorted her to her car.

Lisa climbed from the Volvo and ran her hand over the finish.

"Daddy, this is the kind of car I want when I'm sixteen."

Annette looked at Richard. He looked at her. They laughed heartily.

"What's so funny?" Lisa asked.

"If you get a car like this, you'll have your own money."

"No problem, I'll just save my allowance."

Richard and Annette doubled over with laughter again.

"What...is...so...funny?" Lisa asked.

"Your allowance must be huge." Annette took her keys.

"It's not nearly enough." Lisa laughed. "Thanks for my things."

"You're welcome, Lisa girl." Annette patted her cheek.

Richard opened the car door and she got in.

"Bye," Lisa and Richard said.

"Bye bye." Annette pulled off, hit the brakes and backed up. "I almost forgot. This is for Em." She handed Richard a box wrapped in gold paper and took off.

"Daddy. When are you going to teach me to drive again?"

"It seems like you already know how."

"No, I don't."

"If you can back in the garage, you already know."

Will I ever see Sebastian again?

"I want real driving lessons."

"Not from me, Kiddy Widdy."

"Daddeee, you're calling me Kiddy Widdy."

"I'm never letting you drive my car, and your mother won't let you touch hers, so forget it."

"But I didn't wreck Mommy's car."

"You'd better be glad you didn't." He laughed. "If you had, the beating you got would have seemed like a caress."

"That's not funny." She touched her throat. "Mommy was crazy."

"I see that encounter gave you a little attitude adjustment."

"Attitude adjustment? I'm the same loving daughter I always was."

"Sure," he said, laughing, "Sure."

They walked to the house arm in arm.

"Wonder what this is?" Lisa tried to take the present.

"It's not for you, it's for your mother. Where is she?"

"In the kitchen," Lisa said. "Where's Uncle Junior?"

"In the family room."

Lisa went to see her uncle. Richard went to see his wife.

"Emily, are you in here?"

"Uh huh," she said from the pantry. "Stir the sauce, please."

Richard stirred the bubbling mixture and sampled.

"It needs more oregano," he said and sat at the table.

Emily came out with two cans of sweet peas.

"Feeling better?" he asked.

"Uh huh."

She shook in oregano and let him sample until she got his okay.

"I keep thinking about, Maple Honey." She sat beside him.

"It's only been two weeks, give it time."

"Why didn't I just drive down to see her?"

"Baby, stop torturing yourself."

"I try, but I feel so guilty."

"You know, Maple Honey, loved you don't you?"

"Yes."

"Would she want you blaming yourself like this?"

"No, she wouldn't."

"Would she want you unhappy?"

"No."

"Try and remember that, okay?"

"I'll try."

"That's my good girl." He kissed her and felt the soft caftan. "I knew you would look fabulous in this the minute I saw it at Saks."

"Thanks." She took the box from him. "Is this another present for me?"

"Probably," he said. "But it's not from me, it's from Annette."

"Oh." She dropped it on the table.

"Aren't you going to open it?" He picked it up, hefting it in his hand.

"Put it on the frig. I'll open it later."

"What's happened between you two?"

"Nothing's happened."

"Emily, I've known you too long for bull."

"We're going through a rough time right now," she said. "It'll smooth over." She hoped it would smooth over. When a man came between two women, things rarely returned to the same old groove.

"Do you want to talk?" He opened the refrigerator. "Do you want a soda?"

"No, not now...later maybe."

"What? No to talking about it, or no to wanting a soda?"

"No." She laughed. "To talking about it, yes to a soda." She took the cold can he handed her and popped the top. She would eventually tell him about Milo and her spat with Annette. She told him everything. Well...almost everything.

"I'm ready to listen," he said. "Whenever you're ready to talk."

"Okay," she said. "Has Lisa been acting strangely to you?"

"No! Why?"

"She mopes about. When I ask what's wrong, she acts like she wants to tell me something then says she's fine."

"You think she's pining over, Sean?" Richard asked.

"I don't think so. Nicole seems more upset since he stopped coming around than Lisa does."

"Well, I hope she's not still trying to see him."

"She says she's not, but I can't watch her every minute."

"I know." Richard said. "I know."

"I'll ask Pauline to talk to her, maybe she can find out what's on her mind."

"Okay," he said. "I'm starving, when will dinner be ready?"

"As soon as I heat the peas. Tell everybody to wash up.'

"Okay," he said and left the room.

Emily set a ceramic bowl filled with meat sauce beside a crisp tossed salad bathed in oil and vinegar. She carefully peeled foil back on two steaming garlic loaves and put one on each end of the table. She placed the buttered peas by a piping mound of spaghetti and pressed the intercom.

"Soups on," she said. "Come and get it."

Everyone except Lisa trooped to the kitchen. Emily went looking and found her reading a book in the turret room.

"Aren't you going to eat?" she asked.

"I'm not hungry."

"Sweetie, tell Mommy what's wrong." Emily felt Lisa's forehead.

"Nothing's wrong. I'm just not hungry."

"You'd tell me if anything was bothering you, wouldn't you?"

"Uh huh." Lisa gave her a half smile. "Really, nothing's wrong."

If nothing's wrong, why do you look so sad?

22

Emily took her usual seat in Dr. Chambers' office with two questions on her mind: *Should I give hypnosis a try or should I mention the baby?* She glanced at the brain wave synchronizer and decided "no" to it, "yes" to the baby.

"There's something I want to discuss."

"Go ahead," Dr. Chambers said.

"I don't know quite how to say this." Emily squirmed in her chair. "Don't get me wrong, I dearly love my girls. But..."

After ten seconds of silence, Dr. Chambers said. "But what?"

"I...I..." Emily faltered. "More than anything I want...a...a..."

"Yes?" Dr. Chambers said.

Emily blurted the words. "I want to have a boy child."

Dr. Chambers could barely keep her composure. It had been sixteen years since Sonny first mentioned Emily's obsession with having a boy.

"Why is having a boy so important to you?"

"That's just it," Emily said. "I don't know."

"How long have you felt this way?"

"As long as I can remember," she said. "All my life."

"All your adult life?"

"No!" She shook her head. "Even as a child, whenever I got a doll, I'd pretend it was a boy."

"Did you name your doll?"

"Yes."

"What did you name it?"

"Bunny."

"Why?"

"I don't know."

"Was there a special doll you named Bunny?"

"No. I named them all Bunny."

"I see."

"Does this make me a bad mother?" Emily implored.

"Do you feel it makes you a bad mother?"

"I have three beautiful girls yet all I think about is having a boy. It's like my girls count only until my boy comes along. What if he never does?"

"You'll have to separate your love for your girls and your longing for a boy."

"But can I do that?"

"Yes," Dr. Chambers said. "Of course you can."

"I think I'll lose my mind, if I don't have my son." She remembered her depression when she miscarried a baby boy two years ago.

"I can't promise you'll have a son," Dr. Chambers said. "But I can promise, we'll continue to talk about this until we find out why it's so important to you." Emily looked at the brain wave synchronizer.

"Do you think hypnosis will help me remember the nightmare?"

"It might."

"I want to try it."

"You're quite sure?"

"What do I have to lose?"

"Not a thing," the doctor said. "Sit over there, please." Emily moved to the leather recliner and settled into its cozy softness.

"Put these on." She handed Emily a pair of opaque wrap around glasses and a set of earphones.

"What are these for?" Emily asked.

"The lights and tones slow your brain waves to the alpha state." She turned on the machine and the tape recorder. "Shut your eyes, please." Flashing red light penetrated Emily's closed lids. High pitches droned in her ears accompanied by a soothing female voice.

"Bre...athe deep...ly ex...hale...feel the ten...sion lea...ving your body. Re... lease all...the ten...sion in the little...toe on your right foot."
The exercise continued to the top of her head.

"Emily," Dr. Chambers said. "Can you hear me?"

"Yes."

"When I touch your right shoulder. You will use all your senses to remember the nightmares you have. Do you understand?"

"Yes."

"When I touch your left shoulder. You will awake alert and refreshed. Do you understand?"

"Yes."

The doctor touched Emily's right shoulder. She immediately began to speak.

"I'm in prison. I'm walking around the cell. I see ducks flying through the air. I see ocean waves. I climb over a high fence and jump on a sleeping blue grizzly bear. It chases me up a steep hill. I see little pink piggies in the air. I come to a grove of tall trees. Each tree has its name carved in the trunk. Pine, pecan, cedar. I'm looking for an oak tree and find it in a deep, dark forest."

Emily thrashed about. Her breaths became labored.

"I hear...doves cooing...high in the...oak tree. There is no...bark on the tree. I...step...on a ledge...and the tree leans...forward. Burning hot rain falls...in my eyes. A...rabbit falls from the...tree. "

Emily's terrified screams echoed through the room.

"Emily." Dr. Chambers touched her left shoulder. "Come back. Now!"

"I...can't...breathe!" She clutched her chest. "I can't breathe!"

"Yes, you can," Dr. Chambers assured her. "Breathe in slowly, out slowly, in slowly, out slowly, that's right...that's right."

Emily breathed with Dr. Chambers until her ragged pants evened out.

"How are you feeling?" Dr. Chambers asked.

"Tired," she said. "Very tired."

"Why couldn't you breathe?"

"A heavy weight sat on my chest."

"What kind of heavy weight?"

"I don't know."

"My eyes burn." She rubbed them with her fists.

"Why are your eyes burning? What do they burn like?"

"They burn...like...like..."

"Like what?"

"Like shampoo," Emily said. "No...no not shampoo...soap!" She bolted upright. "Soap! It's soap!"

"Soap?" Dr. Chambers asked.

"Yes. Soap!" Emily swung her legs around and stood. "Why would I remember soap in my eyes?"

"It's another piece added to the puzzle."

"Am I a thousand piece or a million piece puzzle?"

Dr. Chambers laughed. "You're as many pieces as it takes."

"Oh God! I may never find out why I have this nightmare."

"Don't fret. You've already taken the first step."

"What's that?"

"You remembered your nightmare."

"I did." Emily smiled broadly. "Didn't I?"

"Yes, you did. Do you have any idea what any of it means?"

"I don't have a clue." Emily shook her head.

"Are you up to listening to what I recorded?"

"Yes!" Emily became very excited. "Yes!"

Dr. Chambers played the tape. They went over each symbol, every emotion, trying to make some sense of them until the session ended. This time when Emily left Dr. Chambers' office, she saw a dot of light at the end of her nightmare tunnel.

23

Emily stood in the hallway at, I Love To Read, watching Annette and Milo cuddle and coo like love birds in heat.

How can Annette have the gall to bring Milo here after I told her what he said, and how can he have the gall to come?

Emily laughed out loud. Why should Annette care about her, a friend of twenty years, when she had a rich, handsome man who made her orgasm just looking at him? The lovers headed toward the office. Emily hurried to her desk.

"I'm going to have to ride shotgun to beat the women off you if you keep looking so good," Annette said. "Em, look at this finey fine, here!"

"Hello Emily," Milo said. "You're looking as beautiful as ever."

"Hello," Emily said dryly and made no reply to his compliment.

"Milo, you have more clothes than I do," Annette said. "I've never seen you wear the same thing twice."

Milo laughed. He spun around modeling a watermelon colored jacket over a pale pink shirt, black trousers and a peach and black tie.

"Today is Em's birthday," Annette said. "Let's take her to lunch."

"Great idea," Milo said. "Happy Birthday."

"No, thank you." Emily busied herself with the book order.

"Come on, Em," Annette said. "We want you to go."

"I said, no thank you."

"Not another word." Milo jerked her up by the wrists. "You're coming with us, birthday girl."

"Get your fucking hands off me!"

Milo released her and she dropped to the chair.

"Em!" Annette shouted. "What's wrong with you?"

"Let's go, baby," Milo said grimly and escorted Annette out.

Emily stared at the door not believing what Milo had done nor what she had said. Sighing, she threw herself into the book order.

"I Love To Read, Emily speaking."

"Emily," Milo said. "While I'm fucking you—"

She slammed the receiver down so hard it bounced to the floor. She left it there, enduring the agitating noise until she went to lunch.

"What's wrong with you?" Annette hovered over Emily. "Why couldn't you have come with us?"

"Number one, he yanked me up like I was a piece of meat. Number two, I told you what he said to me."

"Don't start that shit again, he...was...kidding. Why is that so hard for you to understand?"

"Was he kidding when he called me talking dirty?"

"Called you when?" Annette glared at Emily.

"Around twelve-thirty."

"He was with me at twelve-thirty."

"He was with you every second?"

"Yes, yes he was." She failed to mention he'd gone to the men's room.

"Open your eyes. He's been after me from day one."

"You think every man wants you, don't you?"

"I do not!"

"Oh no?" Annette said. "Why are you always in Milo's face?"

"I avoid Milo as much as possible and you know it."

"I see you checking him out." Annette put her hands on her hips.

"Checking him out?" Emily said. "You're crazy."

"I'm crazy, alright." She tapped her head. "I know what I see."

"I wouldn't have Milo on a silver platter trimmed in gold."

"You just keep my man's name out of your mouth."

"I don't have to speak his name or yours!"

"See to it that you don't!" Annette put on her right shoe and dropped to her knees to retrieve the left one way under her desk. She grabbed her purse and stalked all the way to the parking lot before she remembered Milo had her car. Too ashamed to face Emily, she called a cab and went home.

Emily was worried.

Milo Trotter is a giant wedge prying us apart. Am I going to let him destroy our friendship? Can I convince Annette he's a dogsnake?

She opened the owner's manual for the answering machine. In the index, she found recording telephone conversations and turned to page twenty-five. The part about compliance with state and federal regulations made her nervous, but a twenty-year-old friendship was more important than the law. When Emily read, this unit does not sound a warning beep when a call is being recorded, she whooped.

"I am ready for you, Milo Trotter. I am ready for your butt, now!"

Emily drove home wondering why Annette attracted the men she did. It was like she had a scent a no good man could smell from a thousand miles. She backed into the garage and climbed the steps with a heavy heart.

Annette is my truest friend. I don't want to lose her.

"Surprise!" A quartet of voices yelled and sang the birthday song.

"Oh my," Emily said, laughing. "Oh my, oh my."

Her family swarmed around her with hugs and kisses and the unpleasantness with Annette and Milo was soon forgotten.

"Are you surprised, Mommy?" Michelle gave her a tiny box wrapped in silver foil. "Are you really surprised?"

"Thank you." She hugged her. "Yes, I'm really surprised."

"Happy birthday, Mommy." Nicole gave Emily her present.

"Thank you." Emily shook the box. "What can this be?"

"Happy birthday, Mommy." Lisa gave her a large rectangular box.

"What can this be?"

"You'll see, " Lisa said, excitedly. "You'll see."

"Thank you, sweetie."

Lisa set all the gifts on top of her big box and carried them from the kitchen.

"Happy birthday, sweetheart." Richard waited until she washed her hands and led her to the dining room.

A blue and yellow sheet cake loaded with candles sat in the middle of the table surrounded by her favorite foods.

"My goodness," Emily said. "How many candles are on that cake?"

"Forty," Lisa said. "Thirty-nine and one for good luck."

"I hope the house doesn't catch on fire." Emily laughed.

Emily sat down and stuffed herself. After dinner, she blew out her candles in seven puffs with a little help from Michelle.

"Did you make a wish, Mommy?" Michelle asked.

"Uh huh."

"What did you wish?" Michelle asked.

"She can't tell or it won't come true." Nicole scooped ice cream in a bowl.

"You can tell me," Michelle said solemnly. "I won't tell."

"If I tell one soul." She put her fingers to her lips. "It won't come true."

"Open your presents, Mommy." Lisa set them by her chair.

"Open mine first." Michelle pushed her box in Emily's hand.

"What can it be?" Emily tore at the tightly taped paper and lifted the top. Nestled in a square of cotton lay the biggest mood ring she had ever seen. Shaped like a miniature crown, the gem looked like a brown roach.

"It's beautiful." She slipped it on and held out her hand, admiring it.

"Do you really like it?" Michelle asked.

"I love it," Emily said. "Look it's changing light blue already." She held out her hand to show Michelle.

"Let me read what it means." Michelle removed the paper from the box. "Brown means sad. Light blue means temperate. What's temperate?"

"It means not happy or sad," Emily said. "But in between."

"Temperate," Michelle said. "I learned a new word."

"Yes, you did."

"Teal blue means you're happy," Michelle continued. "Sapphire blue means you're ec, ec...Mommy what's this word."

Emily looked at the paper. "Ecstatic. It means extremely happy."

Michelle lifted Emily's hand. The stone was teal. "You're happy."

"I'm very happy." Emily hugged Michelle.

"Do you really like it, Mommy?"

"I don't just really like it, sweetie. I really love it"

"Me next." Nicole thrust her gift in Emily's hands.

"What can this be?" She mangled the paper. "Ummm, chocolate covered cherries. You know how much I love these. Thank you, sweetie."

"You're welcome." Emily pulled Nicole close for a hug.

"Who else has a present for me?"

"I do!" Richard could hardly wait his turn.

"Daddy, I'm next," Lisa said. "Your present is always the best."

"Okay, Kiddy Widdy."

"Daddeeee!" She rolled her eyes. "Don't call me Kiddy Widdy."

"Sorry." He bowed to her. "I meant Lisa."

"Here, Mommy." Lisa gave Emily the huge box.

"It's so big. What could it be?" She lifted a royal blue and silver dress from the tissue.

"O-o-o-oh." Emily held it up to her body. "I love it, Lisa."

"It's not exactly like the one I...messed up," she said quickly adding how she got the money. "Daddy let me cash in some bonds."

"Thank you, honey."

"You're welcome." Lisa stepped into her mother's hug.

"Here's mine." Richard handed her one end of a shiny gold ribbon. Last year, Emily found a sable coat on the other end of a mink brown cord. Emily could hardly contain her excitement "Is what I'm getting gold?"

"No clues." Richard laughed. "You have to find it yourself."

Emily wrapped the ribbon around her hand and followed the golden line from the dining room. Her family trailed as excited as she. Down the hall to the turret room, out the French doors, across the side lawn. By the time Emily reached the garage, the ribbon resembled a misshapen beach ball.

"It's not a new car is it?" she asked.

"No clues," Lisa said. "But you're getting warmer."

They tracked around the magnolia tree, back through the French doors into the family room. When Emily reached the kitchen, the ribbon went taut.

"I'm almost there?" she asked, laughing.

"Almost," Richard said. "Almost."

"Don't tell her, Daddy." Nicole scolded.

"Okay." He zipped his lip and made them all giggle.

The ribbon disappeared under the laundry table. Emily dropped to her knees and peeled tape off the object stuck there and pulled it free.

"I'm so excited." She held a large, square box in gold foil. "I'm so excited!

"Open it, Mommy." Michelle insisted. "Open it."

"Yeah, Mommy." Nicole agreed. "Open it."

"Hurry, Mommy." Lisa urged more excited than her mother.

"I'm trying." Emily tore the paper off a black leather case and lifted the lid. Her sharp intake of breath told Richard everything he needed to know. She loved it.

"I love it!" She grabbed him in a bear hug. "I love it! I love it! I love it!"

The girls crowded around, admiring the brilliant flashes on black moiré silk.

"O-o-o-oh it's so pretty." Michelle touched it.

"Look how it sparkles," Nicole said.

"When can I wear it?" Lisa asked.

"Never, Missy." Emily laughed. "Never."

"Let me put it on you." Richard lifted the necklace from the box. Emily held up her hair and he clasped it around her neck.

"Let me see." She went in the half bath to see the diamonds glittering at her throat. Richard followed and stood behind, caressing her shoulders, warming her backside with his raging body heat.

"O-o-oh, Richy." She turned from side to side. "This is the most exquisite thing I've ever seen."

"You're the most exquisite thing I've ever seen." Their eyes met in the mirror with a silent promise of glorious lovemaking to come. Emily reached up and stroked his hand. Her mood ring glowed sapphire blue.

24

"I wonder what time Annette got home last night." Nora asked that morning. "She was still waiting for her car when I left."

"Milo!" Emily said with disgust.

"Milo!" Nora answered with equal disdain.

"What time did you leave?"

"Around ten-forty-five. I offered her a ride, but—"

The wind chimes rang. Annette came in with a cup of coffee.

"Morning." She mumbled and headed to the office.

"Morning," Nora said.

Emily said nothing. They had not spoken since her birthday.

"See you later," she said to Nora. "I have an order to make."

"Okay."

Emily went to the office and sat at her desk.

"How do you like your present?" Annette asked.

Emily started not to answer.

"What present?" she said.

"Your birthday present."

"It's lovely. I sent you a thank you card."

"What about the other present I gave you?"

"What other present?"

"The one I gave you when I took the girls shopping."

"Oh, that one." The box sat unopened in her bedroom. "It's beautiful."

"Just something to let you know I was thinking about you."

"Humph!" Emily said. "I doubt that you think about me."

"Of course I think about you. I love you."

"You haven't been acting like you love me."

"I'm sorry. I know I've been a Meany."

"A Meany? You, my dear, have been the wicked witch of the south."

"No, baby doll, you've been the wicked witch of the south. I only thought pregnancy made you Mrs. Evil."

"I am definitely not pregnant!"

"You've sure been acting like you are." Annette laughed. Emily joined her. It had been a long time since they'd laughed together.

"Guess whose valedictorian at Mitchell Prep this year?" Emily had lots of news to catch Annette up on.

"Who?" Annette said. "Lisa?"

"Yes, my Lisa."

"Great," Annette said. "She beat out all those older kids?"

"Sure did," Emily said proudly. "She's been working on her speech every day. It's really good."

"I can't wait to hear it."

"She got her SAT results back." Emily's chest got tighter.

"What'd she score?"

"Fifteen forty nine out of a possible sixteen hundred."

"Got-dam!"

"She trounced that smart mouth Sean Favor by over a hundred points."

"She said she was going to trounce his ass. Where's she sending her scores?"

"She sent them already," Emily said. "They want her at Harvard and MIT. We haven't heard from Yale yet."

"What about Spelman?"

"They want her, too," Emily said. "But she says she wants to be on her own, far away from us."

"Soon your first little chick will be flying from the nest."

"I know," Emily said, sadly. "I know."

"I'm buying Lisa something special for this."

"What?"

"That red suede suit she raved about in Brill's."

"She'll love that. She's been buying school clothes since last year."

The phone rang.

"I Love To Read, Annette speaking. Hello? Hello?" She hung up. "I guess they didn't want me."

Someone called twice and hung up when Annette answered.

Emily removed the cassette from her desk.

I wonder if that's Milo?

He hadn't called her lately with obscene talk, but she had enough recorded to not only cook his goose, but to fry him to a crisp.

"Annette?" Emily nervously fingered the case.

"Huh?"

"I have something I want you to—"

"I know who Dr. Chambers' lover is," Annette said.

"What?"

"I know who Dr. Chambers' lover is."

"Who? Who? Who?"

"Who do all the men go gaga over at the club?"

"Yolanda Story?"

"Cold."

"Jackie Norton?"

"Freezing."

"I don't know." Emily dropped the tape in her pocket. "Tell me, tell me."

"Guess."

"Uh...I don't know, Glenda Hightower?"

"Nope."

"I give up," Emily said. "Tell me."

"Nope." Annette laughed. "You have to guess."

"Give me a hint then."

"She's beautiful."

"That's no hint that could be anybody."

"Okay...okay." Annette giggled. "She plays tennis."

"Half the women at the club play tennis...I don't know."

"She's a lawyer—"

"Opal Joplin?"

"Nope."

"Uh...uh...Glory Marlowe?"

"Nope."

"I don't know, tell me."

"One more guess," Annette said.

"I don't know." Emily shrugged her shoulders and pulled a name from the air. "Justine French?"

"Bingo."

"You're kidding." Her mouth gaped open. "Who told you?"

"Nobody. I practically saw them fucking."

"What? When? Where?"

"At the club," Annette said. "Justine was feeling the good doctor's titties."

"What?" Emily got angry. "Here Richard is trying to protect her reputation and she's flaunting herself to the world!"

"Actually, they didn't know I was there."

"They didn't?"

"I went back to get my ring from my locker. They came in laughing. Before I could say a word, Justine said, 'I can't wait to get you in bed.'"

"Wha-a-at?"

"Uh huh," Annette said. "I peeked around my locker. Justine had her hand up Dr. Chamber's dress and her tongue down her throat."

"What was Dr. Chamber's doing?"

"Moaning. I got so hot, I almost asked if I could join them."

"Shut up!

"I did." Annette laughed. "I'm smoldering now just thinking about it."

"You're crazy."

"Like a fox." She tapped her head.

"Did they do it?"

"No, they left before they got that far."

"Dr. Chambers and Justine French," Emily said. "Man."

"Justine is the man," Annette said.

"How do you know?"

"Justine was in charge. Dr. Chambers let her do whatever she wanted."

"Man!"

"Aren't you afraid Dr. Chambers is going to feel you up?"

"I used to be, but not now. Man! Dr. Chambers and Jus—"

"Hello ladies." Milo walked in like he owned the place.

"Looking good," Annette said. "Look...ing good."

Not as colorfully dressed as usual, Milo was still impressive in a black and white checked jacket over a black shirt and trousers and a black and white floral tie intertwined with red.

"Thanks," he said. "Baby, I need to borrow your car again."

"Hold on." Annette looked through her purse for the keys.

Emily glared at Milo. He chuckled and wagged his tongue suggestively.
I can't believe he'd be so brazen with Annette in the room.
   "Annette!" Emily muttered. "Hurry up and get him out of here!"
Annette looked from Emily's frown to Milo's angelic smile. He hunched his shoulders in dismay. Annette looked back at Emily.
   "What are you talking about?"
   "Nothing."
   "Milo, drop me at Brill's." Annette tossed him the keys and looked for her other shoe.
   "You have to go this minute?" he asked. "Can't you go when you get off?"
   "No, I can't go when I get off." She mocked him. "They close early on Tuesdays. I'll lose my discount if I don't go today."
   "I'll pick it up." He twirled the keys around his finger.
   "I've gained a few pounds." She felt her hips. "I may need a refit."
   "Your body looks perfect to me."
   "That's not the point," Annette said. "When are you getting your car out of the shop? It's been there how long now?"
Good question, Annette. Say something stupid Milo.
   "You have too many clothes already," he said.
Good answer, Milo. Go-o-o-od answer.
   "What...did...you...say?" Annette stood in one shoe with hands on hips in her don't fuck with me stance.
Get him, Annette.
It was all Emily could do to keep from laughing out loud. She didn't want to disturb her when she was on a roll.
   "I buy my got-damned clothes, not you!"
   "Chill baby, I've got to be somewhere in fifteen minutes, I'll be back for you." He blew her a kiss and hurried out.
   "Milo, got-dammit!" Annette hopped after him, screaming. "You son of a bitch! Come back here! Come back here!"
   "Annette, stop it." Emily pulled her back in the office. "The customers can hear you!"
   "I don't give a shit!" Annette found her other shoe under the computer table and jerked it on. "Can you believe that bastard wouldn't wait for me in my damn car. He's got a woman some fucking where! I know it!" She held her hand out to Emily. "I need to use your car."
Reluctantly, Emily handed her the keys. Annette stalked out.
Did I do the right thing? Suppose Annette catches Milo with a woman and does something stupid?

Negative supposes ran through Emily's mind. Fifteen minutes later, Annette stormed in smoking worse than a four-alarm fire.

"I lost the son of a bitch!" She paced like a caged animal. "But I'm going to kill Milo Trotter before this day is through. I swear to God...I'm going to kill him before this day is through!"

Now was not a good time to play the tape Emily decided and slipped it from her pocket and returned it to the desk.

Joe Webster streaked past the black Volvo and glimpsed the driver leaning across the seat.

There's that bookstore whore.

He U-turned and doubled back. Two golden haired White women stood on the passenger side, laughing down into the car.

The excitement he felt at finally carrying out his plan was closely akin to getting a nut. His only regret was he wouldn't get both whores together. He had missed his chance after the law interfered on Covington Highway.

One at a time will do. One at a time will do just fine.

Joe Webster pulled in the lot and eased off the brakes. The van inched forward and lined up with the Volvo driver's window. Joe Webster slid to the other seat and straddled the two-gallon bucket. He pried up the plastic lid. Dark streaks of congealed blood rippled through liquid brown cow shit. The overpowering odor rushed up his nose and he fought to catch his breath.

"Whe-e-e-w!" He fanned with his hand and smiled wickedly already seeing it covering the snotty bitch. He lifted the bucket. Four fingers dipped in the mess. He jerked them out. A pint sloshed over his pants. "Shit!" He tried to dodge the spill. More sloshed on him. "Shit!" He heaved the container up and dashed the contents down into the Volvo's window.

"Mo-ther fuc-ker!" Milo unfolded from the car with shit from his waistband to his cuffs. He pulled his jacket back and reached for his pistol.

Joe Webster scrambled into the driver's seat and took off.

P-yow! P-yow! The bullets entered the back window and exited four inches then two inches from Joe Webster's head. He screamed louder than the two White women running for cover and careened from the lot.

Milo aimed again. A truck blocked his target. He hopped in the Volvo oblivious to the shit-soaked seat or the soupy liquid, sloshing on the rubber mat under his feet. He slammed the car into drive and stomped the gas. The Volvo shot forward. A red light caught Milo at the second street. He spotted the van in the distance and pulled through the intersection. A truck plowed into the front fender and spun the car around. Milo steered deftly around the swearing driver and hit I-20 East going eighty.

"Help me, Jesus! Help me Lord!" Joe Webster prayed as the car fast advanced in his side view mirror. He veered off at the next ramp. Milo followed and stuck the pistol out the window.

P-yow! P-yow! P-yow! P-yow! P-yow! P-yow! P-yow!
Bullets one, two and five slammed into the side of the van. Six and seven missed altogether. Number three punctured the right front tire. Number four hit the right rear. Curved strips of rubber bounced off the road and smashed into the windshield. Milo ducked instinctively, peering around the spider web crack.

Joe Webster fought the steering wheel for control. The van skidded down the road on the right rims, sending sparks flying like a comet's tail until it veered with a savage halt into the gully.

Milo stood up on the brakes, imprinting four wavy lines of hot rubber on the faded asphalt. He jumped from the car and slid down the embankment.

"Out, mother fucker!" He yanked open the door and aimed the pistol at Joe Webster's head.

"Don't...kill...me!" Joe Webster covered his head with his hands. "I didn't mean it! Don't kill me!"

"Get in the goddamn car."

"Okay, okay." Joe Webster climbed out with his own shit added to his sopping pants and slid under the Volvo's steering wheel.
Milo tossed him the keys. Joe Webster fumbled the catch and fished them from the shit pool surrounding his feet.

"Drive until I tell you to stop!"

"Okay, okay, okay!" Joe Webster pulled away at a crawl.

"Faster."

"Okay, okay, okay!" He accelerated to sixty.
Two miles up the road, the car began to sputter.

"Turn through those bushes and stop!" Milo pointed right with the gun.

"Don't kill me...please don't kill me!" Joe Webster plowed through a hedgerow that sprang up immediately and completely hid the car.

"Get out!" Milo ordered.
Joe Webster opened the door and began to cry.

25

Annette sat at her desk, drumming her nails on the glass. Emily looked at her watch. It was after eleven. She told Richard she'd be late, but didn't say she thought Annette might do something dumb.

"Let me give you a ride home."

"I'm waiting right here until Milo brings my car back." Annette propped her head up with her hands.

"All night?"

"All damn year if necessary!"

"Maybe he's been in an accident. You should call the hospital."

"You think so?" Annette sat up hopeful.

"Maybe," she said. "You can call and ask."

"If you think I should."

Before Annette could open the phone book, the phone rang. She snatched it to her ear.

"I Love To Read, Annette speaking."

"Baby." Milo's voice shook. "Come pick me up."

"In what?" Annette screamed. "Where's my got-damn car?"

"In Rockdale County—"

"What the hell is it doing in Rockdale County?"

"Chill, baby, chill listen...listen."

"Don't you tell me to chill. What have you done to my car?"

"It's almost out of gas and uh...uh been in a...little accident."

"Accident!" Annette screamed. "What did you do to my car?"

"Baby...baby!"

"What did you do to my car, got-dammit?"

"I'll tell you but you need to be calm."

"Calm?" Her voice got higher. "You wreck my car and you want me to be fucking calm?"

"Baby—"

"Where are you?" She stood. "What kind of damage?"

"You don't want to know."

"What?" She shrieked. "What?"

"Baby—"

"Don't you baby me. You tell me what happened right got-damned now!"

"Joe Webster threw shit on me!"

"What?" Annette eyes got big. "Joe Webster did what?" She motioned for Emily to get her phone.

"I said he threw shit on me!"

Emily clasped her hand over her mouth to keep in the scream. She knew this act of terrorism was meant for them.

"Exactly where were you when he threw this shit?" Annette asked.

There was a long pause before Milo answered.

"In...your...car."

"In my car! Annette dropped into her chair. "Shit is in my car?"

"Don't worry. By the time you get here—"

"Get there in what?" Annette hissed.

"Get Emily to bring you."

"Where are you?" Annette asked.

"Out on Lester."

"Where the hell is Lester?"

"Come to Covington and Sigman Road. Go east—"

"Wait a minute." She grabbed a pencil and tore off a memo. "Go ahead."

"Go east on Sigman and hit Lester. Pass the lake and you'll see an oak tree."

"How am I going to find an oak tree in the dark?"

"You'll see it. It's really big."

"Okay...okay what else?"

"Park by the tree and walk into the woods."

"Are you cra...zy?" she said. "Snakes live in the woods!"

"Do you want to see the goddamn car or not?"

"You listen here, mister." Annette blasted him. "You must not know who you're talking to."

"I'm sorry. Can you bring the clothes I left at your house."

"What for?"

"Shit is all over me."

"Oh okay."

"Bring some wet towels, too."

"I'm on my way." Annette hung up in a daze. "I guess Joe Webster wasn't a pussy after all."

"I guess not." Emily replied.

"Will you take me to see my car?"

"You know I will. Come on."

They got lost twice and had to start over at Covington and Sigman until they saw the oak tree. Emily got the beam from the trunk. They stumbled across a field covered with roots coiled like snakes ready to strike.

"What's that?" Annette pointed to a clump of bushes. Emily turned the light on the accordion crush of the hood. In the silence, Annette's gasp sounded like a lion's roar. They hurried forward into a stockyard stench.

"What the hell?" Annette cried.

After Emily refused to go further, Annette took the light and clamped her hand over her nose. She moved toward the car and played the beam over the shattered windshield. A large, dark stain covered both seats. Shit crusted over her name printed in gold on specially made rubber floor mats. Shit crusted the steering wheel. Annette's anger spiraled off the scale.

"Joe Webster is going to die with no balls!" She howled. "That mother fucker is going to pay for this!"

"He's already paid!" Milo said.

Both women whipped about, screaming. Annette trained the light in the direction of his voice. Milo stepped from the shadows in just briefs and looked more like a model for a beach shoot than a man not long ago with shit down his leg.

"Already paid?" Emily's voice quivered. "What do you mean already paid?" She stumbled forward and stood by Annette.

"The less you know, the better." Milo replied.

"Oh God, Milo, what have you done?" Annette cast the light on his face, making it hideous and frightening.

"Don't even ask."

"Did you kill him?" Emily whispered. "Is he dead?"

"Yes!" He laughed cruelly. "He's dead!"

Suddenly the hot night felt chilly and Emily couldn't stop shivering.

"Oh God!" She whimpered. "Oh God!"

"Not so stuck up since you're an accomplice to murder." Milo taunted her.

"I'm not an accomplice."

"You most definitely are. You're in this up to your lovely neck."

"I never wanted him dead," Emily said.

"I never called the police on Joe Webster," Milo said. "You all did."

"Oh Jesus! Jesus!" Annette grabbed Emily's hand.

"Don't you two go hysterical on me. Where're my clothes?"

"In the car," Annette said. "Milo, is he really dead?"

"Do you want to see the body?"

"No-o-o!" They cried together.

"Come on, Annette." Emily pulled her toward the Mercedes.

"Annette." Milo held his black shirt. "Don't you want a new car?"

Annette's interest jumped from Joe Webster to her car.

"Yes! What are you going to do?"

"Torch it," he said. "You can report it stolen."

"That's filing a false report," Emily said.

"What difference will a little arson make? You're involved in murder."

"Oh God!" Emily moaned.

"Jesus," Annette said. "Help us, Jesus."

"Do you want a new car or not?" Milo asked.

Annette didn't take a second to think about it. "Yes, got-dammit! I want a brand new car!"

The Mercedes pulled away minutes before the flaming shirt reached into the Volvo's gas tank. A fireball soared ten feet in the air then fell back and completely engulfed the car.

Friday May, 22, 1981

"Joe Webster's not dead!" Emily shrieked.

"What?" Annette turned lethargically and gave her a blank look.

"Joe Webster's not dead!" She shouted. "He's not dead!"

Annette jumped up and ran to the newspaper spread open on Emily's desk.

"Read this! Read this!" Emily stabbed a finger at the article on page three.

Annette snatched up the paper and consumed the words.

COMATOSE MAN IDENTIFIED
A man found unconscious Tuesday,
May 19, in Rockdale County has
been identified as Joe Webster.
Webster remains in Intensive Care
fighting a massive infection. Webster's wife reported him missing…

"Thank God!" Annette hollered. "Thank you, Father! Thank you Je...sus!"
Emily flung the paper in the air. She grabbed Annette and twirled her around
the room with a gaiety she never thought she would feel again.
Milo had so convinced them Joe Webster was dead, that each time the door
chimes clanged, they looked at each other with frightened eyes, expecting to
be arrested at any moment. Neither of them could eat or sleep, thinking of Joe
Webster's body lying somewhere in Rockdale County rained on and eaten by
wild animals.
"Milo had us believing that bullshit!" Annette fumed. "I'm calling his ass
right now." She jerked up the telephone and jabbed the buttons.
"Hello," Milo said.
"You asshole—"
"I can't answer the phone now, leave a message at the sound of the beep, I'll
get back to you."
Beep.
"Milo, you lying sack of shit, if I were looking at you now, I'd spit in your
eye! You knew Joe Webster wasn't dead when you told us that bull shit!" She
paused to catch her breath. "If I see your sorry ass again, it'll be too got-damn
soon!" She slammed down the phone.
"Looks like that romance is over," Emily said.
"It sure as hell is."
"We should do something for him," Emily said.
"Who?"
"Joe Webster. I was thinking about sending him flowers."
"Send, Joe Webster, flowers?" Annette snapped. "After what he did to my car.
I'm not sending him, shit!"
"You're getting another car. You should be glad he's alive."
"I am glad. I'm just not glad enough to send his ass flowers."
"Well, I'm calling to find out what hospital he's in." She picked up the phone.
"Don't call from here!" Annette hung it up.
"Why not?"

"Don't you know the police wait for remorseful criminals to call in to find out how their victims are doing so they can trace the call and arrest them?"

"That's only in the movies."

"No, it's not. I saw it on TV"

"I only want to know how he's doing."

"Well, I don't."

Emily located Joe Webster at South DeKalb Hospital and anonymously sent him a box of chocolates and a dozen "get well soon" balloons.

26

S ean stayed worried about the lies Lisa had written in that letter.
I'm not a rapist. She asked me to fuck her. I did what she asked me to do.
He flopped on his bed and used the remote to click on the TV.
"Get your new Buick at—"
"Rape is not about—"
"Visit Zoo Atlanta and—"
He flipped back.
"Rape is about anger, control and humiliation."
He flipped forward again.
"Zoo hours are from—"
He flipped back and watched the program on rape greatly disturbed.
I didn't rape, Lisa.
The more he tried to deny he had raped the more convinced he became he had.
I abducted her. I tore off her clothes. I hit her. I threatened her with a rock.
Jesus, I threatened to kill her. She begged me to stop. Oh God! I did rape her!

With that admission, Sean took full blame for his misfortunes stemming from that day in the woods and picked up the phone.

"Hello." Lisa answered. "Hello, hello." She hung up.

Sean called back.

"Hello," she said. "Who is this?" She hung up.

He called back.

"Whoever you are," she said. "Stop playing on my phone."

"Lisa," Sean said softly. "I...I—"

"Fuck you!" She hissed and slammed the phone down.

He called right back.

"Please—"

"Fuck you!" She snatched the cord from the wall so hard, it broke in the jack.

At school, Sean tried to get close enough to apologize. Most times, Lisa spotted first him and hurried in the opposite way.

"Lisa." He cornered her outside the gym. "I'm so sorry about what I did."

"Fuck you!" she said and walked away.

Each time he confronted her, she said "fuck you" and walked away.

Sean followed Lisa and her entourage down the hall to fourth period class. Hoping she wouldn't curse him in front of her friends, he pushed through the crowd and whispered in her ear.

"I'm so sorry. Please forgive me."

Lisa's cold stare chilled him through and through, but when she pressed a note in his hand, his heart cartwheeled with happiness. Before he could speak, she turned sharply and went to her class. With trembling fingers, Sean unfolded the hot pink page and read printed in two-inch high letters 'FUCK YOU'. Crushed, he put it in his pocket and plodded to his class, late again.

Thursday, June 11, 1981

The storm whipped the city with howling winds and slanted rain, streak lightning and bowling-strike thunder. The fainthearted remained indoors but not Sean or Lisa. He followed her cab to the beauty shop and waited four hours for her to come out.

Lisa waited for her cab under the pink striped awning with two elderly ladies. Sean ran up and joined them.

"Good morning," he said.

"'Morning," the women spoke.

"Hey, Lisa" he said. "You look so beautiful."

Lisa stepped into the pouring rain and hurried away.

"Wait a minute." He ran after her. "Let me give you a ride."

"Why?" She whirled about with teeth bared. "So you can rape me again?"

"No...no...I'd give anything to take that day back...Anything!"

"Fuck you! Fuck you! Fuck you!"

"What I did to you was the biggest mistake of my life. Please forgive me."

"I hate you!" Tears ran down her face. "I hate you! I hate you!"

It broke his heart to know he caused her tears and reached out to comfort her. She stepped back.

"Don't you ever touch me again, Sean Favor! Don't ever touch me again!"

His hand froze in mid-air and he stood there and watched her walk away.

"Mommy...Mommy!" Lisa cried. "Mommy, where are you?"

"In here," Emily said. "In the laundry room."

Lisa went in with hair plastered to her head.

"What happened to you?" Emily towel dried her hair. "Did you go to the beauty shop?"

"Mommy!" Her voice quivered. "Mommy!"

She stopped rubbing Lisa's hair. "What? What is it?"

"I'm...I'm...I'm...I'm pregnant."

"You're what?" Emily held Lisa at arms length, shaking her.

"I'm pregnant!" She sobbed. "Pregnant!"

"How do you know?"

"My...my...period still hasn't come."

"You know your periods are erratic."

"I've been throwing up...every morning!"

"When was your last period?"

"In...in...February!"

"February?"

"Uh huh." Lisa snuffed snot up her nose.

"When in February?"

"The...twenty-third."

"How do you know it was the twenty-third?"

"I marked it on the calendar!" She was glad to see it after sex with Sebastian.

"Why did you wait so long to tell me?" Emily slumped against the counter.

"I kept hoping it would come!" Lisa wailed. "I was afraid you'd be angry with me." She fell into her mother's arms. "And you...are!"

"I'm angry because you didn't tell me." She scolded. "Don't cry, don't cry."

This is what Lisa was trying to tell me.

"What are...you going...to do, Mommy?"

"First we need to tell your father."

"No, Mommy...no please…don't tell Daddy."

"He'll have to know."

"Please don't tell him, please don't tell him." She clung to Emily. "Can I have an abortion without Daddy knowing?"

"No, you cannot."

"He'll hate me!" Lisa sobbed. "He'll hate me!

"He won't be pleased, but he won't hate you," she said. "Is it Sean's?"

"I...I..." Lisa's eyes darted away.

"Don't tell me you don't know." Emily shook her again.

"I know! It's Sean's...it's Sean's!"

"When were you last with him?"

"The...the Saturday you...were in...Lacewell."

"I knew something was going on." She turned the calendar back to March and counted the weeks. "You should have come to me sooner."

"I'm sorry! I was afraid!"

"Have you been with anyone else?" Emily snatched tissues from a box and handed them to her.

"No, Mommy, no!" Lisa blew her nose.

"This is no time to lie to me." Emily looked Lisa in the eyes.

"I'm not lying!" A light flashed in her head and suddenly she had the perfect revenge. "It's…it's Sean's!"

"Have you told anyone else about this? Twyla maybe?"

"No, Mommy, nobody."

"What about, Kenya?"

"No-o-o." Kenya would never hear any more of her secrets.

"Good. Maybe we can keep it quiet."

"Don't you think Sean should know?"

"If you have an abortion, why should he know?"

"It's his baby...I...I think he should know."

"You do want an abortion don't you?"

Lisa said nothing.

"Do you want an abortion?" Emily asked again.

"Yes," Lisa said finally. "I want an abortion."

"I'm glad that's settled." Emily's face was grim.

"Sean…" Lisa began.

"Sean what?" Emily asked.

Sean raped me sat on the tip of her tongue ready to dive from her mouth until Corvetta's sad face floated before her eyes.

"Nothing."

"How am I going to tell your Daddy this?"

"I'm sorry, Mommy, I'm sorry!"

"Shhh, shhh don't cry." Emily hugged her tight. "Everything will be fine. Everything will be just fine."

Emily waited for bedtime to mention Lisa's predicament. She still did not quite know how to tell Richard his fifteen-year-old daughter was pregnant.

"Richy?" She fidgeted on the edge of the bed.

"Huh?" He turned the page of his book.

"Lisa's pregnant."

"What?" He slammed the book shut. "How could you let this happen?"

"Me?" She looked hurt. "I didn't let it happen."

"You were suppose to be watching her!" He yelled.

"Well it happened on your watch!" She yelled back.

"What are you talking about?"

"The day you let her go shopping was when it happened."

"Oh my Lord. Isn't she on birth control pills?"

"She stopped taking them."

"You said you put them in her mouth."

"I did. She spit them out."

"What? Why?"

"She said she wasn't having sex, so she didn't need the pills."

"What the hell is that suppose to mean?"

Emily shrugged her shoulders. "She said something about a promise."

"A promise?" He hollered. "A promise to whom?"

"I don't know." She shook her head.

"You should have watched her swallow the damn pills!"

"You shouldn't have let her go to the damn mall!"

"I'm sorry…I'm sorry," he said. "It's too late to blame each other."

"I'm sorry, too."

"Who's responsible for this?"

Fury blazed in his eyes. Emily feared he would do something foolish.

"Calm down, sweetie." She hugged him. "Calm down."

"I am calm!" He shouted. "I asked you who's responsible!"

"She says it's Sean's."

"I'm going to kill the punk!"

"Honey...please keep your head...please!"

"How old is he?"

"Seventeen, I think."

"First I'm going to have him charged with statutory rape."

"Okay...okay." She'd agree to anything as long as it was rational.

"Then I'm going to kill him!"

"Sweetie...just be calm."

"Has she been examined by a doctor?"

"Not yet."

"How far is she?"

"About eleven weeks."

"Does she want this baby? Does she want an abortion? What?"

"She says she wants an abortion, but I'm not so sure."

"She has to have the abortion." He shook his head.

"Why?"

"If Lisa has this baby, then Nicole will want one."

"No, she won't."

"You know Nicole always wants what Lisa has. Then Michelle will want one, and soon we'll have a house full of little bastards!"

"No, we won't," she said. "No we won't."

"How long have you known about this?"

"Lisa only told me today. She begged me not to tell you."

"Why?"

"She thought you'd hate her."

"Hate her, oh my Lord!"

"I told her you wouldn't. She's been crying her eyes out since she told me."

"Is that why she didn't come to dinner?"

"Yes. She's too ashamed to face you."

"She must be scared to death." Richard got out of bed and took Emily's hand. "Come with me."

They went into Lisa's room. She snuffled, crying in her sleep.

"My poor baby." He leaned to kiss her face. "Daddy's poor little girl."

He picked the cover from the floor, spread it over her and returned to bed.

"Lisa wants Sean to know about the baby," Emily said.

"For Christ's sake! Why?"

"I don't know. She wants to meet with his parents to discuss her situation."

"If she wants an abortion, what's to discuss?"

"I asked her that. She seems set on talking with them."

"I don't want her saying one word to the Favors," Richard said. "First thing in the morning, have her give you a urine sample."

"What are you going to do?"

"I'll drop it by the lab and get Groton to test it."

"Can he be discreet?"

"Yes, he can."

"Richy?" Emily touched his arm.

"Huh?"

"What if Lisa changes her mind and wants to have this baby?"

"We'll talk her out of it that's what."

"What if we can't?"

"Then we'll make the best of it." He mused aloud. "It might not be so bad being grandparents."

"Speak for yourself!" She snapped. "I'm too young to be a grandmother."

"Momma and Daddy will be devastated if they knew they were losing their first great-grandchild."

"I know," she said. "And that's exactly why we're not going to tell them."

"My lips are sealed," he said glumly.

"If she has to have an abortion, who would you ask?"

"Bart Lansing."

"I thought he moved away."

"He did," Richard said. "He opened a clinic in Savannah, but we're jumping the gun. Let's wait until Groton does the test, okay?"

"Okay."

Friday, June 12, 1981

Richard came home and did not speak one word. His dismal face said it all.

Saturday, June 20, 1981

At six o'clock, Lisa showed up at Sean's house to discuss her problem. Blake and Margaret Hampton-Favor sat across from her on a green velvet sofa, waiting for an unsuspecting Sean to get home from his summer job.

"You're sure I can't get you something to drink?" Margaret asked. Six feet tall and stout, the Irish green lounging outfit complimented her fair skin and mane of thick red hair. Sean had her striking eyes and enchanting smile.

"No, thank you," Lisa said.

"Your valedictory speech was wonderful," Blake said. He was shorter by three inches and cinnamon colored with a head of shocking white hair.

"Thank you." Lisa glanced about the richly furnished room and stopped at the adjacent wall filled from top to bottom with black and gold framed photos of the Favor family, some taken before the Civil War.

"Have you chosen a school?" Blake Favor asked.

"Yessir, Harvard."

"Sean's going to Harvard, too." Margaret said proudly.

Lisa made no reply. They lapsed into another silence.

A few minutes later, Sean came in the front door whistling.

"Sean?" Dr. Favor said.

"Yeah, Daddy."

"Come in here, please."

Sean walked to the doorway. The tune died on his lips.

Oh shit! Did Lisa tell anyone I raped her? Maybe not, maybe not. If she had, I'd already be dead. I knew Dr. Bennett almost killed a man for touching his wife. How could I rape his daughter?

"Hey everybody." He forced his feet into the room and sat on the sofa next to his mother.

"Lisa says she's pregnant," Dr. Favor said. "And you're responsible."

"Pregnant?" Sean glanced at Lisa's scowling face then averted his eyes.

Lisa held her breath.

If he says the baby isn't his, I'll tell them he raped me. I don't care what people say. If he says the baby is his, my revenge will be sweeter than any what goes around comes around payback could ever be.

"Well?" Dr. Favor said.

"Lisa's baby is mine." Sean hoped his admission would go toward earning her forgiveness.

Lisa glowered, inwardly relieved. Margaret started to cry.

"Don't cry, Momma." Sean patted her arm. "Don't cry."

"I won't see my first grandchild." She looked at Lisa. "Will I?"

Lisa glanced at her hands to avoid the sad eyes.

"Yes you will. My mother will see her first grandchild won't she?" He looked at Lisa. She nodded her head.

"Ye-s-s-s!" Sean jumped up, cheering. "With you as his mother and me as his father, our baby will be the most beautiful baby in the world."

Having accomplished her goal, Lisa stood to leave.

"Don't go." Sean grabbed her hand.

She jerked away and started out.

"Lisa." He hurried after her. "Don't go. We need to talk."

Lisa was almost from the room before she remembered her manners and turned to Sean's parents. "Goodnight," she said.

"Goodnight," they said and followed them to the door.

"I'll walk you home," Sean said.

"I want to talk to you." Margaret glared at her son. He'd sworn to her he'd never touched this child and here he was admitting paternity.

"I'll be right back, Momma."

"Now," she said harshly. "Right now."

"I'll call you," Sean hollered to Lisa. "We need to make plans for our baby."

Twenty minutes later, Lisa came through her front door.

"Lisa Marie!" Richard roared from his den. "Get yourself in here!"

"What, Daddy?" she asked innocently from the doorway.

"Don't play the nut role with me! Get in here and close that door! I just got off the phone with Blake Favor. Why did you go there after I told you not to?"

"I...I...just thought they should know."

"You had no business—"

The ringing phone interrupted his ranting. He snatched it up.

"Hello!"

"Lansing here, returning your call."

"One moment." Richard pressed the hold button. "Go to your room, miss, but by no means think I'm finished with you."

"Yes, Daddy," Lisa said meekly and turned to go.

"Bart, old man. I have a problem."

Lisa heard her father say before she closed the door. Tears formed in her eyes. *I didn't think I could love my baby so much after the way it was conceived; but to have my total revenge on Sean, it will have to die.*

Sean called Lisa. She hung up the instant she heard his voice. Desperate, he called the other number.

"Hello," Michelle answered.

"Michelle," Sean said. "Please call Lisa to the phone."

"Okay." She raced upstairs, yelling. "Lisa...Lisa telephone."

"Is it Sean?"

"Uh huh."

"Hang up on him, Michelle."

Michelle picked up the telephone in her parent's room. "She said to hang up on you, Sean."

"No, no Michelle, please don't hang—" he said before the line went dead.

"Emily," Richard said groggily. "Emily."

"Huh?"

"Get the phone."

"Okay."

"Emily." He shook her. "Get the phone."

"Okay...okay." She mumbled and brought it to her ear. "Hello."

"Mrs. 'B'," Sean said. "Please make Lisa talk to me."

"Stop calling here!" Emily spat.

"Who is it?" Richard squinted at the clock.

"It's Sean." She held the phone to her breast. "He's really beginning to get on my nerves!"

"Give me that phone!" Richard leaned over her. "It's one fifteen in the morning, Sean. Enough is enough. Don't call here again."

"Dr. Bennett, please make Lisa talk to me."

"She doesn't want to talk to you. Don't call here again! You hear me?"

"Yessir," he said and hung up.

At seven-thirty, Sean showed up on their doorstep.

"Nicole," he said. "Call Lisa to the door, okay?"

"I can't," she said. "What did you do?"

Sean hunched his shoulders and stuck his hands in his pockets. Nicole talked to him until her mother passed by and sent him away.

Tuesday, June 23, 1981

"Is he still out there?" Emily asked.

Richard pulled the side curtain back. Sean sat on the steps holding his head.

"Yep."

"Send him away."

Richard opened the door. Sean scrambled to his feet.

"Dr. Bennett. Can you please make Lisa talk to me?"

"She doesn't want to talk to you," he said coolly. "I want you to leave."

"Please, Dr. Bennett I—"

"Leave now!" he said roughly. "And don't come back."

"Yessir." Sean went slowly down the steps to his car.

Richard watched until he drove through the gates and shut the door.

"Did you talk to Dr. Lansing?" Emily asked.

"Uh huh. Everything's set for the twenty-seventh."

"Okay." Emily sighed. "Let's go tell her."

They told Lisa the procedure was scheduled for Saturday. She began to cry and could not stop.

"Mommy, what's wrong with Lisa?" Michelle asked.

"Lisa is sick with a virus."

"I hope I don't get it," Michelle said.

"Me neither." Nicole added.

"What goes on in this house," Emily said with her sternest look. "Stays in this house, do you understand?"

"Yes, Mommy," Michelle said around her thumb.

"Yes, Mommy." Nicole watched her mother walk away and wondered what really was going on.

Friday, June 26, 1981

Richard sat in the family room reading the paper. Emily lounged across from him, reading a book.

Lisa came in and sat beside her father.

"Do you hate me, Daddy?"

"Hate you?" He put down the paper. "I could never hate you."

"But you're disappointed in me, aren't you?"

"I'm disappointed because you're too young to have a baby."

"Daddy...I'm so...sorry." Lisa fell against his chest.

"I'm sorry, too." He hugged her, grieving for the grandchild soon to be lost.

"Daddy."

"Yes, baby."

"Call me, Kiddy Widdy."

"I thought you hated for me to call you that."

"It's your special name for your special girl...am I still your special girl?"

"Oh-h-h, Kiddy Widdy, you'll always be my special girl."

"Forgive me." She sobbed. "Do you forgive me!"

"Of course I do." He looked over at Emily. Her eyes brimmed with tears.

"I'm sorry. I'm so sorry."

"Shhh, baby. It's okay. It's okay."

The doorbell echoed over the house.

"I'll get it." Emily swiped at her tears and left the room. She pulled the side curtain back. Sean stood on the steps with both hands stuffed in his pockets.

"What does it take to keep him away?" She snatched open the door shocked at his haggard face. "Didn't my husband tell you not to come back over here?"

"Mrs. 'B'," Sean said. "Please make Lisa talk to me."

"Lisa doesn't want to talk to you."

"Please...please!"

He looked so pitiful, she couldn't bring herself to turn him away.

"Come in." She moved aside to let him in.

"Thank you!" he said. "Thank you! Thank you!"

"Wait here."

"Yes ma'am." He took a seat in the chair by the door.

Lisa lay in her father's arms with eyes swollen and face puffy. Emily couldn't tell who looked worse, her or Sean.

"Lisa, honey."

"Yes, Mommy?"

"Will you talk to Sean?"

"No. Just hang up on him."

"He's not on the phone. He's in the foyer."

"You let him in our house?" Lisa jumped up, gawking at her mother.

Richard was astounded, too. He knew how Emily felt about Sean.

"Yes I did. Can you at least talk to him?"

"No, Mommy, no!"

"Why?" Richard asked.

"He..." Lisa began. "He…"

"He what, sweetie?" Emily hugged her. "He what?"

"He...he...he's the reason I'm in this condition."

"Maybe you should talk to Sean," Richard said.

"Not you, too, Daddy. Not you, too."

"Did Sean force you to have sex with him?" Richard asked.

Yes. He raped me!

The words swelled in her mouth.

"No, Daddy." She gulped and swallowed the lie.

"Well then."

"He thinks I'm having it."

"Well, tell him you're not," he said. "I'll go get him."

Richard found Sean pacing the floor.

"Hello, Dr. Bennett." He grabbed his hand, pumping it.

"Hello, Sean."

"I'm here to tell you, I stand up to my responsibilities." He showed him a pin head diamond ring. "I'm here to ask for Lisa's hand."

"Lisa...married?" Richard said. "I don't think so."

I have to admire this boy. It takes considerable balls to come to my house to ask to marry my pregnant daughter.

"Okay, okay. I'll pay support, the hospital bill. I have a job, money saved. I'll be a good father."

"What about school? Aren't you going to Harvard this fall?"

"I was. But I'm going to work and go part-time here."

"If you do that, you'll throw away the opportunity of a lifetime."

"No sir, not being with my child is the opportunity I'd be throwing away."

"I see." Richard said. "I see."

Lisa's going to have to tell him about the abortion. I'm not going to be the one to break his heart.

"Come along, son." He ushered him to the family room.

"Do you want us to stay here with you?" Emily asked.

"I'll talk to him alone." Lisa turned her back and wiped her tears.

Sean waited until Emily and Richard walked, then rushed forward.

"Lisa," he said. "We need to make plans for our baby."

"Don't come any closer." She stopped him four feet away. "Don't touch me."

"I won't hurt you." He stopped with his hands palms up. "Don't be afraid."

"Why not? I trusted you and look what you did." She felt her flat stomach.

"I'm so sorry." He glanced at the door and lowered his voice. "Why didn't you tell them?"

"That you raped me?"

"Yes," he said softly.

"Say it!" She hissed. "Say I raped you!"

"I...I raped you." He avoided her fiery eyes. "Why didn't you tell anyone?"

"Because I didn't want to be ridiculed like, Corvetta."

"Oh-h." He moaned. "I'm so sorry, forgive me, forgive me!"

"I'll never have any forgiveness for you."

"I never knew I hurt you so much until I saw a program on rape."

"You had to see a program before you realized you hurt me?"

"I knew I'd hurt you. I wanted you so bad. I was crazy jealous. I love you!"

"Love!" She spat. "Is that what you do when you love someone? What you did to me?"

"No, it's not. I'm sorry!" He showed her the ring. "We can get married."

"Me, marry you?" She sneered. "I wouldn't marry you if you were the only person in the whole universe."

"Okay, okay. We don't have to be married to have our baby."

"I'm not having your baby. I'm killing your baby."

He stared at her dumbfounded. "You're killing my baby?"

"You hurt me. I hurt you back."

"You'd…you'd kill an innocent baby to hurt me?"

"Yes!" Lisa said spitefully. "Yes, I would!"

"I have rights!" He was angry now. "I'll get a court order and make you have my baby."

"You can't make me have anything." Lisa seethed.

"Oh yes I can! I know my rights!"

"If you're not out of my sight in one minute." She wet her index finger in her mouth and crossed her heart. "I swear! I'll tell my Daddy you tore off my clothes and raped me. He'll kill you. You know he will!" She went to the door and jerked it open. Sean left without another word.

                                        Saturday, June 27, 1981

Emily and Lisa arrived in Savannah at the Lansing Clinic before seven a.m.

"This is nice." Emily walked around the suite furnished in Danish modern.

"It looks like the hotel we stayed at in San Francisco," Lisa said.

"It does, doesn't it?"

"Mommy?"

"Yes, sweetie."

"Can they tell if my baby is a boy or a girl?"

"I think so," Emily said.

"I want to know."

I hope it's a boy so I can laugh when I tell Sean I killed his son.

Lisa came to. The baby's sex was the first thing she asked about.

"It was a boy." Emily said.

"Sean's first extension was a boy," Lisa said groggily.

"What's that?"

"Sean says when your blood flows from generation to generation, it makes you immortal."

"What a lovely thought."

"I have no extension. I won't be immortal."

"You'll have your extension one day when you're older and really ready."

"You think so?"

"I know so."

"Mommy…my heart hurts so bad." Tears flowed down her face.

"I know. Each day it'll hurt less and less and one day it won't hurt anymore, but this baby will always have a special place in your heart."

"I'll be glad when that day comes." She turned into the pillow to muffle her broken sobs.

"Shhh, shhhh." Emily climbed in bed, rocking her until she slept.

Back at home, Lisa walked the house, weeping like a mournful ghost. She thought she would rejoice in telling Sean his dead child was a boy, but the mere thought of her baby gone forever brought such grief, she found that information to painful to bestow.

27

Nicole came in the kitchen.

"Morning Daddy," she said and kissed him on the jaw.

"Good morning, Kitten." He looked up from the newspaper. "Where's your mother?"

"Trying to make Lisa stop crying. What's wrong with her?"

"She's depressed."

"I thought only old people got depressed." She shook cereal into two bowls and poured milk in one.

"Young people get depressed, too. How's summer camp?"

"Real good." She got her books and showed him a printed certificate. "I got one hundred on this test."

"Excellent!" He patted her head. "You're my little Math expert."

Nicole's grin went across her face.

"Morning, Daddy." Michelle came in and kissed him, too.

"Good morning, Pumpkin."

Michelle poured milk in the bowl Nicole fixed and began to eat.

"How come you're still here?" Michelle asked her father.

"No appointments until this afternoon."

"You can take us to camp."

"Nope," he said. "I'm just going to read my paper and relax."

"I got chosen to dance in *The Red Shoes*."

He pinched Michelle's cheek. "I'm so proud of my little ballerina."

"One day I'm going to have my own dance company, in New York."

"I know," Richard said. "You're so smart and talented."

"Hurry up, if you're going." Nicole headed for the door.

"Nicole." Richard looked at her then her used dish. "Your mother shouldn't have to empty your bowl."

"Sorry." Nicole poured the soggy circles in the disposal, and put the rinsed bowl in the dishwasher. "Hurry up, Michelle, or you're going to get left." Michelle shoveled cereal in her mouth.

"Slow down, slow down!" Richard admonished and wiped her face.

"The bus will leave me."

"No, it won't."

Michelle drank the milk from the bowl and tossed it in the dishwasher.

"Bye." She grabbed her ballet gear and ran out the door.

"Bye, Daddy." Nicole followed.

"Bye."

"I almost forgot." Nicole hurried back and dropped a paper ball by his plate. "Give Mommy this."

"What is it?" He wiped his hands on a napkin and picked it up.

"A message for Mommy."

"Nicole." Michelle yelled. "The bus is coming."

"Got to go." Nicole kissed him quick and ran out.

Richard flattened the deep creases and read the note.

Call Mrs. Shelton about Leora DuPree. 912-555-3188. Urgent.

He got up for a second cup of coffee, just as Emily walked in.

"Want some?" He held up the pot.

"Uh huh," she said and slumped in a chair. "I don't know what we're going to do with Lisa."

"What?" He set a steaming mug in front of her.

"All she does is cry." She stirred in two sugars and a dollop of cream.

"Don't the sedatives help?"

"A little, but after they wear off, she's crying again."

"I think she should see Rachel," he said.

"I do, too. But will she?"

"I don't know." He touched her forehead. "You feel okay?"

"Uh huh, why?"

"Your face is puffy." He chuckled. "Like when you're pregnant."

"I know that's not the case. I just had a period."

"You were having your period with, Lisa, remember?"

"Yeah, I remember." Emily sipped the coffee. "But I'm not pregnant."

"I thought you took care of this." He handed her the message.

She read it and nearly strangled. Richard slapped her back until she stopped coughing.

"Are you okay?"

"Uh huh." She moved to the sink so he couldn't see her trembling hands.

"I thought you called Mrs. Shelton."

"I kept meaning to call."

"You never called?"

"No," she said lightly. "It's just a mistake."

"Aren't you curious about how our name, address and phone number came to be associated with this other Leora DuPree?"

"It's probably a computer error. I'll take care of it."

"Okay."

He got up and pulled her close. Her arms encircled his neck. He lifted her up and staggered over the floor.

"O-o-oh." He groaned. "You're gaining weight."

"I am not!" She squirmed away and slapped at his hands.

"Oh, yes you are. I'd say ten to twelve pounds."

"Ten to twelve pounds?" She touched her hips. "For real?"

"For real."

I know it's true. I can hardly fit in my clothes.

"I need to step up my exercise program."

"Weight gain, weight gain." He teased.

"That's mean." She pouted. "And unfriendly."

"Whatever you weigh." He hugged her. "You're perfect to me."

"Thank you, darling." Emily fluffed the handkerchief in his jacket pocket and kissed him good-bye.

Richard drove away worried.

Each time I mention, Leora DuPree, Emily panics. Something is going on concerning this woman and it looks like it's up to me to find out what.

He parked by the gates and picked up the car phone.

"Good morning, Dr. Bennett's office."

"Pamela, it's me."

"Yes, Doctor."

"Cancel my appointments and get directions to the Blue Pine Nursing Home."

"Just a minute."

Richard heard the computer working to retrieve the data and took out his pen.

"Here we go." Pamela gave him the information.

"Thank you," he said.

"You're welcome."

"Oh," he said. "Who owns Blue Pine?"

"Dr. Loren Dobey."

"Thanks. See you tomorrow. Bye."

"Okay. Good-bye."

He hoped this trip to Allison would be something easily explained, but he couldn't shake the feeling there was going to be a big fight when he got home.

Richard maneuvered the car through a lot strewn with broken glass and parked beside a black and chrome Harley. He paused a second to admire the motorcycle then passed a rusty metal sign, sagging on bowed legs. A brown brick sidewalk sloped through a dirt yard and ended at three chipped steps.

He tested the rotted porch. The grimy front door he went through, missed a pane, like a lost tooth.

To his right, nineteen or twenty elderly people sat on gray vinyl furniture in clothes several sizes too large.

"Good morning," he said. "How're you all doing?"

No one spoke or looked his way. They either examined their hands or stared into space. Richard couldn't believe it could be so quiet with so many people in a room. Where were the attendants? Down the hall, he saw a person who looked to be Lisa's age bent intently over a desk.

Thank God somebody's on the job.

He followed threadbare carpeting and saw where her attention lay, on her nails, polishing them. Her sparkling white nurse's uniform rode high on crossed nutmeg legs. Richard forced his eyes from them and the cleavage threatening to pop her buttons.

"I'm here to see—"

"One second." She swiped a line of violet down her index finger.

"Is this a nursing home or a beauty shop?"

Her head snapped up. She looked Richard up and down sorry she hadn't paid attention to him sooner. She screwed on the top and smiled.

"Can I help you?"

"I'm here to see, Mrs. Shelton." He read her nametag. "Shahkneequinetta."

"You can say my name?" She smiled bigger. "Can't hardly nobody say it right the first time."

"Is that so?"

"Uh huh."

"I'm here to see, Mrs. Shelton."

"Can't"

"Why?"

"She got fired."

Have I come all this way for nothing?

"Fired when?"

"Last month."

"Who's taking her place?"

"Nobody."

"Then I'd like to see Leora DuPree."

She swiveled in her chair and flipped through a box of cards.

"Here we go." She pulled it out and smeared her polish. "Dammit!" She wilted under Richard's steady gaze and apologized.

"How long has Leora DuPree been here?"

"Almost five months."

"Which way is her room?"

"I can show you the way." She stood, smoothing her uniform over wide hips.

"I think I can find it."

"The doors don't have numbers." She dropped to the chair, pouting like one of his girls.

"On second thought, I'd be happy to have you show me the way." Shahkneequinetta came around the desk with such an exaggerated strut, he battled to keep from laughing.

"Does she have visitors?" he asked.

"Who?"

"Leora DuPree."

"Not while I'm on duty."

They went left into the faint stench of shit.

"Whew!" She wrinkled her nose.

"Who takes care of all those people I saw in the front room?"

"Stella and Francine."

"Where are they now?"

"Somewhere around."

The smell grew stronger the further they went.

"Whew," she said again.

"Who are Leora DuPree's people, her next of kin?"

"Don't know." Shahkneequinetta stopped in front of a door with peeling blue paint. "Here we are."

Richard knocked.

"Help me! Help me! Help me!" Came feebly from inside.

He opened the door. The combined odors of urine, shit and rotted flesh slapped him in the face. Shahkneequinetta clamped her hand over her nose and fled. He stepped in on a cracked tile floor littered with soiled gauze pads and discarded wrappers. An emaciated White woman lay in a filthy bed with her wrists tied to the railing. A soiled gown covered everything except the enormous bed sore on her bony hip. As bad as she looked, there was no mistaking the resemblance. Her eyes and Lisa's were the same pretty green. This woman had to be Emily's mother.

"Help me!" she called weakly and struggled to sit up.

"What are you doing here?"

Richard whirled around. A woman taller than he, in a uniform dirtier than the room stared at him with intense black eyes.

"I'm visiting, Leora DuPree."

"She can't have visitors. She ain't been prepared!"

"Look at her! A decubitus ulcer covered in feces, inhumane restraints." He encompassed her with a sweep of his hand. "I'd say she hasn't been prepared!"

"You a doctor?" Fear showed in her eyes.

"Yes, goddammit. I'm Doctor Bennett." He flashed his I.D. She didn't have to know he was an ophthalmologist.

"Help me! Help me! Help me!" Leora cried like a hurt child.

"Take her out of those restraints." He ordered.

"She'll escape again. She got way to the highway the last time she took off."

"She's drugged out of her mind. She can't run anywhere. Take them off!"

She pulled on gloves and untied the bloody rags.

"When she falls and breaks her as…breaks her neck. Don't blame me."

"Where's Dr. Dobey?" he said. "I want to speak to him."

"He just took off on his motorcycle."

"It hurts." Leora whimpered and rubbed her wrists. "It hurts."

"Do something about her wrists." Richard commanded.

He watched her clean the raw wounds and wrap them in gauze. When she filled a basin and began to bathe the woman, he stepped in the hallway.

"You can come in now," the nurse said thirty minutes later. She walked in a small circle on a floor free of debris, spraying air freshener. The smell was less noticeable, dissipated by a hot breeze blowing past tattered blue curtains.

Leora DuPree lay in a clean gown in a clean bed.

"Do you know, Emily Bennett?" he asked. "Emily Douglas?"

"Emily, Emily." A smile lit her gaunt face. "Emily's, my sweet baby."

"Did, Emily, put you here?"

"Emily's, my sweet baby."

"Has Emily been to see you?"

"Emily's, my sweet baby." Was her answer to everything.

"Get some rest, dear." He patted her bony shoulder.

She obeyed and closed her eyes. Seconds later, she was snoring.

Richard stepped in the hall. Shouts reached all the way from the front desk.

"You had no business letting him see her!" The nurse screamed.

"I do my job!" Shahkneequinetta yelled back. "It's not my fault you don't help these old people!"

"Ain't nobody gonna have a job to do if—"

Richard walked past and she fell silent.

"Mister." Shahkneequinetta caught him before he pulled off. "I could be in big trouble for this." She handed him a memo. "This is Leora's next of kin."

"Thank you, Shahkneequinetta, thank you very much."

"You're welcome." She smiled and ran inside.

Richard read the note. Emergency contact: Emily Douglas Bennett, daughter. A hundred questions fought for answers. One headed the list.

Why did Emily lie to me and say her mother was dead?

"Health Department, how may I direct your call?"

"Dr. Eastman, please," Richard said.

"One moment, please."

"Dr. Eastman's office."

"Richard Bennett, Janet, is he in?"

"Yes, Doctor, one moment, please."

"What's up, Rich?" Daniel Eastman said.

"You're not going to believe what I saw at the Blue Pine Nursing Home."

"It can't be the Blue Pine Nursing Home. We closed them down."

"Well, they're open again. The people look underfed. This poor woman was tied to the bed like an animal. Only God knows what else is going on."

"I can't believe Dobey would be this stupid."

"Apparently, he is."

"I'm sending the troops to close Blue Pine down once and for all."

"I'm counting on you, man." Richard said. "You'll have them out today?"

"My word's on it," Danny said. "Why don't you swing by here? I missed seeing you when I was up your way."

"No can do. I have pressing business at home."

"I'll be in Atlanta next week. I'll drop by your office."

"Great," he said. "What's going to happen to the workers at Blue Pine?"

"Those on the premises will be taken into custody. Why?"

"Just wondering," Richard said. "So long."

"So long."

Richard hung up and dialed the nursing home.

"Blue Pines," Shahkneequinetta said. "Can I help you?"

"They're raiding the nursing home, today. Leave right now."

28

"I wonder why Daddy parked his car by the front door," Michelle said. "He always puts it in the garage."

"Mommy, we're home." Nicole sniffed. "Something smells good."

"Smells like chicken pot pie." Michelle smacked her lips. "I can't wait."

"Me neither," Nicole said. "Wonder where Mommy is?"

"Upstairs probably." Michelle hurried through the door. "Race you."

They ran up the steps into the angry words crashing through the bedroom door.

"I wouldn't let a dog live in that fucking place!" Richard yelled.

"You can't judge me." Emily's voice trembled. "Pauline was your mother. Leora was mine!"

"Don't even try to justify leaving your mother in that hell hole."

"I'm not trying to justify it. I'm trying to make you understand."

"All I understand is you lied to me all these years."

"Sweetie, I'm sorry."

"Don't touch me."

"Okay, okay."

"How could you say your mother was dead?"

"As far as I'm concerned, she is."

"You can't just label somebody dead and forget them."

"With Leora it was easy."

"You sat at the table that day at the club." His voice broke with anguish. "You looked me in the eye and lied. In front of my brother, you lied!"

Emily groped for words to change how he looked at her.

"You lied about, Dr. Chambers!" She hit back.

"I didn't lie. We promised we'd never lie to each other, remember?"

"Stop trying to make me the villain."

"You are the goddamn villain!"

"Don't you dare curse me! Curse Leora! She's the villain!"

"That's right." He jeered. "Blame that poor old woman tied to the bed."

"She wasn't always a poor old woman and she wasn't always tied to the bed. When she was free, I was the one tied to the bed."

"They're going to get a divorce." Nicole whimpered.

"They can't divorce!" Michelle wailed. "We'd be orphans."

"Not orphans, silly, wards of the court."

"I don't want to belong to the court," Michelle said. "I want to belong to Mommy and Daddy. She hammered on the door.

The shouting stopped suddenly. Richard jerked open the door.

"Are you and Mommy getting a divorce?" Michelle asked.

"Pumpkin." He pulled her into a hug. "Of course we're not getting a divorce."

"What's all the arguing about then?"

"We're not arguing," he said. "We're discussing."

"We know arguing when we hear it," Nicole said. "Don't we, Michelle?"

"Uh huh," she said around her thumb. "Please don't get a divorce."

"No divorce!" Emily hugged the girls and glared at Richard for support.

"Mommy's right, absolutely no divorce."

He hugged them, but not Emily. Michelle noticed.

"Daddy's not hugging you, Mommy?"

"I'm hugging, Mommy, too." Richard's arm covered her shoulder briefly and dropped away.

"Who is Leora?" Nicole said.

"Yeah," Michelle said. "Is Leora really our grandmother?"

"Yes," Emily said flatly.

"How come you never told us about her?" Nicole asked.

"Where has our new grandmother been?" Michelle said.

"Thumb out, Michelle," Emily said. "You'll ruin your teeth."

"Yeah." Nicole brought the subject back to Leora. "Where has she been and how come you never told us about her?"

"It's a long story," Emily said.

"Tell us," Nicole said. "We want to know."

"We need to discuss this in a family meeting," Michelle said. "Don't we?"

"Yeah," Nicole said. "We want to know what's going on."

"Tomorrow, after dinner," Emily said.

I wish I could disappear until this madness ends.

"You promise?" Michelle asked.

"Cross my heart and hope to die," Emily said.

"Finish it Mommy," Michelle insisted. "Finish the rest."

"That's enough." She couldn't bring herself to say 'if I should ever tell a lie' in front of Richard. She had already broken his heart and prayed there was enough love left to mend it.

"What's that smell?" Nicole wrinkled her nose.

"My casserole!" Emily shrieked, glad for the first time in her life to have her dinner burn so she could escape Richard's angry eyes.

Saturday, July 25, 1981

After two weeks passed with no reporters storming her door, Emily began to feel hopeful that Mrs. Shelton wouldn't mention her name. She couldn't stand the thought of strangers pointing fingers, whispering when she walked by. 'That's the woman who left her mother tied to a bed to rot at the Blue Pine Nursing Home' They wouldn't understand. How could she expect others to understand when her own husband didn't.

Usually when he was angry with Emily, Richard turned cold and silent. Now he never missed a chance to throw Leora in her face.

"I guess you've seen this." He read the headline. "Blue Pine Doctor Arrested In Nursing Home Abuse." He dropped the paper on the kitchen table in front of Emily. Rather than look at it, she gazed out the window.

"What are you going to do?" Richard asked.

"About what?" She sipped her coffee

"About your mother, Emi-lee-e," he said harshly. "What are you going to do about your mother?"

"I'm not going to do anything about her."

"I don't believe you said that."

"Believe it!" She got up abruptly, sloshing coffee into the saucer. "I told you I'm not helping her and I meant it." She yanked her shoulder bag from the knob and slammed the door on the way to the garage.

"Emily!" Richard hollered down the steps. "You can't run away from this!"

Emily pulled onto Panola Road with her head full of frightening thoughts. Frightening divorce thoughts.

Will my lie about Leora really destroy my marriage?

Richard hadn't touched her since he'd found out about Leora. She'd tried everything to bring him around. She'd cooked his favorite foods. She'd bought the band saw he wanted. She'd told him her sorrow was bigger than Atlanta, all to no avail. He still looked at her like a wounded puppy.

Maple Honey said this would happen. I could have at least seen to it that Leora wasn't being abused.

"Dammit!" She struck the wheel at her stupidity and picked up the telephone.

"Hello," Pauline answered.

"I need to talk to you face to face."

"Come on, baby. I'll be waiting."

"See you soon."

Emily pulled in Pauline's backyard and climbed the steps with the look of doom.

"What's wrong?" Pauline hugged her and rubbed her cold hands.

"Richard's going to leave me."

"What? What happened?"

"It's something I said, something I didn't say."

"Come in. Maybe we can figure something out." She led her to the kitchen.

"Hello Ezell," Emily said.

"Morning." He raised his face for her kiss. "How you doing?"

"Fine," she said out of habit. She was far from fine.

"Coffee?" Pauline lifted a blue speckled pot.

Emily shook her head. She hooked her bag over the chair and dropped in it. Ezell rolled away from the table. "I'll just go watch my cartoons and leave you two to talk."

Emily laughed. Ezell loved his Saturday morning cartoons.

"Want something to eat?" Pauline asked.

"No thanks. I ate already."

Pauline filled her coffee cup and sat next to Emily.

"Now tell me what's wrong."

"I'm so ashamed," Emily said but did not stop until she had told Pauline everything from her abusive childhood up until Richard found Leora tied to the bed at the nursing home.

"Great stars of Mercy," Pauline said.

"What am I going to do?"

"You know Sonny despises a liar."

"I know," she said. "What can I do?"

"Give him time. He'll come around."

"He's never stayed angry at me this long before."

"It's a heavy blow. It's going to take longer than normal."

"We're always arguing. The girls think we might get a divorce."

"Divorce?" Pauline laughed. "Believe me on this. Sonny loves you more than I love Ezell...and you know I love myself some Ezell."

"You think so?"

"I know so. Just give him time."

"Okay...okay," Emily said. "I'll give him time."

"Time is all it'll take."

Emily hugged her. "I've got to get back. Lisa's not feeling well."

"What's wrong with her?"

"A...a...cold." She stammered. "Just a summer cold."

Pauline cocked her head as if processing that information.

"You're sure?"

"Uh huh."

"This will make her feel better." She took a cake saver from the top of the refrigerator and handed it to Emily. "She loves my pineapple-coconut cake."

"Thank you," Emily said. "Let me say good-bye to Ezell."

Pauline and Emily stood on the back porch.

"Take care of yourself." Emily hugged Pauline.

"I will."

"I'll call and let you know how things are."

"You sure you don't have a little loaf in the oven?" Pauline patted Emily's protruding stomach.

"Not you, too." Emily sucked in her gut. "I just need to exercise."

"Uh huh." Pauline looked slyly at Emily. "You can believe that if you want to. I'm making my grandson a christening gown."

"I hate to disappoint you, but you're wasting time and money." Emily went down the steps and buckled the cake in the passenger seat.

"We'll see," Pauline said. "We'll see."

Emily waved good bye and drove away laughing.

Two hours later, Richard showed up in Athens.

"Hey, Daddy." He sat at the kitchen table. "How're you doing?"

"Fine." Ezell lifted the coffeepot. "Want some?"

"No thanks." He got up, pacing the brown tiles.

"You look like you need something stronger than coffee."

"I'm fine." He sat at the table, again. "Where's Momma?"

"Gone shopping," Ezell said. "You don't look fine, what's wrong?"

"I'm troubled, Daddy, deeply troubled." Richard propped his elbows on the table and held up his head.

"What's got you troubled, son?"

"My marriage." He was up, pacing again.

"Is there another woman?"

"No." He laughed glumly. "There's no other woman."

"Has Emily been unfaithful?" Ezell stuffed tobacco in his pipe.

"Unfaithful?" Richard said the word as if unfaithful and Emily didn't belong in the same sentence. "Not as far as I know."

"Stop right there!" Ezell said sternly.

Richard stopped pacing to look at him. "What?"

Ezell lit the pipe and sucked the stem. A sweet pungent aroma floated over the room. Blue smoke undulated to the ceiling.

"If there's no other woman," Ezell puffed smoke with each word. "And Emily hasn't been unfaithful, everything else can be worked out."

"She lied to me, Daddy. She's lied all the years I've known her."

"What did she lie about?"

Richard told about finding Leora in the nursing home. He told how Emily refused to help her in any way. He spoke of how he feared the whole awful story might appear on TV any day.

Ezell listened without comment until he wound down.

"Has Emily lied to you about anything important before?"

"No." Richard shook his head. "Not that I know of."

"Has she explained why she lied about her mother?"

"She gave me some old song and dance about how much her mother hated her. There's no excuse for what she's done."

"You think it's not, but apparently Emily thinks it is."

"Daddy." He shook his head. "Emily has broken my heart, I wish—"

"Be careful what you wish for. You just might get it."

"What did you wish for that turned out so bad?"

"Humph." Ezell grunted. "When I was a young man, I wished I had enough money to give your mother the beautiful things she wanted…you children a good education..." He paused and rubbed his useless legs. "After those logs fell on me, I got my wish. More money than I'd ever be able to spend, but I robbed the very people I wanted the money for, my wife and children."

Richard remembered that tragic time when for nine days his father hovered near death.

"You did more things with us than most men with two good legs. Did you know, all the kids on our block wanted you for their Daddy?" He looked at his father and his chest got tight. "But you were our Daddy...*my Daddy*!"

"I didn't know that," Ezell said. "Have I told you how proud I am of you?"

"Yes sir," Richard said. "Many times, many times."

"Don't judge your wife too harshly." Ezell took a final pull on the pipe and tamped it in the ashtray. "Don't make this little mole hill into a big mountain you can't climb."

"I can't forgive her, Daddy!" He shook his head. "I can't forgive her for this!"

29

"**L**isa turned down her scholarship to Harvard."

"Why?" Annette stopped writing checks and looked at Emily.

"She won't say," Emily said. "She just says she's not going."

"What does Richard say?"

"He's furious, but she refuses to change her mind."

"What about the scholarships from Yale and MIT?"

"They already gave them to someone else."

"Is she going anywhere?"

"Uh huh, to Spelman."

"All right." Annette clapped her hands. "Our alma mater has as much to offer as Harvard."

"I know, but Richard had his heart set on a Harvard graduate."

"In her state, she doesn't need to be that far from home, anyway."

"I know. I can keep an eye on her if she goes to Spelman."

"Is she staying on campus?"

"Uh huh," Emily said. "And coming home some weekends."

"How's her depression?"

"So deep I canceled her birthday party."

"Oh no," Annette said. "And you made all those plans."

"I know," Emily said with a deep sigh. "Maybe next year."

"Did you talk to her about seeing, Dr. Chambers?"

"She says she's not crazy and she doesn't need a shrink."

"Well she's not crazy."

"I know that!" Emily snapped. "I know that!"

"Damn, you're so touchy lately."

"I'm going to the drugstore. Do you want anything?"

"Yeah," Annette said. "I need toothpaste, mouthwash, nail polish remover, soap, cotton balls—"

"You need a list." Emily laughed.

Annette tore a sheet from a note pad and started one.

"I have a coupon for a free jar of that face cream I use." She looked for it in her purse then stopped to answer the phone.

"I Love To Read, Annette speaking."

"Hello, baby," Milo Trotter said in his sexiest voice.

"What the fuck do you want?"

Emily looked at Annette and slowly shook her head.

"I just wanted to hear your lovely voice."

"For what?"

"I can't get you out of my mind."

"You're violating my Tuesday rule."

"What rule is that?" he said with a chuckle.

"I don't listen to bull shit on Tuesdays. I'm hanging up."

"Please don't." He crooned. "Please, don't hang up."

"Why shouldn't I?" She squirmed and crossed her legs.

"Because we're destined to be together...like bacon and eggs."

"Quit it." She bit her bottom lip and swiveled in her chair.

"Like peanut butter and jelly, like...like."

"Like ass and hole?" she said, grimly.

"Asshole?" he said. "Baby, I'm the man who loves you."

"Puh-leeze. Is that the best you can do?"

"I'm not ashamed to bare my heart to the woman I love."

"Please."

"That's how you used to beg me to fuck you, all soft and low."

"I did not!"

"Remember when you came to my house to cut off my dick because I'd lied about killing Joe Webster?"

"Yeah." She spun around. "What about it?"

"Remember how angry you were?"

"Yeah."

"I love to fuck you when you're angry. You're so wild and uninhibited."

"I'm not angry now."

"You're not angry, but you're hot."

"I am not!"

"Yes, you are," he said. "I can hear it in your voice."

"Hmm, hmm." She cleared her throat. "Is there a point to all this?"

"Do you remember all the erotic things I did to you?"

She paused a few seconds.

"Yeah...so?"

"Remember how you moaned?"

"I never moaned."

He laughed.

"Let me make you moan again."

"No."

"Come on, baby. Don't you want to moan for your Milo?"

"I have work to do. I can't just drop everything for you."

"Who do you have to report to? Aren't you the boss?"

"Yeah but—"

"You're on fire, aren't you?"

"No, I'm not." She uncrossed her legs.

"Yes, you are."

Annette swallowed to wet her parched mouth and whispered in the phone.

"I'm not letting you tie me up and fuck me in my ass again."

"You know you loved it."

"I mean it!"

"Whatever you say, baby, what...ever you say." He chuckled. "Are you coming so I can make you come?"

"I'm on my way. Tata."

"I'm waiting with nothing on but a smile."

Annette hung up, laughing. "Let the church say, a man."

"A man." Emily said. "Who is that?"

"An old man," Annette said. "With a new attitude."

"Who could this be? Ty Massey?"

"Nope."

"Jake Scott?"

"Cold."

"Harold DeWitt?"

"Freezing."

"I give up," Emily said. "Who is it?"

"Milo Trotter."

"I want to hear this." Her tone was sharp. "What line did he use this time?"

"Listen, I don't have to tell you shit! You're not my mother!"

"If I were your mother, I'd knock some sense into your stupid, empty head."

"Stupid? Empty head? Watch what you say, Em!"

"How can you be offended? It's obvious you're stupid and empty headed."

"Just stop talking to me!" Annette yelled.

"Who wants to talk to someone who would see Milo Trotter again?"

"You don't tell me who to fucking see!"

"Somebody needs to tell you something because you're pitiful on your own."

"I know what it is." Annette scoffed. "You want Milo yourself."

"What?" Emily stared at her. "If you believe that, then you're more stupid than I thought."

"I'm warning you!" Annette jumped up and hovered over Emily. "Call me stupid again and I'll slap the taste out of your mouth!"

Emily leaped up with fists clenched. "Goddammit! Bring your ass on!"

Annette retreated two paces. They stared at each other until Emily grabbed her bag and hurried outside. Her hands shook so hard, it took ten seconds to unlock her car. She slid under the wheel. The hot seat burned through her slacks. She started to get out, but Annette chose that moment to leave the store and head for her Volvo. Emily endured the heat and drove away heartsick. Leora hated her. Richard hated her and now that the Marshall-Trotter affair was back in session, Annette hated her.

"I'm hungry!" Michelle eyed the bucket of fried chicken. "What's taking Mommy so long?"

"Emily, we're ready to eat." Richard spoke into the intercom and got no reply. "Michelle," he said. "Go tell your mother we're ready to eat."

"I don't want to. Mommy's so mean lately."

"Nicole, you go."

"Please, Daddy. She growls at me all the time, too."

"I guess we'll just have to start without her."

Before he said grace, Emily came in and took her place at the table.

"Mommy?" Nicole said. "How come you never told us about Leora?"

"Not now, Nicole." Emily snapped. "We're eating dinner."

"When can I know? You said you'd tell us at the family meeting, but you called it off."

"I wasn't feeling well," Emily said. "Plus it's a long story."

"We want to hear." She looked at Michelle and her father. "Don't we?"

"Yes, we do," Michelle said. "Where is she now, Mommy?"

"I don't know," Emily said. "And I don't care."

"Do you know, Daddy?" Michelle asked.

"She's in the hospital," he said.

"When she gets out," Nicole asked. "Where will she go?"

"Probably to another nursing home."

"Bring her here, Daddy." Michelle's eyes sparkled with excitement. "We could take care of her, couldn't we, Nicole?"

"Uh huh. We'd get to know her and she'd get to know us."

"Girls," Richard said. "I know you're surprised to learn you have another grandmother, but having her here will require more care than we can give."

"We can do it, Daddy," Michelle said.

"She's very ill. She'll require around the clock care. We can't give her that."

"Yes we can," Michelle said.

"You two hardly want to do the little chores I give you." Emily interrupted. "What makes you think you can take care of Leora?"

"We could at least try," Nicole said. "We can't just send her to a home."

"What about Disneyworld?" Emily asked.

"Disneyworld." Michelle moaned. "I forgot about Disneyworld."

"And that's just how you'd forget about Leora."

"One minute, Mommy." Nicole pulled Michelle in a huddle. When they broke, Nicole said. "I wish to make it known, we have decided not to go to Disneyworld. We're going to stay home and help our grandmother get well."

I can't believe it! I've lost my children to Leora.

"Why would you give up your vacation to look after a mean old woman?"

"Mommy," Nicole said. "How come you feel this way?"

"You want to know why?" She declared. "Okay I'll tell you why!"

She told them everything about herself and Leora DuPree.

"Wow!" Nicole said. "She was mean to you."

"When I saw Leora," Richard said. "She said Emily was her sweet baby."

"I don't care what she said!" Emily snapped at him. "I have never, ever been Leora's sweet baby, and I will not have her in my house!"

She fixed a plate for Lisa and left the room.

"Come in." Lisa answered the knock on her door.

"Hi, sweetie," Emily said cheerfully. "How're you feeling?"

"Fine," Lisa said spiritlessly.

"I brought you some chicken."

"Just put it on the desk."

"If you don't eat, you'll lose all your curves."

"I can afford to lose a few curves." Lisa giggled.

"That's the first giggle I've heard from you in a long time."

"I haven't felt much like giggling"

"I know," Emily said. "Let's go shopping tomorrow."

"I don't know."

"You have a few more things to get for school, don't you?"

"Just notebooks and pencils."

"We can pick that up tonight. Want to go?"

"No thanks."

"You need to get out. You stay cooped up in here too much."

"I know." Lisa covered a yawn.

"Sleepy?" Emily stroked her uncombed hair.

"Uh huh."

"I'll braid your hair when you wake up, okay?"

"Okay," Lisa said.

Emily patted her arm and started out.

"Mommy?"

"Hmm?"

"If a baby is aborted, does it still go to heaven?"

"Sweetie." She returned to the bed. "All babies go to heaven."

Lisa let out a strangled moan and began to cry.

"I...I thought he went to the other place."

"Hush...hush." She pulled Lisa into her arms and held her until she slept.

Emily collapsed on her bed frightened beyond belief. Lisa was slipping away fast. They had pleaded with her to see Dr. Chambers. Her answer was always the same. She wasn't crazy and she didn't need a shrink.

Maybe Pauline can talk to her. She'd have to be told about the abortion, but if she can help, it will be worth her anger over her lost great-grandchild. Maybe Annette can talk to her. Rats! I forgot. We're not speaking, again.

Emily noticed Annette's present atop the highboy and took it down. She shook the box. It sounded like clothing. She shredded the paper and lifted the lid. A blouse the color of fresh blood leaped up in 3–D. Nausea overwhelmed her. She turned toward the bathroom. Pain exploded at her temple and she fell headlong into a charcoal gray abyss.

Emily drifted in and out of consciousness, awaking with a headache worse than the last and vision so blurred she had to constantly blink to focus.

"How do you feel?" An indistinct shape hovered over her and sounded so far away, she strained to understand. "How do you feel?"

"My head!" Her mouth felt stuffed with cotton. She tried to sit up.

"You have to lie still," the shape said.

"Be still, baby." Richard's worried voice called from a distance.

Her garbled reply sounded nothing like. "Okay."

"What's her B.P?" A female voice asked out of her vision.

"170/110."

"This is mobile unit 6545." Her voice reverberated around the ambulance. "We have a female approximately thirty years—"

"Thirty nine." Richard corrected.

"We have a thirty-nine year-old female with a deep laceration to the left temporal lobe, BP is 170/110, respiration 24 and shallow. ETA ten minutes."

"Make way, make way, coming through." The paramedics rushed down the hallway. From her back, square lights, heat vents and black holes in the ceiling tile looked to Emily like foreign terrain. They moved her from the stretcher. She screamed with pain. A nurse snatched curtains around her bed. A doctor flashed a light in her eyes. The same ominous gray cloud floated toward her from the ceiling. She opened her mouth to warn Richard and it surrounded her before she could speak.

The emergency room staff stood solemnly by and watched Dr. Bennett sink to his knees next to his wife's bed and pray for her life.

30

E mily opened her eyes and tried to sit up. Torturous pain buffeted her head and she lay back, tracing a dressing to the huge wad by her left ear. The faintest prod sent out new waves of agony and she stopped and turned slowly to her left. A blue teddy bear grinned atop a machine with one pulsing red light. Across the room, Richard huddled under a blanket, asleep. *Did I have a stroke?*

"I did not have a stroke!" she said to see if she sounded as garbled as before.

"Huh?" Richard yawned and cracked his fused vertebrae with a long stretch.

"Richy." Emily moaned. "Richy."

"Emily! Emily!" In two steps, he hovered over the bed. "I thought I'd lost you!" He sank to his knees, crushing her hand. "I thought I'd lost you! Thank you, God! Thank you! Thank you! Thank you! Thank you! Thank you!"

"Don't cry...don't cry!" Pain pounded her head as she leaned over, stroking his stubbly face.

"I thought I'd lost you!" He smothered her throbbing hand with kisses.

"I'd never go anywhere and leave you behind." She pulled her hand free and lay back. "You know that."

A nurse came in but did not interrupt the joyful reunion.

"I was so afraid!" He laid her hand against his cheek. "So afraid."

"I'm okay," she said. "What happened?"

"You don't know?"

"I remember opening Annette's present, then the room was spinning."

"I think you hit your head on the dresser. Blood was all over it, everywhere."

"No wonder my head hurts so bad," she said, covering a yawn.

"You're sure you're okay?"

"Uh huh." She touched his face. "When's the last time you shaved?"

Richard absently felt his beard. "Five days ago."

"I've been unconscious five days?"

"Uh huh."

"Doctor," the nurse said.

Richard looked back. She held up the stethoscope.

"Okay, Freda." He sat quietly until she recorded Emily's vital signs and left.

"Guess what?" He leaned over the bed, grinning.

"What?" Emily stifled a yawn.

"We're going to have a baby."

Emily remembered the blouse and knew it was true.

I haven't been nauseated by the color red since I was pregnant with Lisa.

"I know exactly when we made him," Richard said with a chuckle.

"Me, too." She laughed. "On my birthday."

"Uh huh," he said. "I always know when I make a baby."

"Sure."

"I do." He touched her stomach.

"How come you're always surprised when I tell you I'm pregnant?"

"Since you carry them nine months, I don't think I should brag."

Emily laughed and patted his hand.

"I hope a little boy's in here," he said.

"I hope so, too."

"Will you be disappointed if it's a girl?"

"No." She lied. "A girl will be fine with me."

"Me, too," he said. "Me, too."

"Do you think," She yawned again. "I hurt him when I fell?"

"I doubt it, but Norm wants to give you some more tests."

"Dear God, please protect my baby." She gripped his hand almost as tightly as he had gripped hers.

"Amen," Richard said.

Emily began to cry softly.

"Don't cry baby. Everything will be okay."

"I'm sorry I lied about my mother."

He understood now about making little molehills into big mountains.

"Shh. It's history."

"I wanted to tell you so many times. Do you forgive me?"

"Sweetheart, there's nothing to forgive. I didn't try to understand."

"You had every right to be angry. I lied."

"Why didn't you want me to know about her? Because she's White?"

"She's Black. She only looks White."

"You favor her, but Lisa looks just like her."

"I know. I never told you about my inheritance either."

"What inheritance?"

She told him about Maple Honey's estate.

"Je-sus Chri-ist!" He grinned at her good fortune. "You're loaded."

"Not exactly," she said.

"What do you mean?"

"There's a stipulation."

"What kind of stipulation?" His grin faded.

"I don't inherit unless I become Leora's guardian."

"That's no problem." His grin returned.

"I'm not going to become Leora's guardian."

"What?" He looked at her with disbelief. "Why not?"

"I'd be a fraud hating her like I do. I couldn't face myself."

"You'd throw away a fortune because you can't resolve your feelings for a woman you haven't seen in twenty years?"

"I can't help someone I hate!"

"Hate destroys the hater not the hated."

"You weren't the one hated. I was!"

"You didn't let that destroy you. You went on with your life."

"I don't care! I won't do it!"

"Look what you're giving up. What you're denying our children."

"Don't bring our children into it. I know what I'm giving up."

"And your decision is the same?"

"I will not be Leora's guardian!"

"I know you're stubborn, but I'm not letting you throw everything—"

Emily raised her hand for silence. The set of her mouth told him it was useless to continue the discussion, now.

"How're my girls doing?" she asked.

"They're doing fine."

"And Lisa?" she said. "How's she doing?"

"Better, she doesn't cry as much."

"Maybe she should have had her baby."

"She wanted an abortion. The best decision was made for all."

"Sean certainly wouldn't agree."

"I know he wouldn't. It wasn't up to him. It was up to her."

"Does Lisa know about our baby?"

"Not yet."

"When are you going to tell her?"

"Tonight. I'll tell everybody tonight."

Emily yawned and was suddenly so sleepy she couldn't keep her eyes open.

"You look awful. Go home, shave, get some rest."

"Okay." He kissed her passionately. "I'll be back this evening. I love you."

"I love you, too."

Before Richard closed the door, he turned for one last look and thanked God again for letting her live.

Friday, August 21, 1981

Annette hadn't heard from Milo in over a month and here he was at I Love To Read in a tacky green jogging suit she'd seen him in twice before.

"Where's my money?" She confronted him at the office door.

"Where's my ring?" He countered.

"You mean Dr. Quill's ring, don't you?"

Milo's danger antenna went up. "Who's Dr. Quill?"

"Puh-leeze!"

"What are you talking about?"

"Don't come here trying to bullshit me. I know you charged those clothes to Dr. Quill. Wrecked his car, sold his coin collection and God knows what else."

"A misunderstanding," he said smoothly. "It's all been cleared up."

"What makes you think I'd believe anything your lying ass says?"

"I'm telling you the truth," he said. "Give me the ring and I'll—"

"When I get my money, you get the ring."

"I saved you from insanity," he said. "If you had been in your car that day, you'd be crazy now."

"Maybe, maybe not," she said. "But if I keep messing with your ass, I *know* I'll be in jail."

"Ba—by, all that's been taken care of."

"Give me my money. I don't want to be a partner in your restaurant."

"I'm a little short of cash right now."

"You're always short of cash."

"You know I'm good for it."

"Why are you here?"

Milo put his hands on his hips and let her survey his body.

Umph! Umph! Umph!

"I just wanted to see you."

"You've seen me. Now turn your ass around and get out of my life."

"Ba—by." He opened his arms wide. "You don't mean that."

"Don't you baby me. I heard what you said to Em."

"When? I haven't even seen Emily."

"On the phone! On the got-damn phone you dogsnake!"

"Dogsnake. That's awful low."

"You're lower than low." She got the cassette from her desk, shoved it in the tape deck and punched play.

"Emily, before I fuck you," Milo said soft and sexy. "I'm going to drizzle chocolate syrup over your body and lick—"

Annette jabbed the stop button. Milo never missed a beat.

"I was joking. You know how I can piss her off."

"I know." She came around her desk. "Get the fuck out of here."

"I was only playing. You know she's stuck up."

Annette flew into him. "You don't call my friend stuck up!"

"Okay, okay. Haughty." He put his hands on his hips, posing.

Shit! He looks good.

Annette remembered his tongue licking warm chocolate off *her* body.

How much longer can I go? No man has touched me since I ran to Milo's house, correction Dr. Quill's house, like a bitch in heat. I should have figured he was up to no good when he held off fucking me until I signed the check. When will I learn?

"I've missed you." He took a step forward.

"Don't start that I've missed you bullshit." Her pilot light ignited. She took a step back.

"I took the shit for you, remember?" He eased toward her.

"No better for you." She moved back. "You wrecked my car."

"An accident." He opened his arms. "Ba—by."

Her next step was against the desk. Milo pinned her there.

"Don't touch me!" She pointed to the door. "Get out!"

"If that's how you want it." He turned and started out.

"Oh Milo?" Annette said sweetly. "Before you go."

He spun about, grinning. "What is it my darling?"

"Joe Webster is out of the hospital."

"Yeah, I know." He sauntered toward her.

"Do you think he'll bother us?"

"You don't have to worry about that mother fucker ever again."

"What did you do to him?" she asked.

"Don't ask questions. Just believe me when I tell you, Joe Webster won't be bothering you anymore."

"What did you do to him? Tell me, tell me."

Milo put his lips to her ear and whispered his secret.

She pushed him back. "You…did…what?"

"He deserved it, didn't he?"

Annette nodded.

He pulled her into his arms. "Now…where were we?"

Annette laid her head on his chest. Milo touched her thighs. When she stayed nestled in his arms, he gathered the dress about her waist and stroked her pussy.

"Mmmmmmm." She purred. "O-o-o-o-o-o-o-o-o-o-o-oh!"

Milo eased down her red lace panties and untied his jogging pants. They and his briefs dropped around his ankles. Annette watched his dick pulse with eyes half closed and leaned on the desk, spreading her legs. Milo eased between her thighs, caught in the tentacles of her *Joyous* perfume.

"O-o-oh baby, Emily, baby." He groaned.

Annette shoved him back and slapped him with both hands.

"What's wrong with you?"

"You called me, Emily, mother fucker! You called me, Emily!"

"I did not!" He insisted, dodging her blows.

Fingernails raked his cheek before he tied his pants and grabbed her wrists.

"Let me go!" She kneed at his crotch. "Let me go, you son of a bitch!"

"I only said that to make you angry. You're so wild when you're angry."

"Let me go!" She wrenched free and almost tripped with her panties around her ankle. A kick sent them flying across the room.

"Let's do a threesome. You, me and Emily."

She screamed and hurled a plant at Milo's head. He ducked. The clay pot exploded, showering dirt down the wall. "Get the fuck out of here!"

Milo scooped up her panties and held them to his nose. "Ain't nothing like the smell of good pussy."

Annette heaved another pot. It hit the door and cracked the pane. Milo stuffed her panties in his pocket and strolled out, laughing.

"Got-dammit!" Annette slammed the door. Safety glass sprinkled down. She kept slamming until the entire window lay like diamond chunks at her feet.

31

The pain in Emily's head subsided, replaced by the agonizing ache between her legs. Well past horny, she constantly daydreamed of Richard naked on their bed with Mr. Roscoe at attention. Her pussy fluttered continually, thinking of the sexual havoc it would wreak.

"You have a thumbsucker." Angela snapped Emily from her revelry.

"Oh no." She grimaced, squeezing the table edge. "Not another thumbsucker." The ultrasound probe moved slowly back and forth over her stomach, extended by a bladder that seemed filled a hundred times its capacity. She gripped her muscles and prayed she wouldn't pee on herself and shame the Bennett name.

"How much longer?" Emily clenched her teeth.

"Not much longer. You're sure you don't want to know your baby's sex?"

"No-o!" Emily cried. "I don't want to know. Please, please hurry!" She had specifically asked not to be told the sex of her baby. It took all her restraint not to look to see if she could determine if it were a girl or boy.

"Hold on." Angela patted her arm. "Almost done."

"I hope my baby's okay."

"I'm sure it is."

The ultrasound results were favorable, but Emily worried still. She'd been doing everything a pregnant woman shouldn't and fears for the baby's well being plagued her. To ease her mind, Dr. Royal asked the head of OB–GYN to talk to her.

What's taking him so long?

Emily clutched her barf bag, hoping she wouldn't need it when the doctor came. She lay on the bed and examined her stomach. It was certainly not the five-months-pregnant-large Dr. Royal estimated her to be. She'd only gained sixteen pounds. When she was five months pregnant with Nicole, she weighed twenty pounds more. With Michelle, forty.

Dr. Groton swept into the room like a gale. Nut-brown with a narrow face and pointed ears, he looked like an elf with chipmunk front teeth.

"Mrs. Bennett," he said. "What are your concerns for your baby?"

"I was X-rayed and didn't know I was pregnant."

He jumped on the bed with feet dangling and consulted her chart. "You're approximately five months along."

"Yes."

"They X-rayed your head?"

"Yes."

"X-ray used the lead apron over your abdomen?"

"Yes."

"You'd have to have more rads than that to cause injury."

"I've been on the Pill all this time, too."

"No problem."

"I've had alcohol."

"How often and how much?"

"I had several glasses of champagne at a business luncheon."

"That's all?" Dr. Groton said.

"Yes."

"No problem." He stuck the stethoscope in his ears. "Open your robe please." He laid it to her abdomen, listening intently. "Strong heartbeat. I see nothing to worry about," he said and straightened up.

"So you think my baby is fine?"

"I do," he said and patted her arm.

"You've eased my mind a great deal."

"I'm so glad. Do you have any more questions?"

"No, I guess not. You've been very helpful, thank you."

"You're welcome." He smiled and hopped down like a small boy. "Give my regards to Richard."

"I will."

He left as he had entered, with his lab coat flapping.

The phone rang. Emily reached over to pick it up.

"Hello."

"Hi," Annette said. "How're you doing?" Her voice sounded as strained as their relationship.

"I'm fine and you?"

"Fine," she said. "I wanted to come see you but...you know."

"I understand."

Annette hated hospitals. She hadn't even visited her own mother when she'd had open-heart surgery.

"I was thinking about coming by when you got out."

"I'd love to have you visit me."

"You would?" Annette sounded relieved.

"Of course I would."

"I'll come by then."

"I'm glad you called," Emily said. "Richard told me how much you helped out since I've been in here. Thanks for getting Lisa settled at Spelman."

"It was the least I could do."

"I just want you to know I appreciate it."

"You're welcome."

There was a long pause.

"I won't keep you," Annette said. "Bye."

"Bye." Emily hung up glad to know there was a spark of friendship left. She hoped it was enough to turn back into a flame.

Richard walked in ten minutes later.

"Hello, baby." He kissed her with much tongue.

"Why doctor." She imitated a southern belle. "Is this the bedside manner you use with all your patients?"

"No, ma'am. Only the fillies with my brand." He traced her scar.

They laughed.

"How do you feel?"

"Ready to get out of here."

"You're signed out and free to go."

"Let's ride."

"Did Oscar get by?"

"Oscar?"

"Dr. Groton."

"Uh huh."

"What did he say?"

"He said to give you his regards and the baby's fine."

"Didn't I tell you that?"

"Richy." Her voice shook. "I can't lose another baby."

"Honey, you won't." He sat on the bed and hugged her.

"I'm so afraid."

"Shhh, you're fine. The baby's fine. Don't worry, okay?"

"Okay."

He picked up the phone and made a call. "Suzy, we're ready."

"Who's Suzy?"

"Your escort. I don't want you waiting here all day."

"What can I do with all these flowers?" Four large bouquets and three potted plants sat on the windowsill.

"They can go to the ward if you want."

"The bouquets can go, but save the potted ones for Mother Nature."

"Who?" He laughed.

"For Annette. Take them to the store. She keeps her jungle there."

"Okay."

A pretty, young Black girl in a pink pinafore pushed in a wheelchair.

"Hello." She flashed a dimpled smile and parked it by the bed.

"Hello, Suzy," he said. "This is, Mrs. Bennett. Emily this is, Suzy Milburn."

"Hello, Suzy," Emily said. "How're you?"

"Fine and yourself?"

"Wonderful, since I'm going home."

Sweltering heat greeted Emily at the door. Richard helped her in the car and put her bag and the plants in the back. When he got in, Emily sat so close to him, she was practically under the wheel.

"This feels like our courting days." She laid her head on his shoulder.

"The rest of our lives will be courting days. I promise you that."

She waited until they pulled off and felt between his legs. Mr. Roscoe rose under the soft pressure of her hand.

"Don't start something you can't finish," he said with a laugh.

"Miss Nina is burning up! Pull over so we can get in the back seat."

Richard slammed the brakes and steered to the curb. Emily laughed like crazy until he pulled her in his arms for a tooth-rattling kiss.

"Mr. Roscoe says Miss Nina is going to be in deep trouble tonight."

"Tell Mr. Roscoe, Miss Nina can't wait until tonight. She wants him as soon as she gets home."

"I think that's going to be a bit awkward."

"Why?"

"Momma's giving you a welcome home party."

"Oh no-o-o! Not a party."

"I couldn't talk her out of it. You know how she loves to throw a party."

"I know."

"If you don't feel up to it—"

"If I get tired, I'll just excuse myself and go to bed."

"And I'll be right behind you." Richard laughed and took a pink, wrinkled paper from his wallet.

"What's that?"

"It may be awhile before you're up to your old sexual self, but I just want to let you know I will be calling in this marker."

"Let me see." She reached for it.

He jerked it back and read. "This entitles the bearer to freaky, freaky sex."

"The last time I saw that." She struggled to keep from laughing. "It was balled up in the wastebasket."

"I know," he said sheepishly. "Each time I thought about what freaky sexual act you might perform on me, I had second thoughts about throwing it away. When I went to get it, Michelle had emptied the trash."

"I saw you going through the garbage." She laughed outright. "I thought you were looking for something important."

"I was." He returned the paper to his wallet. "I was."

32

Richard crested the hill. Emily recognized Ralph holding a big box under the magnolia tree next to Annette. Pauline, Nicole and Michelle sat on the steps. Ezell played cards in his chair. Only Lisa was missing. *Where is she?*

Richard pulled to the steps. Over the front door, a pink and blue "Welcome Home Em" banner fluttered in the hot breeze.

"Mommeeee!" Michelle ran toward the car until Annette restrained her.

"Welcome home!" Pauline hugged Emily. "How're you doing, baby?"

"Fine." She patted her hand. "Just fine."

"I missed you so much." Nicole crashed through and kissed her mother's face.

"I missed you too, sweetie."

"Mommy, Mommy." Michelle cried when she couldn't get through.

"Come on." Pauline cleared the way. Michelle leaned in for a hug and kiss.

"Move back girls and let Mommy out." Richard gently pushed them aside and practically lifted Emily from the car. "You okay?"

"I'm fine," she said. "Where's Lisa?"

"In her room." Nicole volunteered.

"Why is she in her room?" Emily looked at Richard.

"She's upset about the baby," Nicole said.

"Upset?" Emily asked. "Why?"

"She's humiliated because you're having a baby." Nicole explained.

"Why didn't you tell me?" Emily looked at Richard.

"Because I didn't want *you* to be upset."

"Oh dear," Emily said. "Oh dear."

"Em." Annette hugged her and handed her a bouquet of yellow roses. "I'm so glad you're out of that awful place."

"Me, too," Emily said absently. "I brought you more babies to love."

"You did? What kind?"

"A coleus, some ivy and something else. They're in the back."

Annette yanked open the door to look.

"Hello, Emily." Ralph hugged her and removed a huge, yellow teddy bear from the box. "This is his first present."

"Sorry, big brother." Richard held up his teddy bear. "His second."

"You know it's a boy?" Pauline said. "Don't you, Sonny?"

"I don't know, Momma," Richard said.

"It's a boy, all right," Pauline said. "I dreamed it was a boy."

"Hello, Ezell." Emily gave him a hug and kiss.

"Hello, baby. All this woman talks about is her new grandson."

"I'm telling y'all, it's a boy," Pauline said. "I can look in her eyes and tell she's having a boy."

"Pauline." Ezell laughed. "Quit it!"

"Look at her ankles, the right one is bigger than the left."

"Je-sus Chri-ist!" Ezell said. "Now I've heard everything."

Pauline ran her hands over Emily's stomach. "This child is due in December, probably around the twenty-fifth or twenty-sixth."

"Come on, Momma." Ralph laughed. "Sonny, told you that."

"No I didn't," Richard said. "I just found out she's due Christmas day."

Silence fell over the gathering. All eyes turned on Pauline.

"Ya'll know I was born with a veil," she said. "Stop looking at me like I'm possessed and come and eat.

Everyone laughed and followed her to the kitchen. As usual, Pauline outdid herself with the food. Fall off the bone, barbecued ribs filled a roasting pan. Brunswick stew bubbled thick and savory in a blue canning pot. Macaroni chocked with cheese sat beside collard greens full of ham hocks and corn bread squares loaded with crackling. Dessert was her special homemade vanilla delight ice cream and flaming peach brandy cobbler.

"You okay?" Richard hovered over Emily like a mother hen.

"Honey." She reassured him. "I'm fine."

"I don't want you to over-do."

"I won't." She led him to the glider. They sat holding hands, pushing back and forth.

"I'm a woman of my word." Pauline placed a large bag on Emily's lap. "Here's my present for Baby Boy Bennett."

"What bit of knowledge did Momma hit on the money?" Ralph asked. He and Annette set up the card table while Ezell shuffled a deck, waiting

"She knew I was pregnant before I did and told me she'd make something for her new grandchild."

"My mother, the fortune teller." Richard laughed.

"My wife," Ezell said good-naturedly. "The voodoo queen."

Everyone laughed.

Emily removed an ice blue blanket bordered with eight-inch long fringe.

"Oh-h Pauline." She exclaimed. "Thank you! It's gorgeous." She rubbed it on her face. "And so soft. Feel this, Annette." She passed it over.

"It's beautiful, Pauline," Annette said. "Simply beautiful."

"Thank you." Pauline's smile lit up her eyes.

Emily took out an off-white satin christening gown and cap trimmed in lace.

"O-h-h-h! It's beautiful. Look at this, Annette."

Annette ran her fingers over the capital letter B's embroidered in pale blue. "I want my baby's layette just like this."

Misty-eyed, Emily got up and hugged Pauline.

"Will your layette have B's for Bennett, too?" Ralph teased Annette.

At a loss for words for the first time in her life, she shook her head, no.

"What initials do you plan on having?" he said.

"That's to be announced," she said flippantly.

I'm not pinning my heart to my sleeve this time. This time I'm playing it cool. I hope my interest in Ralph Bennett doesn't transmit like a beacon from my face. His eyes have my body burning like a gasoline fire, hot and smoky.

Annette touched her cheeks. They scorched her hand. She glanced at Ralph. He smiled like he knew she was in heat.

"Michelle," Emily said. "Has Lisa eaten anything?"

"I don't know."

"Go tell her to come here."

"Please no, Mommy." Michelle whined. "She's pouting."

"I...am...not...pouting." Lisa declared from the kitchen door.

"What's wrong, honey?" Emily asked.

Lisa stepped onto the deck with eyes red from crying.

"What's wrong?" She screamed. "What's wrong? How could you do this? Everybody is laughing at me. You're too old to be doing it in the first place, let alone having a baby. I hate you! I hate you!" She ran inside, sobbing.

"I'll talk to her," Pauline said and went in the house.

"Uh oh," Annette said. She flicked the ace of clubs on the card table in a furious game of coon with Ezell.

"I'm glad you're having a baby, Mommy," Nicole said. Her parents stopped pushing and let her to climb in the space between them.

"Thank you, honey." Emily gave her a hug and kiss.

"I'm glad, too," Michelle said.

"Thank you, sweetie." They stopped again and let her climb on Richard's lap. Emily and Richard looked at each other and burst out laughing.

"N-e-x-t!" Ezell yelled after he beat Annette. "I'm tired of whipping everybody in sight. Who wants to play bid whist?" he said, rippling the cards.

"Are you feeling okay?" Richard asked.

"Stop worrying about me," Emily said. "I'm fine."

"I'll play." Richard slid Michelle off his lap.

She and Nicole sat by their mother, bringing her up to date on the happenings.

"Daddy." Richard sat opposite his father. "Let's whip these chumps."

"Sonny." Ezell pushed the cards for Annette to cut. "You ain't said nothing but some words."

"Annette?" Ralph smiled at his partner. "Are we going to let them get away with calling us chumps?"

"Most definitely not." She cut the cards and pushed them back to Ezell.

"The deal is in the White House," Ezell bragged. "President Ezell Bennett presiding." He dealt the cards and threw out the last six for the kitty.

"Four." Ralph bid first.

"Five, no trump," Richard said and laid his hand face down.

"He took my bid," Annette said. "I don't know if I can make a six."

"Go for it," Ralph said.

"Wait one cotton picking minute," Ezell said. "Young woman, why don't you just show Junior your hand and you won't have to talk across the table."

"You're mad because you don't have a hand." Ralph laughed. "Bid, baby."

"Six." Annette grimaced and looked at Ezell.

Ezell stroked his chin and looked a long time at his cards. He laid them on the table, picked them up and studied them again.

"Pass." He looked at Annette. "What's trumps?"

"Spades." Annette groaned before she turned over the kitty.

"That's my kitty." Ezell yelled. "That's my dog gone kitty."

"Partner, we'll soon see who the chumps are," Annette said and gleefully rubbed her hands together. She picked up the queen of spades, ten of spades, ace of hearts, king of hearts, queen of hearts, and the jack of diamonds. She discarded all losers except the jack of diamonds.

"Go get em, baby." Ralph put her discard book in front of him.

Annette led off with the big joker. She and Ralph reached for the book. Their fingertips brushed. Her pussy fluttered like a drunken butterfly.
Got-damn!
She kept her hands to herself after that and let him pick up the books.

Annette cleaned house with her trump cards and started her heart rundown. She could easily make her bid, but she wanted to go to Boston and shut the braggarts up. She threw out the jack of diamonds.

"Ah ha." Ezell topped it with the king.

"Not so fast." Ralph threw out the ace and smiled at Annette.

"N-e-e-e-x-t!" She slapped the trey of spades to her forehead. It stuck there for all to see.

"Straight to Boston." Ralph held up his hand for five.
Annette hesitated an instant then slapped her hand in his. A jolt of sexual hunger scorched her panties. She snatched her hand back, blushing.
What is wrong with me? I'm a grown-ass woman not a got-damn school girl.
"Excuse me," Annette said.
I can't stand Ralph's eyes burning holes in my body any longer. I have to go somewhere and cool it down.

Lisa was no where in the house. Pauline headed down a narrow path through a field of lilac flowers. Each flounce of her skirt sent swallow-tail butterflies flitting in the humid air.
Lisa lay on her stomach on a boulder jutting over the stream. Pauline climbed up and sank beside her winded.

"Gram, how could they embarrass me like this?"

"Honey, they didn't do it to embarrass you."

"Nobody would even know they were doing it if they weren't having a baby."

"It's as much a surprise to them as it is to you." Pauline said.

"I'm not surprised. I hear them talking about Mr. Roscoe and Miss Nina."

"Who are they?"

"You know...Daddy's penis and Mommy's vagina. They think they're talking over my head, but I know what's going on."

"I see." Pauline tried not to sniggle.

My candy is Saphronia. Ezell's johnson is Joe-Joe Boy.

"When did you stop having sex? Old people don't do it, do they?"

"Where did you get the notion old people don't have sex?"

Lisa sat up and looked at her grandmother, amazed.

"You still do it with Grandpa?"

"Sex is not just for the young."

"Man, I'd have to leave town if you had a baby."

Pauline doubled over laughing.

"It's not funny, Gram."

"You're embarrassed now, but you'll love the baby when he comes."

"I won't." She leaned against Pauline with a heart aching for *her* baby and a longing to tell someone how badly she felt for killing him.

If I had known Mommy was having a baby, I could have had mine!

"You say that now, but after he's born, you'll adore him."

"I'll hate it!" she said cruelly. "I'll never love it!"

"Lisa, Lisa," Pauline said. "You don't mean that."

"Yes...I...do!"

"Child." Pauline sighed. "Child."

"Please don't call me that. I'm not a child."

"You are a child and you need to stay a child as long as you can." Pauline said sternly. "But, what's the use? You won't listen."

"I listen," Lisa said.

"Did you listen when I told you to save yourself for someone who loved you? I *heard* you were seeing some boy."

"Who told you that," Lisa said miffed. "Daddy?"

"Never mind who. Are you on birth control?"

"I'm not having sex so I don't need birth control."

"But suppose you decide to—"

"I won't." Lisa cut her off. "I won't."

"If you decide—" Pauline said.

"Gram—"

"Let me finish! If you decide to have sex, will you at least use a condom?"

"Okay," Lisa said. "I'll use a condom."

If Sean had used a condom, I wouldn't have gotten pregnant and had a baby to kill.

"I'm serious, Lisa."

"I'll insist on a condom, I promise."

"You made a promise, too, and you broke it."

"I know, but I had to."

"Had to?"

"Yes," Lisa said with a far away look. "He was a very special person."

"A boy will always tell you what you want to hear to get what he wants."

"I know." She looked in Pauline's eyes. "But this was different."

"How was it different?"

Lisa wanted to tell her how tenderly Sebastian had made love to her and that he was not a boy but a grown man. She shivered, remembering how beautiful his body looked naked and how good he felt on top of her, inside her. He had saved her from Zebo and Kenya.

There they are again. Each time I think I've cut them from my mind, they pop back in. Why should I be sorry Zebo is dead? He wanted to hurt me. Didn't he? He got what he deserved and Kenya, too.

In jail for cocaine possession, Kenya had the nerve to call and ask Lisa to forgive her. She had hung up in her face.

"It was different, Gram," she said. "Just different."

"It looks like rain." Pauline eyed dark clouds in the distance. "We'd better get back to the house."

They topped the slope. The red Porsche sat flagrantly in its old spot.

"What is he doing here?" Lisa said dryly.

"Who?"

"Sean Favor."

"Who's he?"

"Someone I—" She almost said detest. "Went to school with."

Pauline's sixth sense buzzed. Something here did not quite meet the eye.

"You don't sound like you like him very much."

"He likes me." She made her voice carefree. "I don't like him."

"I see," Pauline said gravely. "I see."

Lisa stood at the side of the house and watched Sean with her parents.

Don't hug him, Mommy. Don't shake his hand, Daddy. He's a rapist.

"I just dropped in to say good-bye," Sean said. "I'm leaving for school tonight."

I know its crazy coming here after Lisa's threat, but I couldn't go away without seeing her one more time.

"Where're you going?" Ezell asked.

"To Harvard."

"Wonderful," Annette said.

"Way to go," Ralph exclaimed.

"Best of luck to you." Ezell gave him a salute.

"Thank you," Sean said. "Thank you all very much."

"This handsome young man must be Sean." Pauline pushed past Lisa.

"Yes, ma'am."

"Lisa tells me you like her," Pauline said. "Is that true?"

"Yes, ma'am." Sean looked at Lisa. "I like her very much."

"Who're your people?" Pauline asked.

"Blake and Margaret Favor—"

"The Margaret Favor I see in the paper all the time?"

"Yes, ma'am."

"Stop giving him the third degree, Momma." They're not getting married."

"Like I'd marry a rapist." Lisa muttered to herself and headed inside.

"Lisa, come back here!" Richard yelled.

She kept walking.

"Lisa, do you hear me talking to you?"

She slammed the kitchen door and left Sean crestfallen.

"Nicole." Richard ordered. "Go tell Lisa to get herself back here."

"Yes, Daddy," Nicole said and went inside.

"So, my boy." Richard threw his arm over Sean's shoulder. "You're going to be a doctor like your old man?"

"No, sir. A lawyer like my, Uncle Ian."

"Does, Blake, know this?" Richard acted shocked.

"Yes, sir." Sean laughed. "I have his blessings."

Three minutes later, Nicole returned from loitering in the turret room.

"Where's Lisa?" Richard asked.

"She says please excuse her," Nicole said. "She has a terrible headache."

"Well," Richard said. "Okay."

"I'd better be going," Sean said.

"Have something to eat." Nicole invited.

"No…no thanks."

"There's plenty," she said. "I'll fix you a plate."

"Really, no thanks."

"You used to eat everything in sight. I'm fixing you a plate."

"Okay." He took a seat and looked at the house.

Maybe Lisa will come back out.

Nicole carried the plate to the table by the pool and chased Michelle away.

I want Sean all to myself.

"How long will you be gone to college?" Nicole asked.

"Four for undergraduate. Three for law school."

"I'm going to be a lawyer, too," she said. "We can work together, fighting poverty and injustice."

"Yeah." He picked at the food. "That'd be great."

"I'll write you," Nicole said. "Will you write me?"

"I'll probably be too busy studying."

"Me too." She laughed to hide her hurt feelings.

"Do you think Lisa is coming back out?" Sean asked.

"No, she's not coming back out." Nicole snapped. "I told you she has a headache. When she has a headache, she stays in her room."

"Well." He stood. "I'd better be getting on home."

"Don't go." She caught his hand, trying to think of something to say to make him stay. "You've hardly eaten anything."

"I'm not really hungry." He pulled free. "I've got to finish packing and stuff."

"Can I give you a good-bye hug?"

"Sure."

Nicole squeezed Sean fiercely then stood on tiptoes to kiss his lips.

"Bye."

"Bye, S.L.G."

Nicole watched Sean walk in the house.

Will you ever know how much I love you?

Voices at the front door pulled Lisa from her room. She stood by the banister listening to her father carry on like Sean was his son headed to Harvard.

I know he's disappointed I'm not going, but it can't be helped. I have no control over being in the same city with a rapist, but I have complete control over being at the same school.

"Keep in touch," Richard said. "Let us know how you're doing."

"Thank you, sir. I will."

"You know you're welcome here any time."

Lisa groaned.

"You don't know how good that makes me feel," Sean said. "Will you tell Lisa I think about her all the time and I'm truly sorry about everything."

"I'll tell her."

"Well." He shook Richard's hand. "Good-bye, sir."

"Good-bye, my boy."

Lisa held back the curtain and watched Sean walk to his car.

Our baby would have been the most beautiful baby in the world.

Sean looked up, as if hearing her speak. A smile lit his face. He raised his hand and waved. Lisa stood there with tears for their dead child, streaming down her face and let the curtain drop.

33

Emily's nausea stopped as suddenly as it started and she returned to work. "Em." Annette hugged her tight. "I'm so glad you're back. I have so much to tell you."

"What?" Emily said eager to hear the news.

"Let me finish this first." Annette completed an invoice and filed it away.

Emily noticed the empty "in" tray. "You've done a very good job."

"Thanks, little Mommy," Annette said. "I've been working my head off to stay caught up."

Emily put her hands in the small of her back and stretched before she sat at her desk. "What do we—"

The phone rang.

"I Love To Read, Annette speaking."

"Hello," Ralph Bennett said. "How are you?"

Annette remembered how his touch made her wet.

"Fine, thank you. Who is this please?"

"Ralph...Ralph Bennett."

"Oh, hello, Ralph. How're you?"

"Just fine. Are you free for dinner tonight?"

"Tonight? Let me check my calendar. Please hold." Annette pushed the hold button and squealed. "Let the church say, a man."

"A man." Emily jumped startled. "What's wrong with you?" She rubbed her stomach to soothe the kicking baby.

"Ralph asked me to dinner tonight."

"Are you going?"

"Does a bear shit in the woods?"

"I guess that means yes?" Emily laughed.

"Yes! Yes! Yes!" Annette pushed the hold button and said calmly. "Yes, Ralph, I'm free tonight."

"Good, I'll pick you up at home at say...seven-thirty?"

"Seven-thirty is fine. See you then. Bye-bye."

"Bye."

Annette hung up and slid to the carpet.

"Get up, girl." Emily laughed. "Stop acting silly."

"I'm not acting silly. I'm in love." She got up and sat in her chair. "What am I going to wear?"

"What you have on looks good."

"This old thing?" She looked down at the expensive green silk pantsuit. "I can't wear this rag to dinner with the fine Ralph Bennett?"

"From what I saw when I came from the hospital, I don't think Ralph will notice what you're wearing."

"Whatever...do...you...mean?" Annette said.

"I couldn't help but notice the fireworks between you two."

"Oh God!" She groaned. "Was I that obvious?"

"No," Emily said. "I just know the look when you're in lust."

"Ralph didn't say a word. He just kept me on fire with his eyes."

"At the time, he thought you and Milo were an item so he backed off."

"Who told him Milo and I weren't an item?"

"I did of course." Emily smiled. "He's always asking about you."

"He is? Why didn't you tell me?"

"I didn't want you to get the big head." Emily laughed.

"Tell me what he said. What? What? What?"

"You're sure you won't get the big head?" Emily teased.

"I'm a split second off your ass if you don't tell me what he said."

"Okay, okay. I'm not going to taunt you like you do me."

Annette started toward Emily with hands clenched like monster claws. Emily laughed so hard, she could hardly speak. "He wants to know what you like."

"Like what?"

"Your favorite perfume, movies, flowers, travel spots, restaurants." The closer Annette got, the faster Emily talked.

"Did you tell him my most favorite thing is to fuck his brains out?"

"Shut up, Annette."

"You know I haven't had any since I fired..." She scowled. "Milo."

"Long time, huh?" Emily said.

"A got-damned long time. I feel like a nun."

"Sure. I know James Collins came by when I was off."

"Girl, don't you know?" Annette shook her head sadly.

"Know what?"

"James Collins is gay."

"No-o," she said. "He is so fine."

"Every man I meet is either on his way to jail, married or fucking gay?"

"Ralph isn't on his way to jail, married or gay."

"Thank God!" Annette knocked on wood. "Shit!"

"What?"

"What am I going to wear?"

"What about your Ronny Kahn?"

"Yeah." She stood then sat. "I forgot, it's in the cleaners."

"Okay, what about that Ballanalonda?"

"It's in the cleaners, too." She sighed.

"What about your T-H-Y dress with the floral scarf?"

"In...the...cleaners. Everything I own is in the got-damn cleaners."

"You've have two bedrooms full of clothes and you don't have anything to wear. How can that be?"

"I don't know."

"What about your pink suit with your new navy strap shoes."

"Yes, yes, yes." Annette dropped to her knees in front of Emily and bowed three times. "Thank you, thank you, thank you. That's the look I need for Mr. Ralph, sophisticated yet sexy. I'll wear my lace tube top."

"You're so bad. I wouldn't dare wear a tube top."

"Girlfriend, if you can't handle the attention a tube top will get you." Annette jiggled her breasts. "You might as well stay at home."

Emily doubled over, laughing.

"Get off the floor, Annette."

"While I'm on my knees, I may as well put it to some use." She looked toward the ceiling and clasped her hands in prayer. "Dear Heavenly Father, let Ralph Bennett be the man of my dreams. Let him be a loving father to our beautiful children, and please, please let him be the one to make me scream and cream—"

Emily gasped.

Annette stopped praying to look at her. "What?"

"That's blasphemy, Annette, stop it!" Emily said. "You can't ask God to give you a man that makes you scream and cream."

"And who else should I ask, Miss Ma'am?"

"Uh...uh." Emily stammered. "I see your point, pray continue."

"Anything for you while I'm down here?" Annette asked.

"You are totally insane." Emily put her finger to her head in thought. "Could you ask Him to make Leora love me?"

Annette closed her eyes and prayed for her friend.

"Heavenly Father, give Leora DuPree a brand new heart overflowing with love for her daughter, Emily. This I ask in Jesus' name. Amen."

"Amen," Emily said. "Amen."

Annette got up and sat at her desk.

"I should have prayed for Milo before we started."

"Do you think it would have made any difference?"

"Hell, no! Milo is too far gone."

"Why do you say that?"

"You don't know do you?"

"Know what?"

"When you were off, the police came by looking for Milo," Annette said with a laugh. "I thought they were here about my car. I almost held my arms out to be handcuffed."

"You're nuts. Why were they here?"

"Girl, Milo is in all sorts of trouble."

"Wha-a-t?" Emily sat forward.

"They want him for everything."

"Like what?"

"Forgery, theft—"

"Forgery?" Emily said aghast. "Theft?"

"Yeah, girl, and you were right," Annette said. "That house he took me to wasn't his. He was house sitting for those people."

"I knew it. I told you that house belonged to Bob Quill."

"He charged those fine clothes to Dr. Quill's account and." Annette's voice quaked and trailed off.

When she sounded like that, she had done something really stupid.

"What did you do?"

"I…I loaned Milo twenty five thousand dollars."

"No, you didn't."

Annette nodded her head, looking ashamed.

"There's something else, but I'm too embarrassed to say."

"You'd better tell me."

"Milo came by here looking so good I came this close to giving him some."
Annette held her thumb and forefinger a sliver apart.

"If you resisted by that much, you weren't in any danger of submitting."

"Actually, it was nearer to this." Annette jammed her fingers together.
Emily laughed so hard she almost peed on herself. Annette didn't tell her if
Milo hadn't called her Emily, she would have been fucked.

"I'm sorry I didn't believe you when you told me the nasty things Milo said."

"How come you believe me now?"

"I played the tape."

"What?" Emily opened her desk drawer.

"Here it is." Annette held up the cassette and began to cry. "I'm sorry!"

"How did you get that?"

"The tape in the answering machine broke, I played this one to see what was
on it and there Milo was, talking shit."

"Oh."

"Why didn't you play it for me?"

"I was going to the next day. Then I had the accident."

"Em." Annette moaned. "I'm sorry…I'm sorry!"

"Stop crying and saying you're sorry."

"Okay, okay." She blew her nose. "Can you forgive me for doubting you?"

"Of course I can. Now stop crying."

"Em, there's more." Annette dabbed her eyes.

"Oh God, what else?"

"It gets worse."

"How worse?" Emily asked.

"Something personal worse."

"Something personal worse like what?"

"Milo wanted us to have a ménage á trois."

"Son of a bitch!" Flew from Emily's mouth, but Annette was crying so hard
she didn't notice.

"You know the emerald ring Milo gave me?" Annette said.

"Uh huh."

"It's worth thirty thousand dollars."

"Wha-a-at?"

"Uh huh!"

"Sell it and get the money back you gave Milo."

"I can't. Milo stole it from the Quills."

"Where is it now?"

"In my purse." She took it out and handed it to Emily.

Emily tossed it to and fro and threw it on her desk. "Why is it so cold?"

"I keep it in a bag of broccoli, in the freezer."

Emily laughed. "Why in a bag of broccoli?"

"In case Milo breaks in looking for it," she said with a shudder. "He wants it bad. I don't know what he might do to get it."

"Go to the police."

"No-o-o!" Annette exclaimed. "He'd tell them about Joe Webster and burning my Volvo. I'd go to jail before he did."

"Don't be silly. If he told, he'd be in more trouble than us."

"O-o-o-h, Em." Annette wailed. "You said us! You said us!"

"What?" Emily said.

"You said he'd be in more trouble than us."

"Annette," Emily said. "We're friends for life. 'Til death do us part."

"You're better to me than I deserve."

"Stop crying and blow your nose." She handed her tissues.

"I know what Milo did to Joe Webster." Annette said and blew her nose.

"What?" Emily said. "Poor man."

"Poor man nothing. If he had thrown shit on me, I'd probably be doing this all the time." She strummed her index finger across her bottom lip.

"What did Milo do to him?"

"He made Joe Webster drink the soupy shit off my floor mat. He put the gun to his head and made him suck up every drop."

"He...did...what?" Emily cupped a hand over her mouth and ran to the washroom.

Annette followed and beat on the door. "Are you okay? Em, are you okay?"

"I'm okay," Emily said finally.

"Are you sure?"

"I'm sure." Emily came out with a damp paper towel to her mouth and sank in her chair.

"I'm sorry." Annette massaged her shoulders. "I shouldn't have told you in your delicate condition."

"I'm okay," Emily said. "How could Milo do that?"

"Joe Webster did throw the shit first, remember."

"I know, but still—"

"But still nothing, Joe Webster brought it on himself."

"Okay. I won't say another word in his defense."

"You're sure you're okay?"

"Uh huh," Emily said. "I'm fine."

Annette gave Emily a pat on the shoulder and returned to her desk.

"Guess what I've done?" Emily said.

"What?"

"Promise you won't laugh and call me a wimp."

"Cross my heart and hope to die," Annette said solemnly.

"I became Leora's guardian last week."

"I knew you wouldn't let all that money go to the state."

"Don't say that. It makes me look so greedy."

"It doesn't. It makes you look smart. This is a fortune we're talking here."

"Don't think Richard hasn't constantly thrown that fact in my face."

"What made you change your mind?"

"Michelle did."

"Michelle?"

"Uh huh. She said if I continued to hate Leora, I wouldn't be in heaven with the rest of them."

"Out of the mouths of babes."

"Uh huh. She carried on so, I finally told her I didn't hate Leora anymore. She said if that were true, I'd bring Leora to live with us."

"Is Michelle working for, Miss Maple Honey?" Annette laughed.

"It looks that way."

"You're really going to bring Leora to your home?"

"I guess I am," Emily said. "I guess I am."

"Who's going to take care of her? You?"

"No way. Richard hired nurses around the clock."

"I'll bet that's expensive."

"It is, but Maple Honey had a fund set up for nursing care."

"She thought of everything, didn't she?"

"She sure did."

"Everything will work itself out," Annette said. "You'll see."

"I hope so, I really hope so."

"I just decided," Annette said. "I'm giving the ring back to the Quill's."

"Good for you."

Wearing gloves, Annette sealed the ring in a small box and dropped it at the post office. She returned to I Love To Read greatly relieved.

"Come in." Annette answered the door and accepted a bouquet of pink roses.

"Somebody spent a fortune on these," Emily said. "Who're they from?"

Annette inhaled the lovely aroma and found the card.

"Thinking constantly of you," she read. "Its signed R B."

Both women said at once. "Ralph Bennett!"

34

Saturday, October 3, 1981

Leora DuPree arrived at the Bennett house that morning. Richard's orders to the girls were to leave her alone and give her a chance to adjust. He was gone somewhere with their mother. Mrs. Johnson, the evening nurse, was at dinner so Nicole and Michelle decided to introduce themselves.

"Go ahead." Nicole pushed Michelle toward the door.

"You go." Michelle pushed her back.

"Go on, she won't bite."

"How do you know," Michelle said and knocked timidly.

"Enter." A strong voice invited.

Michelle opened the door surprised to find the formerly sunny family room dark and scary. The woman propped up in the hospital bed was barely visible.

"Hello," Nicole said cheerfully.

"Who's there?" The low wattage lamp Leora clicked on cast little light. "What are you children doing in my room?"

"We came to visit. We're your grandchildren."

"Grandchildren?" Leora snapped. "I have no grandchildren."

"Yes, you do, Granny," Michelle said. "You have us."

"What…did…you…call…me?"

"Granny," Michelle said meekly.

"If I had grandchildren, I'd never allow them to call me granny!"

"We only want to welcome you," Michelle said.

"I don't care what you want." Leora clicked out the light. "Go away before I call the police!"

They felt foolish standing in the dark, so they left.

"Did she look White to you?" Michelle asked.

"Uh huh," Nicole said. "But it was so dark, I couldn't see good."

They sat on their bed discussing Leora.

"She's mean," Michelle said.

"She sure is." Nicole agreed.

"Maybe having her live here wasn't such a good idea," Michelle said. "We could have gone to Disneyworld."

"I'm bored," Nicole said. "What can we do?"

"Let's play checkers," Michelle said. "Naw. You always beat me."

"What about pick up sticks?"

"You beat me playing that, too."

"Let's go mess with Lisa," Nicole said.

"I don't want to. She's depressed."

"She's not depressed. She's just faking to get attention."

"I don't know—"

"If you don't go, you're chicken shit."

"I…am…not!"

"You are if you don't come with me."

Michelle followed Nicole and barged behind her into Lisa's room.

"Get out of my room." Lisa sat up and slammed the book shut.

"We don't have to go." Nicole declared. "Unless we want to."

"I'm warning you, Nicole."

"You can't threaten me. I know your secret."

"What secret?" Michelle prodded. "What secret, Nicole?"

"What are you talking about?" Lisa's eyes narrowed.

"That's for me to know and you to find out."

"I'm not worried," Lisa said. "You can't remember your own name."

"I don't have to remember." Nicole looked at the closet. "I only have to read."

Lisa followed her gaze.

"Get out of my room." She rolled off the bed. "Get out!"

"We'll go when we get good and ready." Nicole laughed and folded her arms over her chest.

Michelle sucked her thumb, watching the fray.

"If you're still here when I count to five, you'll be sorry you were ever born."

"I'm already sorry you're my sister."

"One...two...three." Lisa began.

Nicole grabbed Michelle's hand and headed for the door. Before she closed it, she laughed wickedly and patted her butt. Lisa threw the first thing she touched. The box detonated against the door. A cloud of body powder drifted to the magenta rug.

Lisa snatched the key from around her neck and pulled the overnight bag from the closet shelf. The broken lock dangled on half a shank. She groaned and opened the bag. Her letters to Sebastian were gone. Nicole was mean and vicious and would not hesitate to tell everybody what those letters contained. *Oh God! Is the other letter gone, too?*

Panic stricken she hurried to her dresser and pulled out her sweater drawer. She ran her hand under the bottom. The insurance letter was still there and she sighed, relieved to know Nicole didn't have it. Her cheeks burned at the thought of others knowing her secret. Nicole would definitely tell what she had written Sebastian, unless...unless. Lisa got five one-dollar bills from her bank and went to her sisters' room.

"Michelle," she said. "Do you want to make a dollar?"

"Don't listen to her, Michelle." Nicole cautioned. "She's up to something."

"What do I have to do?" Michelle opened the door.

"Just make me a peanut butter and jelly sandwich and bring it up here with a glass of milk."

"Why can't you do it yourself?" Michelle asked.

"Two dollars," Lisa said. "It *has* to be peanut butter and jelly."

"Don't do it, Michelle." Nicole warned. "She's up to something."

"No!" Michelle said.

"Three."

"Four," Michelle said. "I'll do it for four."

"Okay, four," Lisa said.

That should keep her busy until I find my letters. I used all the jelly yesterday.

"Okay," Michelle grabbed the bills and ran for the steps.

The second she was out of sight, Lisa stepped into Nicole's room and locked the door.

"Get out of here!" Nicole jumped off the bed, afraid without Michelle to help her fight. "Get out of my room."

"Where're my letters?" Lisa seethed.

"I don't know what you're talking about."

"I'm going to make you sorry you took them."

"Girls." Richard's voice resonated over the house. "We're home."

"Daddddeeeee." Nicole ran toward the door. "First I'm telling Daddy what you did with Sean, you nasty thing, then everybody in Georgia."

"You're not going to tell anybody anything." Lisa opened a dresser drawer.

"You're not even close." Nicole laughed. "They're not in there."

"But this is." Lisa pulled out the cosmetic bag and swung it back and forth. Nicole's laughter stopped abruptly.

"That's my stuff." She croaked. "You put that back."

"If you tell anything on me, I'll tell Daddy you're a shoplifter!"

Nicole froze a few seconds and grabbed at the jewelry bag. "Give me that."

"Give me my letters." She removed a few of Nicole's favorite pieces and tossed the bag on the floor.

Nicole lifted her mattress and removed a stack of letters. "Here!" She threw them at Lisa's feet."

"Put them in my hand!" Lisa ordered.

Mumbling, Nicole placed them in her hand. Lisa examined the flaps. One was open. She pulled the page out and scanned the sheet.

Darling S. F, I can't wait for you to fuck me again.

"Give me my jewelry." Nicole hissed.

"I'm keeping these for insurance." Lisa dangled the tiny hoops in Nicole's face. "Remember!" She warned. "I go down! You go down!"

Saturday, October 17, 1981

Early that morning, Lisa sat in the kitchen drinking orange juice and heard the night nurse, Mrs. Lincoln, briefing the day nurse, Mrs. Glenn.

"How did she sleep?" Mrs. Glenn asked.

"Pretty good but she woke up asking about her baby."

Lisa's interest peaked at the mention of a baby. She cracked the door, listening.

"That's something new," Nurse Glenn said.

"If she asks about him again," Mrs. Lincoln said. "Say he's sleeping, that seems to satisfy her."

"Okay."

"I had to give her a sedative when it started storming," Mrs. Lincoln said. "I've never seen anybody so afraid of thunder."

"Me neither," Mrs. Glenn said. "I hope it doesn't storm today. I don't think my nerves could stand that squalling."

"It's supposed to stop raining," Mrs. Lincoln said.

"Good," Mrs. Glenn said. "Leora's moods change with the wind, one minute she's sweet as pie: the next the old bitch is screeching and calling me a whore."

"Now Darlene you—"

"You can't call my grandmother an old bitch!" Lisa charged from the kitchen, sloshing orange juice over the floor.

Both women jumped, surprised.

"Uh...uh." Darlene Glenn's face drained the same color of her uniform then went beet red.

"You're an angel of mercy," Lisa ranted. "You should be ashamed. You're suppose to help people not say unkind things about a sweet old woman."

"I'm...sorry!" Nurse Glenn stared bug eyed at Lisa.

"Settle down, Miss." Mary Lincoln's mahogany face was ashen. She stepped between Lisa and her colleague. Lisa slipped around her and continued her tirade.

"What's going on here?" Richard came down the stairs tying the fringed sash of his robe.

Lisa pointed at Mrs. Glenn. "She called my grandmother an old bitch."

"Dr. Bennett, I'm sorry, I...I...I didn't mean—"

"Mrs. Glenn," Richard said. "Perhaps you should go."

She pursed her thin lips and went silently to the hall closet. Richard and Lisa watched her get her coat and purse and drive away.

"Dr. Bennett." Mrs. Lincoln put on her coat and took her purse off the shelf. "I wish I could stay. My husband's on the road and I don't have anyone to keep the kids." She took out her keys. "I'm sorry about what happened."

"That's okay, Mary. We'll get along fine, you go ahead."

"Thank you, Doctor." She smiled shyly and left.

Where can I find another nurse on such short notice? Maybe Emily will help. Richard promptly discarded that idea. In the time Leora had been in their home, Emily hadn't spoken to her. She hadn't even looked at her.

"Today I go in there and demand to know why she hates me!" She'd said the first week. Now, she never mentioned confronting Leora at all.

"How could a nurse say something so cruel?" Lisa asked.

"People sometimes say unkind things, Kiddy Widdy."

"I won't let anyone say unkind things about my grandmother!"

"Good for you." Richard half-listened and called the nursing exchange. Every nurse they employed had an assignment.

"Daddy, I can help with Leora until you can get somebody."

"Its too much work. You'd have to lift her, change her dressings."

"I can do it. Give me a chance."

He looked at her eager face. This was the first time since the abortion she seemed interested in doing anything.

Should I give her a try? Naw. She'll puke her guts out the first time she sees Leora's decubitus even if it is almost healed.

"I don't think so," he said.

"Plee...eeze, Daddy. I can do it."

"Do you think you can?"

"Of course." Elaborate plans of how to help Leora ran through her mind.

"She'll need a bath," he said. "I can give her her medication."

"I can do all of that."

"Are you sure?"

"Of course."

"Looks like it's me and you, kid." Richard hugged Lisa. "I'm going to shower and change. You do the same and we'll meet outside Leora's room at say." He looked at the grandfather clock. "Eight."

"Okay." Lisa shoved the dripping glass in his hand and ran up the stairs.

"Spare me, Lord." He noticed the orange juice trail and went to get the mop.

At eight sharp, Richard waited for Lisa outside Leora's room. At five after, he decided she had made an empty promise and knocked.

"I'm trying to sleep." Leora sounded angry. "What is it?"

"Good morning." He looked around the door. "How're you feeling?"

"Who the hell are you?" Leora clicked on the table lamp, scowling.

This can't be the same woman who had sat quietly with a black scarf tied over her eyes until Junior and I got the drapes hung.

"I'm Dr. Bennett."

"What kind of hospital is this where stupid little children can come in my room and harass me?"

"Children were harassing you?"

"They stood there." She pointed to the bed foot. "And called me granny."

"Let me assure you, it won't happen again."

"It had better not. If I had grandchildren, they'd call me grandmàmà."

"I'm going to help you get washed, now," he said.

"Oh...no...you...are...not!" Leora pulled the blanket to her chin. "Don't you dare touch me!"

"I won't hurt you," he said gently, spreading his hands. "After I get you washed up, I'll get your breakfast." He walked toward the bed.

"Rape! Rape! Ra-a-aape!" Leora grabbed the lamp like a baseball bat.

"Okay." He headed out. "I'm leaving...I'm leaving."

"Don't leave me, Buddy." She begged. "Please don't leave me."

The pity in her voice grabbed at his heart. He turned to assure her he wouldn't leave, but the moment had passed.

"Who the hell are you?" she asked angrily. "Where's my baby? Where have you put my baby?"

"Baby," he said at a loss for words.

"Your baby is sleeping." Lisa came in dressed all in white.

"He cried all night," Leora said.

"I know," Lisa said then whispered to her father. "Sorry I'm late. I wanted to look as professional as possible."

"And you certainly do."

"Thank you," she said. "Excuse me. I need to get Leora washed up."

"Of course." Richard left glad to turn this chameleon over to her.

"Who are you?" Leora squinted at Lisa and put on her glasses. "You look very familiar."

Lisa could only stare at the deep resemblance. *If this is how I'll look when I'm as old as Leora, a little make-up and I'll be kicking.*

"Good morning, I'm Lisa."

Maple mentioned that name a long time ago, but I can't remember why.

"Who're your people?"

"The Bennetts."

"I don't know any Bennetts," she said.

"That's okay. What should I call you?"

"By my name of course, Leora."

"Okay, Leora." Lisa worked at lowering the safety rail.

"You look too young to be a nurse."

"I'm in training," Lisa lied. "Are you ready to use it?"

"Use what?"

"You know, the bathroom, the toilet?"

"Absolutely bursting," Leora said. "How long have you been in training, you stupid girl, push it there." She pointed to a button on the side.

"Oh."

Lisa slid the rail below the mattress. She helped Leora into a robe and house-shoes and got her to her feet, swaying.

"Don't let me fall!" She clutched Lisa's arm. "Don't let me fall!"

"I won't." Lisa walked her to the bathroom and got her on the stool.

"Whe-e-e-w!" Leora said after she finished.

She maneuvered herself to the sink and drained the tepid water Lisa ran and refilled it with steaming hot. She used the pink cloth to wash her face, under her arms and around her breasts. She hung the rag on the rack.

"Where's my booty rag?"

"Booty rag?" Lisa looked puzzled.

"This is my face rag." Leora snatched the pink cloth and shook it in Lisa's face. "I use this to wash my face, now I need my booty rag to wash my booty!"

"You use a face rag and a booty rag?" Lisa wanted to howl.

This is the funniest thing I've ever heard.

"And what's wrong with that?" Leora huffed.

"Nothing." She opened the cabinet and handed her a yellow rag.

Leora finished her wash. Lisa helped her into a clean gown and back to bed.

"I'm going for your breakfast. Be right back."

"Hurry up. I'm starving."

Emily put two sausage patties on a plate with grits and scrambled eggs. She set the plate on a tray with buttered toast, orange juice, coffee and a bowl of strawberries.

"Could you help with, Leora, today?" Richard asked her anyway.

"I'm not ready," Emily said anxiously. "I can't."

"Okay, okay," he said. "Lisa and I can manage."

"Lisa's helping you with Leora?" Emily said surprised.

"Uh huh. She's getting her washed up now."

"I'm surprised she wants to help."

"Me too. She seemed so eager, I thought I'd let her give it a try." He picked up the tray.

"I'm sorry," Emily said. "I'm just not ready."

"It's okay." He reassured her with a kiss. "We'll manage."

Richard met Lisa coming down the hall.

"How's it going?" he asked.

"Just fine." She took the tray and returned to Leora's room. "Here's your breakfast," she said cheerfully and set it on the table across the bed.

Leora attacked the food and ate everything except a two-inch square of toast. That she left for manners.

"Why is there no lipstick on this napkin?" She blotted her mouth on the paper napkin again.

"You're not wearing any."

"Not wearing any!" She declared. "I always wear lipstick and you get it this instant."

"Where is it?" Lisa opened the dresser drawers. "I don't see any."

"I want my lipstick!" Leora slammed her fists on the table, making the dishes dance a startled jig. "I want my lipstick!"

"Let me get this out of your way." Lisa set the tray by the door.

"I feel naked without my make-up." Leora traced her lips with her finger. "I want to look glamorous."

"Wait one minute!" Lisa ran out and returned thirty seconds later with a gym bag full of cosmetics.

"My...my...my." Leora couldn't contain her joy at the array before her. She unscrewed lipstick after lipstick and smeared a tiny line on the inside of her wrist before she settled on an orangey-red called Poppy. She lifted the table mirror and applied the color, transforming her face from pale to radiant.

"Put this on." She handed Lisa a bottle of nail polish called Chili.

Lisa pulled out a manicure kit and filed her ragged nails.

"Your hair is lovely." Leora touched Lisa's curls.

"Thank you."

"Can you do something with mine?"

Lisa felt the dry, brittle thatch.

Her hair needs a lot of work, but I'll try.

"I wish I had my books." Leora said.

"What books?"

"My journals."

"You keep journals? I got a diary for my birthday, but I haven't used it yet."

"I keep all my secrets in my journals." Leora leaned over, whispering.

"You do?" Lisa whispered back. "That's good."

"You should keep your secrets in a journal."

"I should?"

"My journals are in a secret room. No one will ever find them."

"They are?"

"Yes. They are."

Lisa finished her nails and combed the tangles from her hair.

"Scratch it for me," Leora said.

Lisa parted the damaged strands with a small toothed comb and scratched.

Leora moaned. "I haven't had my head stratched since Maple used to do it."

"How do you like it?" Lisa held the mirror for her make-up and limp pageboy.

"I like it." Leora smiled. "I look almost like my old self."

"You look lovely."

"I do, don't I?"

Richard knocked and came hesitantly in the room.

"Leora," he said. "How're you feeling?"

"Wonderful young man." She replied. "And yourself?"

"I'm fine, thank you."

She seemed to not remember him from earlier.

"How about we go outside?" he said.

"I can't," Leora said. "The light hurts my eyes."

"I made you something special to stop that."

"The light won't hurt my eyes?" she asked doubtfully.

"No, it won't." Richard placed the sun guard over her glasses.

"Kiddy Widdy. Slowly open the drapes, please."

Lisa gradually drew them back and let in the sun.

"Does the light hurt your eyes?" he asked.

Leora looked into the autumn sky.

"No, young man, not at all."

"Very good," he said pleased to have done something to help her.

"Do you want to go outside for some fresh air?" Lisa asked.

"I believe I do." Leora climbed into the wheelchair.

Lisa helped her into a sweater and tucked a throw around her legs.

"Don't keep her out too long, Kiddy Widdy."

"I won't." Lisa picked up a book and pushed her onto the deck. "O-oh, the woods are so-o-o beautiful."

"Describe them to me?"

"The sweet gums are bright red. The blackjack oaks are deep yellow next to a grove of bronze. Orange, maroon and russet trees are scattered over the hill to the horizon, mingled with dark green pines."

"I wish I could see it."

"I wish you could, too," Lisa said. "Shall I read to you?"

"Yes."

Lisa began *In The Morning*.

"My old friend, Paul Laurence Dunbar." Leora recited the poem by heart. Halfway through, she began to cry.

"What's wrong?" Lisa asked.

"I miss my friend, Maple. I haven't seen her in such a long time."

Should I tell her Maple Honey is dead?

Lisa held her trembling shoulders until the pitiful sobs stopped.

"I'll see if I can find out where she is." Lisa dried her eyes. "Okay?"

"Yes, please do," Leora said. "Thank you."

Lisa kissed her cheek.

"Why did you do that?" Leora smiled and touched the spot.

"Because I love you."

"You love me?"

"Yes," Lisa said. "I do."

"If you love me, you'll never leave me, will you?"

"Never!" Lisa clutched her cold hands. "Never!"

"Who are you?" Leora snatched free. "What do you want?"

"Nothing," Lisa said. "It's time for your lunch."

"Good." Leora whispered. "These people don't feed me."

"Don't worry," Lisa said. "I'll make sure you get fed."

Lisa wheeled Leora in and closed the drapes. She got her in bed and removed the sun guard. After lunch, Leora took a nap and woke up testy.

"Where're my journals?"

"I don't know."

"Look for them you, silly goose! Look for them!"

Lisa left her ranting and returned with her red diary and a ballpoint pen.

"It's about time, you simpleton!" Leora snatched the book and pen and began to write. "I can't use this!" She screeched. "This is blue."

"What's wrong with it?" Lisa asked.

"This is blue! I only use red!" She threw the pen across the room.

Lisa ran out in search of a red pen. Michelle had one, but wouldn't part with it until Lisa gave her a bottle of nail polish.

"Here." Lisa handed the pen to Leora.

"It had better be red!"

"It's red, it's red," Lisa said. "Try it and see."

Leora twirled the pen in her palm and formed a red dot.

"That's more like it." She turned to page one and began to write. Ten minutes later, she nodded off. Lisa covered her up and couldn't help noticing the open diary filled with one continuous line of the letter e. She flipped through the pages and found one legible entry.

Month, date, year unknown. I am in a strange hospital. Children wander in and out. They won't bring me my baby and don't feed me. How long will I have to stay before Maple comes to take me home?

Lisa showed it to her father.

"Leora has Alzheimer's disease." He explained. "Her mind comes and goes. That's why one minute she can write so you can read it, the next its scribble scrabble."

"Will she get any better?"

"No," he said.

"Will she get worse?"

"Yes, she probably will."

"I'll love her any way," she said ardently.

"Good for you, Kiddy Widdy. Good for you."

How ironic it is that the change in Lisa is a direct result of the woman Emily hates most in the world.

Friday, November 6, 1981

Lisa picked up the letter addressed to her in an unfamiliar hand. Postmarked in Cambridge, Massachusetts, it had no return address.

Sean must really think I'm stupid.

She threw it on the table for her mother to dispose of like the others and went in the kitchen. Lisa usually avoided her pregnant mother, but felt she had put off too long telling her about Leora.

"Mommy?"

Emily whirled around. Lisa hadn't spoken one word to her since her outburst the day she came from the hospital.

"Yes?"

"Leora was crying and asking about Maple Honey."

"Did you tell her she was dead?" She spooned string beans on a plate.

"No," Lisa said. "Should I have?"

"No. I don't think we should tell her yet."

"Okay." Lisa turned to go and turned back. "Mommy?"

"Yes, sweetie."

"There's no secret room in Leora's house...is there?"

The plate fell splattering potatoes, string beans and meat loaf over the floor.

"Secret room?" Emily's voice shook. "Who said there was a secret room?"

"Leora."

"Where? Where?" Her nails dug into Lisa's shoulders.

"Mommy!" She pulled away. "You're hurting me."

"I'm sorry...I'm sorry." Emily tried to massage away the pain. "What did Leora say? What did she say?"

"She said she had a secret room in a closet."

"What closet?" Emily reached for her again.

Lisa backed up, rubbing her shoulders. "I don't know."

"Think, Lisa, think!" Emily looked maniacal. "What else did she say about the secret room?"

"Nothing. She just said she had a secret room in a closet."

Emily slumped into a chair.

"Are you okay?" Lisa sounded worried. "Are you okay?"

"I'm okay. Are you sure that's all she said?"

"I'm positive."

Emily struggled up and tried to clean the mess. Lisa saw how difficult it was for her and stooped to pick up the broken plate.

"I'll do it," she said.

"Thank you, sweetie." Emily sat down. "Don't cut yourself."

"I won't."

"Tell me everything Leora said no matter how silly it sounds."

Lisa cleaned the floor and repeated Leora's words verbatim.

"That's everything she said?" Emily asked finally.

"That's everything she said. Can I go now?"

"Yes."

Lisa pushed through the swinging door then came back in.

"Mommy," she said.

Emily turned, hoping she had more information.

"Yes."

"Do you want to go shopping tomorrow?"

How I've longed to hear her ask me that question.

"Maybe next Saturday," Emily said. "I can't tomorrow."

Tomorrow I'm going to Lacewell and I'm not leaving Leora's house until I find the secret room.

35

Emily scribbled Richard a note and left before daybreak in the rain. By the time she reached Lacewell, the rain had stopped and the sun shone weakly through the clouds.

Emily cruised downtown amazed at how much the city had changed in twenty years. She went left onto Mango Street. It had new liquor stores and juke joints, but drug addicts replaced winos sprawled on the sidewalk. She turned on Nash Avenue. The houses began to change for the better. By the time she reached Reese Street, they were grand indeed.

Leora's house occupied an acre corner lot beneath giant oak trees. White posts supported a wide planked porch filled with wicker chairs. Forest green shutters eight-foot tall covered Palladian windows.

Emily pulled in the backyard, cracking acorns beneath the tires. She got the beam light from the trunk. She stopped at Maple Honey's garden blanketed with kudzu. Before she knew it, she was snatching angrily at the dry vines.

"Stop stalling!" She headed for the house, but stopped again to admire the rose bushes, once no higher than her knee now reached to the chimney top.

Emily marched up steps lined with pots of dead flowers, stuck the key in the lock, yet hesitated, turning it.

Maybe I don't need to know. Maybe I was bad.
Emily had had this thought many times.
If Leora hates me so much, I must have done something to deserve it.
"You're stalling again." She turned the key before she lost her nerve.

The door creaked open. Spider webs thick as Spanish moss swayed above. Rat sized fuzz balls dashed over the thick carpet of dust and hid in the shadows.

Emily clicked on the beam and strode up the steps to Leora's room. She played the light around, startling herself and the baby when it reflected her image off a huge, round mirror.

"Did Mommy scare you?" She rubbed her stomach. "Go back to sleep."

Emily pulled the blue velvet drapes back on both windows. A dust shower set her sneezing and the baby on another kicking spree.

Up went the linen shades. Sunshine slotted through the shutters, caressing crystal perfume bottles lining the dresser. A few tried to sparkle beneath dusty coats and managed to throw rainbows on the ceiling. She opened a chifforobe drawer. Discarded rouges, lipsticks and powders sat in neat stacks. Other drawers held fancy underwear in satin, lace and silk. The nightstand held thirteen fountain pens, ten bottles of red ink, and five boxes of blue stationery with the initials LTD.

The strong odor of mothballs seeped from the bedroom converted into a closet. Emily's stomach churned. She opened the door and stepped in. Clothes hung on thick wooden dowels in heavy plastic bags. Leora arranged her clothes by color gradation. The greens ranged from celery to forest. The yellows from lemon to mustard, the blues from sky to navy and so on with the oranges, reds and purples. Emily's hand rippled across the bags and unzipped one. She lifted out a blue fox pelt with brown glass eyes and tossed it over her shoulder like Maple Honey used to do.

Overhead, fifty or so hatboxes occupied double shelves. She inspected them all, stopping occasionally to try on a few.

"Stop it!" Emily scolded herself. "Get back to work."

Rap...rap...rap. She knocked around the wall, trying to distinguish hollow from solid. Each knock sounded like the last.

A brown chest in the corner caught Emily's eye. Locked, she pried it open with a pair of pinking shears and lifted the squeaky lid. She set the light on the corner and aimed the beam on the contents inside. A soft brown package tied with string. A large white box crushed on one side and an upside down jewelry box with Made in Hungary and *Someone To Watch Over Me* etched on a square copper plate. She removed it and pulled out a red velvet lined drawer. Tinny notes played a few seconds then stopped. She opened another drawer. A strand of pearls lay in a coil. They looked expensive. Another compartment held two gold rings, one a dainty circle, the other a heavy band. The white box contained a lace and satin wedding gown of ivory cream, three limp crinolines and a veil made with yards and yards of tulle trimmed with silk ribbons.

Was Leora married? I can remember no husband. Was she jilted?

Only Leora knew for sure and from what Richard said, her mind leaned closer to total senility each day.

A bundle of letters tied with frazzled pink ribbon lay to one side. The top envelope, addressed to Mr. Buddy Boyd in Gary, Indiana had the endorsement refused, return to sender across the face. A faded maroon hand pointed to a return address in Chicago.

Richard said Leora called him Buddy once. Is this the same man?

Emily picked out the tight knots and flipped through the letters. All were addressed to Buddy Boyd, from July of 1945 through October of 1946.

Why did he refuse them?

Emily felt awful opening someone else's mail, even Leora's, but ripped the envelope down the side and removed the solitary sheet.

July 23, 1945

Buddy My Dearest, Please forgive me!

Love always,

Leora

Emily randomly opened another letter, then another. They all made the same appeal. She felt tremendous gratification, knowing Leora had begged forgiveness of someone just as she had begged it of her. Emily returned the letters and untied the soft parcel. It contained a sky blue baby sweater, matching booties and cap stuffed with ringlets of black hair.

Did Leora have another child?

Richard said she babbled constantly about a baby boy. Emily retied the bundle and laid it in the chest with a loving pat. She noticed the tarnished silver frame under the box and pulled it out. Leora gazed at her from a black and white photo with clear eyes and a half smile. She looked to be in her twenties and had signed it 'To Buddy, From Sugar'. Emily put it aside to give to Lisa. She'd be pleased to have a picture of Leora when she was young.

Emily pulled out a manila envelope with 'important papers' scrawled on the front. She unwound a red string from a brown button and pulled out the top page. It was the deed to Leora's house. Emily spied a red book crammed on the side of the chest. She dropped the envelope and snatched up the book, rippling the pages. All were blank. Disappointed, she closed the lid and did not notice the envelope on the floor until she started out. Instead of returning it to the chest, she set it with the photo to go in her bag. Satisfied she had searched Leora's room thoroughly, she drew the shades, yanked the drapes across the windows, restoring it to its original state of gloom.

With eyes watering, Emily stepped in Maple Honey's room and began the search. She found nothing there or in her old room. The bathroom came up a blank, as did her former prison, the attic.

Emily searched downstairs until the only place left to look was the kitchen. She pushed back the gingham curtains for more light. Storm clouds covered the sky. Frustrated, hungry, cold and exhausted she collapsed in a dusty chair and scanned the room. A door led to the back porch. A door led to the hall. A door led to the dining room. The stove, refrigerator and sink covered one wall. Dark oak cabinets took up everything else. There was no space for a secret room.

Sighing, Emily pulled herself from the chair and picked up the beam. Just as she started down the back steps, it hit her. Pauline had a closet off her kitchen. Leora's kitchen was identical to Pauline's. Where was Leora's closet? She returned to the kitchen, visualizing herself coming in Pauline's back door. The counter sat to the left, the closet to the right. She looked right and groaned. A floor to ceiling built-in cabinet occupied that space.

Emily opened both doors. Coffee, flour, and sugar sat at eye level in plastic containers. Quart jars of string beans, tomatoes and corn sat one shelf up with pickled peaches and pints of pear preserves. Boxes of pasta and assorted cans set in neat rows on the shelf below. She rapped a few spots in the back. Each one sounded solid. She pulled on the frame. It stood firm. She got clumsily to her knees and shined the failing light under the kick plate. She stood precariously on the top step of the stool to reach the highest shelf and knew immediately, Maple Honey never looked up here. Dust eight inches thick set her sneezing again and the baby kicking.

Emily's fingers probed everywhere. They touched what felt like a toggle switch on the far side of the cabinet. She pulled it forward.

Is that a click?

She pulled forward again. Nothing. She pushed to the left. Nothing. She pushed to the right. Nothing. She pushed back. Nothing. Discouraged, she climbed down and pulled on the doors to start over. The entire unit swung away from the wall and nearly knocked her down. She jumped back with a yelp, staring with disbelief at the dark, rectangular opening criss-crossed with spider webs.

Emily picked up the beam with a shaky hand and aimed it in the room. The first thing the fading light hit was an opened book, written in red ink.

Emily batted the cobwebs down and went inside. Red leather journals stood like soldiers with the years 1936 through 1980 on their spines. Emily took 1980 down and blew the dust off Leora's name stamped in gold. She rifled the empty pages, but she found an entry dated December 3.

Maple has lost so much weight. She pretends she's dieting, but I know better. She has always been the strong one and taken care of me. Now it is time for me to be strong and take care of her.

Tears ran down Emily's face. Maple Honey was sick last year and never said one word. She set the book on the shelf. A cyclone of swirling dust started her sneezing. She returned to the hall closet for cleaning supplies. Armed with two rags, she didn't stop until the journals set on the kitchen table dust free. Emily knew she wouldn't be able to rest if she didn't at least take one more peek. She picked up a book labeled 1951 and flipped through the pages.

Emily was almost killed today.

She flipped back and read the entry for April 17.

Emily was almost killed today. I saw the car coming before she slid down the bank and did nothing to stop her. May God forgive me.

"O-o-h." Emily moaned at the hurtful information. She knew Leora hated her but not until this moment did she suspect, she wanted her dead. Too distressed to read more, she loaded the books in the trunk and headed home.

What can this child I carry do bad enough for me to want him dead? Nothing. Absolutely nothing

36

Storm clouds chased Emily down the highway, dropping water down the windshield almost faster than the wipers could flick it away. She crawled along in a man-made mist created by speeding cars and semi-trucks until she spotted the Panola Road exit. Relieved, she hurried up the ramp glad to know she would be home soon.

Emily pulled to the front door of her dark house and unloaded the trunk. By the time she set the last journal on the shelf in the turret room, she was soaked through. Worn out, she went to bed, leaving her family to fend for themselves.

Sunday, November 8, 1981

At one a.m., Emily awoke achy and feverish. She took two cold tablets and returned to bed only to toss and turn, thinking of the awful words Leora had written.

Do I really want to know more?

Her answer was to slip from bed and make her way to the turret room. There she pulled down the first journal and shivering more from dread than chills, wrapped herself in a wool throw, curled up on the sofa and began to read.

November 10, 1936

Today I turned fifteen. I got so many lovely gifts. Mona gave me a bottle of real perfume called Joyous. It's simply divine. Daddy said I'm too young to wear real perfume. He gave me a silver vanity set. I won't mind giving my hair one hundred strokes each night with this lovely brush. Uncle Campbell gave me an ermine muff. It's so soft against my skin. Aunt Emily gave me the best present of all. She gave me you, dear journal. I hate my name but it looked so elegant printed in gold on your smooth, red leather. I love the fountain pen and simply adore the blood red ink.

Aunt Emily said I needed some place to keep my secret thoughts. Mona said I'm too young to have secret thoughts. She wants to keep me a baby, but I have news for her. Last week after choir practice, I let Levi Jacque suck my titties. I got so hot and quivery. He said my nipples are so big. Levi's thingy got so hard. I felt it through my clothes. I let him put his hand under my skirt, but when he touched my coochie, I made him stop. Mona said I could have a baby if I let a boy touch my coochie. I don't quite understand how that works and when I asked her about it, she got all red in the face and told me to keep my dress down. When I asked Daddy, he said the same thing. I let Levi kiss me and he did such a disgusting thing. He stuck his tongue in my mouth. It was too slobbery for words. I might take a chance on having a baby and let Levi feel my coochie, but I sure won't let him kiss me ever again.

Against her will, Emily smiled at Leora's innocence.

November 11, 1936

Here is another secret, Journal. I love Aunt Emily and Uncle Campbell more than I love Mona and Daddy. Everybody at school thinks it's swell to have a doctor for a father and a nurse for a mother, but let me tell you, it is not. They never have time for me. Daddy is always at the hospital and Mona is always doing things with her sorority. I stay with Aunt Emily and Uncle Campbell most of the time. They live in a gorgeous house on Reese Street. Mona is jealous because Aunt Emily and Uncle Campbell are rich. If I had a sister, I'd never be jealous of her. Mona says Aunt Emily is black. She's not really black, like our skillet, but a pretty teacake brown. She wears Joyous perfume, too and always smells like a rose garden. Mona said Aunt Emily may have money, but she can't do a goddamn thing with it. She can't go in the front door of the Varsity for a sandwich, or the Colonial Hotel for a quiet drink. Sometimes Mona and I pass for white. Last month we took the train to Chicago. We stayed at that grand hotel on Michigan Avenue, shopped at the most elegant stores, dined at the finest restaurants and even sailed on Lake Michigan on a yacht. We had a glorious time. When we got home, Daddy called us a disgrace to the Negro race. I cried all night.

November 12, 1936
Mona and Daddy had the biggest fight. It wasn't screaming back and forth as usual. It was much worse. Daddy slapped Mona and called her a slut. She cracked him on the head with the poker and told him to go fuck his black whore! Daddy moved out. I can't stop crying.

November 15, 1936
Mona cries all the time, too. I don't know if its because she wants Daddy back or because she has to get a job. Daddy called to ask about me. I begged him to come home. I told him how much Mona missed him and wanted him back. 'This is grown up business you can't fix,' he said. He sounded so sad. I know he loves Mona and I know Mona loves him. I'll never stop until I get them back together.

December 20, 1936
Mona wants to leave Lacewell. She said this place holds too many unhappy memories. I think its because she always runs into Daddy and his girlfriend, Della B. Mona said she couldn't understand how Daddy could leave her and take up with somebody so short, fat, ugly and black.

Raindrops pelted the windows. Lightning lit the sky. A sonic boom of thunder cracked outside the French doors. Emily jumped startled and rubbed her stomach to soothe the kicking baby.

"Go back to sleep, little one. Go back to sleep."
She got up to close the blinds against the intense flashes, wishing she could deaden the violent rumbles, too. Before she snuggled under the throw again, she pulled down the journal for 1938 and rifled the pages. *Daddy and Della B. got married* caught her eye. She stopped to read.

June 23, 1938
Daddy and Della B. got married today. Daddy invited me. I wanted to go but Mona carried on so, I told her I wouldn't, but the minute she left with her girl friends, I caught a taxi across town to Lacy Acres. Its a section of precious little white houses trimmed in blue, black or green paint. Mona said Lacy Acres is appropriate for Della B., small and cheap. I was prepared to hate Della B.

as much as Mona did but once I met her, I couldn't. She's so nice and cute. She's nine years older than me and is more like a big sister than a stepmother. She's smart and talented. She's a nurse at the hospital where Daddy works. She can really play the piano.

August 11, 1938
Della B. is going to have a baby. My cousin, Maple, came to help. She is four years older than me and the big sister I always wanted.

Emily leafed forward.
October 27, 1938
Della B. lost our baby and almost died. Everybody is sad except Mona. She said she could at least give Daddy a baby which is more than Miss Blackberry could do. I wanted to smack her face.

Emily put 1938 back and pulled down 1942.

January 9, 1942
Mona and I moved to Chicago. The first thing she bought me was a switch-blade knife for protection from the wolves.

July 1, 1942
I got a promotion at work and moved from the steno pool to Mr. Warren's office. I'm so glad Mona made me practice my typing and shorthand. Mona works the cosmetic counter at Marshall Field's. She adores her job. She adores this city. She adores this man named Irving Coven and he adores her. He owns furniture stores all over. They're talking about getting married. I hope they do. It will make Mona so happy. I'm dating a guy at work named Hans Voss. Hans is okay but I'm still looking for the man who will set my soul on fire.

Emily leafed ahead.

August 8, 1942
My friend, Grace Oleski, and I go to a jazz club on the Southside. Before we get in the door, Negro men of every size, shape and color either want to buy us drinks, dance with us or do us. We declined all offers and sat down. Pouting women in tight satin dresses rolled their eyes at us like we were there to steal their men. Hell! We came to listen to some jazz. I don't want any static, but one big, burly individual refused to let me alone. No, thank you, I don't want to

dance, I told him over and over. He jerked me from the chair and pulled me on the dance floor. I reached in my bosom for Switchie Mae. With a flick of my wrist, she jumped open like she's part of my hand. The oohs from the crowd told me I was impressive. Get your hands off me, you son of a bitch! I said in my most threatening voice. I caught him totally off guard. He let me go so fast, I almost fell. I wanted to laugh like everybody else, but I don't and keep my eyes on him until he skulked to the men's room with his tail between his legs. I grabbed Grace's trembling hand and we backed out of the place like bank robbers. Grace wanted to go home. I told her we came to hear some jazz and by God that's what we were going to do. We walked down Sixty-third. The mellowest saxophone flowed from Lou's Jazz Palace. We walked in. All conversation stopped. Before we can take our seats, a new herd of men stampeded us with offers of drinks, dance and dick. No! No! No! We said until they finally got the message and I got to concentrate on the hepcat whaling the sax. My! My! My! Talk about a good looking colored man! He was one. Processed hair fell in thick black waves from his luscious chocolate angel face. He is out of this world in an orange zoot suit with a gold watch chain past his knees. This vision held me captive with such beautiful, hazel bedroom eyes, I could hardly breathe. He finished the set and stepped off the stage with his hand out to me. 'May I have this dance?' He asked politely. I molded myself against his tall, slim body and spent the evening dancing with my head on his shoulder. His name is Orlando Douglas—

Emily stopped reading. Is Orlando Douglas my father?

—and he wants to see me again. I told him I'd be back next week. I definitely want to see him.

August 30, 1942
I went to Lou's last night. The people don't stop talking anymore, when I come in. I climbed on a barstool and ordered a pink lady. Orlando sat with a woman at a table in the corner. When he saw me, he told her to get lost. He said it just like that 'get lost.' She rolled her eyes at me and marched to the far end of the bar. Orlando escorted me to his big black Cadillac and took me by his friend Smoky Jones' house. I know Orlando wanted to show off his white girl and I don't disappoint. I pranced and preened and removed hair from my eyes with a toss of my head. I asked for a cigarette. Orlando gave me this funny looking, little crooked, hand rolled thing. He said to inhale deep and hold the smoke as long as I can. I did and started coughing so badly I don't think I'd ever stop.

He laughed and said it would get better, and it did. Soon, I'm floating on a cloud and so hungry I could eat a cow. I put a bowl of peanuts on my lap and didn't stop until I ate every last one.
We left when I started laughing and couldn't stop. I wanted more reefer. Reefer is what they called that little cigarette. Orlando won't let me smoke in his car. He said I might burn holes in the leather upholstery. I'm still hungry. He bought rib dinners and drinks, but I couldn't eat a bite until we got to his place. He doesn't want food stains in his precious car. We walked up three flights to one dingy room. He cooked on a hot plate. The bathroom is down the hall. I'm surprised a musician of his caliber lived like this. His car looked better than this dump. There are no chairs. The only place to sit is on the bed and I think Orlando had it that way on purpose because after we ate and smoked another reefer he pushed me back on the linty blanket and kissed me until I lost my mind. His hands ran over my breasts and under my dress, touching all my secret places. He made me have feelings in places I never—

Emily stopped reading embarrassed to know the intimate details of Leora and Orlando's love affair.

"Should I skip over this part?" She answered her own question by promptly returning to the page.

—thought I had feelings. Before I knew what happened, I'm naked as a plucked chicken screaming Fuck me! Fuck me! Fuck me! (My cheeks flame with shame even as I write this) Orlando pushed his thingy in me and I'm in heaven for forty-eight hours straight. He was the best I've ever seen.

September 2, 1942
Mona and I had a big fight when I got home. You should be concentrating on Hans, she said. I don't want Hans, I screamed. I want Orlando. What can Orlando give you except a house full of pickaninnies? I'm grown, I told her. You won't ruin my life the way you ruined Daddy's. She slapped me. I slapped her back. She told me to get out. I can't believe she'd put me in the street. I packed a few things and go to work. The only person who asked why I have a suitcase at my desk is snoopy Hortense Weiss. After I told her to go to hell, no one else mentioned my suitcase. I asked Grace if I could stay with her but her house was filled with three nieces and a sister who'd left her husband. The only other person I know to ask is Orlando. I called him. He said come ahead. I rushed home to pack before Mona got off from work and sent them to his place in two taxicabs. He was most upset. My things are everywhere except on the bed. I undressed and crawled on the sheet, he began to smile. I love his smile.

September 21, 1942
Orlando and I moved to a bigger apartment. It has a living room, a bedroom,
a kitchen and a real bath. It overlooked the alley but it's still better than where
we were. I'm fixing it up so cute. The rent is a little steep, but I expect another
raise soon and Orlando's is really starting to get noticed. He has an audition
with Cab Calloway coming up. We're getting married as soon he joins a big
band. I hope it's soon. I feel like a whore, living in sin.

October 9, 1942
Orlando missed the Cab Calloway audition and got fired from Lou's. You're
a great musician. You'll get a gig soon. I told him and remind him I have my
job. He kissed me and smiled. I love his smile.

November 2, 1942
I woke up so sick, I barely made it to the bathroom. If I'm expecting, I know
we'll be married soon.

November 16, 1942
I'm definitely expecting. Our baby is due around the twenty-fifth of April. Our
wedding is set for the Saturday before Christmas. I bought such lovely material
for my wedding gown. I wanted to tell Mona but I know what she will say, so
I kept it to myself.

Monday, November 9, 1981

Up at six thirty, Emily's throat felt like she had eaten glass. She got Richard off
to work by seven thirty. By eight, the girls were off to school. At nine, she
canceled her appointment with Dr. Chambers then called Nora. As soon as she
turned on the dishwasher and took something out for dinner, she returned to the
turret room to read.

December 15, 1942
Mona got my address from Grace and brought me Christmas presents. She
wanted me to move back. I'm getting married. I told her. I'm expecting a child.
Your life is ruined, she screamed. It's my life. I screamed back. I'm not going
to pass for white anymore. I'm going to tell Orlando the truth. I'm going to tell
him I'm colored. She begged me not to tell him. You'll spoil it for yourself if
you do. He thinks you're something special, out of his league. What will

happen when he finds out your blood is as black as his? He loves me! Not my skin color! If you have to tell him, she said, at least wait until after you're married. No! I told her. He loves me. I'm telling him tonight.

December 16, 1942
Mona was right. I shouldn't have told Orlando, not even after we married, not ever. He called me such ugly names. I tried to talk to him but he packed his clothes and left.

December 30, 1942
Orlando is still not back. I'm so worried. I called Smoky. He said he hasn't seen him either. I checked the hospitals with no luck. I guess that's a good sign. If I could just talk to him, I know I can make him understand.

Emily pulled down 1943.

January 4, 1943
I lost my job today. More to the point, I got fired. When I walked in, everybody in the office stopped working to watch me. Before I could sit down, my supervisor, Mr. Trueborn, called me in his office. You can no longer work here. He sneered at me like I was something filthy under his shoe. I asked why. 'We don't hire coloreds.' I knew immediately this was Orlando's doing. I walked out of his office into a buzz of talk. A few former co-workers cursed me. Some looked sad. I bit my lip to keep from crying. I cleaned out my desk and walked out of Galaxy Life for the last time.

January 5, 1943
Grace called and asked what I was I going to do? I told her I had war bonds and money saved. In reality, I had five dollars to my name. She wished me all the luck. I called Mona and told her what happened. She didn't say I told you so, like I thought. She said she'd help me as much as she could. I cried so hard, she drove all the way from Skokie to see about me.

January 10, 1943
Today my heart almost stopped. I saw Orlando on my street. I hope he realizes he really loves our child and me.

January 23, 1943
*The word was out. Orlando and I are a bust. Smoky Jones was the third one of
Orlando's friends to stop by my house talking trash. I been looking at you a
long time, he said. I can't keep my true feelings hidden. I want to be your man.
He grabbed me and tried to kiss me. Get out of my house! I screamed. You ain't
nothing, he sneered at me. I pulled Switchie Mae out and snapped her open.
Smoky's eyes bucked bigger than two baseballs. I didn't mean no harm he said,
and hurried through the door. I think he called me a bitch, but the neighbors
are screaming so loud, I couldn't be sure.*

Emily laughed out loud. "If I didn't hate Leora so much, she'd be someone I'd
like to know."

January 24, 1943
I cut my wedding dress into little bitty pieces.

February 18, 1943
Mona and Irving got married. I hope they'll be happy.

March 20, 1943
*I ran into Orlando today. All I remember is the look Mr. Trueborn gave me and
right before my eyes was the person responsible. I punched him in the mouth
so hard; I split his lip with my ring. That's for calling my job and getting me
fired, you son of a bitch. He called me a black slut and drew back to hit me but
looked at my big stomach and backed off. He wiped blood from his lip with the
initialed handkerchief I bought for his birthday. I wanted to cut it from his
hand. Before he peeled away in his car, he laughed a laugh no human being
should ever laugh at another and left me standing there feeling like a fool.*

April 3, 1943
*My bus passed Orlando's car outside the Swan Tap on Cottage. I got off at the
next corner. Straight to the grocery store I had business and bought a bag of
sugar. I poured it all in his gas tank then bent my nine months with child self
down and stabbed each tire five times for the five months we were together. I
wanted to break out all the windows too, but I was afraid he'd catch me. And
I knew nothing could keep him from beating the hell out of me when he saw his
car. I crossed the street to Kathleen's Diner and took a seat by the front window prepared to sit there all night. I only had to wait three hours. Orlando
swaggered out of the bar and slid under the wheel. He pulled halfway into the*

street before he noticed anything wrong. He got out and saw the flat tire. He went to open the trunk and noticed the sugar on the ground. He unscrewed the gas cap and said 'mother fucker' so loud, it seemed he stood by my side. He got his sax from the trunk and walked away. He looked like he'd lost his best friend and I do believe he had.

April 17, 1943
Good News! At six-eighteen this morning, I gave birth to a beautiful baby girl. She weighed seven pounds ten ounces. I never thought I could endure such agony, but each pain was worth it to have her here. She is so beautiful I can't take my eyes off her. She is the same lovely brown as my dear Aunt Emily with Mona's red hair. I named her after them and take Orlando's name since he will provide nothing else. She is Emily Mona Douglas.

April 18, 1943
Nurses walked past my room to stare at the white woman who had the colored baby. I don't care. I can't express the joy I feel with Emily in my life. She is mine alone. I love her so much.

Emily read that entry five times.
  "Leora loved me once. What happened to turn it to hate?"

April 28, 1943
Mona brought so many baby clothes; I lied and told her I'd named the baby Mona Emily. Mona's smile lit up the room. Little Mona is too dark to pass, she said. I told her I'm glad she won't have that decision to make.

July 18, 1943
I wait tables at Martha's Grill. The pay isn't so great, but the tips more than make up. This job would be perfect if the men would leave me alone. They ask me out and get mad when I say I'm never going to date again. They think a tip gives them the right to touch me. I usually have to slap two fresh faces a day. Today I changed my tactics. I leaned across the table to fill the sugar jar. Cairo Smith squeezed my breast and waited for his slap. I just glared at him. He looked so disappointed. I brought his coffee, boiling hot from the pot and dropped it in his lap. Boy, did he jump out of that booth and away from me.

August 22, 1943
Emily is four months old and getting so big. She looks like a butterball. My

baby sitter, Mrs. Dillard, already feeds her cereal. She says milk doesn't fill her up and she doesn't care what the baby book says, she won't let a baby in her care cry if she's hungry.

August 30, 1943
Emily is so smart. I read somewhere if you read to babies, you can make them even smarter. I read to her each night. I know nobody will believe this, but she cries if I don't read to her. I'm not kidding, she actually cries.

September 25, 1943
Orlando formed a band called the Dark Strangers that's really going places. I also found out he had babies with two other girls here in Chicago.

November 23, 1943
Buddy Boyd sat at my station today. He looked so handsome in his Marine uniform. He's quiet and soft-spoken with a deep voice that made me tremble. Several times I caught him watching me and he'd pretend he was looking out the window then go back to reading his paper. I know he likes me. I know I said I wasn't going to date again, but if Buddy asks me out, I'm going to say yes.

December 4, 1943
I wrote Buddy's usual order of hotcakes and sausage. Is that all? I asked. No, he said. Will you go out with me Saturday? I can't believe it when I told him I was busy. I guess I'm afraid I'll get hurt again.

December 9, 1943
If Buddy asks me out again, I'm saying yes. I mean it this time.

December 17, 1943
Buddy asked me out again. I told him from the beginning, I wasn't white and I had a baby daughter and no husband. He said he knew that.

December 25, 1943
Buddy took us to Christmas dinner at his sister's house over in Gary, Indiana. We had a wonderful time. Emily was the center of attention. Everyone fell in love with her.

Emily took down another journal and flipped through it.

February 2, 1944
Buddy asked me to marry him. I'm so happy, Our wedding date is June 17.

February 13, 1944
I bought lace and satin for my wedding gown. I'm sewing it by hand so Emily can wear it on her wedding day.
Tears welled in Emily's eyes. Sheepishly, she wiped them away.

June 3, 1944
I never knew I could feel this way about any man except Orlando. Buddy and I compliment each other in every way. He loves my Emily and wants to be a father to her. He wants a baby right away so he can experience fatherhood from the very beginning.

June 17, 1944
Its over. I am Mrs. Boyd. I have to write quickly. Buddy is in the other room. When he comes to bed and takes me in his big strong arms. I won't have time to write...smile.

September 30, 1944
Dear Journal, The most wonderful news. Emily won't be an only child. I'm expecting a baby in March. Buddy is thrilled.

October 25, 1944
Mona said its bad luck to buy baby things before the birth. She's too superstitious. If I had listened to her, I wouldn't have gotten this lovely oak layette at the flea market. Its lopsided and missing a roller, but Buddy can fix that.

February 12, 1945
My beautiful Emily rests her head on my huge stomach and looks at me in wonder. I think she hears the baby's heartbeat or feels his kicks. I know its a boy. Buddy won't let me do anything strenuous. Emily is such a pudgy wudgy, he forbids me even to lift her on my lap. She has a tantrum when I won't. Yesterday, I had to move her crib. She threw her teddy bear through the window.

Man, I was a handful.
Emily stopped reading and went to cook. After dinner, she took a nap with intentions of reading more and slept the whole night through.

Tuesday, November 10, 1981

Feeling much better, Emily dressed in real clothes for the first time in two days and went to the turret room to read.

March 9, 1945
My beautiful son entered this world at eleven seventeen p.m. We named him David Evan Boyd, Jr. His father has already nicknamed him Bunny—

Bunny! David! These names had plagued her all her life. David was my baby brother. What happened to him?
April 23, 1945
Emily is jealous of the baby. Yesterday, I put him in her crib. She tried to throw him out the window.

Emily turned the page. There was no entry there or beyond.
What happened? Did I hurt him?
She pulled down the journal for 1946 and found one entry.

July 15, 1946
My heart breaks with sorrow. My beautiful baby boy is dead.

"Oh-h-h no-o-o!" Emily moaned. "Oh-h-h no-o!"

A year has passed and I still hear the layette crash like thunder above my head. I still see David's tiny body crumpled on the floor, washed in sunlight so dazzling, it hurts my eyes. Why did Emily kill my baby?
"What?" Emily read the last sentence again. "This can't be right. Kill my baby brother? Me kill my baby brother? I couldn't do such a thing." Her mind fought the acceptance of this horrible information even as a bubble of memory of a baby's cry grew in her mind, but fizzled before she could grab a hold.
Leora is wrong! I can't kill anyone, let alone a baby!
She forced herself to read on.
Why didn't I see her jealousy? Why did I leave her alone with him? Buddy wanted me to give Emily away. When I refused, he packed his clothes and left. He is the third man to leave me. First my father then Orlando. It's all Emily's fault. I try so hard not to hate her. Sometimes it is all I can do to keep from doing what Buddy wants. Emily made me lose the two most precious things I had in this world. I will never forgive her for that.

When Emily calls me, I don't answer. She sits at my feet sobbing Momma until she cries herself to sleep. I feel no guilt, remorse or shame.

Emily's tears fell on the page, obliterating the cruel red words written by a grieving mother. She removed the envelope marked 'important papers' from the desk and looked inside. A State of Illinois marriage certificate proclaimed Leora Tate DuPree and David Evan Boyd united in holy matrimony. Stapled to the back was their divorce decree. David Evan Boyd, Jr's death certificate was stapled over his certificate of birth. Emily scanned the yellowed page for the cause of death and saw crushed skull.

"Oh God! Please don't let me have thrown him out the window!"

"Dr. Chambers' office." Millie answered.

"I...I...need...to...see the...doctor."

"Mrs. Bennett, is that you?"

"I...I...need to see her!"

"One moment please," Millie said.

A few seconds later Dr. Chambers spoke.

"Yes, Emily," she said. "What's wrong?"

"I need...to see you."

"What's wrong?"

"I...I..."

"Can't you tell me what's wrong?"

"I...I...can't tell you...over the phone."

"How soon can you get to my office?"

"Thirty...minutes."

"Come ahead."

37

Emily trudged into Dr. Chambers' office and dropped in the first chair she reached.

"What couldn't you discuss over the phone?" Dr. Chambers asked. She repeated the question twice before Emily answered.

"I...I...she...she...said...I...I...I..."

"Take your time," Dr. Chambers said.

"I don't want to take my time!" She sobbed. "I want to die! I want to die!"

"Why do you want to die?"

"I can't...say what she said about me."

"What who said about you?"

"Leora!" She screamed. "Leora!"

"What did Leora say about you?"

"It's...so...horrible...what she said I did."

"What did she say you did?" The doctor urged.

"I don't want to say."

"You know its better for this knowledge to be free than chained in your mind, don't you?"

Emily nodded. "She...she...said...I...ki...ki...killed her baby!"

"And did you?"

"How can you ask me that? I couldn't have! I couldn't have!"

"Do you have any memory of such a thing happening?"

"No...no...I...don't...I don't."

"Perhaps you need more insight."

"I don't want to know! I don't want to know!"

"Don't you want to find out more about these accusations?"

"You don't think I did it?" For a second, she looked hopeful.

"It's important to find out one way or the other."

"But...but...what if I did kill him?"

"If you did, you will have to call on your reservoir of strength to deal with it, but what if you didn't?"

Without a word, Emily got up and sat on the recliner. She put on the earphones and glasses and slumped back drained.

"Are you ready?" Dr. Chambers asked.

Emily snuffled trying to stop crying.

"Yes," she said finally. "Yes, I'm...ready."

"Let's begin." Dr. Chambers switched on the synchronizer and the tape recorder. "Emily, can you hear me?"

"Yes."

"I will direct you to return to an earlier time in your life, however, you will return not as a child, but as a reasoning adult. Emily, do you understand?"

"Yes."

"I will touch your right shoulder, you will return to the level of your memory that can explain a baby brother. When you reach that level, you will remember with clarity all the information you need to resolve all conflicts associated with the claim against you. Do you understand, Emily?"

"Yes."

"I will touch your left shoulder, you will return to the present refreshed and rested with all memories intact. Do you understand, Emily?"

"Yes."

Dr. Chambers touched Emily's right shoulder. She began to speak.

"I'm in a pink room."

"Where are you in the pink room?"

"I'm in a baby bed,"

"What are you doing?"

"I'm on my knees. My face is pressed against the bars, looking out."

"How old are you, Emily?"

"I'm two years old."

"What do you see?"

"The floor."

"What do you see on the floor?"

"A blue rug on linoleum imprinted with ABC blocks."

"What else do you see in the room, Emily?"

"A dresser with blue ducks. An oak layette."

"What else?"

"Leora is singing a lullaby to the fair skinned baby. I stand and hold up my arms. "Take, Emily, out!" I say. "Take, Emily, out!"

Leora kisses my head and shows me the baby. 'Give Brother a kiss.'

"I hold his hand and kiss to his cheek. Take Emily out."

'In a minute, sweetie, Momma has to bathe, Brother.'

"Take Emily out."

'You used to be little just like this, but you're Momma's big girl now.'

"Leora holds the baby out to me again."

'Give Brother another kiss.'

"I kiss him and caress his soft hair. I reach out for another touch and she turns away. Touch, Momma, touch."

'In a minute, sweetie.' Leora says.

'How's my boy?'

"Buddy sounds like a tuba, big and deep. He comes in with a washpan full of water and sets it on the layette."

'How's my girl?'

" He lifts me from the crib and kisses my—"

"What is it Emily?" Dr. Chambers asked. "What do you see?"

"My scar!" She exclaimed. "I don't have my scar! My forehead isn't scarred yet, it's not scarred!"

"Calm down, Emily," Dr. Chambers said. "Take some deep breaths."

Emily's breaths got deeper then slower.

"That's right, stay calm, stay calm."

"I cling to Buddy's neck like a monkey, laughing."

'Buddy.' Leora said annoyed.

'Huh?'

'This thing came off again.'

'She shakes it gently and gives him a roller."

'It's off balance.'

"I start to cry when he puts me back in the crib and kneels down to inspect the leg of the layette."

'This cardboard will hold it steady until tonight. I'll fix it then, okay?'

'Okay,' Leora said.

"He stuck several layers of cardboard under the leg and got up."

'How's Daddy's boy?'

"The baby begins to cry. Leora hugs him, talking softly in his ear."

'Got to go catch that mule.'

"Buddy kisses us all and leaves."

"Come back. I start to cry again. Leora lays the baby on the layette and removes his clothes."

'Daddy's going to work.'

"Leora begins to wash the baby. Take Emily out."

'In a minute.'

"Leora sprinkles on baby powder and pins on a diaper."

'Where are those belly bands?'

"She searches her apron pockets, pulls out all three drawers on the layette, and walks from the room. I stand on my stuffed animals at the end of the crib. I lean over and try to touch Brother's hair. He kicks and waves at me. I wave back and swing my leg over the railing. I balance there a few seconds then swing the other leg over. I take an extra long step down to the rug. I see Brother's legs kicking, I see his toes, but I can't see him waving. I go to the layette. The floor is cold under my feet. I stand on tiptoe trying to see him. I grab the brass knobs and stick my toes on the thick ledge at the bottom. I pull myself up. The layette starts to wobble...the basin...tilts...soapy water...falls in my eyes...my eyes... are...burning...burning...so...I can't...open them to see. I'm falling...back- wards...I'm...I'm...falling back. The...the...layette crashes...on top...of...me. The brass...knob...cuts into my forehead...I hear...the...baby cry...I hear...the baby cry...I hear the baby cry...I try...to lift the layette off...us...but I can't! I hear the...the...baby...the...baby...cry. Then he stops crying. Mommmmmma! Mommmmmma! Mommmmmmma!"

"Come back, Emily," Dr. Chambers said. "Come back. Now!"

"It's true! It's true!" She yanked off the glasses then the earphones.

"Calm down, calm down."

"I did it!" She sat up, rocking back and forth. "I killed Brother!"

"It was an accident." The doctor knelt, by the chair, rubbing Emily's cold hands. "An accident!"

"I did it!" Emily's tears flowed. "I killed, Brother!"

"It was an accident, Emily, an accident."

"I still did it! I still did it!"

"Calm down, Emily, calm down."

"How can I calm down when I'm a...a killer? A killer!"

"Emily...listen to me, you're not a killer. What happened to Brother was an accident, the layette wasn't level. It wasn't level. You were a baby, a two-year-old child. It's not your fault! It's not your fault!"

Emily stood and unsnapped the keys from her purse.

"I've got to go!"

"You need to come to terms with this."

"I've got to go!" Her voice got shrill. " I've got to go!"

"You're in no condition to drive. Let me call someone to pick you up, okay?" She led her away the door. "Sit here."

Emily sank obediently onto the chair. Dr. Chambers went to her desk and pressed the intercom.

"Yes, Doctor?" Millie said.

"Call Dr. Bennett and have him come here at once."

"Yes, Doctor."

Rachel went back to her patient.

"Emily," Dr. Chambers said. "Emily? Emily?"

Emily blinked her eyes to focus.

"I know it seems insurmountable, but you can work through this, you can—"

"No wonder Leora hates me. I killed her baby!"

Dr. Chambers pulled up a chair and sat across from Emily.

"It was an accident," she said. "A terrible, terrible accident."

"Brother is...dead because...of me!"

"Listen to me, Emily. Look at me! Look…at…me!"

Emily raised her head and gave her a detached look.

"I want to die," she said softly. "I want to die."

"None of that," Dr. Chambers said. "None of that."

"I want to die, Dr. Chambers! I just want to die!"

"You're not going to die," the doctor said. "You need to talk this out."

Emily dissolved into tears. The intercom buzzed.

Dr. Chambers went to her desk to answer it.

"Yes...what is it?"

"Dr. Bennett is not in his office."

Dr. Chambers looked back at her patient.

"Emily, do you know where Sonny is?"

"No." Her voice sounded hollow and lost.

"Who else can come pick you up?"

"Annette." Emily gave the number and stood to put on her coat. A warmth trickled between her legs. "Oh no."

"What's wrong?" Dr. Chambers asked.

Before Emily could reply, a cloudy fluid gushed from her vagina, ran down her pantyhose and saturated the carpet. Emily looked into Dr. Chambers equally astonished face before pain like a mule's kick bent her double.

"O-o-o-o-h!" She screamed. "My baby's coming! O-o-o-o-o-oh!"

"Stay calm, stay calm!" Dr. Chambers grabbed the phone and called an ambulance. "There's a woman having a baby in the Lawson Building. Her water has broken. She's in suite 2526. Hurry! Please hurry!" She hung up on the dispatcher asking who she was and ran to Emily.

"O-o-o-oh!" Emily screamed again. "He's coming! Help me! Help me!"

"Help's on the way. Hold on! Hold on!"

"I...can't...hold...on!" Searing pain ran across her back. She dog panted and slumped forward. Dr. Chambers supported her weight and kept her in the chair.

"Millie! Millie!" She yelled. "Come quickly!"

Millie ran through the door. "Oh my God!"

"Help me!" Dr. Chambers shouted.

Together they eased Emily to the floor.

"Get a blanket!" Dr. Chambers commanded.

Millie rushed to do the doctor's bidding.

"Hold on!" Dr. Chambers said. "Help's on the way!"

"O-o-o-oh!" Emily screamed. "A-a-a-a-a-a-ah." A second fluid gushed from her body. This time it was blood.

"Oh, Jesus! Jesus!" Dr. Chambers' stomach flip-flopped. Bile soaked her mouth. She swallowed, fighting nausea.

Millie returned with two thin, blue blankets and spread one over Emily.

"Where the hell is that ambulance?" Dr. Chambers wedged the other blanket between Emily's legs to stop the bleeding.

"Paramedics! Paramedics!" A male voice called minutes later.

Millie ran to the outer door.

"In here! In here!" She beckoned to the two men hurrying toward her. The tallest one had K. Drake embroidered on his jacket and held a jump kit. P. Willis carried a stretcher and OB case.

"In there!" She pointed into the office. "In there!"

"We've got it now, ma'am." P. Willis went down on one knee beside Emily and took a stethoscope from his case.

Dr. Chambers gladly relinquished her spot and went to stand by Millie.

"Help me get her out of this coat," K. Drake said.

They tugged it off. P. Willis pushed up a sleeve, pumped up the cuff and took her blood pressure.

"O-o-o-oh." Emily panted. "Help me...help me!"

"We're going to help you." P. Willis pulled the stethoscope from his ears. "Pressure 90 over 60, pulse 120 and weak."

"Check the baby," K. Drake said. "I'll start a saline."

P. Willis put the stethoscope to Emily's abdomen. "It's real faint." He pulled the bloody blanket from between her thighs. "Help me here."

They pulled off her underwear and propped up her legs. P. Willis tore open the delivery field and tucked it under her hips.

"It's crowning," he said. 'Get ready."

They did not have long to wait. Seven minutes later a baby, weighing less than four pounds, shot into K. Drake's gloved hands.

"It's a boy," he said.

The blue-tinged infant covered in blood looked lifeless. K. Drake stroked the sole of his foot and barely got a knee jerk reflex and no cry.

"He doesn't look good." P. Willis clamped the umbilical cord and cut it. "What's his Apgar?"

K. Drake scored the baby with a glance.

"Respiration slow and irregular, skin tone blue, muscle tone limp, responsiveness none, heartbeat." He warmed the diaphragm with his hand and laid it over the child's heart. "Fewer than ninety beats per minute, I'd say he's a real bad two," he said. "But let's see if I can't pump him up some."

He wiped blood from the infant and wrapped him in a linen blanket, then an aluminum sheet. He placed a tiny respirator over the child's face and squeezed gently until he slowly turned rosy pink.

"I still don't like the sound of his breathing. How's she doing?"

"The placenta's out," P. Willis said. "But she's bleeding real bad."

"Let's try this." K. Drake ripped Emily's blouse. Buttons popped in every direction. He pulled out a swollen breast and put the baby's mouth to her nipple. He refused to suck. "Massage her abdomen." He suggested another technique to stop the bleeding.

P. Willis kneaded her flabby stomach a few minutes. "It's getting worse."

K. Drake felt Emily's forehead and lifted her eyelid.

"She's shocking! Run the I. V. wide open let's go, let's go!" He threw equipment in the case and slammed it shut.

"On three," P. Willis said.

"One, two, three." They counted and lifted an unconscious Emily onto the stretcher. P. Willis pushed her out. K. Drake carried the baby.

"I'm going, too." Dr. Chambers grabbed her mink coat and purse and ran after the quartet in a race with death.

38

With the mink draped over her shoulders, Dr. Chambers paced the waiting room chain smoking and glanced at her watch, again. *Damn!*
Only three minutes had passed since she had last looked.
What is taking so long?
She crushed out the half-smoked cigarette in an ashtray overflowing with broken butts and went to look for a phone.

"Dr. Chambers' office," Millie said.

"Did you contact, Sonny, I mean Dr. Bennett?"

"He's on his way. Annette is, too. How's Mrs. Bennett?"

"I don't know yet. Nobody's been out to tell me anything."

"Why don't you go in?"

"I'll just wait here," Dr. Chambers said.

If I see anymore blood, I know I'll pass out.

"I hope she'll be okay."

"I'm sure she will be," Dr. Chambers said. "Did you get anybody to clean up that mess?"

"They're doing it now."

"I hope they can get all the blood out."

"They said they could since it's fresh.

"Okay. I'll see you tomorrow."

"Okay," Millie said. "Good-bye."

"Bye," she said and returned to the waiting room.

Ralph and Annette rushed through the emergency doors.

"Emily Bennett," Annette asked the clerk out of breath. "How is she?" The hospital smell had her lightheaded already.

"Are you a relative?" She closed her magazine and stood.

"Yes. I'm her sister. He's her brother," she said. "How is she?"

The clerk gave Annette her I'm not stupid look and said calmly.

"I can't give out that information. Doctor will have to tell you that."

"Why the hell did you ask if we were relatives if you weren't going to tell us shit?" Annette yelled.

The clerk turned her back and returned to reading her magazine.

"Don't you turn your back on me!"

"Baby, come on." Ralph pulled on her arm. "She's only doing her job."

"Shit!" She resisted at first then let him lead her away.

"Junior!" Richard ran up to them. "How is she? How is she?"

"I don't know. We just got here."

Richard turned and ran inside to find his wife. Ralph escorted Annette to the waiting room and spotted Rachel pacing the floor.

"Rachel," he said. "What are you doing here?"

"I'm so glad to see you." She walked into his arms, hugging him as if many years and ill feelings had not passed since they were last this close.

"Did you know Emily's in here?" He held her shoulders and couldn't help fingering the soft fur.

"Excuse me." Annette refused to wait patiently for Ralph to introduce her to the woman who had broken his heart.

I wonder what Justine French would say if she could see her woman all up in my man's arms?

Ralph looked back and pulled her beside him, smiling.

"Baby, this is an old friend of mine. Annette Marshall, Rachel Chambers."

"How do you do?" Annette shook her hand.

"I'm pleased to meet you," Rachel said.

"Love your coat." Annette said. "I need to get mine from storage."

"Thank you," Rachel said.

"How come you're here?" Ralph asked.

"I came," Rachel said haltingly. "With Emily."

"Oh?" He looked baffled.

"Em's been seeing Dr. Chambers a while now," Annette said.

Rachel looked at Annette with gratitude over her face.

"Come on, let's sit down." He escorted them to a tweed sofa and sat across on the oak coffee table. "What happened to Emily?"

"Her water broke in my office," Rachel said.

"The baby's not due for seven weeks!" Annette said.

"He was born about an hour ago."

"What?" Ralph and Annette said together.

Rachel nodded.

"Is he okay?" Annette asked. "Is Em okay?"

"I don't know a thing," Rachel said. "Millie did get in touch with Sonny."

"He just went in," Annette said. "Maybe he'll be back to tell us something."

"I hope so," Rachel said. "I hate this waiting."

"You can leave." Ralph squeezed Annette's hand. "We're here now."

"I want to stay. You know you guys are like family."

"Speaking of family," Ralph said. "Jerry called me last night."

"Me, too," Rachel said. "He wanted me to go check on Mother."

"How's Miss Merlie doing?"

"She's fine. She asked about you."

"What did she say? Something nasty I'll bet."

"No. She said you'd turned into a fine man."

"Miss Merlie said that about me?" He was pleased. Her mother had never liked him.

"Uh huh, she sure did."

Annette saw they cared for each other and had secrets only they shared.

Am I jealous of a lesbian?

"Who's home with the kids?" She broke up the reminiscing.

"Just Leora and the nurse," Ralph said.

"Somebody needs to tell them what's happened," Annette said. "I'll stay with them until Richard can make other arrangements." She stood.

"You want my car?" Ralph stood, too and pulled out his keys.

"No, I'll catch a cab to the store and get my car. I want to pick up a few things from home in case I have to stay a while."

"Okay." Ralph peeled a twenty from a clip and gave it to her.

"What's this for?" Annette asked.

"Cab fare."

"You're so sweet." She kissed his cheek. "Ooops!" She wiped off cherry red lipstick with her thumb.

"I'll be right back." Ralph turned to Rachel. "I need to call Momma and tell her about Emily and the baby."

"Uh...uh...okay." Rachel stammered suddenly nervous.

"See you later." He gave Annette a quick kiss.

Both women watched him walk away.

"Junior's a great guy," Rachel said.

"Yes, he is." Annette had fought the sickening smell for as long as she could. She had to get out of there. "It was nice meeting you."

"It was nice meeting you, too." Rachel walked Annette to the door. "Emily will be out of here before you know it."

"I hope so." Annette shook Rachel's hand. "Good-bye."

"Good-bye."

Ralph stuck a finger in his ear to block out a noisy gurney and told his mother what had happened.

"What'd she have," Pauline asked. "What'd she have?"

"A boy."

"I knew it!" Pauline shouted. "How're they doing?"

"I don't know."

"Is Sonny there?"

"Uh huh. He went in about fifteen minutes ago."

"Who's with those chil'ren?"

"Annette's going over there."

"Annette don't know nothing about taking care of chil'ren." Pauline huffed. "I'll come stay with them."

"Annette can supervise those kids. They're not babies."

"Junior." She spoke sharply. "I said we'd come stay with them."

"Okay, Momma." Ralph chuckled. His mother had adored Annette before they started dating. Now she wasn't good enough.

"Let's not waste time talking. We're on our way. Bye."

"Bye." Ralph returned to the waiting room and found Rachel pacing again.

"Come here and sit down." He led her to the sofa.

"Is your mother coming?" Rachel asked.

"Uh huh."

"Is she in Athens?"

"Yeah, they're just leaving out."

Rachel looked at her watch, reasoning an hour plus from Athens, longer in afternoon traffic. She could talk to Junior a while but she had to watch the time. *If Pauline Bennett is coming here, I want to be far away when she arrives.*

"Want some coffee?" Ralph asked.

"Huh?"

"Want some coffee?"

"I never drink coffee from machines," she said seriously.

"Why not?"

"Because it puts hair on your chest." She laughed.

"I need several gallons, then." He laughed. "My chest is bare as a cue ball."

"I know." She looked away from his piercing eyes and took out a cigarette.

"I'd light that for you, but I stopped smoking ages ago."

"That's okay." Rachel lit it, inhaled deep and blew smoke over his head.

"Is that what I think it is?" Ralph took the gold lighter from her.

"I was wondering if you'd recognize it."

"I can't believe you still have it. I'm surprised it still works."

"I had a new unit put in a few years ago. The inscription is faint, but you can still see it." She took it back and held it at an angle.

"I know what it says by heart," he said. "To R. C. C.- Our Love Is An Eternal Flame-From E. R. B."

"Twenty-eight years old and still going strong." She dropped it in her bag.

"Twenty-eight?" Ralph said.

Our baby would be twenty-eight, if she had lived.

"Do you ever think about Tina?" he asked.

Rachel's head snapped up. She had the saddest look.

"Christina?" she said. "Sometimes."

"What's wrong?"

"Nothing." She stubbed out the cigarette and patted the hand covering hers. "Nothing's wrong."

"Rachy Bachy." He called her the pet name he'd given her when she was ten. "This is Junior. I know everything about you, remember?"

"Is Annette someone special?" she asked.

"Yes, very special."

"Marriage special?"

"Yes, marriage special." He'd finally said out loud what he'd been thinking. *I'm going to ask Annette to marry me. We've only known each other a short time, but we're perfect for each other.*

"I'm so glad, Junior, I'm so very glad." She squeezed his hand. Perhaps now the guilt she had carried since she broke their engagement would go away. She glanced at her watch, figuring fifteen more minutes before she had to leave.

Ten minutes later, Pauline pushed Ezell into the waiting room and spotted Junior talking to a woman across the way.

"Yoohoo...Junior." She hollered and headed over. "Yoohoo."

Rachel jumped up trapped between Pauline and the door.

"Momma, Daddy!" Ralph looked at his watch. "That was fast."

"She did ninety all the goddamn way." Ezell grumbled. "It's a wonder we ain't both dead."

Pauline pulled back on the wheelchair and brought it to a stop.

"What the hell is she doing here?" She sneered at Rachel.

"Momma," Ralph said calmly. "Rachel came with Emily."

"I don't care who she came with." She got louder. "I want her out!"

The entire waiting room abandoned their activities to give their undivided attention to the short, Black woman performing in the corner. The clerk came timidly from her office, debating whether or not to call security.

I will if it gets any louder.

"This ain't your hospital," Ezell said. "You can't tell nobody to get out."

"I can if they're a filthy bull—"

"Be careful what you say, Momma!" Ralph spoke harshly to his mother for the first time in his life. "Be careful what you say!"

"Be careful what *I* say!" Her eyes blazed at her eldest.

"You know what she is and you're taking her part over mine?"

"I've forgiven her. Why can't you?"

"I'll never forgive," Pauline ignored Ralph's warning. "A nasty bull dagger!"

Pauline turned the chair and headed out. Ezell grabbed the wheels.

"What's wrong with you?" She hollered at her husband.

"Nothing's wrong with me. I don't want to be pushed now."

"You shouldn't want to be in the same room with that...that thing!"

"You're my wife." He snorted. "Not my goddamned mother."

"Then stay here, goddammit!" She shoved his chair and stalked out.

Humiliation burned Rachel's face.

"I'm sorry about, Momma." Ralph said. "Come on. I'll take you home."

Rachel turned to Ezell but couldn't meet his eyes. "Good-bye, Mr. Bennett."

"Good-bye, baby." He kissed her hand. "Take care of yourself."

"Thank you, I will."

"Come on, Rach." Ralph took her arm and led her out.

Pauline stomped in the second they left.

"You put your lips on her!" She screamed. "Don't you ever kiss me again!"

"Don't start with me, woman." Ezell took a deck of cards from his shirt pocket. "We've been here ten minutes and still don't know how Emily and my grandson are doing thanks to you and your mouth."

"They're doing fine. Mother and child are doing just fine." Pauline said, but her furrowed brow didn't seem to agree with her words.

Baby Boy Bennett lay still as death in the isolette. Richard stood over him and counted his fingers and toes. They were the first things Emily asked about when she awoke. He held his open palm over him as a measure.

You're no bigger than my hand.

"Be strong, little boy." He gave his son his first fatherly advice. "Hang in there for Daddy."

Dr. Groton came in and stood beside Richard.

"Don't worry," he said. "He'll make it."

"You pulled my Emily back, Oscar!" Richard's voice trembled as he shook his hand. "You pulled them both back!"

"God's the pilot, Bennett." He patted Richard's back. "I'm just the co."

"I'll never be able to thank you enough!"

" Kevin and Phil made my job easy. They're the ones you need to thank."

"I will...I will," he said and hurried to tell Junior and Annette, his wife and child would live.

39

Richard's fears for Emily's mental health already had him distraught. Rachel's call later that night scared him to death.

"Daddeeeee, telephone." Michelle yelled. "It's Dr. Chambers."

"Rachel," he said. "What's up?"

"Watch her, Sonny!"

"What?"

"Watch her, Sonny!" she said again and hung up.

He had gone to the hospital immediately. Between his brother, his parents and Annette, Emily was never alone. They all watched her battle her demons and prayed she would win the fight.

Three days later, she went home and left her son, David Evan, at the hospital to gain the pound and a half he needed before he could join her for good.

"Sweetheart." Richard begged. "Tell me what's wrong."

"Leave me alone." She wailed. "Just leave me along."

"Let's go to dinner and the movies. You need to get out of here."

She refused all offers and only left the house to visit the hospital to nurse her baby or see Dr. Chambers.

Monday, December 21, 1981

"Emily." Richard pleaded with her again. "Tell me what's wrong."

"Leave me alone!" She cried from the bed surrounded by tear soaked tissues.

"You need to get dressed for your appointment with Rachel."

"I'm not going!"

"But you need to go!"

"I'm never leaving this house again!"

"What about our son? How will he get his milk?"

"Oh, My God!" Her hand covered her open mouth but not her guilt stricken eyes. She had totally forgotten about her baby.

He sat on the bed and pulled her into his arms. "Tell me what's wrong."

"I can't...I can't." She sobbed into his chest. "I can't!"

"Okay...okay. You don't have to tell me, but please...please see Rachel."

Emily wanted to say no, but he looked so frightened.

"Okay," she said listlessly. "But you have to help me."

Richard bathed and dried her off. He chose her outfit and clothed her like a child. She sat quietly at the vanity while he combed her hair. Downstairs, he buttoned her coat, drove to Atlanta and deposited her with Millie.

"How're you doing?" Dr. Chambers asked.

"The same." Emily answered.

"Have you had the nightmare at all?"

"No."

"Is there anything you want to talk about?"

"No."

"Hasn't talking been helpful in the past?"

Emily nodded docilely and closed her eyes.

"Do young children know about the laws of physics?"

"The laws of physics?" Her eyes snapped open. "No."

"Would a young child know mechanics is a branch of physics?"

"No."

"Would a young child know how a stationary body reacts when a moving body exerts a force upon it?"

"No." She closed her eyes again.

"A young child wouldn't know a missing roller on a lop-sided layette might cause it to overturn would he?"

"You mean would she don't you? You mean me!"

"Did you know anything about gravity when you were two years old?"

"Buddy was the other man with red eyes," she said. "He'd been crying for his dead son. He thought I killed him."

"Did you kill him?"

"Yes." Emily opened her eyes.

"Did you mean to kill him?"

"No." She shook her head, sadly. "It was an accident."

"Is there anything you would say to Buddy if you could?"

"I'd say I'm truly sorry for what happened."

"Is there anything else you want to say?"

"All my life I've wanted Leora to beg me to forgive her, when I should have been begging her to forgive me."

"Remember, Emily," Dr. Chambers said. "It was an accident."

"Buddy was going to fix the layette when he got from work," Emily said. "If I hadn't climbed on it, none of this would have happened."

"You need to accept that it was an accident," Dr. Chambers said. "Can you try and do that?"

"I'll try," she said. "I'll try."

Many things Emily had wondered about were explained. She no longer fingered her scar with that hollow yearning to know how she got it. She knew how she got it. She hated how she got it, but at least she knew. She knew why Leora hated her. She hated why she hated her, but at least she knew. For the first time in her life, Emily felt sorry for Leora. To lose a child was sad, but to lose a child so horribly was the cruelest fate.

Each session with Dr. Chambers brought her closer and closer to the realization that her brother's death was an accident.

Monday, December 28, 1981

"Why do you think you wanted a baby boy so badly?" Dr. Chambers asked. Emily paused, pondering the question.

"I think maybe...it sounds crazy."

"Crazy how?"

"I think I wanted to give Leora back the baby I took from her."

The anvils dropped from her shoulders and Emily thought her demons dead. On the way home, she told Richard everything and watched the fear leave his eyes. It was not until the ice pick stabs began down her forehead later that night that she knew at least one demon lived.

40

L isa stood in the doorway to her parent's room staring at the mahogany cradle. She had only seen the baby from a distance and today some powerful force pulled her here. Glancing both ways, she went in and stood over the infant.

My baby should be sleeping here.

She stepped forward. Her foot hit the rocker and startled the child awake.

"Don't cry, David." She reached in to soothe him. "Don't cry."

He gripped Lisa's little finger and smiled. Dimples punctured each cheek before his eyes rolled back in his head and he returned to sleep.

In that split second, Lisa fell hopelessly in love with the little creature she had despised since she first learned of his existence. Carefully, she lifted him into the crook of her arm and carried him downstairs.

"Leora," Lisa said. "Look who's here."

"Who?"

"David." She placed the child in Leora's outstretched arms.

"Oh-h-h-h Da-vid." Leora hugged him to her breast. "Where have you been? Momma's been looking everywhere for you."

She then laid him on the bed and removed his sleepers.

"Where's his undershirt and his belly band?" She searched the diaper. "And the safety pins?"

"You don't need safety pins with these." Lisa laughed. "It's too warm in here for an undershirt. What's a belly band?"

"A belly band goes on his belly you silly goose. How do I take this thing off?"

"Pull this little tab," Lisa said. "I'll get some and show you how it works."

Leora removed the wet diaper pleased at how nicely his navel had turned out. *I won't have to tie it down with a silver dollar anymore.*

"Here're the diapers." Lisa showed her how to put one on.

"What will they come up with next? Did you get his belly band?"

"Where is it?"

"In the top drawer of his layette and hurry up."

Lisa went to the kitchen to ask Nurse Brown what a belly band was.

David awoke crying.

"Are you hungry?" Leora unbuttoned her gown and picked him up to nurse. The child pulled several times at the dry nipple and screamed.

Grimacing, Emily filled the baby bottle with milk and placed gauze pads over her oozing nipples. She had breast-fed her other children without a problem. Now her breasts were almost too tender to touch. She left her bathroom to feed David and found him gone from the cradle.

Richard, Michelle and Nicole were in Athens. Leora never came upstairs. Miss Brown was having lunch plus she wouldn't dare take him out. Lisa was the only one who could have taken him. Fear grabbed Emily as the horrors inflicted on defenseless babies by jealous siblings flashed through her mind. *Lisa won't hurt David, will she? No, she won't. She's seeing Dr. Chambers twice a week and coming to grips with the loss of her baby. Isn't she?*
She went as quickly as she could to Lisa's room. It was empty, as were the other bedrooms. She headed downstairs. Halfway the steps, David's wails warbled from Leora's room.
Lisa took my baby in there?

Emily sprinted to the door in time to see Leora toss David in the air.
I have to face her today. My baby's life depends on it.

"Stop that!" Emily moved into the room prepared for hostility.

"Emily," Leora said. "Come in, precious."

Emily paused on guard.

"Say hello to Brother," Leora said and buttoned her gown.

"What?" Emily edged forward.

"Say hello to Brother. Give him a kiss."

She doesn't remember what happened! She doesn't remember what I did!

"Hello, Brother." Emily's voice shook.

"Give him a kiss." Leora held up the child and let Emily kiss his cheek. His head jerked in her direction. His screams turned to shrieks.

"I don't understand." Leora looked distraught. "I had plenty of milk for you, but none for him."

"Here." Emily showed her the bottle. "Let me give him this." Without a second thought, she handed Emily the baby and watched him attack the nipple.

"That's what he wanted." Leora looked up at Emily and frowned.

Here it comes. Here...it...comes.

"How did you hurt yourself?" Leora pointed to the scar.

"Something fell on me," she said, inching away.

"Oh-h." Leora grabbed Emily's hand and pulled her on the bed. "Let Momma make it all better."

Emily leaned into her mother's arms and let her kiss away all the pain.

About the Author

Kieja Shapodee began writing in 1992 after she took a writer's workshop at a local university. Several courses and many seminars later, she began her first novel, *Written In Red Ink.* She is currently working on a second book about the Bennett's entitled, *Broken Beyond Repair.*

Order Form

Order additional copies of *Written In Red Ink.*

Call 1-800-929-7889 to order by credit card.

Copy and mail this form to:

Award Publishing, Inc.
P. O. Box 3248
East Chicago, Indiana 46312.
(219) 397-0585 (219) 398 4641-Fax

Name_____

Company_____

Address_____

City, State, Zip_____

Daytime phone_____

_____ copies of Written In Red Ink at $18.95 each.   _____

Shipping costs $4.00   _____

Indiana residents add 5% tax per book   _____

Total   _____

Payment:_____Check_____MasterCard or Visa

Card#_____Exp. Date _____

Signature_____

Ask about our quantity discounts on orders of 5 copies or more.
Visit our web-site at www.spannet.org/awardpub.